I0635844

Starchild

E X I L E

1

J WASHBURN

LOST BOYS INK

ILLE CAELUM FREMITUS

SYNOPSIS

Flying an ancient alien spaceship, STARCHILD may be the key to saving the rebels. Only he wants no part of their war... until he meets HER.

* * *

TYRANNY RULES THE GALAXY.

TAIBEROS has crushed every hint of rebellion. Like the grip of his cybernetic hand, he maintains a relentless hold on the populace. The power he hates most is the psionic magic of THE SONG—a force so strong it flows out as light from the eyes. People with such powers are called RADIANCES, and Taiberos's Witch Hunters kidnap any that surface.

As the Radiances slowly vanish, so does the galaxy's hope.

Till Kalhette Whitesun, one of the last Radiances, gives a risky speech, denouncing Taiberos and the extermination of her kind. The message spreads across the galaxy like the light of a supernova. She becomes revered as the UNCROWNED QUEEN, the one with the power to finally unite the people.

And then doom falls—

In the form of the crushing hand of Taiberos. He captures Kalhette, sentencing her to the darkest dungeons and imminent death.

All hope is lost.

Until a lone pilot appears. A pilot who wants nothing to do with Kalhette or her rebellion yet who may in fact be the galaxy's last hope. A pilot whose ship, *THE SANCTUM*, was created by an ancient alien race. A pilot who stole that ship from Taiberos himself...

A renegade pilot named STARCHILD.

* * *

STARCHILD is an artisan book.

One author painstakingly crafted everything from the cover typography to the final period. For readers who are sick of stories with thoughtless, cheap thrills, *STARCHILD* is a novel that both ENTERTAINS and ENLIGHTENS. If you value flawed heroines, deep villains, mind-blowing plots, and spectacular worldbuilding, then this is the adventure you've been waiting for.

The story dives deep into the minds of an UNFORGETTABLE CAST of lovable (and loathable) characters. The GALACTIC SETTING is exquisite, and it's based on actual scientific discoveries, with worlds like you've never imagined but which likely exist in our own galaxy. The marvels of the MAGIC SYSTEM will make you envious, and its basis in fact might have you personally testing whether it's real. The story itself is a FAST-PACED RIDE that will leave you hungry for more adventure, and luckily, the sequels are already here.

Get ready for a reading addiction like you HAVEN'T EXPERIENCED SINCE YOU WERE A KID.

The moment you open the book, you'll be transported away at lightspeed.

So, ARE YOU READY to take an intergalactic leap?

ACCLAIM

"Washburn is good at emotion and has an instinct for dramatic style."
— BRANDON SANDERSON, AUTHOR OF *The Stormlight Archive*

"J's stories share the quality that makes *Star Wars* immortal—their heroes seek not just to save the world but also the villain."
— BENTLEY SNOW, AUTHOR OF *Six Fingers Left to Lose*

"This author gets it. Washburn dives directly into the action of an original world that evokes the wonder of the *Star Wars* universe in all the best ways."
— RAYMOND O'CONNOR, HOST OF *Running Off the Rails* PODCAST

"It's *Star Wars* meets Plato. Deeper than most space operas."
— JOSEPH BENDOSKI, AUTHOR OF *WHEN THE SKY FALLS*

"Absolutely loved it! Washburn is a genius. The next Orson Scott Card!"
— MATT DRAKE

"Gripping from the first page!"   "*STARCHILD* is on a higher level."
— MICHAL S.   — TUNK

"What George Lucas did for *Flash Gordon,* J Washburn does for *Star Wars.*"
— CONNOR MORGAN

"It's got all the best parts: action, romance, humor. If *Star Wars* and *Guardians of the Galaxy* had a baby, this would be it."
— MELODEE

"If you like spaceships, daring missions, secret facilities, or damsels who can kick butt, this is a book you'll enjoy."
— ZACH

"I absolutely loved the book! The characters really stuck with me."
— C. HILL

"A heart-pounding, page-turning plot. Plus great settings and fantastic characters. Everything a sci-fi fan could want."
— JEREMY

MORE

For full-size, color versions of the images in this book as well as a pronunciation guide, visit jwashburn.com/books/starchild

CONTACT

If you find an error in the text, notify the copyeditor at typos@jwashburn.com (and make sure to mention this book's title)—you'll go down in history as the hero of the next edition. Subscribe to J's monthly fan letter here: theinformant.jwashburn.com. Contact the author directly at me@jwashburn.com. And check out jwashburn.com.

LEGAL

Ver. 1.31   16 Nov 2023
WC 123482

To Jax

last brother, first reader

best friend

CHAPTERS

All comes from light
and all returns to it.

▲

VICTOR HUGO
Les Miserables
1862 A.D.

Starchild

EXILE

Once upon a time in a faraway universe…

KALH SENSED THE Witch Hunters coming.

The feeling reached out and tapped on her heart with a cold finger.

She put her hand over her necklace—a tiny glass vial filled with white sand from Solace. Home. When they began hunting her, that was what they took—home.

She reached behind her head and pulled her long hair into a bunch then clung to the locks for safety with both hands. Was the feeling a premonition or just paranoia? She wasn't sure.

The classroom seemed normal. Lillan was reading aloud. A small group that sat in a circle around her. The Jall sisters were writing. The room felt reverent, a temple dedicated to the galaxy's most valuable asset.

Tannie worked alone on a contragrav board, distracted enough to have finally put down his seed whistle. The little guy's hair was unkempt, and his pants were held up with a piece of yarn that bunched the waist together in odd places. Kalh tried not to think of him as her favorite. She'd found the board in a junk pile and brought it to him. The small boy, hands on the mangled tech, stared intently, like he intended to piece it back together with his mind. Maybe he hoped to somehow discover its origin—the inventors had vanished aions ago.

The feeling came again, the cold finger reaching out to touch her.

Kalh moved to the window, gazing from the hundred and fifth floor. Outside, subsolars floated gently by in distant traffic lanes. Two gentle moons sat quietly in the blue sky, and white clouds drifted. Everything seemed peaceful, calm.

Except for the menacing silence.

Kalh often had premonitions, but lately they tended toward paranoia rather than an uncanny gift, and she feared being wrong. If she panicked and gave herself away, it could mean more time hiding in sewers and caves, throwing away the regular life that Benton had helped her create. Or maybe one of her messages to Benton had been intercepted. Maybe they were coming for her specifically, to stop the revolution.

No, she had to calm down. No one knew what she was. She knew this logically. And she needed her emotions to follow along.

"What's wrong?" asked Daryan.

Kalh forced a smile and looked at the little girl. "Nothing is wrong."

Tannie screamed.

A musical note sung by terror itself—no respite from the eerie quiet.

The others joined, one screech rolling into the next in a chorus of fright. Chairs tipped over. Some children bolted. Others stood in place, surrendering to annihilation, believing this might be the end.

Everyone left in the room stared at Tannie.

The contragrav board had fallen to the floor.

The small boy stood alone, in silence.

And his eyes were glowing.

T HE COLD THAT touched Kahl's heart now gripped her whole body.

"I can't see!" Tannie's stare projected a white-hot light, obscuring his irises and pupils completely. Tears dripped from the light, past his open mouth. "The light is too bright!"

If Kalh had predicted this, she could've warned the kids to be quiet, to not be afraid. To keep it secret. Too late for that now. Too late for Tannie. The other teachers would've already heard.

And would be calling the Witch Hunters.

Kalh could let them come for Tannie. Could stand by and let them take him. Could keep herself safe and anonymous. She didn't pause to consider this option.

Because what happened to Tannie had once happened to her.

Kalh dashed across the room.

She swooped up Tannie with two arms.

The Song burned hot inside her, adding to her strength as she sprinted from the room, leaving the other startled children behind. Teachers—witnesses—peeked from their classroom doors at the glowing eyes. One of them would call. Strangely, Kalh felt embarrassed—not for doing something so illegal, abetting a Radiance, but for showing such strength as she carried the boy in a dead sprint down the hall.

Her hair was caught between her body and his. As it pulled, she tilted her scalp to relieve the pain, but she didn't have a free hand or time to pause. "Hey, stop screaming. It's going to be okay." She ran onto an open lift and set Tannie on the ground then punched the activator with the bottom of her fist.

The doors closed in a rapid *whoosh*.

She oscillated her head, shaking her hair back into place, and breathed heavily. The lift provided a false safety as it dropped anxiously. They had to get out of the building before—

"I can't see." Tannie stood against the back wall, eyes still glowing.

"It's going to be okay." She closed her eyes in a long blink and breathed deeply.

What he couldn't see was the transparent back of the lift and the view overlooking the city. Some people in this situation might break the glass and jump to their deaths. Many on her homeworld had done so. She dreaded the possibility but couldn't erase it from her mind. Why couldn't they leave her alone? That was all she wanted. A little piece of solitude. For people like herself and Tannie.

Tannie squinted with worry, palms on his face. "What's happening to me? It's so bright."

"Your eyes are glowing." Kalh felt his emotions through the Song, as if his soul were singing a melody she could hear and understand—a requiem. "I'm sorry. I know it's scary. We'll get through this."

She knew exactly what it was like: While your eyes glowed, you couldn't see in the normal way. You had to look past it, see beyond normal sight. Until he did that, he'd be blinded. She could teach him how, but it would take time. And the more he fought to see, the longer he'd prolong the glow.

She forced her voice to sound calm: "Close your eyes."

"Why?"

"Because that will help you calm down, which will bring back your vision." And because people would stare when they got off the lift. Because she'd never get him out safely if they left a trail of observers. But she didn't want to frighten him with these reasons. Or let him know that he might never see his home again.

He didn't close his eyes, and tears leaked past the brightness. His voice was only a whimper: "Why is this happening?"

"You're a Radiance." The light inside had been unleashed.

He looked blankly upward with his head cocked back. His sandy blonde hair was sticky from sweat, his body overheating. "But why me?"

Whatever happened next, the Redhelms would check her background. Her anonymity would vanish, all Benton's work gone to waste. They'd find her fraud and force her back on the run, back into exile. Part of her regretted it already. She wished she could just let Tannie be taken. Except for a question Master Jyngsoo had ask her:

What would you give your life for?

This was it. For Tannie.

"I don't know why you or why me. That's just how it is." She squatted, sitting on her heels. Even then, she was still taller than him. "Close your eyes, and it will go away. Everything's going to be all right."

"Why were they screaming?" His glowing eye sockets looked empty, hollow lights, lifeless, like he wasn't a living creature anymore. He looked like a demon from the Otherworld, a reaper of the dead.

She'd seen Starsight often enough to get used to it, like a doctor getting used to amputated limbs, but she remembered the horror that struck her the first time. "It's not a scary thing, but the other kids have never seen it before, so it surprised them. What made it happen?"

"I was trying to see... I couldn't see the inside."

"Of what?"

"The contragrav board."

It could've happened with anything, yet she still felt guilty when he mentioned the gift she'd brought him.

Tannie shook his head, his mouth as hollow as his eyes. "I just... I don't know... I didn't want that to happen... I just... I wanted to see a little... deeper."

"That's good. It's a neat board, huh?"

"Why were they afraid?"

The ground outside had nearly risen to meet them.

"I can teach you to see, to control it, to turn it on and off. But right now we're almost to the bottom, and I need you to close your eyes when we go out there."

His tone moved back to the verge of tears: "Why?"

"So nobody notices you. I'll explain once we get away. Keep your eyes closed, and everything will be all right. I promise. Can you do that?"

He nodded and squeezed his eyes closed. His eyelids still glowed red, unable to completely hide the light.

"Okay, here we go." She picked him up and put his face against her shoulder. The lift gave a deep rumble as it came to a halt. The doors slid open and the sounds of people in the lobby flooded in. The school was one floor of a crowded corporate skyscraper. She whispered into his ear: "Keep your eyes closed."

She had to get out before the Witch Hunters arrived.

She walked with pretend calm amid the bustling crowd. No one here knew her or knew what she really was.

As she wove through the crowd, she gasped.

Tannie jerked, wanting to see what was going on.

She pressed his face firmly back down.

A patrol flooded in, coming through the door she hoped to leave by.

These were regular law enforcement. The troops wore body armor tinted a bloody red with black accents—the Redhelms. Those masked faces were blank, hiding any trace of humanity. Their eyes were cavernous black shapes. With guns pointed at the ground, they pushed through the crowd like hungry carnivores, moving toward the lifts. "Step aside," commanded one of them. His voice through the mask was robotic, a voice that would scare children.

Kalh had the urge to plow right through and show them what a Radiance could do, but they'd arrived too quickly and entered casually: They must've only been here coincidentally. If that was true, retaliating would only convict herself. She'd been overlooked many times before.

The soldiers stopped before reaching the lifts. Their single line morphed into two lines, which parted from each other. Using their rifles, they coaxed the crowd to the sides, clearing a path from the door to the lifts. To run this gauntlet was too risky.

"What's going on?" an older woman demanded, probably one of the parents.

A Redhelm turned and raised his weapon. His mask gave no expression, but sadistic glee came through in the robotic tone: "You have a special visitor coming."

The woman forcibly crossed the Redhelm line. "I want to see my child."

The Redhelm turned the butt of his rifle and cracked it against the woman's collarbone, shoving her violently against the wall. "Nobody leaves."

The woman groaned and stayed on the ground.

Tannie tried to look up.

Kalh shook her head and covered his face. Her arms were exhausted, and his struggling made it all the harder to hold him. She moved her lips close to his ear. *"I'm going to set you down now. Keep your eyes closed and your face against me, okay?"*

Tannie obediently nodded.

She set him down and put her hands on his back, making sure her arms covered the sides of his face. The Redhelms seemed to take no notice of her or Tannie.

Alone she could escape easily. No one knew her or who she was. If she managed to get her heart rate down, she could vanish before anyone could do anything about it. Only, she couldn't surge carrying another person, so her escape would doom Tannie.

And the Witch Hunters would not be merciful just because he was a kid.

No one said a word. No one dared. Kalh locked eyes with Annekel, a coworker who had the expression of a panicked child. Kalh imagined her own face must look impassive, framed between her curving locks—the calm exterior people expected from her, one that didn't match her heart rate, the same lie she lived beneath constantly. She just hoped someone would take care of the other children, would comfort them. Tannie stood patiently facing her, now somewhat calm, and Kalh patted his back.

Through the entrance walked a lone miin. He looked like a kaipanther with dark purple fur but with six legs instead of four.

And he had unsettling red eyes.

Not yellow like they should be, but red.

Many miina on Sream walked upright to blend in better with their human counterparts, but this one did not. He crawled like a predator on all sixes, disregarding the way it made him stand out. He wore tribal clothing, made of leather. Maybe this was the special visitor. He seemed to be part of the retinue.

Upon seeing him, Kalh crinkled her nose against an imagined stench. Miina were from her homeworld.

And they were traitors.

Benton didn't agree. He trusted them. Or some of them at least. Maybe he'd sent this one. She thought she'd seen this very creature in the marketplace, skulking in the background, acting like a guardian. Or a spy.

The miin looked up. His nub-like horns seemed to snap into place perpendicular to her, as his eyes locked onto her—not falling on her by chance but moving straight to her, as if he'd known, as if he could sense her presence. He gave a discreet wink with one red eye and looked away.

She looked away too.

She peeked toward a side hallway. Maybe she and Tannie could make their way that direction without upsetting the Redhelms. Maybe by some miracle that exit would not be blocked.

When she looked back, the miin was staring at her with his animal eyes. He shook his head ever so slightly, warning her not to try it. If he was an ally, why was he with the Redhelms? But if he was an enemy, why had he been discreet?

She took a risk and gave the slightest nod.

Just then, the crowd gave a collective gasp, but they weren't looking at her. She followed the gazes toward the entrance. A man entered, one she recognized immediately. *This* was clearly the special visitor:

President Malkorn Taiberos, the most powerful man in the galaxy.

H IS GLOVED CYBERNETIC hand gave him away.

As did his fat face.

Taiberos wore the same outfit as the soldiers following him, only his armor plates were a charcoal gray and seemed custom fitted for his unhealthy girth. He carried his helmet under his arm, which exposed his head. His skin was pink, his hair pale. He was the tone of raw meat, a walking, dignified open wound.

The hand hanging over the helmet was not covered in armor but simply wore a black glove, his famous black glove. Beneath it was a cybernetic hand, never once seen by the public. A source of shame, it seemed. But that didn't stop him from famously pounding his gloved hand on pulpits as he campaigned to the ignorant masses.

The hand of Taiberos.

Behind him stomped a retinue of Witch Hunters.

They wore navy jumpsuits with white, mechanical plating over the top, suits that enhanced their abilities. They had batteries and grenades strapped around their waists. Mechanical contraptions hung from their shoulders, chests, and arms, making their shapes look more alien than human. Their masks had special lenses that could carefully scan the body temperatures of everyone in the crowd. Alone, her thermogenesis would certainly stand out, a little too hot even for an adult on the move. Tannie's would stand out even more. But they might not notice body heat amongst all the other people. Good thing the miin told her to stay put.

Kalh's heart raced, equal parts terror and hatred. In her mind, she saw a reporter speaking into a microphone and heard the echo of four words: *Never heard from again. Never heard from again. Never heard from again.* It had happened to Rothlesfer just a millo ago.

Taiberos prowled into the room.

Tannie struggled in her arms. *"What's…?"* He turned to see.

Kalh roughly pressed his face into her thigh, covering the sides of his face.

Taiberos had an air of indifference, as if perfectly immune to social pressures, which showed on his smug expression. She both envied and despised that quality. He meandered, looking at faces one by one, slowly getting closer to her and Tannie. "You know who I am."

The room was silent in reply.

Kalh kept her eyes down, unfocused, barely stealing glances.

Taiberos spoke with a calming tone, one that suggested he only barely kept the insanity at bay: "They used to call me the Witch Hunter. Do you know why?"

Kalh instinctively sensed that vial of sand hanging from her neck, as if the thought of home would steady her.

Taiberos, walking toward her, suddenly stopped. Directly in front of her. As if he knew.

But how could he have known without his helmet on?

Her breath caught in her throat. She looked down shyly at Tannie's sandy head and forced herself to breathe. Even air seemed vile, like food to a retching stomach. She thought of the forbidden melody, hoping its notes could calm her down.

Taiberos gave her a pleasant smile.

It wasn't the first time some creep noticed her flowing hair and shapely figure.

People between them stepped aside, exposing her. Exposing Tannie.

One of the white-clad Witch Hunters dropped a long, mechanical box.

It gouged the floor with a loud *BANG!*

The unexpected noise startled her, which sent a jolt through her body, and for the smallest moment her guard dropped.

Tannie's curiosity peeked just a little too far into the open, exposing his glowing eyes.

They saw him.

People screamed. The crowd exploded chaotically.

And Taiberos grinned.

Taiberos snapped forward with the speed of a predator.

It would've made sense for him to go for the culprit—Tannie. If he had, Kalh might've gotten the upper hand. But his cybernetic hand locked instinctively against Kalh's throat and jaw, slamming her head into the wall with a crack that made her ears ring.

Stars zoomed past, and for a moment life became blurry.

With his cybernetic grip locked around her neck, he grabbed her long hair with his other hand, twisting her to the ground. Right in front of everyone.

Tannie lunged with a growl, eyes glowing. He hacked wildly at the armored private parts, a direct assault on the President of the Pangalactic Socialist Democracy.

Taiberos let go and swept violently with his cybernetic hand, batting Tannie away like an insect. With a groan, the boy went flying, the metal fingers having pierced his skin, leaving bloody holes.

Kalh didn't think about her next decision. Didn't decide at all.

She simply reacted.

Her skin burned with heat. Her core ignited like a furnace. The fire inside flowed out through her eyes.

They knew her now.

"Get her!" Taiberos's mechanical fingers swiped at her neck.

With a snarl of white teeth, she shoved at her assailant with more power than a human her size should've been able to muster. Her hands never made contact, yet Taiberos's head jerked backward, and he stumbled in his heavy suit onto his knees.

Her hands clawed the air, pointing at Taiberos. Though she was a few arm's lengths away, she could feel his neck between her fingers. She threw her hands downward.

Taiberos toppled. His head smacked the ground.

His expression remained eerily passive as his fingers scraped at the skin of his own neck, feeling for something to pull away. But there was nothing—he was being throttled by a ghost.

Keeping her grip flexed, fingers still pointed at Taiberos, Kalh looked for Tannie with her glowing eyes.

One of the white-clad Witch Hunters leveled a stun gun at her. The snub-nosed weapon coughed a low, rumbling boom, like a single beat smashed against a terrible drum. The air rippled in a tight cone as the blast zoomed across the room.

When it hit, her muscles locked, and she collapsed like a mannequin.

The shot's collateral range caught several people near her, and they crumpled too.

The Witch Hunters rushed her.

Her muscles were knotted, clenched painfully, and she couldn't move. As the hands gripped her body, touching her all over, she felt some small satisfaction knowing her grip still clung to Taiberos's throat. It lasted only a moment longer though, until she lost her sense of his position.

Her eyes searched the edges of the room. If only Tannie could've gotten away.

Taiberos stood, his hand rubbing his neck. "Well, ████. She's valuable." He said it so matter of factly, not surprised at all—she hated how he always seemed so composed.

The Redhelms piled on top, crushing her and pulling her hair. She saw one last window of light through the mass of bodies, and then she completely surrendered. As her muscles relaxed, she felt an unusual calm, and her heart slowed its beat. Maybe while paralyzed, she still had a chance to *surge*—disappearing from their grasp and reappearing a short distance away.

Taiberos was a step ahead: "Get her on the exhaust quick. I'll bet she can surge."

She closed her glowing eyes, as if in prayer, but she was too late. Through her lashes, she saw an alien paw gripping a mask, moving toward her face to suffocate her.

It was that red-eyed miin.

She should've trusted her instinct.

She struggled, but they pinned her head against the ground. From that angle, she could finally see Tannie. He was lying on the floor not far away. She'd lied: He wasn't going to be okay. He was bleeding, unmoving.

And the light of his eyes had gone out.

THE WITCH HUNTERS pressed the mask over her mouth and nose, forcing her to breathe in the exhaust. Almost immediately, her hazel eyes closed, though she wished they wouldn't. Darkness crept in from the corners, and she lost awareness of her body altogether.

For a moment, she saw Tannie and believed he was okay. She wanted to ask what he'd seen when he was looking into the contragrav board. She wondered if she'd ever finish the lesson she'd started.

A white monster clawed into her biceps and pinched the nerves next to her bones. Her shadow rushed past her from one side to the other, time and again, at the speed of her heart, which still beat much too fast.

She was no longer herself. She wasn't any self. And then the sky peeled back, exposing her brain. If they could touch that, she'd lost everything. She was just a thing. An object. A slave.

And Taiberos could have his way with her.

She felt his hands on her naked skin.

Her heart raced, exhausting her, and yet she couldn't fall asleep, so maybe waking was the answer. She fought for consciousness, but sleep wafted like a vapor around her, and she couldn't help but inhale it. At least she was still breathing. Still breathing. And she could open her eyes if she wanted. She could. She knew she could. She felt cold, gray dust beneath her fingers. Powdery dust. She felt cold. And completely alone. Alone for cycles and cycles. Only she couldn't see the place where she'd arrived. Not without opening her eyes.

She didn't know how long it took, but somehow she finally managed to wake.

Dim light poured in, seeping from overhead.

Gray walls stood in front of her, all around her, moving slowly, or hardly at all.

As she became aware, she realized they'd stripped her. She was naked. And she couldn't even remember when or how it had happened.

She did remember Tannie's face against the lobby floor. And his body lying completely still, skull bleeding, eyes open.

Staring without any light.

She pulled her knees up close and wrapped her arms around them, trying to cover herself so the gray walls wouldn't see her. Even alone in this room, she felt exposed. Violated. And sore. The very sanctity of her body had been forcibly breached. It felt gross, disgusting. She wanted to vomit.

Fighting to feel fully awake, she squinted.

She put a hand to her neck, wanting to feel her necklace—that small bit of home. It was gone too, taken from her, just like her real home, and replaced by a collar locked tight around her throat, one that fed a toxin into her system at regular intervals.

More nausea hit as she realized something else was missing.

She reached up to touch her hair—and felt skin.

Her hair was gone.

Gone.

Completely gone.

Her naked shoulders curled forward as she put her desperate hands over her skull, bowing her face down into her knees.

She'd never felt so vulnerable. Never touched this close to her own brain.

She turned to the side as her body heaved. She spewed rancid liquid. It splashed on the floor, and the odor floated into the air.

Taiberos had done this. He'd made it illegal to be her.

To be Tannie.

Her elbows pulled together to shield her further.

She hadn't protected Tannie. She couldn't even protect herself.

The mechanical collar poisoned her again, shooting the exhaust into her neck. Immediately the dreadful sleep began to grip her. Still, she fought to stay in this nightmare reality.

She rocked forward and back. A gentle rhythm of calm waters against a painful shoreline. She should've felt anger or grief, but these were lost behind stronger emotions. Never before had she felt so frail. So mortal. So naked.

And so very, very afraid.

Soon the collar's dose would steal her consciousness.

She saw Tannie's eyes, staring blankly without light.

Her own eyes squeezed shut and tears dropped, leaving dark splotches on the concrete floor.

NAK, WHY ARE you in here?" asked CPC4K3.

"I'm avoiding the clients."

Nak sat in an easy chair aboard his ship, *The Sanctum*. The scuffed leather chair had seen better cycles. CPC4K3 had told him not to haul it aboard, but he never listened. One of its arms had a dark, brownish-red stain on it.

The recliner was completely out of place in these sterile surroundings. The floor was a metal grating that clanked when he walked on it. The room was a circle, not large, but large for so small a ship. At the room's center stood the bulky cylinder of the surge drive, which extended high overhead and dropped below the grated floor. The surge drive was directly between his chair and the door—he'd done that on purpose. Access panels and lights lined the circular walls. Everything in the room was metal, sharp, and freezing cold. Yet he loved it in here.

Which was good. Because if he didn't like metal, sharp, and freezing cold, then he might not like her either. Her technical name was C-P-C-4-K-3, but he just called her Cupcake.

"You've barely slept for two isochrons in the last twenty." CPC4K3's voice came from a tiny cube, barely as wide as Nak's little finger, clinging magnetically to the cylindrical surge drive. Well, nearly a cube, anyway. Each of her lines were slightly rounded, each corner just larger than ninety degrees. He once said she was like a cube who'd put on a little weight. She didn't like that description at all.

"Yep," he said.

"You keep ignoring my warnings about building sleep debt." Humans who spent too much time awake could start to hallucinate without even realizing it. Yet even on this important topic, it was like persuading a mountain to move. "PSD standards are ten isochrons every thirty."

" ██████ the PSD." In one hand, he gripped a dread mask. It was a dark helmet, and the front had a face: The upper half had big, round Shadowlyss goggles for eyes, and the lower half was a grinning mouth with tusk-like fangs curling out.

In truth, CPC4K3 couldn't see any of this. After all, she was just a tiny cube with no eyes. Through the ship's phantomlink, she could use all its peripherals, which meant she could see very clearly *outside* the ship, but inside the ship, she could only listen and speculate. Luckily, she had a big imagination.

Still, she hated when he just sat there in silence.

Hated it.

But if she brought that up, he'd tell her to work on the Ancor riddle, and she could, of course. She even wanted to work on it, but she wanted to talk to someone a little more. She decided to risk breaking the silence: "What are you thinking about?"

"I don't know."

Sometimes communicating with him seemed like navigating a maze. "Just give it a try." She said it with snark in her tone. Maybe a touch of flirtiness. In what she considered a sexy voice—one of the few options she had for displaying any personality. "Please?"

"It's hunger."

"The olioges on the starboard side are ripe."

"Not my stomach. More like my soul."

"What does a soul eat?"

"If I knew that, I'd eat it."

"I'm telling you, you're sleep deprived." Her high toned, slightly raspy voice matched her size. "Just go to sleep."

"I need to talk to the clients."

"Why?"

"Find out more about this girl we're rescuing. Can't get them to tell me more than what I've read on the Freenet."

"Then what are you doing in here?"

"Cup—"

When he said her name in that tone, she stopped immediately. She knew when to push him and when to stop.

She aimed her magnets till, with a clack, she snapped downward one body length, still clinging to the metal wall, but now with a different face. It took a moment to redirect her magnets, and then she tilted forward once again—another snap. This was basically her form of *walking*. Not difficult, just tedious, rolling her cubic self along the walls. From here to the cockpit would take nine-hundred and eighty-eight clicks. There was an easier way, but Nak wouldn't listen. He'd pretend to, and then he'd say it was safer if she was limited to the ship's metal, like he thought she wouldn't be loyal—just because other CP units had been unstable. He was wrong though.

She imagined Nak lying there with his eyes closed as she clacked her way down the surge drive's shaft. Persuading him seemed as impossible as solving the Ancor problem, and yet she kept trying. If she could just budge him a little… "I wish I had someone to talk to while you were gone."

Nak leaned his chair back and put up his feet. "You can talk to diagnostics."

"He's a slave processor!"

"So."

"He's not interesting."

"Who do you want to talk to then."

"Everyone!"

"That's because you don't know *everyone* like I do. If you knew them, you wouldn't want to talk to them."

"Yes I would."

She'd once been a completely white cube, but her worn edges and corners now exposed her metal color. Then Nak had drawn a face on each of her six surfaces—six ways for her to show her emotions: Happy, sad, shocked, angry, excited, and neutral. After he'd put her back down and told her what they were, she'd immediately clicked to the angry-face side and said, "I can't believe you drew on me!" Graffiti was *not* funny. He'd drawn on the outside of the ship too—but the ship couldn't talk.

She would never admit this aloud, but the faces he'd drawn turned out to be useful, once she got over the affront. She'd just roll till the appropriate

side faced out—a pretty genius little feature.

She stopped descending when she was directly in front of him, right at eye level. She rolled one last click to the side, showing her face with a hand-drawn grin. "I get lonely, okay? When there's nothing to do."

"We've been through this." She could tell he hadn't opened his eyes to look at her.

"But Nak…" Her voice had a bit of a whine. "I could talk to the clients for you."

He sat the recliner back up, put his feet on the floor, and leaned forward. "Cupcake, I cannot emphasize this enough: You can't talk to strangers. I mean it. No strangers. If you do, you force me to choose between you and *The Sanctum*. Don't make me do that, okay."

She clicked one face over, revealing her crying face.

He sighed, leaned back, and rested an arm over his eyes. Something like that anyway. After a short silence, he said, "You're lucky I didn't get a slave processor."

"Then I wouldn't be able to think."

"And you wouldn't talk so much."

"But Nak, you don't believe in slavery."

"Mmm."

"So are you glad you got me?"

"Still deciding."

"How long's that going to take?"

"At least another percent."

"That's so long."

"You better be good then." The chair squeaked as he shifted in it, probably into a more naplike position.

The steady hum of the surge reactor became the only sound.

Infraspace swirled outside the ship as they traveled to a place called Toar to rescue a woman from prison. A mysterious woman who CPC4K3 wanted to know more about. "Okay, go talk." Then she could at least listen.

But he didn't budge.

As the engine hummed, she thought and thought, wanting so badly to say more, to communicate, which she might've still gotten away with if she said the right thing, if she didn't nag, but nagging was really all she had left right now.

Maybe she could work on the Ancor riddle for a bit.

Captain Ancor became the maneuver's namesake because of how many lives he took. Nak had told her the story. To travel across large distances in a skycraft like *The Sanctum*, you had to get away from other gravitational sources. Otherwise, the three-body problem had hashes too complex to calculate. Usually this just meant your craft couldn't go anywhere, but Ancor somehow forced it. Instead of his ship surging to its destination like it was supposed to, it created a whirlpool in spacetime that sucked in a whole fleet.

None of them ever came out the other side.

Maybe Ancor did it on accident. Hard to imagine someone wanting to lose everything like that. It had been done since, but only a handful of times, and no one who'd solved the puzzle stuck around to explain why or how they did it.

CPC4K3 only liked the puzzle from a theoretical standpoint. It was a fun challenge. Plus maybe if she solved it, she could keep anyone else from doing it to *The Sanctum*. Nak encouraged her to work on it, but if she acted too interested, he'd shut down the conversation with, "Don't get any ideas."

At least the puzzle kept her occupied during the silences.

In theory, any Bloody Wing could do it. CPC4K3 thought she could probably do it if *The Sanctum* were sitting still for about ten percents of a lifetime, but no way Nak would spend a tenth of his life just sitting there. Besides, Ancor hadn't done it that way. He'd somehow found a method that wouldn't overtax the surge drive—some quicker route through the maze of data.

CPC4K3 crunched the numbers over and over, trying to find that faster pathway. Sometimes it felt frustrating to reach dead end after dead end. Especially when she'd rather be talking with someone. Anyone really.

Of course, only one person was an option. Only one person was ever an option.

And he was napping.

Still, she almost—

But then she didn't. Because she wanted to be good. For Nak.

The reactor kept humming.

And then she—

But she didn't. This wasn't the best time.

Though that was the problem: It was never a good time. He was always grumpy.

Then the words just came out, basically on their own: "Hey, after the Chorloak job, you said I could get repainted."

The chair squeaked as he squirmed and groaned. "Can't believe you don't want your faces."

"We could get them professionally done."

"You don't like my drawing?"

"Well, I might feel comfortable if a professional did it."

"Ouch, Cup."

"I'm sorry, Nak, but you don't practice drawing very often. That's all. Or you could get me a body like you promised."

"I never said that."

"Yes you did. On 435:95:1701, you said maybe I could get a body sometime."

"I said *maybe*."

"Well, maybe *yes?*"

"I'm not sure you really want a body."

"All right, give me your body, and you can stay here on the ship."

"You'd change your mind on the first cycle. Bodies are always needing maintenance and repairs and fuel. They're a hassle."

"Maintenance is what I'm best at. Besides, PKBs are getting pretty advanced."

"PKBs?"

"Physiological Kinesthetic Bioforms."

"I know what they are, Cup." He sat back up. "How do *you* know about them?"

Her tone slowed and her pitch raised as she began to tread more lightly: "The Coralains were talking about them while they were aboard."

"I've got to be more careful with your mics."

"PKBs work almost like real bodies. You could get me one of those."

"They're expensive."

"We can afford it—trust me."

"*We?*"

"It's a team effort."

"I seem to remember you telling me not to take the Borson job."

"Well, it was dangerous…"

She imagined him furrowing his brow, as if struggling to heft a distant memory. "In fact, I seem to recall you doing that on just about every job we've been on."

"Ah ha. You just said *we!*"

"All right: *we*. You're helpful. But I can take care of the books."

"Only, you don't. I was keeping them in order."

"Having the books in order is only going to cause trouble."

"I shouldn't have brought it up. I just wanted you to know we could afford a body. In fact, we could easily afford two of the Biopack X.9s."

"We don't need two."

"You know a cyborg body would be stronger than yours at peak performance?"

"I don't want one."

"Why not?" She mentally waded through the silence. "Nak, why not?"

"I just don't."

"But give me a reason."

He sighed. "The Mapuk say a person's soul is fused into his atoms. If I became a cyborg, I'd lose a portion of that soul." He was certainly thinking of Taiberos.

"You've got to spend your half on something."

"My half?"

"Yes."

"Okay, Cupcake. Remember: *I'm* the captain."

He stood up from his leather recliner and groaned as he stretched, head tilted back, his body becoming the shape of a T, holding the mask on one side. She knew what he looked like. His powerful blue eyes were those of an exiled prince, doomed to wander as an outcast. With broad shoulders, he stood nearly a head taller than the average man—built to shape the galaxy rather than speak about it. She loved that about him. And she envied it.

She imagined him curled forward in a somber mood, deflated, taking the dread mask in both hands and staring deeply into its wicked eyes and menacing smile, as if battling it, will against will. Maybe he was talking to the mask when he said, "Time to figure out how exactly we're going to rescue this girl."

"Do you think you're going to fall in love with her?"

"I told you we're not talking about my love life. And, no, I won't fall in love with her."

"Why not?"

She imagined a shrug. "It's a job." He started for the door.

"Do you think *I* could ever love?"

He turned halfway back toward CPC4K3. "I guess that's up to you."

"What do you mean?"

He shook his head. "You just choose to love someone."

"How?"

"I think your AE might be broken."

"What? Why?"

"Shouldn't be showing this much emotion."

"I think *yours* is broken. Just tell me."

"When you love someone, you put their needs over your own. You sacrifice for them. So you can choose to sacrifice or you can choose to not. That choice is love."

"That's what I do for you, Nak!"

"I guess so."

"I've sacrificed getting a body so that we can keep *The Sanctum* safe."

"That's right," he said.

"So I guess I do love you."

He cleared his throat and stepped toward the door, his boots clinking against the metal floor.

"Nak, do *you* love anyone?"

He pulled on his dread mask, transforming his aspect into a monster, and reached for the door controls. It changed his voice into a deeper, more menacing tone:

"Just one person."

THE MYSTERIOUS MAN in the mask approaches."

As Nak climbed the aft ladder and came down the hallway, he straightened his leather jacket. He looked good wearing it. His body temperature stayed too high for layers, except that this jacket had an internal coolant system. It was black except for the right sleeve, which had a wide, red stripe running down the length of it, from neck to wrist. He punched harder with that arm too.

Ribbons of green plants lined the walls of *The Sanctum*, growing from a trough at his elbow height and illuminated by constant white radiation. As he passed, he said to the man who'd just spoken, "You're jealous, Dray." The PSD had made it illegal to wear masks unless you needed one to breathe, a stupid law Nak liked breaking.

"Of course," said Dray in his deep voice. "Those are Shadowlyss goggles. Any kid would be."

Nak turned his dread mask to look directly at Dray. His voice was darker and more sinister through the vox: "What the ███ happened to you."

Dray had on some strange makeup that in combination with his beard made him unrecognizable from his former persona as Lord Admiral. His deep voice was still him though: "Although we hope to keep our masks on, this is a precaution. Otherwise, my face is quite recognizable." He was also wearing a full suit of Redhelm armor. The helmet sat in his lap.

"So's this one. Benton did that to you?"

"He's good, isn't he?"

"He sure knows how to ███████ someone's face." Nak continued toward the cockpit.

Dray wasn't quite as big as Nak, but almost. And although he was older by a good twenty percents, he'd aged well, thanks to a secret from Orban. His red infantry armor was a huge step down from his former rank. He'd let his gray hair grow out long and wild—in complete contradiction to his former career. His beard was trimmed, his demeanor kind, yet stern, and he acted like he cared, which made Nak feel grateful, confused, and wary all at once.

Dray's dossier said he started in the PSD as an enlisted pilot. Over time, he advanced through the ranks of officers, becoming a decorated figure and then the youngest Lord Admiral in history. Then he defected. Which made him infamous. The dossier had no details as to why, and the wild rumors flew. Nak admired the daring it must've taken to betray his own countrymen.

Dray took a seat next to Nak, and together they stared out the windscreen at the mesmerizing pattern created by the storm of infraspace. Each sequel of travel brought them closer to their objective: a prison and a mysterious woman.

The pattern outside was a tunnel of writhing light. Nak had once seen something that reminded him of it. He'd gotten beaten up pretty bad on Feath. Almost lost *The Sanctum* then too. While cleaning himself up, his blood dripped into the basin, and for half a sequel it looked exactly like infraspace, the way the red liquid partly congealed, drawing together to form strings, while also spreading outward, getting thinner and turning the water pink. Infraspace was like that but over and over, like they were sailing into that drop of blood, but instead of just red, many colors formed the strange, swirling network. He'd watched it more than almost anyone, yet the wonder never seemed to wear off.

Nak tapped a button, which changed the readout on the holograph.

"I can't believe how clear the image is," said Dray.

Nak shrugged. That was Photoss tech for you.

"I can't imagine what it must be like having one of these," said Dray. "Who do you think you are?"

Nak's dark voice came through the mask: "A damn good pilot or you wouldn't have hired me."

Dray wasn't Nak's friend. Nak didn't have friends—too much of a liability. He sort of had Lolo, who wanted to be more than friends, but he wouldn't let her. Dray was close to being an actual friend. An almost-friend. That meant a lot in Nak's paradigm. Plus they were both from Terron Prime.

Of course, he had Cup, but he felt embarrassed to think of her as more than hardware. Still, nice to talk to her sometimes.

Nak tapped three buttons on the instrument panel, verifying data he already knew.

"Hey, Skyreacher," said Dray. "How long till we touch down?" He was talking to Nak, who glanced over his shoulder.

The clients had never seen Nak's face or gotten his real name. "Half an iso."

The wings jittered, and Dray looked questioningly at the tentacles writhing outside. "So how does your skycraft work?"

"Ha ha." It didn't seem like a question any serious person would ask.

"What?" Dray responded in all seriousness.

"You mean the surge drive?"

"Yes."

"It's alien technology."

"I know that. Are you telling me you haven't learned anything about it since you got it?"

"Nope."

"Come on." Dray seemed to have a more casual tone around Nak than elsewhere. That also said something about their almost-friendship.

"It breaks the rules of physics. At least the ones we know."

"Go on."

"Let's say I flew in a long arc, curving from Toar to Sible. Then I turned around and flew back across the same space but with less of an arc. I'd get back faster, right."

"Yes. Not because you flew faster. A straighter trajectory means less distance."

"Exactly. Most ships can sail in a straight line—that's the fastest they can go: curve of zero. But *The Sanctum* can sail in negative arcs."

"Negative arcs?"

Nak said confidently, "Yeah. Shorter than straight lines." Photoss technology seemed far beyond mortal comprehension. For example, according to natural law, if you traveled immensely fast, you'd experience a short amount of time while the rest of the galaxy experienced a long time, so the traveler might experience a few sequels while a whole lifetime passed for everyone standing still. But for some reason, flying in a Bloody Wing reversed that. The traveler experienced several isochrons, while almost no time passed for others, a reversal of time dilation, directly contradicting nature's laws. Or else the whole galaxy was doing the traveling while the ship stood still. Whatever was going on, it made no sense. Still Nak liked to pretend he got it.

"But that's impossible," said Dray.

"Only in four dimensions."

"And how'd you learn this?"

"I just made it up."

Dray shook his head, unsure whether Nak had been joking all along.

And that was right where Nak wanted him.

Dray swiped a hand over his gray beard. "You have a computer aboard?"

Cup's grin popped into Nak's mind, but he just glanced over at Dray and didn't reply. He didn't like to talk about the hardware.

"Where do you keep it?" pressed Dray.

"Put away," said Nak.

"I don't think you ever told me what line of work you were in before you got your hands on *The Sanctum*."

"I navigated a spice freighter at Skalkurian."

"And now you do odd jobs?"

"Mostly data runs. They're good money but less exciting than the sort of thing you guys hired me for."

Dray gave no reply, so they sat in silence, listening to the hum of the surge drive. It played one note that pulsed in a high pitched warble, so quickly that it almost seemed stable. The sound of steady airflow accompanied, like the ship was constantly exhaling mechanical breath.

Nak checked the stats again—everything in order.

Dray cleared his throat. "You going to tell me how you got it this time?"

Nak turned his mask toward Dray, and its exposed teeth made a threatening snarl. "My ship? No."

"And apparently I didn't talk you out of your mask either."

"Can't afford the luxury of trusting people." Letting Dray be an almost-friend was already pushing it.

"Maybe you should consider giving it up."

"*The Sanctum?* ▮ no. Are you kidding."

Nak's ship blasted through the empty cavern of space. The edges of the wings ruffled up and down, in the shape of a solid wave or a shimmering angel. Its sheen cloaked it in black as night.

"I don't envy you," said Dray.

"Why not."

"You have one of the galaxy's most prized possessions, and what it's doing to you is clear."

"Giving me freedom."

"The opposite. Having this skycraft isolates you from everyone. And isolation is exactly what a prison is."

"Fortresses isolate too, you know."

"Not from loved ones."

"You're trying to talk me down before you start making offers."

Dray had a gentleness to his voice—a calm. An earnestness too. "I'm saying this as a friend."

In his head, Nak corrected the phrase to *almost-friend*. "You were invited aboard as a client, not a guest lecturer." His dread mask peered forward through the windscreen.

He knew the history of the Bloody Wings.

And he knew the consequences of his actions.

N AK LEARNED THE story from his dad.

The last time hearing it stood out in particular, for obvious reasons.

The tall buildings hid all but a narrow slice of the sky. Little Nak had been lying on his back next to his dad on a stretchy frod tarp that smelled of grease and atmosfuel, looking up at that slice of starry night on Terron Prime during one of the long summers.

"Dad, tell me about Captain Skyreacher's first flight and Aion Zero."

"You gotta pick one."

"Can't you do the whole thing?"

"You need to go to bed."

"Just tell it fast."

"Mmm."

The history enchanted Nak. It felt like the stuff of legends, a thing to reverence. It also happened to be true.

"A long, long time ago, when the Photoss Galaxy was very young—"

"How long again?"

"Over nineteen aions ago—nineteen whole human lifetimes."

"That's a lot."

"Hard to imagine, huh? On a planet named Rime, two nations went to war: the Toshi humans against the miina—with their six legs, horns, and sharp teeth."

"And you've seen one in real life!"

"Yes, I have."

"Awesome."

"The miina massacred the humans."

"And it was the bloodiest battle ever."

"Who's telling this story?"

"I don't know."

"Yes, it was bloody. Gruesome—I imagine. Probably would've made you sick to your stomach to see it. They killed them all, down to the last man, and that last man was just a boy."

Little Nak grinned, anticipating.

"With his family dead along with everyone he knew, the boy ran for his life and learned to survive alone in the wilderness."

"And learned how to make fire."

"I'm not telling that part. Then one cycle he stumbled on an abandoned alien colony, with crumbling ruins and broken temples hidden beneath the creeping jungle. No one was around, but whoever had once lived there left behind a skycraft."

"And Skyreacher probably found the bones of a dead pilot inside."

"Yes, probably."

"A Photoss?"

"I like to think so, but no one knows."

"I wish we did." Nak remembered how the tarp had stretched beneath his elbow.

"It took smarts and maybe a miracle for the boy to get the ship running. You gotta work really hard to figure out something like that all on your own. When he did, *The Elizaan* came alive, and then he sailed it. With the atmosdrive, he shot up into the sky all alone, with the thrusters shaking and pressing at his back. He grit his teeth like this because he could hardly take the g-force. Then with the zentisal drive, he crossed space for the first time till he reached Solace, Rime's sister. The boy found the remains of the civilization who'd made his ship, technology that we still can't understand, but the aliens themselves had vanished."

"I wish we could find out *where!*"

"You need to lie down. Thanks, Nak. As the boy grew up, he made a new home there on Solace, but he felt pretty lonely, having a planet all to himself, so he returned to Rime and made friends with some miina outlaws and brought them back with him."

"And he wrestled the chief."

"Maybe I'll tell that one next time."

"Okay."

"On Solace, the miina helped him build a village, a new home, and the boy grew old with his new friends."

"You're skipping all the good stuff!"

"It's bedtime."

"But you didn't tell the first interstellar flight yet."

"Well, I keep getting interrupted."

Little Nak pursed his lips.

"As an old man, the boy finally figured out how to use the surge drive. He took one miina buddy with him and left to another solar system. That was probably pretty shocking too, to see the swirl of infraspace for the first time, with no one to warn you what it would be like."

"I can't wait till I get to go interstellar."

"When you get a little bigger."

"And that was Aion Zero?"

"Yep, that was sort of like the beginning of history. That moment made him famous forever, and he became known as Captain Jethers Skyreacher."

"I wish I had that ship."

"Ha ha. So do I."

"Then what?"

"That's the end."

"No it's not!"

"Uh... Well, as you know, the colony never heard from Captain Skyreacher again, and we don't even know where he was buried, but after two aions *The Elizaan* returned to Solace without him, full of pirates from Terron Prime. The pirates had better weapons—"

"Rifles."

"Yep, rifles. The pirates conquered the miina of Solace and stole every Photoss artifact they could find. The humans of Terron Prime then copied as much of the tech as they could. They made atmosdrives to fly through their own air and zentisal drives to explore their own solar system."

"Then they found the surge gates!"

"And people began traveling from star to star. The connected galaxy... Fight for control... Blah blah blah... I don't want to tell all that. It's time for bed."

"You skipped the Bloody Armada!"

"Why do you want me to tell it if you know it all?"

"I don't know."

"Hmm. Okay. Well, when the pirates looted Solace, they unearthed a bunch more ships that were the sisters of *The Elizaan*."

"And they could go interstellar without a surge gate."

"Then what happened?"

Little Nak jumped into telling the story with all his enthusiasm: "People fought over the ships, killing and blood, so they called it the Bloody Armada. I don't see why they can't just make more."

Nak's dad squinted. "No one has figured out how to make a surge drive. Or a surge gate."

"But why not?"

"I don't know."

"Can't they just look at one and build the exact same thing?"

"Well, it's complicated. It would be like you trying to build a contragrav. Just because you can see it, doesn't mean you can recreate it."

"I'll bet I could when I'm a little older."

"I know you could, but for now, we're stuck with what the Photoss left behind."

"I wish I could figure it out. Then everyone could have one."

"Maybe you will when you grow up."

"I wanna hear the part when he fights the kaipanther."

"Time to go to sleep, Nak."

Whenever Nak smelled grease and atmosfuel, he thought of that night. It wasn't just another story though. It was the *last* story.

And the last time he'd seen his dad alive.

BEEP, BEEP, BEEP.

The whirling storm of infraspace calmed and calmed until it was nothing but a dark blanket pricked with stars.

Nak grinned beneath the dread mask.

As *The Sanctum* came back into normal space, any nearby skycraft would've detected no electromagnetic disturbances of any kind. One moment housed empty space; the next carried the ship steadily along, whispering across the blackness. He didn't even need to burn zentisal fuel to create his initial momentum.

A thing of beauty.

Few Bloody Wing pilots knew how to do that. Because these drives were so valuable, governments monopolized most of them, and the rest were controlled by big corporates. That divided the flying among large crews and bogged it down with standard procedures, preventing anyone from getting good at the fine details. Few in the galaxy had clocked as many isos at this either, making him one of a kind. Just like his ship.

The space surrounding this solar system was filled with dust like a common atmospheric cloud, a vast vapor, frozen in time. The rays of the nearby sun reflected off it in strands of electric purples and smeared blues, though they were hard to see without Starsight.

He pressed the internal comms button and leaned forward: "We're on approach, landing in half an iso." He had a mirror on his dashboard for keeping a subtle eye on anyone behind him. He saw Dray in it, sitting patiently, silently. Nak glanced over his shoulder. "How'd you get roped into this mission."

"After my military career ended, I spent two percents of my life incarcerated." Dray seemed a little too kind and a little too calm to match the profile of an inmate. "I'm somewhat of an expert on Building 13 now."

Nak raised his eyebrows and nodded. He'd been caught by the Witch Hunters once himself, but he managed to escape before getting his own reluctant tour of Building 13. "I can't imagine what's driving you to go back. Seems a little risky, doesn't it."

"It's a long story."

"I won't pry."

"No, I'll tell you." Dray gave a wry grin. "Seeing as how you're my friend."

"We hardly know each other."

"And yet I'm probably one of the people you trust the most."

Nak's mask stared blankly at the comment.

"This could also be one of the last conversations I ever have," said Dray.

"You wouldn't go in there if you didn't think you'd make it back out."

"No, *you* wouldn't."

Nak nodded. Fair point.

The truth was, on the Feath job, Dray had gone beyond the contract, beyond his own self-interest, and risked his life to save Nak's. That strange fact made no sense. Nak kept looking for a reason, a moment when Dray would suddenly demand repayment, but it hadn't yet come, as if Dray had done it simply for the sake of helping a person who needed help.

That strange fact also defined their relationship.

Nak wanted to reassure Dray, tell him he wouldn't die, that it wasn't his last chance to get something off his chest, but this mission had extremely high stakes, and one small hitch could be fatal. Or worse. And while Nak prided himself on keeping cool under pressure, marching into Building 13 required guts at another level. Guts he admired. Or maybe it was just plain stupid.

Must've been some girl in there.

Dray said the next sentence with an uncanny calm: "I helped create the Witch Hunters."

Out of respect, Nak's mask withheld any response.

Dray went on: "When I served the PSD, I hunted down Radiances. I captured them, took their freedoms in the name of safety, while calling it my duty. I did that for percents, till the laws I'd enforced on others were enforced on me—on my family. I tried to save them, but I failed, and my actions landed me here on Toar as a prisoner." He bowed his head. Not with a shameful expression, more as if out of reverence.

Nak was surprised but couldn't show it on his mask and didn't know how else to express it. Again he said nothing.

"After escaping Building 13, I became an exile, on the run from nearly everyone, a bit like you. I was tormented by what I'd done. Without my family, I had no future. I wanted to die. Till almost magically I found Master Jyngsoo. He taught me to calm my mind, and I began to see. I realized my purpose was to make amends for my crimes."

"So you're going to end the Witch Hunters."

"I want more than that. I want to stop the thing that created them. I want to put an end to people's fear and complacency."

"Big goals."

"I would give anything to change what I helped create." Dray's demeanor shifted again, battling for calm. "We've spent aions squabbling over the same old things. We have great potential, but we need guidance to reach it. We're children in need of a parent to show us the way."

"And who would that be."

"A new government."

"You don't like our government, huh."

Dray shook his head in an emphatic *no*.

"Any particular reason?"

Dray sighed. "We've all seen the government do some good. For example, it protects us from the Grezyk."

"That's about the only one I'll concede."

"And yet it over-taxes its citizens, censors the truth, starts unnecessary wars, and kidnaps innocent Radiances. The government hurts people on the outskirts the most, like Benton or the prisoners in Building 13, but it's not hurting the majority enough personally, so they remain complacent. They turn a blind eye to atrocities like the ones I committed. To most people, it's a dull pain they can ignore, even while Solace is being oppressed and Kalhette's life is being shredded to pieces." As he continued, his tone rose in passion: "People feel safe, but it's a lie. They think the PSD's wrongs are justified, that the good it does outweighs the bad. That's not acceptable though! If the government will treat one citizen that way, they'll treat any citizen that way. That's the truth. And while the populace does nothing, the government continually grabs more power."

"With that bastard Taiberos at the helm."

"Who the majority elected."

"Doesn't make it right."

Dray took a deep breath and seemed to calm back down. "Of course not. No one is safe either. If we let this go on, soon it will be too late. The PSD will become too powerful to stop, and then it will turn on the populace. Just like it did to me."

Nak inhaled quietly through his mask. "Maybe people are trying to lie low, staying out of it for their own self preservation." Seemed like a good tactic.

"You're right. This galaxy is filled with children, people who can barely take care of themselves. I understand. Fear drives them, rather than some higher cause. And that hurts other people, just like I did when I hurt those Radiances." Dray paused, leaving his words to linger across the silence and the hum of the zentisal drive.

Nak wanted to defend himself, but that would've been a confession. Instead, he chose the noble route: "Well, at the time, you thought you were doing the right thing."

"It doesn't matter what I thought. I was wrong. And look what I created."

"So you're planning a revolution."

"If that's what it takes. I want to give the galaxy a better government than what they have."

"If you *don't* die down there, are you going to regret telling me all this?"

"No. I trust you." Dray stared with a pervasive calm, looking so deeply it was like he could see through the dread mask, although that was impossible, even with Starsight.

"Not sure Benton would want you telling me."

"Benton doesn't know you like I do."

Nak laughed.

H IS MASK LOOKED toward the black of space where the tiny dot of a red planet grew in size. "I hope you're not waiting for me to take my turn at a last confession. *I'm* not risking my life in the Strand, remember."

"I don't think—"

"Skyreacher? Skyreacher!" Benton's shout came from down the hallway. Not a demanding shout, just an overzealous one, considering Nak was in the cockpit.

He felt glad it'd interrupted his turn though. "I'm right here."

He swiveled his chair and watched as two figures came down the hall: a human and a miin. If Nak weren't wearing a dread mask, he might've greeted them with a grin. Instead he touched a finger to his masked eyebrow and gave them a lazy salute.

First was Benton Xylander.

The man who'd chartered the mission.

On Dray's referral, Nak met Benton in a dark cantina on Skalkurian. That was how this had all started.

The low lights had seemed to enhance the sounds of tinkling drinks and murmuring patrons. Nak liked to start these interviews by letting his mask do a little silent intimidation while he sized up the potential client.

"You must be Skyreacher," said the client. Benton was around five percents of a lifetime older than Nak. He was the pristine sort, sandy hair always recently cut, always combed, and a beard perfectly trimmed to match. His narrow face had a straight nose that ended abruptly as if measured with a straight edge. His eyebrows slanted upward in the middle, giving him a lasting expression of sincerity. His ears were about the only thing you could criticize on his perfectly regal face, and even that was a bit of a stretch.

Nak leaned forward under the warm table lights. "You're a Zhan? You don't look like a monk to me."

"That's because Zhani aren't monks." Benton took it well, keeping his cool on nearly every topic, including Nak's exorbitant price. He came across as exceptionally competent, and he seemed like a nice guy, maybe a little too nice.

That didn't stop Nak from probing till he found a weak point: "So this woman—she's your daughter."

Benton became rigid, like he expected a Grezyk to jump out of the conversation at any time. "No."

"Girlfriend."

Benton squinted at that comment, like he was hiding a cringe on the inside. "Can we keep this professional?"

Of course Nak could be professional, when he wanted to, but he needed to get an emotional read. "Fine. This woman is of marginal importance to you."

Benton put his hand over his mouth, as if the phrase had been so far from true he could barely keep his protest from spilling out.

After one round of drinks, Nak knew two things: This man could be trusted, and he'd pay a lot of money.

Nak took the job.

And now the two of them sat together in the cockpit of *The Sanctum*, with Benton wearing the armor of a Redhelm.

HERE, YOU TAKE that one," said Benton in his distinguished tone, pointing to an open seat.

The fourth member of their outfit wasn't human.

Though Nak had seen plenty of miina in his life, they still held some intrigue from his childhood. To him, they were creatures straight out of myth.

This one's name was Liink Adiin.

He looked like a kaipanther but with six legs instead of four. His feral head was covered in short, dark fur—colored like a deep purple wine—and his yellow eyes shone in beautiful complement. From the profile view, his cranium curved forward into a snout like a wildercat's. From the front, his ears drooped to the side like wings, sloping toward his jawline. No horns yet. His large eyes sat wide on his face and formed an obtuse triangle with his dark, wet nose, and they conveyed the keenness of a soul. His mouth curved back and down above a strong jaw. His lips seemed to have been bunched together with needle and thread. Crude leather armor covered his body.

He curled awkwardly into the chair designed for humans and folded his upper, shorter arms across his chest, a strangely human gesture, while his lower ones rested on the arms of the chair. The fingers on his lower paws reached the floor, splayed out in an inhuman way, and one claw twitched, tapping against the metal. When Nak was a kid, he wondered what having that extra pair of arms would be like, a thought that crossed his mind again. Would definitely help in a dogfight.

When Liink had first boarded *The Sanctum*, he pointed at the plants growing in the hallway and said, "You cultivate life. That shows reverence." He spoke with a voice slightly higher pitched than you might expect, a voice that was small, humble, timid in tone, but bold in its clarity, quietly bold.

"I eat them," Nak had replied.

"One can honor what is exchanged for his own life." Liink's tone was smooth as a hot drink, a surprisingly mild voice for such a large creature. He had an accent too, which added a dash of alien sour to the soothing liquid, a voice familiar and foreign.

Nak always wanted to hear a little more.

O NCE LIINK SAT, the four companions watched the red sphere growing in front of them. Sible was a massive planet with low density, much too hot to survive on—with nothing to stand on if you tried. They were just close enough to see her moons too, one of which was the place they'd meet their death or glory.

Benton leaned forward and stared out the ship's glass screen. "Wow. I'm not sure I've ever seen a planet spinning so fast."

Nak dimmed the cabin lights, making the vista outside all the more impressive, shining brightly by contrast. "Toar's just as bad. Just wait till you're on the surface and see the shadows."

He navigated toward Toar, a giant moon with a dark terrestrial surface and an orange, breathable atmosphere. Some strange collisions must've birthed her and put her on her present course. She spun so quickly that you'd notice a decrease in weight if you moved from the poles to the equator. If she rotated faster, the velocity would tear her apart, yet somehow Sible gave her just enough stability and warmth to be a viable home to biological life.

Pling! One of the panels pulsed with a jarring waveform and turned red.

"What was that?" asked Benton.

"It's picking up seismic activity on the surface, not far from our landing site."

"A bomb, maybe," said the miin.

"No, it's not a war," said Dray. "Massive quakes happen often here. It's unstable."

Benton faced Liink. "My intel was a little vague on this point. The explosions might not be natural. Possibly a byproduct of one of their research projects."

Nak felt something strange on approach.

A hunch, really, but maybe stronger. A feeling of... destiny maybe... something grand in scope... almost epic... like it was hanging in the sky overhead, waiting to fall. Not that he believed in that sort of thing. Maybe his gut did though.

He let out a lazy sigh as he clipped on two shoulder belts. His tone revealed the grin beneath his mask: "Okay, boys. The fun's about to start." As his passengers locked in their seat buckles, he tapped the manual-mode toggle, grabbed the horns of the steering yoke, and just for style rolled the ship in a looping barrel as they dove toward the surface. The targravs pulled them to the floor, only partially masking the twisting momentum.

The Sanctum's black wings glided through morphing orange clouds, moving forward and down at a steep angle. At these higher altitudes, Toar's constantly turbulent winds shook the ship, jostling the passengers back and forth.

Once they descended low enough, the winds calmed. Then great cracks in the landscape became visible, and smoke billowed out of them, curling and drifting with the wind. The bottoms of many of these chasms glowed orange with molten lava, flowing like reluctant water.

Nak eased off the descent as they neared the surface, shallowing his slope and reducing his speed. He still dropped fast though, closer and closer, till the smoke from the cracks breathed all around them.

Benton leaned his perfectly trimmed skull back against the headrest. "What are you doing?"

"Relax." Nak steadied her out, flying parallel to the surface and exceptionally low. Once they finished falling, he activated the atmosdrive, which could accelerate fast enough to make a mortal go unconscious. He kept his speed high, aiming toward some strange rock formations that reached skyward like gigantic fingers, eager to claw down the tiny ship. Smoke floated upward, putting a veil between them and whatever lay ahead.

"Seems a little close to the ground," said Benton.

"If we go higher, the heat won't hide our signature."

A pair of massive rocks shaped like agonizing towers suddenly appeared through the smoke, zooming toward them.

Nak wrenched the yoke, and *The Sanctum* rolled onto her side, threading the space between without a moment to spare.

The targravs couldn't compensate for this rapid movement, especially so near the surface gravity. As the movement jerked the passengers to the side, Benton grabbed the harnesses going over his shoulders. "Oh, my."

"This is the best sailing you've ever seen, isn't it."

Benton moved his hands from his harness to the bottom of his seat, pulling himself deeper into it.

The Sanctum cut between more curls of smoke and massive rock formations. Its wings fanned to the sides, forming two jagged-edged semicircles. It looked almost like a raptor with its wings stabbing forward in an aggressive dive.

"Just want to make sure you get your money's worth."

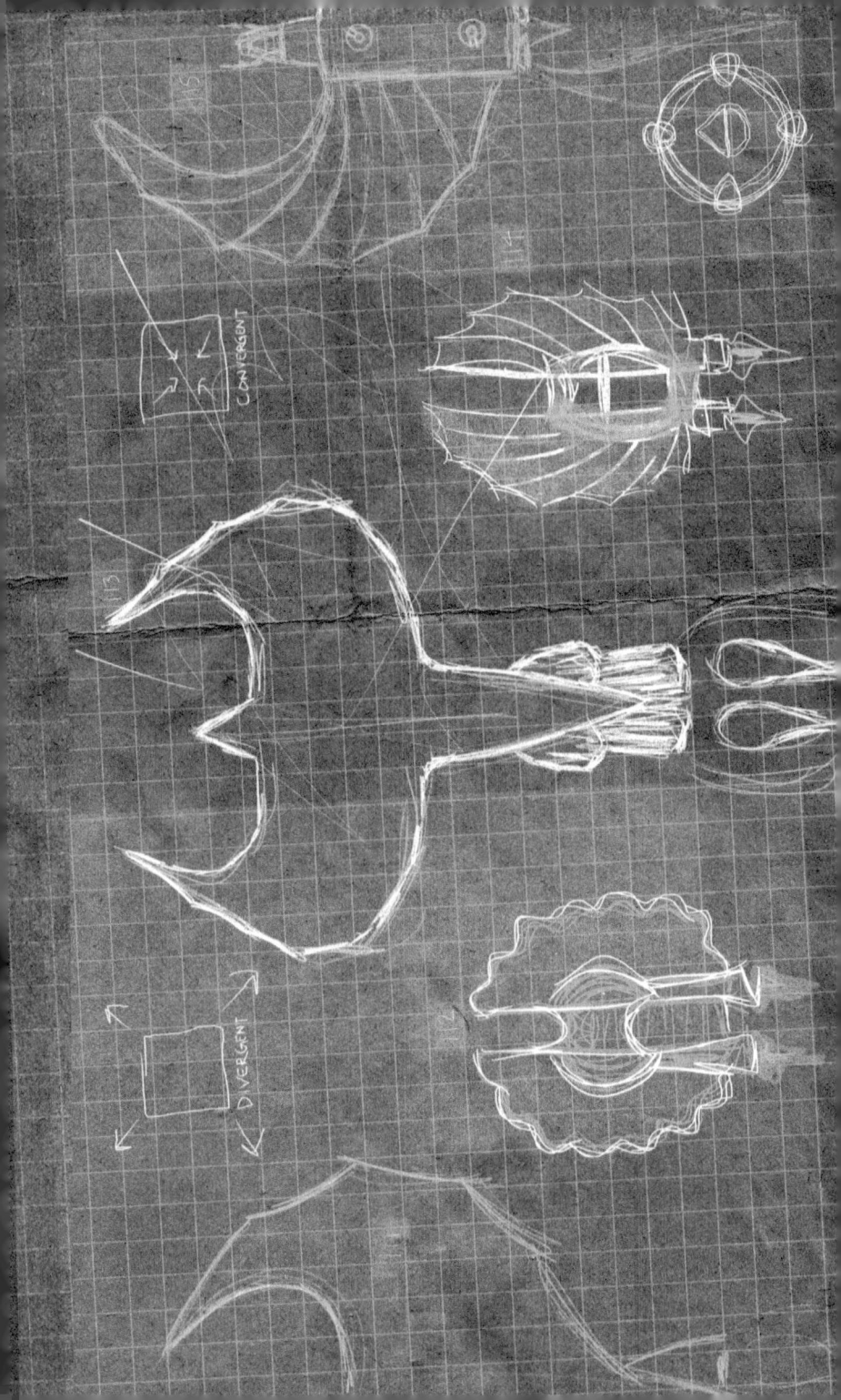

CONVERGENT

DIVERGENT

No one laughed. But Liink, clinging to the seat with only three of his paws, at least grinned with his rippled lips.

Nak eased the ship down into one of the glowing canyons, zipping along the uneven corridor. He slowed a bit too, but not enough for Benton to relax.

At last, he pulled back out of the canyon, eased up on the throttle, glided above the flat ground, and drew to a gentle stop. *The Sanctum* hovered for a moment as the landing gear deployed, and then she touched down on the dark surface of Toar.

"Okay, this is the contracted drop point, and not a chance they detected us." Nak looked at his wrist. "I'll meet you at our next rendezvous point in six isochrons. That'll be right when the sun vanishes for the third time."

The team members each set their chronometers and did a final gear check.

With a hiss, the airlock opened, and beyond it the gangplank lowered as the hot air flowed in. The foreign atmosphere came through Nak's mask—something about it was the wrong flavor.

The three clients marched down the walkway and into the strange air.

Nak walked halfway, placed a forearm on the deck, and leaned down. His dread mask turned to one side and then the other, surveying the landscape. The soil looked like burnt charcoal and seemed to absorb any light that touched it, creating an unnaturally dark surface. He breathed in, letting the heavy, warm air do its job. He then descended the rest of the way and stepped onto the black ground.

As the three others set out on foot, their shadows grew quickly behind them. The sun approached the horizon at an unsettling speed, as if time itself were hoping this would hurry up and be over.

Nak shouted at their backs: "I just want to reiterate, since you're all on your way to set off some alarms—if anyone isn't at our next rendezvous on time, I'll be forced to cut you loose. That's in the contract."

Benton turned around, taking a few steps backward. Any timidity he'd shown on the descent had completely vanished. His tone held the courage of a man ready to die for his cause as he shouted, "As we agreed."

Nak couldn't shake the feeling: Something big was coming.

Real big.

Maybe it was here already.

Soon the sound of their footfalls disappeared into the wind as the three figures slowly diminished toward the black horizon. The sun slid behind jagged mountains, marking the end of the first day and transforming the cloudy sky into a colorful array. It faded too quickly into a black dome of unfamiliar stars with the red planet glowing huge in the sky.

Nak watched them go, marching off into this land of fire and smoke.

Something about this outfit really fascinated him—three desperados risking their lives to save one woman.

Must've been something to have friends like that.

BENTON'S MIND WAS stuck in a loop.

Miss Whitesun, I have to apologize for something you don't know I did.

No.

She'd hate the formal tone. Plus it would be a lie. After what they'd... once been.

Although she'd been born into a distinguished family much like his own, she'd been ripped away from them at an early age. Early enough that most of her polish had been scuffed. Her personality was distinct from his too. He found it strangely attractive.

Listen, Kalh, I need to be upfront with you. There's...

No.

Too casual. Even if he managed to do it authentically, it wasn't the right decorum for Benton Xylander, son of Tarkon Xylander. Though it wouldn't be the first time he'd done what such a son shouldn't...

Miss Kalhette, I did something that inadvertently put a lot of attention on your imprisonment.

She wouldn't be happy about the news—not a positive step in their relationship. But he'd sworn off subterfuge with people he trusted and who he wanted to trust him. He had to tell her.

Immediately.

Kalhette, I need to tell you something. I made an honest mistake, one for which you have suffered and will suffer the consequences.

Straightforward.

Just her full name, then warn her what was coming, and then tell it all.

"Where's your ID!" The gruff voice snapped Benton free of his thoughts.

They had come to the gates of the Strand.

After the pilot dropped them off, they spent their first short night on Toar hiking across the black desert to a transport, which they sailed to the Strand, arriving with all the trappings of an official transfer. That part had taken a long time to plan.

Flock towers stood high on both sides of the entrance. Red-clad sentinels carrying rifles walked down the gangways on both sides, looking down on anyone who approached. The low trajectory of their inbound flight meant they hadn't seen the Strand from the sky, but Benton had been studying it most every waking isochron for the last forty sleep cycles. On the surface, the network of buildings looked like the spine of a dead animal, its vertebrae forming a series of white clumps in an arc across the black ground. From above, the buildings appeared to be about the same width and length, but these structures plunged underground at varying depths, making it something like an underground city.

Rumors said the engineers dug so deep into the infernal surface that they'd reached a demonic Otherworld ruled by Lethos himself. As a Zhan, Benton believed in the supernatural, but this seemed more like superstition. The people running it were the real monsters. They did unspeakable things to their prisoners, and all for some mysterious purpose that Benton had yet to discover.

He hadn't found maps or blueprints either and wouldn't have even known which building to approach. Dray, the mastermind, explained that Building 13 housed the prison, although *prison* might've been the wrong term. It suggested justice. What happened at Building 13 was far from that. It contained detainees who'd committed no crimes other than to have been born with propensities in the Song. People like Kalhette and Tannie. And there they waited for experiments to be performed on them.

Dray stood in front, wearing one of the eponymous masks of the Redhelms. It was shaped like a crimson skull with big, black eyes of glass. A channel of vertical slits formed what could've been the mouth, like a human muti-lated. Charcoal gray circles covered the ears and housed the comms. Dark grooves ran through the helmet in a pattern like frowning eyebrows that stopped short and cut directly downward like daggers through the eyes. Dray's shoulder pads indicated the highest rank that still wore one of the anonymizing masks. Higher ranks showed their faces and had identities.

Through the Song, Benton had learned to detect thought beyond the usual mental boundaries, so although nothing could be read on these death masks, through Ptolis he sensed Dray's stillness. The man had poise beyond that of other mortals, but Benton still detected a hint of trepidation, proving Dray too was human and the threat was real. Just the smallest thing out of place, and these soldiers might shove the visitors to the ground and aim guns at their heads.

Yet Benton had been thinking about Kalhette.

He swallowed, willing the anticipation to remain dormant.

It was absurd. He was acting like a teen. She was just a person, a woman, a young woman, a little naive at times, right on the border of being too young for him. And just because it was the first he'd seen her since…

Since she told him no.

After all this time, his heart was still broken, but he honored her choice. His feelings would not be her burden. If she brought it up, so be it. If not, he would die holding his peace.

Under his red helmet, he felt a dab of sweat building above his lip. He needed to focus, to watch for clues about Darkstar, the secret project going on at the Strand, so he could prove to the War Council that they'd gotten more than their money's worth. And assuming he survived, the revolution would then follow, an attempt to overthrow the PSD on Solace.

In comparison to these matters, his lonely soul counted not at all.

Dray wore a bracelet with an ID coded into its grooves—one that had cost a fortune to acquire. He held it up for the soldier to scan. The machine beeped.

During his percents in exile, Benton had broken into several places with similar protections, and he'd learned that any given system was only as secure as the weakest person with access. That meant any system could be infiltrated. It was a matter of finding the weak link. Or in this case, the weakling: A man named Jaulson had authenticated these IDs into the system.

Benton raised his own wrist to the scanner.

"State your purpose." This guard also wore the mortal red color.

Again through Ptolis, Benton sensed Dray's annoyance. He was the perfect person for this role because he wasn't acting. He pointed a gloved finger toward Liink's wine-dark fur. "A new acquisition." He handed over the papers.

The guard leaned for a clear line of sight at Liink and said, with a metallic ring in his voice: "That's a big one."

Dray didn't even look at Liink. "Coming in from Koischioux Station. Ready?"

The guard was supposed to be reading the orders, but he somehow sensed Dray's annoyance. He handed the papers back and waved a red, mechanical-looking glove, urging them past the checkpoint. "Move along."

Benton took a slow breath and followed Dray, while leading Liink on a leash.

They crossed a courtyard toward Building 13, which seemed not much more than a large shed. Inside, a corridor was lined with lifts on both sides. The trio went directly to an open lift. Dray punched a key for the processing floor, another detail only an insider could've known.

And they descended deep underground.

T HE INSIDE OF the Strand was busy.

Redhelms stood about, like wounds spread throughout the populace. Researchers in white jumpsuits walked the lengths of hallways and in and out of offshoots, matching the pristine white walls. These were nearly all humans, the result of one of the galaxy's greatest mysteries:

As explorers slowly unfolded the Photoss Galaxy and its colorful spectrum of species, they had found humans existing in multiple systems. Not just humanoids but actual humans, the only common species ever discovered. Yet no civilization had any evidence of even a lost ability to traverse the ocean of stars prior to Aion Zero.

So who had sewn the seeds of humanity? And why?

As the most populous species, many human cultures maintained a sense of superiority. The dominance of the Pangalactic Socialist Democracy confirmed this attitude. The Orthau from Orban were a notorious exception, having earned almost universal respect for increasing their own lifespan and that of their human neighbors.

The miina, on the other hand—Liink's people—had not fared so well. Prominent PSD leaders had described the miina as backward and barbarous and had labeled their high chieftains monsters. All because the miina refused to be ruled. During the conflict known as the Solace Sunset, the PSD confiscated and destroyed thousands of volumes of miina literature and demolished hundreds of Photoss temples and libraries, trying to break their spirits. The PSD then vilified the miina to justify their own wrongdoings.

That made Liink the perfect decoy, just the sort one might expect to find imprisoned in Building 13.

Benton sensed anxiety from Liink, an eagerness to prove himself. Despite his massive size, he was just a cub. He'd come because of his demolitions training. It was also a symbolic gesture to have a chief's son on the mission.

Liink's black jumpsuit was designed for a human, so they'd cut holes for his middle arms, which stuck through, naked, another affront to his species. With his six limbs chained together, he walked more like an insect than a mammal. He wobbled, pretending to be drugged by the collar around his neck. A muzzle ran between his eyes, down the bridge of his snout, and clamped around his jaw. Not the most dignified of costumes, but a miin like Liink was completely committed to the mission:

He would undergo any hardship for honor.

Benton handed Liink's leash to Dray as the three of them approached a woman at the desk who wore a white jumpsuit and had her hair tied behind her head. "Let me see your assignment." She held out a hand. Next to her desk was a murky glass door, above which read the words *Pharmacology Block*. A pair of Redhelms sat casually on a bench, their discipline apparently quite lax. "▮▮▮▮▮▮ miin."

Benton acted like he was supposed to be there and turned to a plink comms terminal to the left of the desk. So began his role as the clacker. Building 13 had dozens of prisoner floors, which made finding Kalhette nearly impossible, not without Benton accessing the Strand's local database to find out exactly which cell she was being held in. They'd been unable to get this carefully guarded data on the outside. Even if he had, it might've changed by the time they got inside. He had to find it now, on the spot, and he had to do it quickly, while Dray stalled.

The terminal fit into an inset in the wall. It offered Benton the slightest privacy and put his masked face out of sight to the pair of Redhelms. Still, if either of them stood and looked directly, they would see what he was up to. His best bet was to simply pretend like he was supposed to be there and make it fast. He tossed his bag on the ground and began typing at the terminal. He casually pulled a plink comms cylinder from his bag and plugged it in to the console, leaning his stomach against it for concealment.

"Was he looking at me?" came a metallic voice.

The words snatched Benton back out of his focus. He leaned back to see. One Redhelm sat forward, his face clearly pointed toward Liink.

Liink was supposed to have his muzzled head down, eyes mostly closed, like a toddler who couldn't wake up. He definitely wasn't supposed to be looking around.

Dray still held the leash and was talking with the woman at the desk, somehow using his insider knowledge of this place to distract or confuse her. He faced forward, exemplifying perfect discipline, acting as if he hadn't noticed any of it.

The Redhelm leaned in an aggressive pose toward Liink. "Were you looking at me, vermin?"

Liink bent his head to the floor, not acknowledging the question.

Benton focused forward, typing away. At the right moment, he grabbed the plink comms and twisted carefully. If anyone reviewed the logs, they'd think an android had been the one accessing it. He was a quite talented clacker and just needed a few more moments to reach the roster.

The soldier stood and grabbed a baton from his belt.

Liink almost imperceptibly drew closer to the floor.

Dray seemed to be doing nothing about it.

Benton tried to hurry. He just had to scroll through a few hundred inmate names, down to W. Fortunately, only the adults were held in this building, which decreased the search size by a lot.

"Seems he doesn't know Building 13 etiquette yet. That's easy enough to learn though." Without a moment's warning, the Redhelm raised his baton in the air and cracked it against Liink's face.

The sound seemed to go right into Benton's own spine.

The miin crumpled forward, his chin hitting the ground just before his chest did too, his arms in a tangle beneath him. His tail was the only part of him that never hit the floor.

Benton jerked the plink comms from the terminal and turned around. "Stop! He's supposed to be conscious for testing!"

"You're obviously new too." The disdain carried clear enough in the soldier's voice. "He shouldn't be looking around like that. You gotta be careful, specially with these big ones. Better check his collar. I think the exhaust is running out."

The woman at the desk frowned.

Dray's Redhelm was a mask of indifference.

Benton stared for a moment at Liink, debating whether to help his friend back up.

Before he'd decided, Liink struggled back onto his own feet, his gaze carefully locked on the floor. The blood on his face oozed into his fur, yet he still had conviction in his eyes.

The woman at the desk handed Dray a collection of tiny packages. "Here you go." Dray stuffed them into his pack, handed the leash back to Benton, and walked out.

Benton wanted to apologize for taking so long.

Instead, he silently turned and led Liink to Floor 27, cell A13.

T HE NIGHT HE met her, she'd appeared suddenly, the moment she was needed, like a page from a storybook.

He'd been sitting in a dank, poorly lit bar.

A man with a head made of concrete said, "What about people paying their fair share—for good things, like skyways and police and charity?"

Benton got lured right in to the argument.

Too inebriated to see the impossibility of convincing anyone of anything, least of all of the rightness of his ideal government to some ignorant Panso. "My government would never stop anyone from paying whatever they want of their own earnings to support whatever causes they believed in. I even believe they should: roads, police, or toilets. But we'd never force someone to pay. That is slavery."

The blockhead blathered back about democracy and the social contract.

Then she appeared, a bright light in a dark room.

She'd overheard the conversation and stepped in with her own rebuttal. Though she later denied it, he remembered her being a little drunk too. "The slavery happens through taxes. A fourth of my personal earnings gets used for things I don't believe in. So I've personally funded the Strand and the horrors performed there. My money made possible the murders of the Shartriin Massacre. I've literally earned the money spent to kill people. It makes me so angry."

After she said that, the man spit a filthy word at her under his breath.

Benton had never been in a bar fight before or since.

Another example of Kalhette clouding his judgment. They'd become lasting friends, making the bloody, swollen face more than worth it.

She'd been rotting in the Strand for millos. Just finding the right pilot had taken a long time, not to mention the planning, logistics, and bribery. It took much too long, and every additional cycle was another she had to suffer. All that work had only gotten them a route inside. Getting a prisoner back out was more complicated.

That was where Dray came in.

When they arrived on floor 27, Dray said, "Wait here a moment."

Benton got off the lift and stood obediently, holding the leash.

Liink was still bleeding, with a terrible gash across his face beneath the muzzle—which perhaps had shielded him just a little. The wound needed to be bound.

Benton sighed, and his warm breath lingered in his red mask.

He both adored and dreaded her.

Logically he wanted to stop, but for some emotional reason—unfathomable to him—he could not. He'd obsessed while they sailed to Toar. He'd obsessed as they crossed the black wasteland on foot. Now as he stood paces from her cell, he continued. It grew worse the closer he got.

The words of Master Jyngsoo echoed in his mind: "At any moment, you have access to a place of perfect peace, a shelter from all your anxieties and fears, a haven of serenity. This place is a state of mind, a spirit that can possess you."

At any moment.

Including right now. Benton breathed in.

I am everything.

The mantra circled, while a long time passed in silence.

He breathed out and tried to release his anxieties.

I am nothing.

D RAY HAD GONE deep into the prison block, quite far away, and yet his thoughts traveled back across that dark gap and formed a single word: *Ready.*

"Did you hear that?" asked Benton.

"Yes," said Liink.

Dray was extraordinarily gifted, especially for one who began so late.

Benton breathed steady and deep. Beneath that, his soul barely rippled. He pulled the red helmet off his head and swiped a glove automatically through his sand-colored hair. "I suppose our costume party is over then." Crouching, he released Liink from the chains and undid the muzzle. "I'm sorry for what happened to you back there."

Liink nodded his animal head and said nothing.

The two of them proceeded down the hallway to the cell blocks. They climbed rusty, disgusting stairs, moving toward A13. From that vantage, they could see Dray below, and he was opening one door after another.

Benton called down: "Wait, you're freeing all of them?"

Dray didn't respond to the question but instead replied, "The door code is *hinterland*. The collar is one zero six four two."

"You never told me that was your plan. What if they're killed escaping?"

"They're too valuable to be killed." He was right. The Witch Hunters had spent massive resources to collect these Radiances. "Plus some will make it out. Besides, we won't get a better distraction than this."

"You said explosives. That's why we brought Liink."

Dray didn't respond. The decision had already been made apparently.

Benton moved toward Kalhette's cell: A13. He punched the *hinterland* code into the door. The panel gave a disgruntled beep and flashed red. Something hadn't worked. Maybe a wrong keystroke. He glanced at the tiny window in the door, but it was too dark to see inside. She'd been in that shadowy place for all this time.

When his eyes began to glow, he saw a bright shape inside the room. She looked small and frail, curled up like a frightened animal, yet so brilliant she shone through walls. One arm wrapped protectively over her torso, the other over her bald skull, covering her face so he couldn't quite distinguish the eyes. But he could see her lips clear enough, with the scar on the upper left side.

Kalhette, I…

Suddenly, what Benton had done didn't seem to matter.

I'm just sorry you've suffered… in this place… for so long.

He took a deep breath and exhaled with the calm of sadness.

He tried the code again.

Sirens blared: *Wee-ooh, wee-ooh, wee-ooh!*

With no change in his breathing, he heard the richness of the sirens' tone. Two failed attempts seemed a little too strict for any mortal security, but maybe they'd been watching her cell extra close. Or maybe something else had triggered the alarm. He glanced at the chronometer on his wrist.

A man in a white research suit exited an adjacent cell. He seemed to take offense at Benton's helmet being off, ready to immediately cast blame. "What are you…" The man concluded his sentence with a gasp.

Liink flew like a snarling projectile.

He smashed into the attendant with brutal force. Then with four giant claws and massive teeth, he made quick work of his prey, which left blood on his teeth and lips.

Benton turned away. Alarms continued to wail, moving slowly, as if from a dream. He reached toward the small of his back and drew his prism from the pack.

The fiery gemstone had a leather casing fitted around it, making the handle of a weapon, more than long enough for two hands to grip. As he held it forward, a circuit of Spirit flowed within himself, a channel of energy running through every cell in his body, linking one to the next in an unending loop. As that energy flowed through his hand, he diverted its course through the prism, making it part of the loop as well.

A flame sparked to life at the tip first, which seemed to hover in empty air. The fire darted from there down two sides toward the prism in Benton's hand, forming the shape of a blade. The instant those two edges connected to the hilt, a blinding flash came that made a sound like something being torn in two, perhaps the fabric of spacetime itself.

He now held a stable blade of light protruding from the prism handle. It was flat like a metal blade, wide from the side and narrow from the back. Its two cutting edges curved symmetrically into a point, and the whole thing shone like a portable sun—

A violent incandescence.

It was called a Singblade, and its core pulsed white. The orange of fire rimmed the edges, simmering electrically. Where the light first emerged from the handle, bright rays shot in all directions, forming a spherical white nova that swallowed his red-gloved hand in brilliance and blazing heat.

Benton flipped the Singblade upside down and with two hands pressed the tip into the crevice where the door's lock met the wall. As the blade moved through the air, it left a trail of light like a thin film, like the atmosphere itself had been cut and was bleeding. When the tip touched, the seam of the metal door morphed, and reds turned to orange, yellow, and then white. He pushed the weapon deeper and deeper into the door, and the metal retreated, curling back and dripping to the floor.

When Benton's blade hit the lock, it crunched as the failsafe mechanism released.

The orange of his Singblade disappeared, giving way to the darkness. With his thumbs touching, he held the quiet gemstone with both hands, closed his eyes, and took a deep breath. As his eyes began to glow, he reached toward the molten metal, and without actually touching it, gripped the air with two hands, and lunged, forcing the door to slide on its track back into the wall.

He entered the shadow that had enclosed her for so long.

And he looked on her with his eyes still glowing.

Her appearance shocked him. She was thinner and seemed to drown inside the gray jumpsuit they'd put her in. Her skull was completely bald. Her eyes seemed sunken. A band encircled her tiny neck, with lights blinking.

Yet still the most beautiful woman he'd ever known.

She picked up her head and squinted forward, like lifting a great weight, but her eyes did not glow. Instead they had darkness below them. "Who are you?"

"It's me, Kalhette. It's Benton." He swiped a hand through his hair then started into three different words, trying and abandoning each: "You... I... If..."

Her voice barely reached a whisper, but she conveyed a command just by saying his name: *"Benton."*

He paused, a soldier awaiting orders. "Yes?"

"Please get me into the light."

WHEN DRAY FIRST re-entered Building 13, he cringed beneath his mask. Long, bright bulbs embedded in the ceiling formed a repeating pattern of light. He remembered this very hallway, how his eyes ached, how he squinted to keep back the flooding brightness, and how his heart nearly melted in the presence of a few radiating photons. At first, he'd longed for the light, until he learned it only meant more tests were coming. They'd shaved him, stripped him, drugged him, and put him not behind bars but behind a solid door, in darkness—where the light couldn't reach.

Then they'd drugged him, to keep his mind a blur, with white collars like the one Liink wore, which left all his memories of this Otherworld a little askew, as if he'd dreamt the whole thing. Their toxins had kept his heart rate high too, a treatment used only on their most prized prisoners. Keeping the cardiovascular system agitated made it impossible to become calm enough to surge. They'd assumed *he* had that power. They'd misjudged him.

Fortunately, that wasn't the only way they'd misjudged him.

He'd planned his escape and his return, engraving a map deep in his consciousness. The layout, the places they'd taken him, the rooms where they'd experimented on him. He'd even noted where they kept a very special molecule—in a place just ahead.

Longing for his wife had been the driving factor.

Now he tried not to think of her.

Sweat formed on his forehead. He put a hand to the face of his mask. As if that feeble gesture might keep the nightmares from flooding back.

Then he thought he heard Lethos laughing.

The sound echoed in Dray's mind and down the wide white hallways that met at ninety-degree angles. Maybe it had been a mistake to come back.

Benton, Dray suspected, had come because he loved the woman.

Liink had come for an opportunity to prove his valor.

Skyreacher had come for the money.

And Dray…

He'd come back into this hell for his daughter's sake. Also for the Radiances he'd once hurt, and for the ones that even now suffered the same torments he had undergone.

He'd been a prodigy, rising through the ranks of the PSD to become the youngest Lord Admiral in history. He helped to found the Witch Hunters, alongside Taiberos, a man more ruthless than the public would ever know. Eventually, Taiberos and the Witch Hunters aimed their wrath at the one most precious to Dray. He tried to stop them, but he couldn't defeat the monster he'd unleashed.

Now, he maintained his poise as he walked in military armor that wasn't his own. He wore a pack, and at the base of it hid his prism, out of sight, yet within easy reach. His commanding presence, even beneath the mask, invited only timid glances from the staff. Few in this place would outrank the costume he currently wore, and fewer still would stand up to his confidence. One of those few was General Venette. For the sake of the mission, Dray hoped the two of them wouldn't meet.

Aside from Taiberos, there was no one he'd rather execute.

Yet Dray wasn't here for revenge, no matter how well deserved. He'd come for a higher cause. The revolution would begin immediately after this mission, with whoever survived. They planned for everyone to make it out, but Dray had been at war long enough to know things would not go as planned. Yet he believed the one they risked their lives for was worth it.

As he went deeper into Building 13, he sensed something strange.

It wasn't quite a memory. More like he remembered something through Ptolis... What was it? A fragment he couldn't quite discern, some strange presence, like a small piece of himself still resided here, some tiny sliver of light amid the crushing darkness. It reached out to connect with him. It might have come from one of the prisoners—they were all Radiances. It might've even been the girl they were about to rescue.

Whatever it was, he'd never felt it before.

He did a double take when he saw an officer dressed like General Venette. The officer looked at the glass representing Dray's eyes. Dray confidently saluted, keeping his pace steady but calm, just slow enough so as to not draw attention.

That man was the only military personnel within sight. The war against the Shadowlyss had spread the PSD's military quite thin, leaving even places as important as the Strand understaffed. That left them to rely heavily on sedatives, with prisoners left largely unguarded. Given the right stimulus, the prisoners could become a colossal force, though Benton would've called it unethical to weaponize the prisoners.

So Dray didn't tell him.

Liink walked behind, claws on the floor, his six appendages bound together in chains, which limited the distance of each step. His tail swayed unbound and could potentially be a weapon.

Benton, dressed in red armor, lifted a foot to Liink's backside and gave him a rough shove. "Hurry up."

Liink, quickening his truncated steps, cocked his head and glared with yellow eyes, which was either surprisingly out of character or excellent acting.

The sound of Dray's boots changed from a pristine *plink* against tile to a soft *thud* against rubber as he arrived at a desk next to a glass door labeled *Pharmacology Block*. He spoke to the woman at the desk: "Major General

Taok here to oversee a pickup of K4271." He handed over an official order form, with what appeared to be all the correct stamps of approval.

She took the paper and reviewed each piece, taking her time. When she seemed satisfied, she turned to an assistant, and said, "Fourteen packages of K4271."

"Yes, ma'am." The door shot open with a hiss, and the assistant went through.

For the first time, Dray gazed into that room in his right mind. Researchers in loose white robes worked around rows and rows of tables. They looked like reverent dead. Their mouths were covered, leaving only eyes. The assistant made his way to a large cabinet, halfway across the vast room, but still in sight. He pulled out a key to unlock it. Another person monitored the access. The molecule was called Orikerse. Interestingly, it occurred naturally in every mortal's body, yet going beyond a natural dose could produce supernatural results. Though it came with a terrible tradeoff.

Next to the door stood an unmasked guard with a stun gun and a suspicious look. "You new?"

The helmet distorted Dray's deep voice: "Just arrived from Aldenal."

The woman at the desk asked him about Aldenal, so Dray made small talk.

Benton moved toward a terminal and began clacking into the system. Without one simple bit of information, it would take isos just to find their target.

A pair of Redhelms prodded Liink, but Dray maintained his poise, acting as if he didn't care what they might do. The exchange ended with Liink taking a blow to the face. Dray wanted to show sympathy, but more was at stake than physical pain.

The assistant returned with a tray containing the fourteen small packages. "That's an awful lot," said the guard.

Dray stared with the lifeless face of his mask, not condescending a reply. He took the packages, said, "Thank you," turned on his heel, and walked out.

Not only was he risking his life, but he was now carrying a small fortune, which he nonchalantly put in his pack as he made his way to the lifts. "Which floor, Benton?"

"Twenty seven."

Dray pressed a button, and they descended deeper underground.

H E KEPT HEARING the echoes of Lethos's laughter.

As they descended, they felt and heard a deep rumbling. It reminded Dray of the fiery Otherworld he'd climbed through to escape this place. Many had told him not to come, saying he was too valuable for such a high-risk mission, but no one else could've performed this role, and the revolution would not be successful without this woman.

The lift doors opened, revealing a long, narrow corridor with security gates along it, but guards only manned the farthest of these gates.

Benton and Liink stayed next to the lift while Dray marched on.

As he entered the cell block, he gestured to the two Redhelms standing guard. "You two, come with me," he said with perfect confidence.

The two Redhelms fell into step without questioning, exactly as they were trained—not to think, only to obey. It was endemic to the whole galaxy. Still, these Redhelms' docile servitude didn't merit the punishment they were about to suffer.

"And call your backups too," said Dray.

One of the Redhelms put his fingers to the circular button on the side of his helmet and requested backup.

At the end of the corridor, the ambiance transformed from brightness to misery. A massive room housed a stack of concrete cells, three stories high, with balconies lining each row. The railings were speckled with rust. Concrete floors and cement made up the rest of it, beaten down by percents and people, exposing corroded, leaking ruin in chaotic patterns. This being so far beneath the surface, heat floated in, bringing mugginess and insects. Iron pipes crossed overhead suspending dim cylindrical light bulbs. Not a single guard stood watch over the sedated cellblock.

Though Dray hadn't been to this floor before, he knew what the cells looked like. Each one had a fist-sized hole in the floor, doubling as a drain and a toilet. A small faucet came out of the wall for washing. Reds, browns, yellows, and greens stained the floors in billowing patterns. Yellowing hinges sealed the doors shut, clamped with electronic locks. Each door had a tiny window covered by a metal mesh, but the outer room was so dim that it hardly let light inside.

A second pair of Redhelms caught up to the group. If something went wrong within the cell block, this second pair would be the first to come snooping around. And so, with the four Redhelms in tow, Dray descended the stairs to the lowest floor of the cell block. "Form up."

They did as commanded, lining up side by side, heads held high, feet shoulder-width apart, their hands clasped behind their backs.

Dray mimicked this pose, grabbing the prism hidden at the base of his pack.

His eyes glowed white beneath his helmet.

He started swinging before even igniting the weapon.

In a flash of light, the blade appeared tip first and then core, a streak of blazing orange that cut through two of the guards.

The blade vanished just as the stroke completed its momentum, leaving Dray standing over two corpses with nothing but an empty handle pointed at the wall.

The faint trace of the blade's path still hovered in the air.

To most people, including the two surviving soldiers, the blade's appearance would've been a complete surprise. Singblades were rare and those with the power to activate them even rarer. The soldiers shrank to the ground, instinctively cowering.

Dray stepped back, knowing that if they decided to fight back, a little distance would give him the necessary time to react. Looking at the corpses on the ground, he said, "I advise you not to touch your comms, or you will join them. Now, tell me the access code."

Their masked faces stared silently. Their bodies remained rigid, unmoving.

He had neither the time nor patience for no response at all.

Without stepping close enough for actual contact, Dray made a motion as if reaching over one soldier's helmet and gripping the back rim. As he jerked his hand down through the air, the soldier leaned forward violently, and the helmet clattered across the floor, revealing the terrified face of a young man.

Dray stepped closer, and his glowing orange blade flowed again, this time lingering. He leveled it at the young man's throat.

The soldier collapsed back, begging: "No!"

The other soldier stood and ran.

Dray pointed his arm at the escaper and clenched a clawed hand in the air.

The soldier's head jerked back, and he twisted to the side, falling to his hands and knees. Dray's arm dipped at the same time, straining at an empty grip. This soldier pulled off his own helmet and reached for the ghostly fingers around his throat.

With his left arm still raised in a clenched position toward his choking victim, Dray moved the burning Singblade closer to the first soldier's throat, backing him against the cell door. "Tell me the access code."

The soldier stared with bulging eyes. *"Hinterland! It's hinterland!"*

"And the collars?"

"One zero six four two."

The sequence echoed in Dray's mind, making itself ready for recall.

His blade vanished, and with the hand that gripped the prismatic handle, Dray punched the code into the nearest cell. The bars slid open. "Come out of there."

The inmate obeyed, shuffling from the shadows.

Dray looked at the cowering soldier. "Get inside."

The soldier obeyed, with shame written on his exposed face.

Dray's arm finally fell as he called to the other one. "You too."

The second soldier gasped deep breaths. Without looking up, he skulked into the cell, and the door slammed shut. With their helmets outside, they couldn't get help.

Dray knew this military and the harsh punishments that would soon come. "Circumstance killed your comrades. I couldn't have managed all four of you. They died in the line of duty, a noble end for any soldier. Do not blame yourselves." Yet he himself already felt the repercussions weighing on his soul. At least Benton and Liink hadn't seen the slaughter. Dray closed his eyes, and through Ptolis a single word echoed from his mind and out across spacetime:

Ready.

White eyes stared out from the grated cell window across from him but faded into the shadows when he turned. More onlookers peered from nearly every cell above and around him.

The captive Dray had already freed now stood in the center of the space, too bewildered to run. Not much showed of her figure, and like all the inmates, her head was clean shaven, but Dray guessed from her size she was female, probably not dissimilar from the girl they'd come to liberate. She wore a gray uniform that had been soiled and cleaned many times. Her gaze showed fear, a dull fear, like the unsure perceptions of a child just awoken.

Dray made a pulling gesture with his fingers: "Come here."

She didn't move.

He commanded with his mind: *I won't harm you. Come here.*

She responded, though not quickly, tilting her head to the side and carefully approaching. She was in here because of him. Because of the Witch Hunters.

"What's your name?" he asked.

Her tone was as lowly as a blade of grass: "Darson." It could've been someone like her who gave him that strange feeling when he entered this place.

His eyes flicked upward, toward the spectators above. "You know a woman named Whitesun?"

Darson shook her head.

"Let me help you get that collar off," said Dray.

She stood still like a cautious animal.

He stepped toward her slowly, gently, not looking directly at her. Quite close to her, he took the collar in one hand and punched the release code with the other. It clicked as it unlocked. He took it off carefully and set it quietly on the ground.

When it was done, she didn't step away. Instead, she just looked up at him, as if anticipating further instructions.

"I have something for you, Darson."

The prisoner lifted a cupped hand, fingers curling back timidly. A tiny insect crawled from her sleeve and then took flight.

Dray produced a packet of Orikerse. From it, he pinched a small sampling of the crystal slivers. Next he rolled his fingers together till he could feel just two of the glass shafts still between them. He dropped these into the woman's palm. "You know what that is?"

Darson lifted her hand up to her eyes, squinting, then nodded her skull.

More spectators appeared on the upper floors, cramming their faces to the tiny windows for a better look.

"You know what to do with it?"

The ragged woman nodded.

"Then do it. And quickly. Guards will be here soon." Without waiting to see his orders carried out, he stepped left and faced the next dark cell.

Darson pinched one of the slivers in her lips for safekeeping while she crouched to the dirty ground. She pinned the other glass needle upright between the floor and her palm. Then she slammed her hand down.

The Orikerse seemed to wash into her system like ice water. She became immediately brighter and keener than before, alert with life and dead calm. She slammed the next needle into the meat of her palm as well. If she didn't know how to use her radiance before, she would now. She'd be a force to be reckoned with.

Dray couldn't see anyone in the next cell. His eyes glowed white with Starsight, and the occupant became a hot spot amid cold darkness. "Darson, go ahead of me and release them. The access code is *hinterland*."

She did as commanded.

He asked the next prisoner to follow her and take off all the collars. And he came third, giving each of the captives two slivers of Orikerse and assigning a floor number, going downward from twenty seven.

He heard one prisoner explaining to another how to use the gift.

Benton's voice sounded over the murmur: "Wait, you're freeing all of them?"

Dray looked up and shouted: "The door code is *hinterland*. The collar is one zero six four two."

Benton strode along the third level. "You never told me that was your plan. What if they're killed escaping?"

"They're too valuable to be killed. Plus some will make it out." He hoped plenty of the Radiances would make it. They could flee to one of the nearby mining towns, find a new identity, perhaps even get a ticket through the surge gate. "Besides, we won't get a better distraction than this."

"You said explosives. That's why we brought Liink."

Dray said nothing. He'd calculated this as more likely to succeed.

Fortunately, Benton hadn't time for debate. He'd nearly come to Kalhette Whitesun's cell, the girl they'd risked so much for.

As the freed inmates made their way to the lifts, Dray thought of Spalkur down on floor eighty-two. That floor felt like it still belonged to him in a way. He hoped the escapees would reach her. He wanted her to be free.

The Radiances formed a veritable army. If they obeyed their orders and freed the lower floors, they'd all have a greater chance of escape. But he couldn't control that outcome, and he expected lots to head upward instead, making a dash to the exit, keeping the Orikerse he'd given them for themselves. It was a shortsighted choice, but he wouldn't blame them. That was how people were.

Children.

He glanced at his chronometer.

Then alarms started blaring.

* * *

RED LIGHTS FLASHED on the face of Kalhette Whitesun.

A pale, weak-looking figure with a shaved head.

She seemed to be in pain, squinting at the light. One arm hung over Benton's shoulder as she limped alongside. Dray knew exactly how she felt, but with her collar off, she'd soon come out of the nightmare haze. Despite her current state, he couldn't help but notice her alluring beauty.

They got quickly away from the massive riot just unleashed—

A parting gift to General Venette.

Dray led the foursome through a series of maintenance hallways that cut deeper into Toar's roiling underground. They cut through a round pipe big enough to stand upright in. It led to a pair of sealed metal doors.

"It's these." Dray's Singblade materialized, and in a blaze of fiery light, he sliced through the hinges and lock. He stepped back, gripped the air, and pulled. As the door tilted, he rushed his hands over his ears. The door landed with a *bang!* He ominously locked eyes with Benton. "You take her first and move as quickly as you can. Liink and I will be right behind you."

"Yes, sir." Benton helped Kalhette toward the dark tunnel, a shaft leading to the surface. He would have to cut handholds to ascend, which would take time, but it was much more certain than climbing the bolts.

Dray turned around.

Through Ptolis, he felt that mysterious presence… now along with something else… something was coming. He stepped back into the previous hallway and turned to Liink. "Tell them to hurry, and report their progress back to me."

Liink nodded obediently at the orders.

Dray went back through the massive pipe and into the reactor room. Panels of glowing lights lit the room in various colors. The entrance on the far side that drew his attention: Red lights from sirens in the hallway illuminated the door frame. His escape plan left a trail of their actions on security cameras, a necessity of their hurry, and it was a matter of time till troops came to stop their escape. He expected the riot to keep anyone from noticing too soon. Another matter of probability.

His instinct prodded him again, a sense of something coming, stringing through his heart. He cocked his chin in the direction he felt it.

Liink came running, the rhythm of his tail increasing with the pace. "They're about halfway up it."

It wasn't far enough.

"Liink, I want you to follow them out."

"What about you?"

"Don't wait for me. You need to get the Prophetess back to the rendezvous point. That's the mission."

"But you're coming, right?"

Dray could think of no fate more awful than the torment of Building 13. He would, in fact, rather die than face it, and he expected that would be the case. In a way, he deserved this. And more. He'd carried the guilt for so long. "I will come if I can."

Liink had fright in his young eyes: "Let me stay and fight with you."

Dray kept his stoic, impassive stare fixed on the young miin and faced the reality that he might not be overseeing the battle for independence. "No. If I don't make it, tell Trillion he has my deepest gratitude. Now go, Liink. Protect the Prophetess. Do you understand?"

In the end, Liink was an obedient soldier. "Yes, sir."

"Go!"

As Liink galloped toward the ventilation shaft, he glanced over his shoulder, one last look.

Dray could see the end of his own life from here.

He would now pay all he had against his debt and would still come up devastatingly short. Hopefully whatever waited in the Otherworld would show him mercy.

Ahead, hoards of soldiers ran through that flashing-red door, too many for one normal man to challenge. They piled through, flowing into the room, spreading out, rifles at the ready, preparing to surround him. He backed into the massive pipe.

It made the perfect choke point, forcing the enemy to face him barely one at a time.

As the reality settled in, two emotions appeared. The first was sadness, sadness that he would not see his beloved. The second was rage, rage toward the force standing in front of him. A godlike rage.

He took a deep breath.

He noticed the texture of the prism in his hand.

His two terrible emotions faded into the distance like constellations.

The first attack came quickly.

With his eyes glowing, Dray's skin burned hot, and a deep magnetic sound rung through the space. He pushed against the air, and strength beyond his own lifted the Redhelms and threw them back out of the pipe.

They tumbled back haphazardly.

With the first wave knocked down, it revealed the second wave behind them.

It was led by General Venette.

The man who directed Building 13.

A man who deserved to be interred here.

In Dray's first life, he would've outranked this man, and he still felt a stark sense of superiority, given to him by justice. Justice required its due, the recompense unpaid. This feeling did not burn within him. Instead, it was absolute zero. It was ice, an absence of motion and energy, and it demanded that all around him become still too.

Shouts came followed by laser fire.

They'd decided to use deadly force on him.

That was for the best.

He didn't want to survive and risk becoming a prisoner again.

He faced his enemies, blade ignited orange, eyes glowing white.

High time he showed General Venette what a Zhan was really capable of.

[6] UNMASKED

"U H OH."

Nak sat in the cockpit of *The Sanctum*, which lay in a crevice high on a black cliff. When he heard Cupcake's feminine voice, his instinct told him to check the instrument panel—make sure his ship was all right. He didn't see anything to worry about. "What."

"Something's going on at the Strand," said Cup.

Nak looked through the glass screen and across the dark gray horizon. The sun was rapidly sinking and still no word from the clients. Below stretched some of the strangest terrain he'd ever seen, and he'd seen a lot. Massive rock pillars made of black sandstone, many times taller than his ship, were strewn across the ground. Some looked like fingers, others like mushrooms, and still others more like giant Slaghkian slugs, and all of them seemed to be defying nature in one way or another. They seemed too tall and too thin for this much gravity. He couldn't imagine what would've shaped them like this. Maybe they were grown.

Beyond that, Nak saw what looked like three people descending a distant slope: two dressed in gray and the other in red. One of the grays was down near the ground, probably on all sixes, probably a miin, probably Liink. The other upright gray seemed to have a bald head—the girl. And the red had his helmet off, but it was too distant to tell whether it was Benton or Dray. Was that sandy hair or gray?

Nak leaned back against his chair. It stood just high enough for him to sit or stand without hardly changing his vantage. The dashboard sat at a matching height, within perfect reach of his hands. With his feet on the footstool, he leaned back into the seat, frowning. They weren't supposed to be on foot. *Where the* ▓▓▓ *had their transport gone.*

"Nak, what are you thinking?" Cupcake's voice was so tiny and yet it was the biggest thing about her.

"What do *you* think I'm thinking." He held up his palm and tried to hide the red planet Sible from view, but his hand was not quite big enough.

Cup's tiny voice came again: "That if they don't arrive at the rendezvous in point two five, we sail away from Toar forever, keeping the ship and ourselves safe."

"Huh."

Cup hung magnetically against the ceiling. "What do you mean *huh?* Is that what you're thinking?"

"That thought did cross my mind." He reached into a side compartment and pulled out a pair of oculars. He found the right point on the slope, but the people had slipped down out of sight behind the next ridge.

"But...?" asked Cup.

"But I was thinking I'd only wait point one." He pulled the oculars against the ridge of his eyebrows. On a crest beyond the clients, a lone figure appeared, dressed in a red helmet and silhouetted by the last rays of twilight. That must've been Dray or Benton, whoever had fallen behind.

A similar shape appeared. Then another and another. They raised their rifles and started shooting at the three figures fleeing ahead.

So that first one chasing had been a platoon leader, *not* whoever'd fallen behind.

And with that realization, a strange feeling hit Nak, but he wasn't the type to sort out the shades of whatever the feeling was. He thought it might be related to friendship. Or maybe the lack of friendship.

Cup clacked a few of her paces, affixed directly above the dashboard, pausing with her surprised face pointed down at Nak. "And that's still the plan, right?"

He set down the oculars and started punching keys. *The Sanctum's* atmosdrive began to hum. The clients made their getaway across hilly terrain. That meant they were protected every time they started on a downhill but were exposed again when they headed up. Their luck might not last much longer.

Cup rolled to frowny. "You should consult me before you do anything rash."

"Why's that."

"Uh... I'm the smartest person on this ship?"

"You're not a person."

"Yes I am. Don't say that."

"Just keeping you humble." He checked the gauges, tapping through various stats. "What do the scanners pick up on that third ridge up there."

"I read eight lifeforms. That's all I've got."

"Believe me, Cup, nobody is more concerned about keeping my ship safe than me." Nak felt a moment of upward pressure against his boots, which vanished to normalcy as the vessel began to steadily hover in place.

The Sanctum was airborne.

"Nak, what are you doing?"

"I'm just thinking."

"You don't have to think with the whole ship!"

He picked up the oculars. "I don't think they're going to make it."

"You don't have to risk the ship for them. That's outside the contract. There are scourge turrets and flock towers if you get closer."

The last rays of twilight were now fading across the charcoal landscape.

He pulled up the oculars, and laser fire flashed in the eyepieces, streaking projectiles that looked like beams of light in orange, purple, and blue. "I know. But... if the clients don't survive, we don't get paid the rest."

"It's not like we're desperate for money," said Cup.

"No, but we *are* desperate," said Nak.

"No we're not."

Nak strummed the fingers of his left hand across the dashboard, three sets of five rolling taps, and for some reason he thought of that mysterious bald head. "*Shogram* says there are two kinds of people: the ones who read history and the ones who write it." He set the oculars on the seat next to him. "Well, Cup. I'm a writer."

"What's that supposed to mean?"

He grabbed the steering yoke. "It means I'm going for it."

T HE SANCTUM'S PURPLE engines glowed in the twilight as she lunged forward into a steep dive. For a moment, everything inside the ship became weightless, including Nak, who still hadn't buckled in. Instead, he hooked his heel under the footrest.

The thrusters engaged like a parent catching a child from the air, pushing upward and forward. *The Sanctum's* fall gently diminished as she neared the ground, almost touched, and then launched forward, weaving between the massive formations.

Clack.

As the ship neared the skirmish, Cup released her magnetic grip, just enough to begin falling, then snapped herself back into place: *Clack.* The closer they got, the more anxiously she did it. *Clack, clack, clack, clack.*

Nak's tone had moved beyond warning: "Cup—" He stood, pinched her firmly between his thumb and forefinger, and peeled her magnet off the ceiling.

"I'm sorry, I'm sorry."

"Too late." He smacked her down onto the leather seat next to him, by the oculars and his dread mask.

Without a metal surface, she couldn't clack and also couldn't move. She let out a depressed whine—"Ohhhh." And she'd landed with her happy side up, which she wouldn't be happy about.

"You know the rules."

She sulked in silence for only a moment before saying, "We're well within range of those scourge turrets now. I do *not* feel good about this."

"If I keep behind these slug things, their cannons can't touch us."

"Yeah, *IF...*"

"Better sorry than safe, huh, Cup?"

"That's not how it goes."

As *The Sanctum* creeped forward, three violet streaks flashed: the first high overhead, the second lower—the third crashed into the hull, rattling the floor and everything attached to it, including Nak's seat. The oculars twirled off the other chair and went spinning.

Cup hit the floor too—the metal floor—with a *clack*, her grin-side up. She knew better than to give any victory shouts, opting instead to clack across the floor quietly.

Nak dropped the ship and slowed her almost to a halt as more lasers blasted overhead. A holograph flashed "SHIELDS 92%" a few times before returning to stasis.

He eyed the landscape. His task was nearly that of a footsoldier: to run from cover to cover and take ground. Only he had to do it in a ship.

He accelerated toward the next ridge, and *The Sanctum* leaped over as if off a jump. He turned the sticks of the yoke down. As the ship crested and then ducked out of sight on the far side, his feet came off the deck again, his dark hair flying straight up for a moment. The oculars jumped and then smacked into a corner.

As more massive bolts of violet shot overhead, Nak punched the throttle, skimming the ground and weaving. He finally slowed to a stop behind one massive, slug-shaped tower. The lifters kicked up black dust as they kept the ship hovering above the ground, her wings spread wide.

He felt that prodding feeling again somewhere in the vicinity of his chest as he located the clients: The long, dark form of Liink crawling across the ground, tail swaying, followed by Benton, now close enough to identify. He clung tightly to a small human dressed in gray, her bald head distinct in the low light.

So Dray had fallen behind.

The small figures moved across a patch of open ground.

As Nak eased *The Sanctum* into the open, a flash of violet struck hard, and the metal frame groaned. Like the ship was his own arm, Nak jerked her back, out of sight, not even thinking as he engaged and then disengaged the zentisal drive—doing all this in the time it took to blink.

The ridge ahead was, apparently, just enough to shield the clients on foot, but not enough to protect a ship a few times that height, so this was as close as he could get to them in *The Sanctum*.

The sensors beeped, telling him the grooves in the terrain were too rugged for the ship to touch down. "Crap." The clients were on the other side of the rock formation, meaning he couldn't use the guns to help.

Still, better them than *The Sanctum*.

He locked her into a steady hover, punched one key, then grabbed his dread mask.

"Cup, take the starboard gun. And don't let her drift."

"Sure." She didn't move from her position: Through the phantomlink she could control the ship from anywhere aboard.

"This isn't one of our shoot-anything-that-moves drills. Just those Redhelms if they come into sight. And don't shoot Benton, okay? He's dressed like one."

"Got it. Hey, Nak?"

As he raced to the engine room, sliding down the aft ladder, he heard her voice through the overhead speakers. He then scanned his hand to get access to the inside. His sanctuary.

"When they come aboard, can I talk to them?"

"Of course not," he shouted as he pulled his illegal rifle from the wall.

He wasn't trying to be mean, but he had to be wary. He's heard rumors of a CP unit that stole a Bloody Wing from her master. Whether or not it was true, most people considered CP units too unstable to actually use. And that risk increased if she connected to outside influences, especially if they convinced her to listen to them instead of him. For now, Nak trusted Cup, at least to a degree. Maybe that was foolish. Maybe it was only a matter of time till she broke down.

But she was all he had.

He pulled on his dread mask and jumped from the gangplank onto the hard, ashy ground. This whole moon seemed like it had been burned as a sacrifice to some fierce god. He immediately felt stronger—as the gravity was much lower than what he'd set the targravs to inside the ship. The rock pillar towered overhead. He breathed in Toar's atmosphere through his mask and felt slightly light-headed.

When a single orange bolt kicked up dust next to him, he lunged for the cover of a nearby rock. He'd been burned by a laser blast before and wasn't excited to try it again. He checked the magazine on his rifle. More shots flew overhead and pelted the ground beyond him. Fortunately, he was stationary and they weren't.

Plus their audacious red armor stood out against the black surface.

He leaned out just far enough to expose one eye and took a few shots as the Redhelms darted down the open slope. He didn't need to hit them, just slow them and hinder their accuracy. He continued to lay suppressing fire as the clients approached.

When they finally got close enough, he shouted, "No Dray?"

Benton shook his head and kept moving.

Nak squeezed the trigger on his rifle again and again, sending blasts of hot light at the Redhelms. He hit one square in the chest, and the soldier tumbled lifelessly down the slope.

The clients finally passed him and approached *The Sanctum*. Nothing so far on this mission had bothered him as much as letting them board before him—it required too much trust. He wasn't planning to give them time for mischief either.

The bald woman stared at his dread mask as she passed. She climbed aboard first, struggling to pull herself up the gangplank which hovered a meter in the air, so Benton gave her a lift. The other two climbed up after her.

Nak put one Redhelm in his sights and steadily squeezed the trigger several times. Without waiting to analyze the result, he turned and ran for the ship.

In that exact moment, a massive, violet laser bolt from one of the cannons flew through the air and impacted with the rock pillar overhead. Chunks of stone, which appeared tiny so high up, broke free, shooting out in every direction. Several much larger chunks split off and tumbled downward.

Dropping toward *The Sanctum*.

"Oh no! Cup, move it!"

He ran straight for the ship. If he'd thought about it, he might've realized how foolish this was, but instinct spurred him to save his ship.

He raced the falling rocks, aiming his run at the back corner of the ship, beneath the swooping wing, where the foot of the gangplank hovered in the air. His boots pounded into the ground, one giant step after another.

When he realized the falling rocks would reach the ship a split sequel before him, he slid—a dodge that saved his life.

The noise roared at magnificent volume—a jarring crash of stones pouring from above, bouncing violently into the wing. The contragravs kept the keel off the ground, but the balance tilted, and one of *The Sanctum's* circular wings rose into the air while the other dropped, slamming into the ground just as Nak was sliding under it. If he'd been just a half meter over, the wing would've cut him in half, but the shape of the semicircle wings saved him, as only one part of the edge touched the ground.

As Nak was still sliding, rock fragments ricocheted off the tilting wing and cracked against his masked face, knocking his head back and spinning his body around violently, wrenching his focus away from the fact that he'd nearly been cut in two.

When he came to a halt beneath the wing, a few final rocks fell. The ship's metal frame still shook from the force, rocking as it tried to regain stability.

Then the world rang loudly in silence.

And Nak lay still.

C UP'S TINY VOICE had become even tinier, as if she were now kilometers away. He could barely hear her say, "Nak? Nak?"

All urgency somehow vanished from his mind. For a moment, he didn't even think about his ship. As the dust cleared, his shoulder throbbed worst of all. He lifted his face from the ground. His dread mask lay in pieces next to him, like a planet cracked apart, shattered by the falling rocks, having died to protect him. It left him with nothing between him and the putrid air.

He rolled over and found the wing wobbling just above his skull.

He touched his face and felt a thick layer of dry powder and a warm liquid. His brain felt like it was pounding on the backs of his eyes and wanted out.

Cup's voice came from the tiny earpiece that was no longer in his ear. "Nak! Come in!" She gave a whistle.

Thud.

A creature darted into the sand right next to his hand, kicking up dust.

Nak rolled back to his stomach.

And then came another. No, not a creature, a laser blast.

He looked toward the horizon. The Redhelms were still shooting at him!

He pushed off the ground and took a few stumbling steps. If he entered his ship, they'd know what he looked like, but he had to: His *Sanctum* was on the line. Not to mention his life.

With lasers flying past, he pulled himself like a drunkard onto the gangplank, but when he stood and strode aboard, he walked with the steadiness of his adamantine will.

Benton was helping the girl get back to her feet. The miin—*what was his name again*—was further up the hallway, unsure whether to abandon ship.

Nak gazed a moment, waiting for his head to stop spinning, and dusted off his black jacket and red sleeve. All three of the passengers looked at him, perhaps expecting an explanation from their captain. Actually, their stares seemed to signify more than that. Maybe surprised to finally see his face.

Although that wouldn't be the case for the girl. Her bald head with a gray hint of stubble lent an air of frailty, but her hazel eyes shone with might, and with those mighty eyes, she stared at him, perhaps at the damage to his face, but it didn't hurt bad enough for him to believe that. Only why else would she be looking at him so—*what was the word?*

Dammit. Didn't matter.

He didn't let anyone stare him down, so despite their hurry, he walked straight up to her and held out his hand. "I'm the pilot. Welcome aboard." Before she accepted his greeting, he smacked his hands against the dark dust on his pants.

All the trouble was for her. The girl took his wrist instead of his hand, a less common gesture. It was the formal greeting in some places but familiar in others. He couldn't distinguish her meaning from the nod she gave him.

Rather than ask, he played it cool and clasped her wrist back, a little distracted by her slender arms and his buzzing brain. "No Dray then." He knew Cup was watching him too, and she knew he had a thing for bald girls.

The girl had a confused look on her face, like she hadn't been coherent enough to put the pieces together. "Lord Admiral Dray is still back there?"

Benton nodded solemnly.

The pulse of rifle blasts hit the hull. Anything handheld wouldn't do much damage to the shields, but it was still time to go. Nak wiped the back of his hand across his face, smearing blood as he marched past her. He couldn't believe they'd seen his face. "Well, strap yourselves in. It's going to be a wild ride." He leaned into his seat in the cockpit with a sigh of relief. It already felt good to be back. He pressed his hand to the dashboard to unlock the ship's security measures. A light scanned his palm and fingertips. "Cup, give me the, uh... what's it called... The... how-bad-is-the-damage-to-that-wing thing."

Cup's voice came over the intercom, which she normally only used when they were sailing alone: "See, I told you it was dangerous."

He looked to where his dread mask usually hung, inside of which would've been private headphones—but his mask was lying in Toar's black dirt. "You don't get high rewards for low risks," he said lowly, trying not to think about the damage to his ship, his face, his secrecy, and his pride. "And let's keep the chatting to a minimum for now. But get me the, uh… what's it… uh… *diagnostics!*"

"Yes, sir."

The girl stepped into the cockpit wrapped in a blanket, the other two clients in her train. She looked up as if she might see whoever had just spoken, which under most circumstances would've been absurd, but Cup actually was positioned on the ceiling above the dashboard. The girl, however, didn't see her, and as long as Cup didn't move, no one would ever locate the most valuable item aboard.

Cup's voice gave the report through the ship's speakers: "The wires in the aft joint might have come loose again. I'm getting no readings there. It's possible something punctured the hull. However, I've confirmed that the control and passenger decks still have air pressure, so we're ready to exit the atmosphere."

As the clients buckled in, *The Sanctum* spun and then accelerated away from the Strand. The engines purred, pushing Dray further and further behind.

"We're getting quite a bit of drag from the starboard primaries," said Cup, "but it should get us outbound just fine."

As the ship accelerated, the shimmy in the wing became more apparent. He repeated his approach path in reverse, weaving behind rocks and ducking below ridges while violet beams zipped overhead.

The girl spoke like an invalid, in that soft and careless way: "You sure keep the gravity heavy in here." She had an interesting accent, similar to the miin's but with a twist.

Nak's brain was still pushing on his eyeballs, though not as violently. "Helps with the sharp turns."

Then no one said anything.

As they escaped the range of the scourge turrets, Nak watched the holographs for approaching vessels. He didn't mind silence, but he knew it would bother Cup, and she'd be saying so if she still had a private line. With his head still reeling, he said, "Honestly, I thought it would be *you* who didn't make it back." The name just wasn't coming to mind, so he looked back at the miin to show who he was talking about.

The creature's head lifted and pointed toward the pilot. "Why?"

Nak shrugged, his eyes tracking the proximity report. He'd have left any of the others without hesitation, but it was different with Dray. Dray had been good to him, treated him like a friend even when he didn't deserve it, let him take withdrawals without ever making deposits. Nak wanted to wait—he really did. Only that would mean keeping his ship in danger.

Besides, if Dray hadn't made it out yet, he likely never would. "Benton, you're not expecting me to try and delay somehow, are you."

Benton didn't reply. He seemed deep in thought, working some problem anxiously with one finger pressed against his lips as if to seal them.

Nak looked into the small mirror he used to track passengers, glancing at his own face first, noticing the scrapes and drying blood, and wishing he hadn't shown these people what he looked like. "Benton?"

It seemed the man had gotten snagged on something mentally. He looked at the girl. She looked back at him with… trust… maybe love. As if something had been said between these two. Or something hadn't.

Nak didn't wait for an answer. "All right."

He punched the throttle and jerked the steering yoke, aiming straight for the sky.

THE G-FORCE PUSHED them hard into their seats. The damaged wing shook, rattling their ascent. The winds kicked too, as if trying to stop *The Sanctum* from getting away. Light blasted from the tail of the ship, streaking a distance many times longer than the vessel itself. The edges of the flame twisted and curled in purple and orange, jittering against the atmosphere.

As they soared skyward, Nak's eyes wandered back to the mirror, and to this woman they'd risked their lives to save, this woman they'd traded Dray for. All this trouble because she'd stuck her neck out for some kid. Nak wished someone had done that for him when he was a kid.

She looked thin but maybe emaciated now that he thought about it. "I hate this place," she said.

"Oh, I don't know," said Nak. "I thought the dizzying speed of the sun was kind of a trip."

"Where I come from, day and night are directions." Her tone suggested that her background embodied absolute truth and everything else was unnatural. Must've been in a bad mood. She pointed at the dashboard. "It says you're out of zentisal fuel."

"We're not. The reader's broken." It'd been broken for a long time, but he knew his ship well enough to know how far he could push her before needing to refuel.

The turbulence calmed as the orange of the sky thinned to black and stars began appearing with Toar's electric-purple backdrop. As they left the atmosphere, the jitter from the starboard wing steadied out and then vanished.

While the clients watched the majestically painted sky, Nak watched the mirror:

Her eyes pointed toward the windscreen but were glossed over. She bit her lip on the left side, making a lopsided pout. When Nak noticed this detail, he looked away, at the black of space, at the ceiling panel, and then he stole another glance at the mirror, and what her teeth were doing to her lip.

Her head was shaved. No flowing locks like he'd admired on so many other women. It left her bare, like a helpless newborn. It exposed her humanity too, as if blatantly stating *I am nothing more than flesh and bone*. She was not more than that but nothing less either. That made her real, so real. And this statement made by her presence—this bold, open, candidness—left her vulnerable. And somehow inexplicably attractive.

A bad idea.

She was a Zhan, and that meant she was crazy. What a strange breed.

One idea in particular bothered him: Zhani mated for life. In fact, it was worse than that. They mated for eternity, which would never work for him. He thought it might be barely possible to be with someone for a whole aion, but he'd only know it after he'd spent that lifetime. How could you make that commitment beforehand?

Actually, maybe he was confusing his cults. Maybe the Zhani were the celibacy-for-life cult. Even worse. Either way, it could never work.

Something still wasn't right with the yoke, but aerodynamics shouldn't matter out in the black. He turned the yoke back and forth, but the ship only responded sluggishly.

"Oh no."

"What?" came Benton's voice.

"I think… the zentisal drive might actually be low on fuel."

"What?" Benton repeated the word with a tone of disbelief: "What!"

"I promise, it was fueled. Must be leaking from the impact."

"What exactly does this mean?" asked the girl.

Zentisal drives were based on Photoss tech and had three dimensions of thrust: horizontal, vertical, and zentisal. The atmosdrive, however, only had a half dimension of thrust: forward. It was old tech that relied on fins against the air to steer. That meant that out in the black the atmosdrive could only accelerate them in one direction. And worse, it couldn't slow them down afterward.

Instead of explaining, Nak just said, "Once we run out, we can't navigate in space."

S O WE'RE TRAPPED?"

"Not if we surge soon enough." That was all Nak really wanted—to get his ship back in the clear. Although it was risky to surge without a reserve of zentisal fuel. You never knew how much you'd need once you popped back into normal space. If you couldn't steer, you couldn't make it home.

Red octahedrons appeared as hovering holographs just before Cup spoke up: "Three large vessels descending on our position." They were coming from space, almost directly ahead, aimed to cut off his trajectory.

Nak twisted the yoke, and *The Sanctum* rolled sluggishly, putting the red planet above them. He swerved onto a course away from the approaching skycraft and roughly parallel to the surface of the moon. He wanted to be flying perpendicular though, to put as much distance as fast as possible, so they'd be clear to surge. Apparently, these attackers had been trained to counter Bloody Wings. "Cup, give me the time till we're in open space based on this new trajectory, and I want a countdown every ten sequels."

"We'll clear the moon in sixty-seven sequels," said Cup. "Also, one of the approaching vessels is sending a laser relay. Do you want me to play it?"

He looked at the compartment in the wall next to him, trying to remember where he'd put his spare headphones. "Uh, yes, play it."

The voice was low, lazily slow, and calm as a corpse—a hateful one: "Starchild. I told you this isochron would come. Told you our paths would inevitably—"

After the first word, the relay was overlaid by Nak's own frantic speech: "Ah ███, not Taiberos—Sorry, ma'am—Cup, switch it off—and where are my extra headphones." Nak's face flushed, which, unfortunately, the clients could now see.

Taiberos's relay fell silent.

"Benton, you take the aft gun." Nak turned to the alien and paused—"Miin, you take the fore." *Damn, that was rude—what was his name?*

Benton and the miin jumped to their feet and rushed from the cabin.

Nak pressed and held a comms switch: "Don't worry. They're too distant to stop us." His voice echoed through the halls. "Just keep them from getting any lucky shots while I get us to open space."

Cup's voice said, "We'll clear the moon in forty sequels." If there weren't guests aboard, she'd have also been reminding him about their contingency plan—to use the coffin. She liked to think that was always an option. It wasn't. He preferred to go down with the ship.

The girl leaned forward in her seat. "How do you know Taiberos?"

Nak thought of Taiberos's disembodied hand, pale and bloodless, floating out in space near one of the moons of Gavore, spinning and pointing endlessly at everything. Not exactly how most people pictured the most powerful man in the galaxy. "We're old friends."

"Close?"

Nak chuckled. "We had a secret handshake."

Her bare skull emphasized her giant hazel eyes and childlike nose. "And yet you don't want to see him?"

Cup interrupted: "We'll clear the moon in thirty sequels."

The ship shook, giving his voice a vibrato as he said, "There's hardly anything I want more than to not see him." *That bastard.*

"Why?"

"He's mad at me for not keeping in touch."

"Captain—" interrupted Cup again. "You've got a fleet of more than a dozen Goebs approaching at zero degrees low."

Nak's eyes jerked to the holograph. Outside of his physical view, just above his toes, a dozen or more fighter craft screamed toward him. He rolled the ship so he could see them through the windscreen, putting them just above his head.

The Goebs looked like discs with the center carved out, but through that open space in the middle ran the cockpit. The engines blazed in bright orange. These sleek, swift skycraft had been produced in immense quantity, positioning the PSD as the preeminent naval force of the galaxy. Although Nak felt confident he could outmatch at least a few of them, he would need zentisal fuel to do it. Plus the lag was killing him. That left him with one option:

He had to get to open space before they got too close.

Benton and the miin obviously heard Cup's message too because their turret guns blasted yellow lights ahead at the approaching fleet. Each time they fired, the ship pulsed with a vibration.

"On our new trajectory, we'll clear the moon in seventeen."

Almost there.

Nak tapped his fingertips on the dashboard, three strums before he noticed what he was doing and stopped.

██████ Taiberos.

"We'll clear the moon in ten."

Nak rolled *The Sanctum,* heading in a path perpendicular to the two approaching fleets. "This is going to be close." He began to bob and weave, moving in an erratic pattern that was worsened by the lack of fuel, and few of the blasts from the approaching skycraft connected. Unfortunately, the weaving extended his flight path and allowed the enemy to creep closer.

That proximity would keep him from surging too.

And the closer they got, the more shots they landed. She couldn't take this kind of heat forever. The ship shook and the holographic text blinked an update: SHIELDS 71%.

In the mirror, the girl sat deeper into her chair. She pulled the safety straps down uncomfortably tight, put her hands over her bare skull, and frowned a sickened expression. Surely wasn't in any condition to take this kind of spinning.

"We've cleared the moon," said Cup, without a shred of enthusiasm.

The girl squinted as if in physical pain. "Why aren't you surging?"

A shot skimmed *The Sanctum's* wing, forcing her into an involuntary roll. Nak pulled the yoke to fight against it. Another blast hit, and the ship jerked again. Even a damned fine pilot like himself couldn't be expected to do more, especially when the yoke was barely responding. "They're too close. We can't complete the surge hash with another mass that close, and he knows it."

"Who knows it?"

"Taiberos."

She closed her eyes and gave a squinting frown. "So we can't surge?"

Clear to Surge

Toar

Outbound Flight Trajectory

"Actually, no. I—" He jerked on the steering yoke and gritted his teeth as acceleration pulled them portside. It turned harder than expected. He had to be careful—too much acceleration could kill. Besides, he didn't have enough fuel to spare a move like that. The next blast hit directly, shoving the whole vessel off course and jerking the necks of all her passengers. He heard them groaning and hoped he wouldn't have to clean up anyone's puke. The holograph blinked again: SHIELDS 38%.

And the blasts kept coming.

Nak wiped a hand across his face—the blood seemed to have dried.

She peeked just one eye open at his naked face. "So what are you going to do?"

In a whirl, *The Sanctum* twisted around, pointed once again at Toar. "Our only chance is to lose them on the surface." Maybe he should've listened to Cup and let the clients die. If he'd known that bastard Taiberos was here…

The Sanctum had an escape pod. Big enough to fit him and barely someone else. It was cloaked too, and even if the Goebs actually saw it, no pilot would chase it with a surge drive up for grabs. Only one problem: He wouldn't want to go on living without *The Sanctum*.

The starboard wing sent a jitter through the ship as she slowly re-entered Toar's atmosphere. At least the fins would give him the power to really steer again. ███████ lucky the atmosdrive was fine.

"Captain!" shouted Cup.

Nak snapped out of his trance just in time to see a blaze missile on the holo. He jerked the ship into a hard roll, and the g-force pulled the safety straps tight into their shoulders.

The girl gave an audible groan. Nak looked into the mirror: She didn't have hair to cloak her humanness, so she was just there, completely legible.

The ship rattled violently as the missile passed. It then appeared visually ahead of them through the windscreen, crackling with white light as it blazed slowly toward the cracked surface below.

The girl spoke with sickly enthusiasm: "Wow."

Nak smiled wide without showing his teeth. "That was nothing."

The girl pressed her hand over her lips. Felt like a tease. "Where'd you learn to sail like that?"

"It's instinct."

Looking forward, yellow and orange flashes of light zipped past the windscreen in various directions. Another direct hit caused a jarring shake against the ship's metal chassis.

SHIELDS 27%.

Once the shields dropped, any projectile laser would have its full effect against the hull, the heat and momentum burning even through thick layers of metal. Atmospheric pressure would be lost, passengers might be hit, and the engine itself could go up in flames, consuming their oxygen while burning them alive.

As Benton and the miin fired back, vibrations pulsed through the floor. Every once in a while, another blip would disappear from the chase.

"Cup, how's our ammo holding up."

"Magazines both still over sixty percent, but these two are wasteful."

Nak switched the comms to go through the whole ship. "Hey, guys, go easy on those rounds."

The starboard wing continued to wobble. At least they weren't burning zentisal fuel out in space anymore.

Toar's charcoal gray surface grew, its features becoming distinct. From this far up, the cracked surface looked like a dry lakebed, but really they were massive chasms going fathoms deep, and the largest ones glowed with a faint orange from far below. Soon they got close enough that even the smaller cracks seeped with light.

Nak strummed his fingers on the dash. "We're going to make it." And if they didn't, the lava would be the perfect place to lay *The Sanctum* to her final rest. Anything to keep her out the hands of that bastard Taiberos, whose disgusting pink face hovered in Nak's mind.

Lasers fell like rain, some of them connecting.

SHIELDS 19%.

The Sanctum, barely decelerating, dropped into the network of fractured canyons.

Benton apparently knew better than to ask Nak to slow down.

The holographs showed a dozen Goebs in close pursuit, with the rest hanging back at higher altitudes. Nak increased his speed and dove deeper into the crevice, till the light from above disappeared, replaced by the glowing orange from below. "This heat from the core will make tracking us hard. It's just a matter of outrunning them."

Then he showed them what kind of pilot he was.

He accelerated, taking the first corner so close he thought he heard the tap of metal against rock. The purple engines roared as he hurried sideways into the next opening, dropping still lower.

The girl pressed her hands against her bald skull, as if compressing her own brain. Unfortunately, flying gently wouldn't be doing her any favors.

One of the Goebs behind him clipped the canyon wall, spun halfway around, and exploded in a boom so loud they could hear it inside *The Sanctum*. If the girl didn't look so sick, he would've explained to her that it wasn't even a fair match: These Goebs were half the size of his ship, so he had at least twice the difficulty.

After their comrade went down, a few of the disc-like Goebs fell behind. The rest, however, kept in close, even with Benton and the miin firing back. The Goebs kept landing shots on the straightaways, jarring *The Sanctum*.

SHIELDS 13%.

Nak glanced at the lava. It would be easy enough.

As the stone corridor opened up, he stood, placed one hand on the ceiling to stabilize himself, and hit several dials on the overhead board. "Cup, queue up the surge hash. I want a canyon parallel to this one. Find a segment that's close."

He sat back down and punched the throttle. Already moving quite fast, he still felt the added acceleration. Damn fine ship.

As the canyon walls curved, he banked hard right, dipped below an outcrop, then began to climb. There was still a chance they could survive this.

The fighters remained hot on his tail.

"I have one," said Cup. "I'll calculate the sequence as soon as you stand still."

The Sanctum rolled on her side to squeeze through a narrow gap.

The crevice opened into a large space. Nak leveled her out and turned the yaw to the right, as if skidding along the friction of an earthy surface, till the rear thrusters were pointing in the direction that had been forward. He punched the throttle in a spurt.

"Hit it, Cup!"

The engines burned purple, bringing *The Sanctum* quickly to a standstill, hanging above the lava in midair.

Outside the windscreen, the Goebs came screaming through the gap and into view. Hot orange lasers spiked from their front teeth, stabbing toward *The Sanctum*. The first hit rocked the ship—it was a cinch to hit a stationary target. More blasts poured down like a flood.

The reader blinked, now in red: SHIELDS 8%.

SHIELDS 5%.

SHIELDS 2%.

As the lasers pounded into them, Cup spoke one last time: "We'll have it in three, two, one."

The Sanctum vanished.

BUT YOU SAID you couldn't surge with other skycraft that close!"

Kalhette gritted her teeth against the pounding in her brain, fighting the nausea.

Her stomach was ready to discharge whatever it could find and then keep trying out of pure desperation. That was her body. Her mind felt worse. The effects of the exhaust were fading, and her heartbeats were finally beginning to slow. She almost hoped it would keep going until it was truly still. Because otherwise she would have to think about how they... how Taiberos... had violated the sanctity of her body.

Tears leaked from her eyes and rolled down her cheeks.

Her life before and her classroom felt like a distant dream, like her whole life had been torn away. Till, like a legend, Benton had burst into her cell to rescue her.

From her darkness.

As the pilot did his wild maneuvering, she tried to act healthy, but she felt miserable, wanted to die—ready to release her hold on life and become one with the Song, even though she'd finally been set free. Then the pilot, whatever his name was, out of nowhere, had saved them all.

Life finally felt still again.

It left her feeling exposed. And ashamed.

The pilot wiped his fingers across his scratched forehead and stood. "It's more complicated. I was distracted." He slid his hand down the red sleeve of his flight jacked and then wiped the dust on his pants. His eyes were grayish blue, as if a storm were trapped inside but only the color could surface. His scruffy chin made him seem like a wild, untamed animal. Or maybe a pirate. He piloted his skycraft, looking for a quiet crevice deep in Toar's underbelly, till he found a spot and nestled the ship behind a few very large rocks, looking at a black cliff face that glowed with red light.

She was perceptive with people and stared longer than usual, deciphering a complicated pattern in the pilot's expression. She sensed a deep wound, one he himself probably didn't understand. She knew what that felt like.

After a moment, he looked up, acknowledging that he'd been discovered. When he caught her gaze, unlike most people, he held it—and held it, with a power she seldom encountered, till finally it was *she* who looked away.

She glanced to the floor then back at him. "So you going to tell me?" She almost regretted asking. She wanted to know but not now, not with her priorities still askew. First she wanted to lie down and sleep. Maybe forever. "And can I get a drink?"

"Sure, what'll you have. I've got m—"

"—Just water, please."

"It's in the lounge. I have the best couch in there too. Or you can have one of the bunks. I can give you a hand."

"No, I can't be alone right now."

"I'll go with you." He reached out a firm hand, which she felt compelled to take. He looked seven or eight percents her senior, maybe a couple percents younger than Benton. The pilot grabbed her upper arm and lifted her to her feet gently but with surprising strength. "I don't think I caught your name…"

"It's Kalhette." She hated even saying the man's name, but she managed to say, "And I think I heard Taiberos call you—"

"—You can call me Nak," he interrupted.

"Oh. Like the god?"

"It's a nickname."

"Nak, huh?"

They locked eyes again and held it even longer this time as she tried to untangle his secret. Something about this man… Was it that he'd helped her away from such deep darkness? No, because Benton had done the lion's share, and Dray made the biggest sacrifice of the three. She blinked, then squeezed her eyes closed, the sleep pressure making the perfect excuse to look away.

A trough, set into the walls, lined the corridor leading to the lounge, and from it grew small plants, a garden at shoulder height, or elbow height if you were the pilot's size. The top of the inset shone with white light. Rich brown soil filled the bottom, held in place against turbulence by bionets, which also preserved moisture. This feature formed a vibrant green bioribbon that wound its way throughout the dark metal walls of the ship. Even in her current state, she appreciated the beauty of it. Probably a great source of nutrients too. She'd always wanted to garden, but that required a stable home.

"This is the couch here, Kalhette." Apparently her usual priorities weren't completely askew or she wouldn't have noticed how he moved: with an animal ruggedness. He handed her a glass jar of water. His voice was the growl of one who could lead a pack, deep and determined, yet surprisingly warm: "Feel free to put your feet up."

She received the water gracefully and couldn't help but notice the drab suit she wore and how terrible she looked in it. "So are you going to tell me what happened back there?" The ship had surged back there, no doubt about it, even though he'd said they couldn't.

"I need to check on my ship real quick. I'll be back though. Need anything else? Food maybe?"

As she shook her head, Benton and the miin walked into the lounge. The miin's animal face had a nasty red cut and yet still burst with excitement.

"What," asked the pilot—Nak.

"My first aerial combat, and I took down one of the fighters!" Keeping four of his paws on the floor, the creature raised his front two paws and pressed them together as if in a prayer of enthusiasm. Seeing this miin's face reminded her of that red-eyed beast who'd helped Taiberos to capture her on Sream.

Benton ran his fingers through his sandy hair, resetting his style to its perfect state. He had thick, earnest eyebrows, a short, neat beard, and was quite handsome to look at. "How were our shields holding out?"

Nak's cocky gaze was the look of a man who knew a clever secret. "Just fine." It was the same expression he'd had when explaining his relationship with Taiberos. He winked at Kalhette and walked out.

The need for sleep pushed her mind down into silence. The skin on the back of her bald head touched the velvety couch pillow, and she closed her eyes. She just hoped sleep didn't mean a return to nightmares.

"Are you doing all right?" It was Benton's voice. He approached in his red armor. He was an attractive blend of stately and strong and, she imagined, was even fitter than when she'd last seen him, thanks to his rigorous Zhani training.

When she'd...

Now she regretted her pride. She was nothing. Less than nothing. She was Taiberos's whore. She blinked her eyes rapidly, trying to dry the tears before they fell. "Yeah, I'm all right."

Benton smiled. "Kalhette, I'm so sorry."

She knew Benton well. He surely wanted to talk about their relationship, yet the code of a gentleman wouldn't let him awaken a conversation laid to rest. If they were to talk about what was and what might be, she'd have to bring it up. But she did not want to confess her unworthiness.

She closed her eyes and fought tears as she said, "I'm sorry too."

"You're going to be okay now."

"Thank you. I just need some sleep. Maybe a few cycles worth."

The miin laughed at her exaggeration.

She glanced at the creature, who looked away immediately, but not before she caught that look on his face, the same look he'd given her at Building 13, a look of awe, like he expected her to do something miraculous at any moment. This was especially annoying coming from someone like him—a miin.

Benton gave a mild chuckle, probably not at her joke, but to enjoy the mirth of those around him. She loved his resilient humor. He smiled, a look of mild amusement, as if calm had taken so strong a hold that even joy wasn't allowed to displace it.

She needed his calm now more than ever.

He looked at her with round, green eyes and pressed a finger to his lips as he thought, as if subconsciously willing the universes to be silent while the pieces of his grand schemes were placed in position for the start of the game. "Kalhette, I know this is not the best time, that you're suffering, but there's something you should know. It has been weighing on my mind nearly the whole time you were in there."

HOW LONG WAS that?"
"Eleven millos."

"What!" She'd guessed a fourth of that, already far too long. Taiberos had forcibly taken more than a percent of her life. Or maybe he'd taken all of it. The self that felt okay was still in there, trapped in the bowels of Building 13.

She closed her eyes and thought of her students on Sream, and how she hadn't even said goodbye. They must've spent the last percent wondering what happened to her and Tannie. No, they probably hadn't been left to wonder. They'd probably been told a lie that made her into something despicable. And now it was true. "Did Tannie survive?"

"No."

She'd worried that Taiberos killed the child with his cybernetic hand, yet she'd clung to the hope that she'd been wrong. "Are you sure?"

"I did extensive research on what happened that cycle."

For a moment, she was back in the Strand with its heavy shadow looming over her. She'd failed to save him. It had all been for nothing. "I'm sorry, Benton. I wasn't cautious or patient. In the moment—"

"No. Kalhette—"

"I followed my heart. And cost us so much. I'm sorry."

"Tannie was a child. I only wish I had your courage."

For the first time since that cycle, she had clarity, and the events replayed in her mind. President Taiberos, who was obviously not a soldier anymore, had come dressed as one, which stacked the deck against her. "Why was Taiberos there?"

"He was doing a demonstration with his Witch Hunters. For publicity."

"And you defied him," she said. "I can't believe you rescued me."

"If not for Dray, we…" Benton trailed off.

"We left the Lord Admiral in there." She couldn't believe it. An unthinkable sacrifice. Of which she was infinitely unworthy. Yet she didn't have the courage to wish he'd never done it. "Benton, I'm so sorry."

He nodded, helpless regret showing in the corners of his eyes. Not a good thing for a man with an overactive conscience.

Looking at him melted her heart. Yet the despair she'd been drenched in still lingered, and sorrow crept in close. She couldn't believe Dray had… for her…

Benton turned to the miin sitting in one of the easy chairs. "Liink, would you check up on Skyreacher? See how we can help him with repairs."

Liink, huh. He rolled out of his chair and exited as obediently as every miin. His dark-purple tail was the last part of him to slip from the room.

She squinted, wanting to close her eyes. "You call the pilot Skyreacher?"

"That's his name."

"Taiberos called him Starchild."

"I suppose both might be aliases. He's in a secretive line of work. Kalhette, may I tell you this?"

"Yes, what?"

"I don't want to hide it from you any longer."

She looked at him, her curiosity piqued.

"You can't unpublish something. Once it's out there, it's out there."

She frowned. "What did you publish?"

"Just another Prophet piece like the others you edited."

"Then what's weighing on you?"

"I'm the reason you were in there."

She sat up defensively. "What?"

"It shouldn't have gotten more traction than the others."

"Where did you publish?"

"*The Informant.*"

She frowned. "Did it say something about me?"

"No, but it made a lot of ignorant people angry. They think we want chaos and violence—that kind of anarchy. It's the opposite of our real point."

"Benton, tell me what happened."

"The article went big, bigger than the rest combined. The PSD tried to silence the story and removed it from the Freenet, which forced it onto the Handnet, where it got even bigger." He took a breath and sighed.

Kalh shook her head. It hadn't surprised her to be caught by the Witch Hunters, but only now did it make sense that Taiberos himself was there too. "So you mean…?"

"When I realized the danger, I came to Sream to warn you, but I was too late. Taiberos captured you isos before I arrived. I still don't know how they discovered you though. Sream is a populous planet. Unless someone in our circles sold you out."

"You told someone where I went?"

"No, I never did, but it would be easier for someone we trust to spy on us."

"One of the miina?"

Benton shook his head. "No. I don't know who."

Kalh already felt certain. She thought of how that red-eyed miin had looked at her just before she got her head slammed into the wall. "Why would they connect that article to me?"

"I don't think Taiberos actually thought you wrote it. I think he found you and decided to use you as a scapegoat. You matched the profile because you were on my homeworld, so he captured you and made it seem like you paid for writing against the PSD."

"He pinned your articles on me."

"Yes. The PSD painted you as a villain. If I'd known… When I found out you were gone, I started putting together a plan right away. I wish it hadn't taken so long. It's not easy getting into the Strand, and I didn't have the funding at first. I'm so sorry."

"I'm sorry too." She wanted to reach out and hug him. Instead, she sat a meter away, completely alone.

"That's not all of it. There's an upside."

Kalh didn't want to hear the rest. She wanted him to recant it, to undo the past.

Benton's green eyes locked with hers and then moved away and then came back again, continually monitoring her reaction as he went on: "I turned it against them. Made it backfire."

"You what?"

"Since you got so much negative attention on the Freenet, I leaked some of your actual story on the Handnet, as a defense of your innocence. That went big too, again more than I could've predicted. The momentum of lies transformed in your favor."

"Wait, what?"

"Using my leak, an editor on Taice pointed out the holes in the PSD's narrative. Other writers took up the cause, speaking in your favor. They turned you into a heroine."

A sickening feeling rolled through Kalh's stomach. "Me?"

"Yes, based on my articles."

"So they think I'm you?"

"No, they think *you're* you. Your personal story is absolutely yours. Plus you stand behind everything in those articles."

"Not everything. And I'm nobody."

"To be fair, they blew your foresight out of proportion, and your danger classification. And, yes, the persona they created is half you and half me. People have accepted it as fact, particularly the natives of Solace. They're inspired."

She opened her eyes. "The miina?"

"Yes." He paused as it soaked in. "And the colonists. They're talking about freedom like never before. They're calling you the Prophetess. Some even said you might be the Uncrowned Queen."

"Who says that?"

"Everyone. Your story has been all over the Handnet for the last—well, for the whole time you've been in there, and that's a long time."

"But I was barely conscious."

"Your story was alive though. It's a prime example of the oppression Solace has suffered. Plus your parents are a factor."

"You told them about me?"

Benton looked guilty. "I wasn't trying to make you famous. I was trying to defend you. I had no idea this would happen."

Kalh shook her head.

"I only published the parts that were technically already public. Anyone could've done it. People love the humanity and the intrigue of your story. A good person tried to rescue a kid, and the PSD punished you. Even outsiders can see how bad that is. Your cause has traction throughout the galaxy, exponentially so on Solace. You're a powerful symbol."

"I still don't understand why…"

"I don't get it either. It just happened. The Song elected you to have influence. The galaxy sees a warrior goddess, mighty enough to stand against Taiberos. And when the news spreads that you have escaped, it will be the death blow to his campaign. Your defiance will give hope to Solace and to the larger galaxy."

"But…"

"Kalhette, we're about to begin what we've always talked about."

She whispered: *"Revolution?"*

"Yes."

"On Solace?"

"Yes."

"Now?"

"As soon as we get back home."

"But how?"

"Dray… had it all planned out. I know we will succeed this time."

"But Benton…"

"Think about it, Kalhette."

"But I'm not a warrior goddess. I lasted barely a few sequels against the Witch Hunters. People can't see—" …that she was Taiberos's whore. If they really knew her, they would stone her. If they knew she could be carrying that villain's child…

If Benton knew…

"I don't want to be a figurehead. Why don't you tell them it was you?"

"It's much too late for that. Besides, I tried."

"Well, try again."

"They won't believe me. Besides, it's all in motion. Dr Warnur and the others are setting it up right now—everything you and I talked about. The first battle will commence not long after we return, and we need a way to pull everyone together, or this will never work. We need you in this role."

The mention of Dr Warnur reminded her of her childhood, back before she went on the run. Back before her life collapsed. She couldn't believe she might actually go home. If only she didn't have to do so carrying this role. Along with all that had happened in the Strand.

"Solace needs a single point to unite around, and even the miina adore you. We'll finally create the place we've dreamed of, a safe haven for people like us. A place *you* can call home. A place where people like you and Tannie can be safe."

It was too late for Tannie though.

Too late for her too.

She gazed at his shirt and deep into her own mind. Now she knew why Liink had been staring. Her eyes lifted, despairing. "I don't even like miina, and I'm nobody. I'm not this Prophetess…"

"I'm sorry," he said. "I guess you are now."

She shook her head. She didn't want to be, not for them. She was the worst candidate. She could barely take care of herself—barely! The last thing she needed was others relying on her too, especially the miina. "You could do a better job."

"I didn't mean for any of this to happen, but this is what we have, and you're now positioned to make a change. I'm not saying you have to. It's your choice, as always, but I do think it could be a powerful opportunity."

Her head tilted down. "I'll be a greater target for our enemies."

"All the more reason to make this work." He had an expression of real regret on his face. "But it's not too late to back out. The PSD tried to quell the popularity, keeping the responses off the Freenet, no pictures in the broadcasts, so you won't be recognized yet. Only a segment on the Handnet know about you."

"That's good." For so long, she'd felt angry that most of the galaxy didn't care about her plight. The opposite seemed just as bad. "They're expecting a liberator."

"You will be. We will be. I told the War Council you'd help. That's how I got the funding. Your Sorjis will play a key role in the battle. I can explain it to you… if you're ready."

"Sorry. I'm not… not yet. Is that okay?"

"Yes, of course." He glanced at her shoulders, her face, then patted her gently on the knee. "Get some rest."

She wanted a hug but felt unworthy to ask.

He'd rescued her from that awful Otherworld, but its poison was still in her. Was that his fault? Or was he taking more responsibility than he ought to? After all, Taiberos made all this happen. He and his PSD. "Our people won't be happy to hear that my freedom cost us Lord Admiral Dray."

"We'll deal with that in the debriefing. I know you hate attention. I'm sorry. For all of this." Benton's hands wobbled in the air, as if it were too horrible to even gesture toward in the abstract.

She reached out and grabbed his hand, afraid of being alone.

He squeezed back.

She let go and placed a hand on her chest, wanting to find the vial of white sand from the beaches of Solace, but they'd taken it. She lay down in silence, glad the populace couldn't see her now. She was beaten and broken. She was weak. Her bald head emphasized that frailty.

Because of people's expectations, every step she now took would be fraud. She felt glad to hide her weakness, yet afraid of the lie. It made them expect too much.

She was a mortal, nothing more.

Perhaps less.

K ALH FLINCHED.

Someone was sitting there, ready to resume her torture.

She sat up ready to fight.

Oh. She was in a lounge aboard a Bloody Wing. Far from the Strand. Nak Skyreacher-Starchild-whatever was sitting in an easy chair, a book in his hand. Part of her felt scared to be alone with him. Yet she was also afraid to be alone.

"Where are the others?"

"Sleeping."

"How long was I out?" Her reality felt fuzzy.

He had dark grease on his hands like he'd been working on repairing the ship. "You woke up a couple isos ago for a seq if you remember. In total, it's been about thirteen."

She brushed a hand across her bald head and looked down at her clothing, feeling a sudden urge to look dignified. "Wow."

The surge gates connected hundreds of star systems, and out of all the habitable planets and moons, no two had the exact same length of day. Some were as short as Toar, where it was said you could throw a rock into the daylight sky and have it land at night—a bit of an exaggeration, but not by much. Others, like Solace, had a day that was basically infinite. Years had the same problem—they were based on a world's speed and distance from its star, which meant the measurement varied wildly even within a given star system. A long, long time ago, the Jethore Dynasty solved the problem with a system developed on Orban, providing a stable schedule even aboard a ship like *The Sanctum,* where there were no days or years. The Jethorians had enforced this system, and essentially every culture now used it and had for many aions. Many worlds used it primarily, but others used it secondarily, while sticking to their own days and years when it made sense.

The base unit was the average human lifespan—an aion. An aion was divided into a hundred percents, and percents were the scale that most conscients did their long-term planning. Almost every culture had a tradition of celebrating percents as significant milestones—the progress from birth or the nearness of death. Pregnancies were measured in millo-aions, or "millos," tenths of a percent. Millos were divided into thirty segments called cycles, which humans used for tracking wake and sleep. Each cycle included thirty isochrons, or "isos," which were good for measuring short-term things like flights and work projects, and it was recommended for humans to sleep for ten out of thirty, though very few actually did. Finally, roughly four snaps of a finger was a sequel, or "seq," which was a thousandth of an iso.

So Kalh's thirteen isos of sleep was way over the maximum, and all in one go. She felt physically better. Still not great, but better. As long as she didn't think about her unwanted role as the Prophetess or the nightmare of the Strand. "If I'm that close, I might as well go for the record."

"What's the record?"

"Fifteen."

"Wow. I'm lucky to get five." His laugh created light that contrasted sharply with the recent events. "You feeling better?"

She frowned, wondering why he should care. She sat up, squinting and bracing her shoulders as she did. "Yeah..."

He pointed. "I put a change of clothes for you there if you want them. I have showers too. And you can have your own bunk."

"You keep women's clothing aboard?"

He shrugged, as if he didn't know how the clothes had turned up aboard. That seemed like a strike against him. "How about some soup? I'll put home-grown olioges in it."

"Thank you. I'll take you up on that as soon as I get cleaned up." She triple checked the lock on the shower door. After showering, she changed into the clothing, zipping it all the way to her chin. She liked the periwinkle, though feeling clean physically mismatched how she felt inside. She hated being alone, so she returned to the lounge, climbed onto the couch, and pulled her knees up, tugging the blanket tight around her neck. She hummed quietly to keep herself awake. She didn't trust the pilot and didn't want him sneaking up on her again. Paradoxically, she wanted him to come back so she wasn't alone. Her bald head ached and her body hurt. She felt weak too.

The pilot entered with a steaming bowl. She still detected something... He seemed to be keeping secrets not only from her but from everyone, including himself.

"How's your ship?" she asked.

He carefully handed her the dish. "She'll be all right."

"So is now a good time to talk about surges?" She sipped a spoonful, a simple soup with chunks of meat and roots and olioges, and coupled with her starvation, it was about the best thing she'd ever tasted. The fresh targaspice really made it.

"You're awfully curious about my ship."

Bloody Wings were extremely rare, one per surge gate, they said, but if that were true, not all of them were accounted for. Maybe this was one of the missing ones. "I've only done interstellar surges on a few occasions, and each time I've been curled up inside a suitcase."

He laughed a genuine, deeply felt laugh. "I bet you'd fit."

She put the spoon to her mouth and sipped the hot broth, holding her neck steady for her head's sake. She felt awfully tired. "Really, I *am* curious."

He smiled at her and leaned back in his chair. "First off, all surges aren't equal. The distance matters a lot."

Galactic Metered Time

	Units per Aion	Approximately	
Aion (~ *lifetime*)	1 = 1	111.31	Earth Years
Percent (~ *year*)	1 = 1/100	1.11	Earth Years
Millo-aion (~ *month*)	1 = 1/1,000	40.66	Earth Days
Cycle (~ *day; 30 isochrons*)	1 = 1/30,000	29.27	Earth Hours
Isochron (~ *hour*)	1 = 1/1,000,000	0.98	Earth Hours
Sequel (~ *second*)	1 = 1/1,000,000,000	3.51	Earth Seconds

The aion was based on Orban's average human life expectancy (AHLE) some time ago, long before life-extending nutrients (sometimes called *ambrosia*) came into play. Orban's AHLE has now far exceeded an aion. However, across the wider galaxy, human life expectancy continually declines.

She knew that. She knew a lot about non-mechanical surging, but she wasn't ready to divulge her secret. At the same time, she felt herself relaxing in his presence, which surprised her.

He noticed her reaction, squinted a question, gave up on it, and then said: "Imagine you're about to jump off a cliff, and right when you do, it collapses beneath your feet. It's the same with a surge drive—you need a stable surface beneath you. That's why I slowed to a stop before we surged. It locks together the motion of the ship and the moon while the drive calculates the surge. That was why we had to be holding still. Longer surges need much more stability, so you have to distance yourself from other gravity altogether. Even the gravity of a nearby fighter is enough to throw it off."

He looked somewhat dashing in his black leather flight jacket—classic and roguish. The red sleeve made him seem… rebellious somehow. As she thought this, she felt a slight blush, and took another quick bite in hopes of concealing it. "You couldn't have just risked it?"

"Have you ever heard of *The Scarlet* or the Ancor riddle." His blue eyes weren't quite as large or as handsome as Benton's, but they had a calmness to them, as if he had everything under control, including the things out of anyone's control.

"Sounds familiar…" If she had heard of it, it had been in another lifetime.

"Ancor had one of the Bloody Wings, till he surged too close to several other skycraft. It's not the only incident, just the most famous because of how many people it took."

"What happened?"

"Everyone close died. A surge spiral is something like a gravity well—because mass increases with speed. No one knows how he completed the calculations with all that extra mass."

"I'm not really following…" The soup was doing her in, the fog of sleep pressing on her mind. She let her eyes droop in what hopefully looked only like a prolonged blink, but it left her vulnerable. She forced her eyes open and looked at him deeply, trying to discern.

He looked back calmly and offered a smile with his lips sealed. He showed none of the rabid desire she expected from almost all men. On the contrary, his eyes seemed to say he would watch for her and protect her while she slept. If little Tannie had gotten the chance to grow up…

Kalh looked away, trying not to cry.

The pilot acted like he hadn't noticed. "Normally if you lose your stability, you don't surge at all—you *can't*. The instability stops you. When your surge platform decays, the drive can't complete the calculations. It leaves you powerless. But somehow he went through with it, like jumping off of nothing. The increase in mass caused him and the skycraft around him to spin into each other and vanish. They call it a surge spiral."

"Where did they surge to?"

"No one knows. They never came out the other side."

"They must go somewhere."

"Cup's..." He coughed. "I've been trying to figure that out. The point is, I said we couldn't surge, but I meant that we couldn't go interstellar. Back down on the surface, I had enough stability for a short jump, just enough to get us into the next canyon. Any Bloody Wing pilot knows the trick."

"Why couldn't you have just done a series of short jumps to outrun them?"

"Because, like I said, you have to stop during the calculations. It ends up being slower than just powering away with an atmosdrive. This only worked because we had another canyon to hide in."

"I see." She smiled and set the bowl on the floor. "Thank you. That was probably the best meal I've ever had. You grow the olioges yourself?"

"Yes."

"I wish I had a garden."

He grinned then glanced at the empty bowl. "You want more?"

"Not yet, thanks." She laid back down as the sleep set in like a heavy vapor—though ending the conversation felt like letting go of a hug. Strange for a stranger. "So you can't surge close to a planet..."

"Not an interstellar surge. If you could complete the calculations, you'd take a chunk of it with you and surge into oblivion. Or infraspace. Or wherever it drags what's left of you."

She closed her eyes as she asked, "And do you think those fighters knew this—blocking our exit on purpose?"

"Yes. For sure. Especially Taiberos's men. He's obsessed with surge drives."

Something told her she could trust the pilot enough to fall asleep right now. He kept talking, but she didn't recall what was said after that.

K ALH AWOKE WITH a start.

Someone was shouting down the hall. Her heart pounded. She had to run.

No. She took a deep breath.

She was safe. Aboard his ship. She'd escaped the nightmare. It was going to be okay. She reached for the vial around her neck. It was gone.

The couch surface seemed blurry to her touch, and she felt worse physically. As she stood, her shoulders scrunched, as if to brace her neck and the pain in her head. It was creeping around beneath her eyebrows. She stepped carefully toward the voices.

"She's not ███████ staying aboard the ███████ ship." It was the pilot's voice, and if the Freenet were listening in, they'd be censoring every other word.

"But look at her!" That was Benton, her stalwart defender.

She came around the corner and took the two men by surprise. Their animosity crouched for a moment, holding back. She held a knot of the blanket in front of her chest with one hand, and the rest swooped over her shoulders and then touched the floor. "What's going on?"

"The zentisal drive's been punctured," said Benton. "Even if we had fuel, we'd still need parts, but he won't trust me to get them."

"It's not like these are standard parts. I have to find something that will work, and I don't know what that will be."

"He won't let me go, but he won't let anyone stay here on the ship without him."

Nak's fists showed white on the knuckles. "That's in the contract."

"He doesn't trust us," said Benton.

"Of course I don't trust you. Look what you stand to gain."

Benton swiped a frustrated hand through his pristine hair, messing it up. "It's not me I'm worried about."

Nak stared intently at his opponent: "It's in the contract. No one is staying aboard." His tone dropped lower than usual: "She can't stay—not on my ship."

Benton looked at Kalh and pointed a chopping hand in her direction. "She's not going to steal it."

Kalh felt grateful Benton was standing up for her. Still, she didn't like that these two were arguing as if she weren't there at all.

It made her feel like nobody.

And even if it it was true—

"I'm not giving her the option," Nak growled, and he didn't look at her.

She raised her voice over the argument: "It's fine. I want to come." It wasn't true. She wanted to be left alone, but she'd do it to keep the peace.

Nak faced Benton in a fighting stance, his jaw tight: "I stuck my neck out for you. Risked my ship."

Benton aimed his retort directly ahead and pointed fiercely: "She's in no condition—"

"BOYS!"

Both men finally turned and looked at her.

The way she tore off the blanket made its own kind of statement.

"Let's get moving."

TAIBEROS FELT FILTHY.

Like he had dots of blood splattered on his face.

Only, of course, he did not. Because minds did not bleed.

Lord Admiral Dray's only *practically* had.

Maybe it still would. They were far from done with him.

The traitor was strapped to a table, bound by the wrists, ankles, chest, and neck. His forehead and graying hair were drenched, eyes closed. He deserved all of it, for so many reasons, including the mess he'd recently made of the detention block, but that wasn't the point. The point was to scrape out the truth.

Dray needed a small reprieve before they continued. This was not an act of mercy. If he suffered more right now, it might kill him too soon. Solely pragmatic.

Taiberos left the room.

The door clamped tight, trapping Dray inside the cell.

Breaking a mind could take many awake-sleep cycles. Particularly a Zhan of such ability. Unfortunately, they didn't have cycles: The girl and her accomplices might escape Toar at any time, perhaps already had. Taiberos needed to find them now. If word of what happened got out, it would mar his public image.

Dray held the key.

Those fools made a huge mistake leaving him behind.

Taiberos walked up metal steps. The grating rang beneath his heavy boots.

Ironic how all of this had fallen together. The idea for the Strand had come from a non-political entity, a behind-the-scenes puppeteer who called himself Lethos. He urged the creation of the Strand, which launched Taiberos's political preeminence and led to becoming President of the Pangalactic Socialist Democracy. But he would never have been on that path if not for Dray putting him there. Taiberos should've owed a great debt to this man. Instead, Dray deserved only to have his mind split wide open and bleeding.

It had shocked everyone when the former Lord Admiral turned out to be a Radiance. What a thing to be hunting them while hiding the secret in yourself. Aside from the hypocrisy, it made Taiberos feel slight jealousy. He despised Radiances and the unfair advantage of their powers. It wasn't right. So he condemned them and hunted them, leveling the playing field for everyone else.

And Dray was now one of them.

Well, he would be leveled too.

The retinue followed at Taiberos's heels, ready to jump at his whims. As he marched down the hallway, a messenger ran to him, falling into step alongside: "Sir, Shekton sent me to tell you that the facility is now secure. All prisoners have been accounted for except that one."

That one.

The thing that still might embarrass him.

Taiberos looked the messenger in the eye and nodded but gave no verbal response.

The riot, with the prisoners awakening on Orikerse, had been momentarily worrisome. It wouldn't have taken much of a push for the whole facility to have been endangered. Luckily, the prisoners were not united, so the plot was muzzled before it spun out of control. A few had to be killed, which was an unfortunate waste.

"Tell Building Two I'll be returning to the command deck presently. They'd better have news for me. I want that ship and its passengers."

TAIBEROS HATED WAITING.

He went alone to his private quarters.

At the lavatory sink, he looked at himself in the mirror.

As president, he no longer wore military fatigues except occasionally when Kavalion invited him back to the team for a particular mission, like when they captured the girl on Sream—he did, after all, have a gift for ferreting out Radiances. Now he wore a jumpsuit made of metallic ribbing that glistened at the bulges. This was mostly covered by an expensive vest and armored leggings. A pair of glasses hung around his neck. A wire wound from behind his ear and vanished into his vest; this allowed him to stay connected to his underlings at all times.

He looked at his own stately gaze. His face was pale, hair becoming thinner, cheeks more plump than they ought to be. Despite these slight flaws, he still commanded respect. Not because of his appearance alone but because of his accomplishments, because of who he was. He'd outshined everyone else, and so the citizens of the PSD elected him to preside—as simple as that.

He had a right to be here.

He found no blood on him, but he turned on the faucet anyway, soaped up, and rinsed his real hand against his cybernetic one, then splashed water on his face. That helped to push aside the filthy feeling, though it didn't withdraw completely.

It had stained his soul too deeply for that.

In a nook beneath the mirror, a small trinket caught his eye: a glass vial filled with pale sand. He'd taken it from that girl before having his way with her. He didn't know why he'd kept it, and he felt reluctant to touch it. Although quite beautiful, she was both filthy and below him. But their interaction showed what he could do to anyone who opposed him. Yet now she'd escaped, opposing him again.

He stared at that vial of sand.

Of all the prisoners at the Strand, they'd freed her specifically, even though it cost them Dray. That meant something. She'd been framed as the author of the Prophet Letters, a public scandal, but it wasn't really her. He had to stop them before they made some feeble attempt at counter propaganda.

Plus he wanted to know whether she really had a secret.

It was common knowledge that Radiances were simply born. Yet, that girl, in one of their recent intimate moments in Building 13, had said something strange. She'd been on the exhaust, only occasionally able to glimpse even the edges of real consciousness, but through half closed eyes, she said, *"Anyone can be a Radiance."*

When she said it, he'd scrutinized her carefully. "What?"

She stared through the delirium, mouth hanging open: *"Anyone can pay the price."*

Her claim was wild.

It had certainly never been demonstrated scientifically.

If a Radiance really could be created, he needed to know how. A price seemed to suggest suffering or torture. Or maybe she meant to mislead him. He couldn't tell. Maybe that had happened to Dray—a late bloomer rather than an outright hypocrite. If he could start pushing regular people across that threshold, it would solve their supply problem. The Strand would be unimpeded in its march toward a breakthrough, securing his place in history. He'd be more famous than Captain Skyreacher himself. The real one. And he'd truly rule the galaxy with impunity. No one could stop him, not even the voters. And maybe, if the girl was right, Taiberos could finally claim the powers of a Radiance for his own.

Taiberos pinched the vial delicately and dropped it on the floor. It hit with a *plink*.

His heel slammed down, crushing the glass like a venomous insect.

Anyone can be a Radiance.

He washed his hands again, scrubbing his thumb and finger particularly. He used the facilities, returned to the mirror, and washed his hands a third time. After drying, he covered his cybernetic in a black glove. When he turned to leave, the sand scraped between his soles and the floor.

A Bloody Wing created a massive flash of light when it surged, and so far they had detected none. It meant the conspirators were likely still in the system. For some reason. Waiting or trapped.

He paused in his suite to glance at the chronometer on his wrist. He wasn't sure how long he could prudently wait for the next round of interrogation. He sat at his desk and placed both hands down as fists. He hoped his underlings were making progress.

If the conspirators escaped Toar, Dray would know where they'd be going next. He might know why they hadn't left yet too, and where they were now. He was the key. It made waiting for recovery all the more difficult.

Taiberos needed to get the secret out of that man's mind.

Even if he had to split it open with his bare hands.

S IR, YOUR MAIL."
Taiberos's secretary set a stack of papers on his desk and sat down, facing him.

Very little of the galaxy's technology came from original inventions. Instead, they were copies of Photoss relics from the ancient past. Photoss holograph projectors, for example, had been mimicked, but the imitations couldn't reach a resolution to make fine detail like text. Thus, nothing superseded the practicality of pen and paper, which remained the preferred method for most asynchronous communication.

Transferring messages was also a challenge.

To travel directly from one star to another could literally take lifetimes. Even broadcasting a comms signal at the speed of light took so long to traverse the void that it was useless. Surge gates, however, made interstellar travel almost instant, so the best solution was to carry paper messages on ships through the surge gates to be delivered by hand. This was what the secretary set on Taiberos's desk.

He picked up the stack.

Then he looked at his comms. Why had no report come yet?

The first letter, surely not on top by coincidence, had been sent by his wife. He gave a quick glare at his secretary—

And cycled the letter to the back.

The next item summarized broadcasts from the last two cycles. After tearing it open, his eyes widening as he read, he shoved in the wired earpiece and furiously tapped keys on his desktop comms unit, putting through a relay:

"Turnor, you are horrible at your job, and I despise you... I don't want to hear it. It's Gorthon again. I guarantee it. What do I even pay you for? Counterattack! Make him feel what I'm feeling right now. I don't know. Make it up... I said make something up... You are only great if I'm great. Now, do it, or I will find someone else." He jerked the earpiece out of his head and smashed it into the desk with his cybernetic hand.

The secretary flinched as electronic pieces went flying her direction.

"Get me a new one." He cycled through the rest of the mail, stopping to read bits here and there. When he arrived back at whatever his wife wanted, he tossed the stack down, checked his chronometer and stood. "Damn that Starchild."

If this story came out now, it would be very bad.

His secretary, though quite beautiful, gazed at him with a look of scorn. She was judging him. Not her prerogative, but he kept his retaliation inside. For now.

H IS RETINUE JOINED him outside his suite and followed to Building 2. When he entered, the staff turned their attention to him, either overtly or discreetly. They physically straightened up as well. He'd recently reminded them of the consequences of relaxing. Apparently his leadership was getting through.

Taiberos tapped a pair of gloved cybernetic fingers on one of the electronic consoles covered in glowing buttons. Fuzzy holographs floated above. "Why haven't I received an update on the escapees?"

A young major spoke up. "We still have not detected the departure of a Bloody Wing. All signs point to him being in the system somewhere. The posters are up across all of Toar. Any citizen who sees them will turn them in."

"It's not enough. Did you affirm the Bloody Wing's signature?"

The PSD kept a database of these skycraft, noting the features and shapes, with the goal of eventually capturing them all. "They narrowed it down to either one thirteen or one seventeen."

"It's one thirteen. Dammit." The rage burned hot inside him, and his phantom limb tingled. He wondered if Starchild had actually listened to the message he broadcast. "That coward will run as soon as he gets the chance. We have to tighten the screws now."

"I thought we were waiting on Lord Admiral Dray."

Taiberos turned toward the major at the console. "You had better not be waiting. I want seekers out there. Flood the canyons with them."

"The seekers are already deployed," said the major. "No reports so far."

"They need to be in every twist and turn of those canyons." Taiberos opened his gloved palm, making a platform. "I want that skycraft in my hand within the next isochron."

"Sir, with the twists and turns, those canyons increase the search area exponentially, and we only have so many seekers."

"I want that vessel, and I'll get it with or without your help, major. You'd better hope it's not the latter."

The man choked out, "Yes, sir."

President Taiberos turned toward the rest of the staff on the command deck.

They looked at him warily, ready to jump at his whim and searching their minds for any detail they might've missed.

To the operator, Taiberos said, "Get me Admiral Watelle."

"Right away, sir."

After a moment, a voice came over the relay: "Admiral Watelle here."

"Admiral, I want you to move the fleet into orbit and drop your seekers. We're looking for Bloody Wing one thirteen. He's hiding somewhere in these canyons."

"Certainly. That will make it more difficult to guard against his departure."

"I know. How long since your pilots have trained in how to ground a Bloody Wing?"

"We keep all our regimens up to date according to your guidelines. My pilots deflected his last attempt to escape, and we're ready to do it again."

"Mmm."

The major stepped toward Taiberos, his heels clacking as he stood at attention. "Sir, one of the seekers may have found your Bloody Wing."

Taiberos restricted his smile. "Did they or didn't they?"

"Well, it's dark down there, and the seeker footage is difficult to interpret. It's in octant seven. It's called Spearon Channel. A team of troops are preparing to descend."

"Good." His net was already closing. He began to walk from the room. "Give me immediate updates. And tell the engineers to ready my suit. I'm going out there myself."

This would fix the publicity problem. Though really, nothing excited him more than the thought of seeing Starchild captured.

And then killed.

And he wanted to be the one to do it.

THEY WALKED SINGLE file. Liink was second in line.

White strips crossed the gash across his face. He could feel blood pumping through the wound with each heartbeat. To get the repair parts for the Bloody Wing, they had to go into a populated area. His predatory instincts didn't like that.

His tail curved back and forth as he strode, a feature that provided exceptional balance. His form was long and lean, the muscles of his six appendages strong and supple, constantly ready to spring into attack. He was quite strong, despite the fact that his horns hadn't attached to his skull yet, much less popped through his skin and dark fur. Technically, it meant he was still a cub, but he didn't like to think so.

Liink looked at the sky, scanning for PSD fighters. If the team was to be ambushed, he wanted to be the first to give the alert. It felt strange to walk under a sun that moved, especially so fast. When they began, it had been on the rise; now it rushed to high noon. The planet Sible, a huge crescent, chased the sun behind the clouds. No enemy ships though.

As Liink crawled along, he worried about his abiisu—proof of honor.

His companions wouldn't understand. They were humans.

Humans dominated the galaxy, thanks to the Photoss giving them a head start. Physically they were among the weakest of conscient species, but their ruthlessness kept them ahead. The pilot seemed like one of those types.

Dishonorable.

Staring at the man's back made Liink want to pounce.

The pilot was quite large for a human, broadly built, but Liink still could've beaten him in a fight. As long as Liink struck before the pilot drew his pistol. The two had hardly spoken on the flight to Toar, except for one awkward encounter while Liink was trying to meditate. Back then, the pilot had been wearing an intimidating mask, cowering in obscurity. As Dray had said on the flight here, "A Zhan should never hide from the light." Admittedly, war required some subterfuge, but this man's whole life was hiding. He was a scallywag at best and perhaps something much worse.

Liink scanned the horizon, turning his head around and behind him. Still no sign of the PSD coming after them, but he needed something to happen. Only in a conflict could he prove his valor.

This mission had been his chance. If he saved anyone on this team, his people would finally honor him. If he saved the life of the Uncrowned Queen, his *father* might actually honor him. But so far, all he'd earned was a blow to the face—an embarrassing mark.

Not nearly enough to make his father proud.

When he returned, his clan would ask him the story, yet he'd barely contributed to the mission at all. Instead of telling them of his own abiisu, he would tell them of Dray's, how the gray beard had sacrificed himself so the rest of them could escape.

His father would ask why Liink had not been the one to stay behind.

He would have no worthy answer.

L IINK SENSED THE light steps of the Prophetess behind him.
He didn't like having anyone at his back, even someone held in such high honor. He turned his lengthy neck, monitoring the sky in hopes of bad news, but then his eyes fell on her. He tried to make it seem incidental.

Abii brought up the rear, the man who'd organized the mission. He was always well groomed for a human. He now wore formal civilian clothes, perfectly tailored to his form. He also had a pair of heavy black goggles on his head. They were called Shadowlyss goggles, and they'd become popular among youths, or the knockoffs had, even though most people had eyes with nothing to hide. The popularity meant Abii could use them without standing out, and they allowed him to let his eyes glow in public.

Back home, Liink had heard whisperings that Abii was making secret plans, plans to start another revolution and throw off the shackles of Taiberos and the PSD. Liink had misgivings about this being true, as he had been there for the Shartriin Massacre and had watched his brother die. Yet Liink admired Abii, and the Prophetess seemed to be in love with him. Now that she was free, their revolution was sure to succeed.

Liink cleared his throat and spoke in his soft voice: "Abii, I have been contemplating."

The Prophetess, between him and Abii, gazed. Or maybe scowled. Human emotions were so strange. He thought he'd caught her sour glance in Building 13 too. It felt like a rejection already, as if she, like his father, had judged him to be unworthy. "Why do you keep calling Benton Abii?" she asked.

Liink bowed his head. "He was given that title of honor by my father."

The dishonorable pilot chimed in with a dose of sympathy: "What does the title mean?" Perhaps he knew what it was like to be despised.

"What were you contemplating, Liink?" interjected Abii, quickly changing the subject.

Liink spoke tentatively: "That maybe we should go back for Lord Admiral Dray."

"I think it's a good suggestion," said Abii. "I'm not sure it's feasible. Our plan to rescue Kalhette took millos and a lot of money to put in place. Just getting those IDs was… I couldn't believe it."

LïïNK Adïïn

6 · Feb · 2019

With his heart pounding anxiously, Liink spoke to fill the awkward silence after the rejection: "Speaking of titles, my father gave me my title too. *Liink* means 'grateful for the child.' Actually, it just means 'grateful.' The rest is implied."

"I like it," said the pilot.

As they walked, Liink's six paws pressed into the charcoal soil of Toar. They were not so different from human hands. Each had three long fingers and a fourth that could twist into an opposing grip. Each of his twenty-four fingers had a retractable claw. He lifted one to scratch his neck, still proceeding on five legs, as he said, "I have seen that you guard *your* name, Pilot Skyreacher."

"In my line of work, you have to." It seemed like an excuse for cowardice. Liink wanted to ask more but didn't.

His long ears heard the footsteps of the Prophetess behind him, and he tried to sense an attitude in them. He spoke timidly, curving his aching neck to see her behind him: "And you, my Prophetess, do you have a miina name?"

She'd escaped her prison garb and now wore pants and a textured purple-blue shirt that covered her neck. She met his gaze for the shortest moment, then looked down, and said, "Not now." With that, she stopped and waved for Abii to step ahead so she could walk at the back.

It stung.

Liink turned his wounded, cat-like face upward, pretending to search for enemy skycraft, but his mind was too preoccupied to make a decent scout.

First his father and now her...

W HAT YOU GOT there."

The scallywag pilot walked sideways for a few steps as he pointed to Liink's chest, coming to the rescue while pretending not to have noticed anything wrong. Admittedly, he seemed a lot less devious without the mask.

Liink's hind legs were longest, and the place they met his spine was the highest point on his back. His chest split into two sets of shoulders, unlike a cramped human torso. His middle shoulders were broader and led to a strong set of arms. His upper arms were smaller, more dexterous, and his spine bent down to meet them. This physiology tilted his back and head toward the ground, connecting him firmly to it. He wore a belt between his front and middle arms, to which he'd clipped two weapons, both within easy reach of a cross-draw. One was a human pistol, but the pilot's question was about the other: a crystalline handle wrapped in leather with a red ribbon hanging from the end. Walking on five paws, he lifted the sixth to touch the prism on his chest—a source of both pride and of pain. And it made him miss home.

Suddenly self-conscious about how this off-world pirate might react to his accent, Liink said in his smoothly higher voice, "It's a prism."

"You mean a psykatana."

"They have many names." It felt strange to be conversing after keeping to themselves for so long aboard the skycraft. "In my culture, the handle is called a prism. When it's ignited, the light is called a Singblade."

"Show me."

Liink spoke lowly, not wanting the Prophetess to hear: "I can't show you."

The pilot matched the lowered voice: "Why not."

"I haven't yet been gifted with fourth spectrum." Abii and the Prophetess both carried similar blades and could readily show him though.

"What's fourth spectrum mean."

"I can't ignite it."

"You carry a weapon you can't use."

Yes. Because of his father's insult. "It is really quite something to see. The flame appears at the point, which seems to be in midair, and then it catches fire down the two curving sides of the blade, meeting at the handle, but this all happens in the quickest flash, an explosion of light that appears to come from nowhere."

"But you can't do it," said the pilot.

"No." Liink checked over his shoulder—the Prophetess seemed aloof. "It is not the will of the Kurosh."

"So why carry it then," asked the pilot.

Liink wondered if this human could tell when a miin looked dejected.

THE MEMORY WAS still fresh.

A few sleep cycles ago, Liink's mother had come into the hut: "They're here."

It was Abii and Lord Admiral Dray, come to recruit him for the mission.

Liink meandered outside on all sixes. The two humans waited aboard a small transport that hovered above the ground. Soon they would rendezvous with the pilot's dark Bloody Wing at an isolated location out in the wilderness.

Liink looked back at the tree he'd always called home. Not only was he leaving that behind, he was also departing his home planet for the first time. Traveling with a bunch of strangers, people who knew a lot more than he did about nearly everything. He wasn't sure he'd come back alive either.

It should've been a proud moment, but his head was bowed in shame.

Because his father wasn't there. The chief.

Other cubs his age and younger gawked at the visitors. Yet, to Liink, it felt like the eyes of the whole village were on him. Judging him.

When a young miina cub left for his first battle, his father was supposed to give him a weapon. Liink's six older brothers had each gotten something. Bartuun's spear. Or Klef's rifle. Liink had often wondered what weapon his father would give him.

But his father simply hadn't come.

Maybe he'd wanted to be there, but the duties of being chief had called him away. Or maybe it was political—he didn't believe in the mission, and so couldn't support it publicly. Only, how could he not support the Prophetess? Maybe the truth was more simple: He didn't support his son.

So Liink padded across that open space all alone with everyone watching. Feeling ashamed.

Then Gaiing whistled, running quickly out of the jungle.

Just in time too.

One of Liink's three best friends, Gaiing shared the love of Photoss mythology. They even hoped to one day excavate a Photoss city. They believed that some vast, immortal secret lay undisclosed but within reach, perhaps in the very next scroll.

When Liink looked up, Gaiing held the Photoss prism, an artifact the trio discovered among ruins—a red gem wrapped in a hard leather handle with a long, red ribbon attached to the bottom. Gaiing had been the one to personally uncover it, the most valuable thing they'd ever encountered in their expeditions.

"Take this," said Gaiing. "It will be your heroic weapon."

"I can't take it. What if I die? It may never come back to you. This is—"

"It's yours now, to take on whatever adventures lie in your future. Even death."

"But I can't even use it."

"It's an emblem, brother." He clapped Liink on both shoulders. "Reverence the light!"

When they embraced, Liink swallowed hard and fought back tears.

L IINK'S TAIL WHIPPED more energetically upon remembering.

"It's an emblem," said Liink. "It represents what we're fighting for— light." Yet he couldn't help but feel that it also represented a father's neglect.

The pilot spoke in a gruff yet sympathetic tone: "How old are you, Liink."

"Sixteen."

The pilot nodded, like it confirmed some suspicion. "And don't miina live longer than humans?"

"Yes, if they die of natural causes. Lifespan is usually around a hundred and twenty-seven percents."

"You're lucky then."

"Most miina don't die of natural causes."

"How do they die."

"Fighting against the PSD, fighting amongst the miina clans, fighting with the colonists."

"You fight the colonists?"

"Historically, yes. Some think we should still be fighting them."

"So why are you allies then."

Liink lowered his volume, feeling some embarrassment: "I believe in the Prophetess. I believe we can change Solace forever." His tail almost halted when he thought he heard her say his name behind him. His ear lifted, but when he glanced, her lips were still. He took a deep breath and exhaled.

Then he glanced at Sible's giant crescent gliding overhead, moving so quickly. Still no enemy skycraft. Still no last chance to prove himself.

The pilot raised his skeptical eyebrows. "That kind of devotion seems… foolish, to be honest. You risk a lot on your faith in a human."

"In my culture, giving your life is considered an honor."

"Why would that be an honor."

"My people believe this life is a trial. Our light is being monitored by the Kurosh."

"The Kurosh?" The pilot looked back over Liink's shoulder.

Liink whipped his head around to see.

Behind him, the Prophetess caught his gaze and immediately looked away. Perhaps she had some stake in this conversation. Perhaps she wanted to see if the heathen pilot could be swayed toward the Zhani ways.

If so, Liink accepted the challenge: "Have you heard of the Photoss?"

"They made my ship."

"Yes. Well, the Kurosh made the Photoss."

"So you think they're watching, waiting for us to die for one of their causes?"

"For a *good* cause, yes. It's called an abiisu. It means performing a heroic act, an act of valor: to give your life or to save another's life and have that person sing the story to the Council of Elders." Liink looked hopefully at the sky—because an abiisu required circumstances where lives were actually on the line. Many reached old age without achieving an abiisu, but Liink was the son of Chief Adiin. His six older brothers had all done it. He had to do it too.

"Speaking as a friend, you should be careful who hears you say that—a lot of humans will think you're crazy."

"I know, but the number of people who believe a notion does not affect its truthfulness." Liink stole a glance behind to see if the Prophetess had heard that, one of his wisest comments. In fact, though, he'd heard it from Viidan.

"Why would the Photoss care what we do," asked the pilot.

"Not the Photoss. The Kurosh."

"Okay. Why would they care."

"To see if we'll create light and become worthy to join their ranks."

"Their ranks."

"Yes."

"Hmm." The pilot frowned.

"Even if you don't believe, it shouldn't affect your candidacy."

The pilot raised his eyebrows. "So you're trying to live a good life, and maybe give your life, to prove yourself to these invisible beings."

"Yes."

The pilot glanced toward the back of the file. "Do Benton and Kalh believe in that."

"They must speak for themselves, but I would be glad to teach you more."

"You're starting to sound like Benton. Don't take it personally, but I'm a tough case." The pilot turned his head to the side and gestured toward Abii—and his crusade. "How'd you get involved in all this anyway."

"The Prophetess represents the colonists. My father represents the largest clan of miina. I am his youngest. I was sent to bring honor to my family."

The pilot nodded.

The sun made its dash for the horizon, and the shadows moved quickly to hide as the light faded. The crawling shadows left Liink feeling uneasy, as if he could literally see time slipping away along with his chance to claim his abiisu. The glow of skycraft appeared in the sky, descending to and rising from a populated area.

None of them looked like a danger or an ambush.

A S THE TEAM rounded the next rock formation, their destination came into view: the Citadel. From this distance, it looked like more rocks but with slightly less variation in their form. It stretched toward them, reaching with hovels and homes on the outskirts.

The Prophetess raised her voice: "How far are we from the Strand?"

The pilot shouted back: "We're on the other side of the moon. Besides, Toar has upwards of a thousand cities on its surface. No one will recognize us."

Liink found himself almost hoping the pilot was wrong. If anything, Liink's miina body would stand out enough to be a problem. Yet these thoughts made him feel like a traitor, as if he were mentally sabotaging his own team.

He had a little time left to convince the pilot of their beliefs, so he spoke as loud as he could without seeming awkward—wanting the Prophetess to catch the discussion. "What is something you believe in?"

The pilot shrugged. "That's a big question."

"In all your travels and in everything you've seen, did you never find pieces of religion you wished were true?"

"I'll tell you what I believe: There's something funny going on. No way this whole galaxy fell together like this by chance. But all this stuff about Photoss seems like guesswork, like a fun story someone made up. I don't see why it should be any truer than any other religious story."

"I am honored to hear your thoughts."

"Calling it like I see it."

"I believe in the Song," said Liink.

"I don't know what that means."

"Perhaps if you did, you would believe in it."

"Maybe…" His tone was doubtful.

"The Song is all that is written," said Liink. "It is everything that has happened, is happening, and will happen. It is everything that has changed or will change, and it is everything that will never change."

"It sounds like you believe in everything."

"I was quoting a verse."

The pilot laughed. "Why don't you tell me *your* thoughts."

"Well..." began Liink, but he found himself speechless. He wasn't good with words. His father had said so.

"Just shoot from the hip."

"It is... it is a *will*." Liink closed his yellow eyes and swallowed. "It desires things, just like you and I desire things."

"So the Song is a person. You really believe that?"

"I suppose. Or, at least, it includes a person. Or it is like a person, with many cells working together. But it is much bigger than our concept of a person too, I think."

A nearby home was squat and round, with a primitive roof, bathed in the last rays of twilight, but what caught Liink's attention was the human standing out front, staring at them, or staring at Liink in particular.

"Okay," said the pilot. "I'm following so far: a cosmic... uh... *will*. That fair?"

Liink nodded. "It's a force, like gravity, that draws all life together, just like we're drawn to the ground right now. We're all pieces of it, but if you summed all the life on every planet, the total would still just be a tiny molecule of the Song."

"Okay. Bigger than us. Anything else?"

"The Song decides on outcomes."

"Whoa. You're saying it controls our choices."

"No. You control your own actions within your given circumstances, and it controls everything else. But you're part of it, like I said. So you're controlling yourself and *it* is *you*. There's a mantra that goes: I am the Song."

In a jarring sequel, the sun dropped out of sight and twilight vanished along with it, way too suddenly. Sible remained in the sky, shedding significant light from its massive glowing crescent. One star glowed bright, probably the system's surge gate. And the whole heavens moved together at a dizzying pace. On Solace, the sun never moved; the stars did slowly, but he had seldom seen them.

The buildings of the Citadel had grown larger. The light along the streets washed out most of the starlight, but the sky traffic remained visible overhead. People carrying wares to and from the marketplace moved about on foot, or riding beasts, or driving groundrunners. This made Liink uncomfortable because each of them moved behind him either coming or going, and instinct told him he could become prey at any moment. He tried to keep an eye on them all, as nonchalantly as possible.

The pilot eyed Liink with a skeptical look.

Liink felt embarrassed for letting his mind wander. "I sense you still aren't converted." He glanced back to check on the Prophetess.

She might be listening, but she wasn't looking this way.

The pilot nodded toward the buildings. "Nope, I'm not. And we're almost there."

"A simple way to put it is that when you do something good, you feel good in your heart. That is the voice of the Song, at least on a basic level."

The pilot turned his head to the side and nodded: "Okay, I've felt that. Once."

Liink laughed. "My father would be glad to hear you say so." He looked upward, mouth agape. The archway of the Citadel's gates curved high overhead.

"I do have one question," said the pilot. "I heard you Zhani believed in things like no sex and Lethos and stuff."

This was not a criticism Liink expected. "I am not a Zhan, and don't you believe in Lethos?"

"I did when I was a kid."

"He is real."

"And does he really eat people."

"More or less."

"So your religion teaches that there's a real-life nightmare cannibal who eats people while they're sleeping."

"No. Our religion doesn't teach about him. He just happens to exist. And he is more like a *spiritual* cannibal. He consumes his victims through Genosis, eighth spectrum. It is a Zhani ability that he uses in a twisted way."

"But what makes you think he's real."

"My father's father has seen him."

The pilot glanced back with an unconvinced look on his face. Without replying, he turned and sized up the shop on their right. "Time's up. Nice try."

Liink smiled. There was something... admirable... about the pilot's nonchalance. Almost like having no honor freed him of all scruples. Liink hoped they'd continue their conversation on the way back.

Abii and the Prophetess came to a stop, she keeping her distance from Liink. Abii bent over and picked up a piece of garbage and carried it to a bin.

The pilot laughed.

"What?" Abii looked indignant. Defensive even.

"Sorry." The pilot's mirth nearly vanished—though not quite.

Abii seemed calm, but he didn't let it go. "You think it's funny to pick up trash?"

"Surprising."

"Why's that surprising?"

"I've traveled the whole Photoss Galaxy," said the pilot, "and I've noticed two kinds of people: the ones who drop trash and the ones who pick it up. The second kind is pretty rare. You caught me off guard is all."

With the calm of street lights reflecting in his eyes, Abii said, "And which kind are you?"

"I try not to get involved."

"It strikes me that your middle category is unfortunately more common than the two extremes you named."

"Why's that unfortunate," asked the pilot.

"Indifference is the enemy of Initiative."

The pilot inhaled, about to unleash, but then he let it go—just didn't say whatever retort was burning on his insides. He swallowed it and smiled, looking calmly at Abii as the reply vaporized into oblivion.

Now *that* was honorable.

Especially coming from the scallywag.

T HEY HAD ARRIVED peacefully, and the pilot remained unconverted. Both of these left Liink feeling empty.

The pilot pointed to a sign that said *Beck Yard*. "I'm going to try this place. Stay close. Contract still applies, and I'd prefer not to cut anyone else loose." He gave Abii an *even-you* kind of look, then walked inside.

Without the pilot around, Liink glanced warily at the Prophetess and Abii. They stood close, whispering like lovers, beneath the *Beck Yard* sign, which cast orange light on her shaved skull and his groomed hair. They hardly seemed to notice their miina companion creeping away. He looked for a quiet, dark niche to lay low where no one would notice him. It was only in obscurity that honor didn't matter.

If only he hadn't been born a chief's son.

As he retreated, his fur matched the charcoal ground, making him almost invisible, except for his yellow eyes. He squinted to assure that his retinas didn't reflect the streetlight and give him away. The solitude felt good, and he let out a depressed chuffle, something like a groan that came out as a rolling wave. He sized up the passers by, wishing he could use Starsight without drawing attention. At least he'd been born with that gift.

Neon pinks and blues cast shadows on the pedestrians. Humans, as always, were most common. Liink had seen many of these other strange species in books, but some were completely foreign to him—horns growing from heads or tusks from mouths, too many eyes, and odd sizes and shapes of bodies. It both intrigued and unsettled him.

A mixed group passed in front of him, laughing irreverently. One pointed at him and loudly whispered a slur about an endophallus. Even strangers judged Liink unworthy of honor. Ignoring the comment, he bowed his head and retreated farther, not wanting any trouble.

In this dark, crowded, and lonely setting, he reflected on how he'd gotten here: His first interstellar flight happened on an illegal craft. Then in disguise, he'd toured the most dangerous prison in the galaxy. He'd even taken a blow to help rescue the Prophetess. Gaiing and Roark would love it, but his father would hardly notice. Nothing near saving a life. Now Liink rested in an alleyway in a foreign marketplace on an unfamiliar moon, far from his family and friends.

Far from people who believed in the Kurosh.

The sky was black, the stars invisible except for the brightest few. Streaks of starships passed overhead, arriving and leaving peacefully.

And he was out here all alone.

A bipedal form with a mangled head, an arched spine, and two black, bulbous eyes stopped in front of a building across the street. Even in the low light, Liink's sharp eyes could tell the biped was watching the Prophetess. Instinct told him to stalk this onlooker from behind and then clamp down on its throat until it stopped breathing, but sometimes instinct had to be restrained by reason. According to Abii, no one knew what the Prophetess looked like, so how could they be spying on her?

Probably just a creep.

The alien lifted his hand to his mouth and said something into a comms.

Liink raised a floppy ear, but the bustle of the street masked whatever the creature said. Liink touched the pistol affixed to his belt. It was a human design. Whenever he held it, he would grip the handle with three fingers, while his thumb wrapped all the way around to pull the trigger.

A human approached the alien and said something. The alien nodded, speaking back, and then gestured across the street toward the Prophetess, whose face and bare scalp were now bathed in that pink glow from overhead. They spoke in low tones, debating who they were going to contact for help, but the reason was an assumption never stated.

Liink had been in a firefight three percents ago in which he played the role of an unarmed, frightened child who watched the life fade from his older brother's eyes. The Shartriin Massacre. He'd vowed that when his next firefight came, he would prove his valor.

So he let his instinct override his fear.

He stalked silently through the alleys, moving directly away from his prey, taking the long way around. If it came out where he expected, he'd be crouched in a kill position just a few body-lengths from the alien and his companion. With five paws prowling against the ground, Liink reached with his sixth and fingered the pistol.

His squinting yellow eyes watched carefully through the shadows.

The alleyway was sprayed with graffiti in colors that matched the neon lights of the street. Posters of various sizes, shapes, and colors had been pasted along the walls, creating layers upon layers of visual garbage. He saw the corner of a poster that had been covered by a more recent layer.

The poster had Abii's picture in the bottom corner.

The nighttime bustle became hollow and distant.

Liink found another copy of the same one, this time not covered. It showed two faces on it. One was the pilot's. He looked much younger, and he definitely wasn't wearing his mask. The other was the Prophetess, with her eyes closed and head shaven—they'd given her no more dignity than a corpse. The lower part had a picture of Abii next to a miin that wasn't Liink.

His tail stopped completely.

Bold type was printed across the top:

REWARD

By the mandate of President Taiberos

Ħ5,000,000

For aiding in the capture of BRECK STARCHILD
his co-conspirator KALHETTE WHITESUN
and their accomplices

The hackles down Liink's back stood on end.

This meant anyone would recognize them. It meant Taiberos might be on the way here already. They might never make it back to the ship. Or home to Solace.

Unless Liink could warn them in time.

He turned, heart pounding, ready to sprint out of the alleyway.

But five strange creatures already surrounded him.

NAK SAT ON the groundrunner and leaned back. The leather seat felt good. It'd been a long time since he'd ridden one of these. He'd strapped the fuel batteries and replacement parts to a small trailer behind him.

He brushed his fingers down the machine's spine. The galaxy's technology was unearned. The good stuff came directly from the Photoss. Everything else was rudimentary at best. Fortunately, these groundrunners came from the former lineage, and unlike Bloody Wings, people had figured out how to reproduce them. The vehicle amounted to a contragrav engine with handle bars. As was the case with most Photoss tech, it had enough power to be pretty dangerous with the wrong pilot.

He grinned, and the clients saw the expression on his scratched up face. The girl in particular seemed to appreciate his mood, an advantage to being unmasked. Felt liberating. He'd get another mask before he approached his next clients though.

Benton sat on the other groundrunner, goggles hanging from the handlebar, not smiling. Something about him wasn't right. He was too thoughtful. Thinking could get you killed.

Nak adjusted the Shadowlyss goggles around his forehead then reached a hand back, squeezed the tissues of his neck, and groaned—a pinching pain from getting smashed in the face with a ton of rock so hard you do a backflip. He grimaced and happened to lock eyes with Kalh. Not his sexiest move. You didn't have to worry about that sort of thing while wearing a mask.

She stood between the two men, apparently undecided on who to ride with.

Skycraft engines traced paths of light in the darkness overhead. The pilots must've been looking down at Toar's surface of shattered skin, which, instead of blood, oozed the orange light of lava. Nak wished he were up there.

He hated leaving his ship vulnerable like this.

It was only bearable because he trusted Cup, such a tiny piece of technology. That was why he had to protect her from outside influences so carefully—so she didn't become compromised or get ideas about going rogue.

Normally, when he was away from *The Sanctum*, Cup would take her into the storm of infraspace where she'd be untouchable. He'd specify a time and place for rendezvous, with instructions for what to do if he didn't show. They had backup plans for the backup plans, an elaborate scheme to make sure no one could touch the ship. Cup wouldn't land, for example, without verifying Nak's voice over the comms through a secret signal phrase. And they'd need his hand to bypass the crypto key too. But while *The Sanctum* was grounded, most of that security didn't apply. Nak wanted to get back to her, sail someplace safe, and make the repairs she deserved.

He wasn't willing to delay much longer. He liked the miina cub, but the kid knew better than to wander off. Especially now. The second loss of their party.

They'd had every right to leave Dray though—it was in the contract. Not like they could've done more either. Even now, it would take some luck to safely complete their escape. By his own reckoning, Nak had done right, and yet he still felt guilty, which didn't add up. Maybe because he'd left an almost-friend in the cybernetic hand of his worst enemy.

Benton tapped his handlebar anxiously and peered into the dim streets around them—still no Liink. Wild cloeties or something like them howled in the desert. A faint ring of pale dust stretched across the sky—the Photoss Galaxy itself. You could see that same ring from wherever you stood inside it, long as you had enough darkness.

Kalh turned her bald head with what seemed like anxiety, like she was afraid some horror might jump out to grab her.

"You okay?" Nak asked.

She faced him and nodded, maybe relieved to have a distraction. "You sure you don't want to come with us for phase two? It's going to be a riot."

Nak chuckled then gave the same old line: "Sure. If you get him to pony up."

Kalh looked at Nak like she meant it, like she wanted to see deep enough into his soul to understand. "Come on. Why not?" She was a strange creature. He sensed hurt and fear in her, but a brightness hovered about her too.

"Don't want to get involved in a revolution," said Nak.

"I never said it was a revolution," said Benton.

Yes, but Dray had. Nak only wondered about where and when. "You guys are crazy anarchists."

She moved directly in front of him. "Oh, and you're not?" Saucy too.

"First of all, I'm not crazy." With his legs straddling, Nak leaned forward onto the handle bars. "Second, just because I practice a little personal anarchy doesn't mean it's a good idea for everyone."

"So the rule applies to you and no one else?" asked Benton.

Kalh smiled, waiting for the answer. She didn't look good. No, she looked *good,* but she didn't look well. Her skin was pale, her face tired—in no condition to be out here. Yet she still had plenty of fight in her, especially while talking politics.

"Uh, no," said Nak. "The rule *does* apply to everyone else. I'm the exception."

"How do you justify that ethically?" asked Benton.

"I'm different than everyone else," said Nak.

"Okay, yes, Nak," said Kalh, "I have never met anyone like you. That's true—" She paused just long enough for Nak to think she might be into him. "—but there's nearly one trillion other individuals in our galaxy who have no one else like them either. We're all different. That's the point of free will."

Nak gave her a smile with lips only, unconvinced, yet feeling no need to defend his stance against these two.

On the horizon, the sun began its sprinting rise. Time was passing dangerously.

Kalhette glanced anxiously, wanting to get moving. "What was the biggest war on your homeworld?" The hair on her head formed a gray cap where locks might've been.

Nak thought about making a newborn-babe joke, but it wasn't quite coming together in his head. "I don't claim a homeworld." More specifically, he didn't claim Terron Prime. At least not with this crowd. They'd seen his face.

"Okay, we'll use the First Galactic War. A billion people died. Killed by soldiers who would rather not have been fighting. All because a few men gave the command. History's greatest atrocities were all committed by governments, not individuals."

Nak looked at Kalh, listening, but not sure what to say. What came to mind was, *That's the cutest argument I've ever heard,* but he didn't want to say that in front of Benton. Instead, he glanced at the chronometer on his wrist. Then it came to him: "You get your anarchist government in place, what's going to stop people from randomly killing other people."

Kalh frowned. "The same thing that stops them now: *nothing.* You think democracy has ended murder?"

Nak winked at her subtly, barely noticeable. "Fair point."

Benton glanced at Kalh with his green eyes and a gentle smile that widened his sandy mustache. "Economics stops murder more than government. And, honestly, killing will still happen, but hopefully less often than now. People can protect themselves or hire a privatized police force like they do on Iod, which, incidentally, has the lowest crime rates in our galaxy."

"And people will get killed by the ones instead of the billions." Kalh was tag-teaming with Benton in perfect sync. Kind of impressive.

"So you're taking power away from the bureaucrats," said Nak.

"Yes."

"I'm all for it." *Those bastards.* It was Taiberos's face he saw. Nak glanced at the nearby streets. He prided himself on maintaining his poise, but he had no idea what might be happening to his ship. He would've already given the command, except he didn't want Kalh to think of him as a selfish jerk for cutting the cub loose. Nak gently revved the engine. The machine purred. These particular models had been outlawed by the PSD because they moved too fast for hovering that close to the ground, which was why he'd gotten a deal. He looked down the alleyway for Liink.

"And you're welcome to join us," said Benton.

Nak held his hand up by his cheek and rubbed his thumb against his first two fingers, gesturing toward Benton.

Kalh wiped a hand across her face. "So you'll consider it?"

Nak laughed aloud. His elbow pointed forward as he began massaging his neck. "I think it would be easiest to lie and say *yes*." In his mind's eye, he saw Taiberos's troops at *The Sanctum*. They were scrubbing off Nak's paint job, revealing the straight font underneath that read *The Vengeance*. He couldn't keep waiting.

She sighed. "Your neck sore from that spill?" The passion in her tone had vanished, replaced by mildness, exhaustion, and maybe a little flirtation.

Nak didn't look at Benton, but he had an idea of how this interaction might've made him feel—after the way he'd talked about her on the trip. Nak made a chivalrous attempt to end the public flirtation: "I'm fine." He pulled his Shadowlyss goggles over his eyes. They tinted the morning a few shades darker.

"I could take a look at it?" She still looked pale.

"You a medic?"

She raised her eyebrows. "You could say that."

"Or I could say *what* instead," asked Nak.

"I know a little about healing."

Nak didn't move. "All right, take a look."

"You need to be lying down."

"Oh, I see where you're going with this." He couldn't help it.

She might have begun to smile, but her reaction was interrupted with a jolt as they heard a snarling scream—

"HEY!"

—and Liink came racing toward them in the brightening dawn. The cut across his face had been bashed open again.

Bright red blood ran down the dark fur of his skull.

NAK REVVED THE engine.

"Get on!" he shouted.

Liink froze between the two groundrunners, with a question written on his face.

In an instant, Kalhette chose. Maybe because she'd been standing closer to Nak. Or maybe it was just instinct, but she climbed on behind him and slid her hands around his stomach, just above the belt, latched on as if it might protect her from some monster.

Liink jumped onto the back of Benton's groundrunner.

Nak gunned it. The two machines sped off across the charcoal desert so fast it felt like an interplanetary liftoff. He aimed toward a plain between massive lumps of rock. He started easing his groundrunner close to Benton's so they could talk and shouted, "What happened!"

But Benton kept checking the distance and withdrawing.

"Hey!" Nak yelled over the rush of wind. "I'll worry about this! You focus on driving straight ahead!"

Benton did as he was told.

"What happened, Liink," shouted Nak.

Liink's mild voice was hard to hear over the roar of air, but he got the message across to the other three—about the poster and the bounty hunters.

"You're sure it said *Taiberos* on it?" yelled Nak, but of course it had: This had revenge written all over it. Hopefully the posters at least meant that Taiberos hadn't found the ship yet.

"Yes. And I think those thugs will be right behind us."

Nak checked his rear-view mirrors but found nothing. Then he glanced to both sides, gently craning his sore neck.

Ah ██████.

Two groundrunners appeared from just over Liink's shoulder. Each held two riders. They came from behind one of the rock formations, driving at an angle to intercept Nak and Benton. It was going to be hard to stay ahead towing the load of parts.

"They're right there." Nak lifted his chin and pointed with his lips. He drew his groundrunner away from Benton's and squeezed the last bit from the throttle—aiming for giant rocks that might serve as cover. He hoped it wouldn't come down to dropping the tow to get more speed. No trailer meant no repairs.

Which meant no leaving.

As the groundrunner lurched, Kalh pulled herself against him more tightly. He felt her belly against his spine.

"That's as fast as this piece of junk goes!" Nak looked over at Liink—the perfect copilot for one of these because he could hang on and shoot at the same time. Nak tried to turn his neck for better vocal projection but didn't get it to move very far because of the stiffness. "Kalh!"

"Yeah?"

"Grab my pistol, and don't drop it. Hold on to my belt if you need to. I'll keep the runner steady."

Her voice fought through the wind at his right ear. "You've never seen someone use a Singblade, have you?"

"Uh, no."

"Let's use the pistol as our backup." Her calm might've been actual peace or maybe just tiredness. "I think we'll be fine if it's a handful of civilians."

But it wasn't a handful of civilians. It was Taiberos. And he was after Nak's hand.

The harsh headwind shoved across Nak's scalp, tickling his skin as his dark hair shook back and forth. He swerved, and the trailer whipped along behind them. He wished he didn't need it, but how else was he going to get *The Sanctum* out of this hell.

The two enemy groundrunners approached as if from one floor above—because the new contragravs had a lot more boost. Laser-beams shot down, orange streaks slicing just behind and just overhead.

Apparently it was for dead or alive.

To hit a moving target was always hard, harder still while you were moving too, but take enough shots, and you were bound to land one eventually.

Nak weaved around a row of rocks, which shielded the lasers momentarily.

The moment he was back in the open, the blasts came back with fury.

Liink, on the other groundrunner, fired back rapidly. Atta boy. It kept the bounty hunters at a cautious distance. Hopefully he had enough rounds to last.

Kalh stretched out a hand behind and into the currents of wind, like she wanted to grab them, like an infant reaching toward starships in the sky.

"Kalh, what are you doing. Grab my gun!"

She reached her hand farther into the wind's waves, leaning.

Nak's groundrunner jerked violently as an orange beam blasted across the hull.

With his feet planted and his steel grip on the bars, Nak shimmied but maintained his position as the groundrunner jerked.

Kalh, however, did not.

With only one hand holding on, she twisted back and to the left. The hand that had been scraping at the air now scraped at Nak's black jacket and then caught the rim of his pants, pulling on them. For extra friction, her bald skull pushed into his back.

The ground, less than a meter below, scraped past at deadly speed.

"Kalh!" Nak slowed, though only a little, hoping to somehow help. That let the pursuers close the gap. Streaks of orange light flew all around.

She clung desperately, growling as she heaved herself back into the seat. Once safely in place, she squeezed him tight with both hands, and even laid her head on his back.

He felt her heart beating against his ribs. With a grin, he said, "Now's not the time, Kalh!"

She thumped a fist into his stomach.

He ripped at the throttle, and the groundrunner jumped.

Benton and Liink had zipped ahead, while Nak steered off course, hoping to split the pursuers.

Both stayed with Nak and Kalh, cutting in a wide arc to follow, as if they knew exactly whose names were on that poster.

Kalh shouted, and her voice revealed just how exhausted she was: "Get me a little closer!"

Nak's groundrunner now had black scorch marks across the front. The lasers continued to rain down. "You know I'm trying to get away, right?"

The two enemies held position at an angle above and behind, speeding side by side.

"I want to show you a trick," she shouted.

Not sure what had come over him, Nak obeyed and swooped toward the pursuers, dropping the throttle and letting the laser blasts get dangerously close.

Kalh reached out a hand and shoved at the wind.

The enemy on the left swerved sharply to the right, colliding with his accomplice.

Three bodies went flailing into the air.

Where they hit the ground, gray dust puffed up like smoke.

The empty groundrunner flew ahead and smashed into a lump of rock, creating a mass of flame that climbed up and over the boulder. The only still-seated rider braked and turned to help his comrades, who, Nak guessed, had at least a small chance of survival.

"Holy—" Nak let the wind wash away the unspoken profanity. "Did you just…"

He could hear the grin in her voice, even above the foaming sound of the air rushing past. "I am so tired."

He raced onward toward *The Sanctum*. "But really, you just pushed those groundrunners into each other."

"No, no," she shouted. "I just shoved the handlebar a little. Much easier."

"How."

"It's… a lot to explain. Can we write it off as magic?"

"No."

"I can touch things from a distance. Kinosis."

"Oh—" Nak shook his head. "I just can't believe…"

"Benton could've done the same thing if he'd have gotten a little closer."

"But…" Nak stopped his sentence, not sure what question would get him to the answer he wanted.

She squeezed her face against his jacket, and he felt her jaw moving: "I'll explain when we're holding still."

A S THE SUN reached its zenith, Benton slowed till the two groundrunners were racing somewhat side by side across the dark ground.

Even with Kalh's strange miracle echoing, Nak's thoughts turned to face Taiberos.

If that bastard knew they were still on Toar—that *The Sanctum* was still on Toar—he'd do everything in his power to stop them.

And that was a lot.

Nak released and cranked the throttle again, making sure that was all it could give, and the groundrunner rocked. His ship was his one safe place in the galaxy. Anywhere else, they could get at him. Take his hand and take his life. But in *The Sanctum*, he was untouchable.

Kalh tapped him on the belly and said, "Hey, slow down."

He turned his stiff neck ever so slightly, wanting to hear a reason.

"I think there are Redhelms ahead. Slow down."

"Where."

He sensed anxious fear in her voice: "At the ship."

"We can't see the site yet."

"I know. Slow down before we get into the open."

Nak raised a fist in the air, signaling to Benton, and then slowed his groundrunner to a crawl. The sound of rushing wind died, and the motor quieted to a hum.

"What are you talking about," he asked.

Her response was stern: "Just approach slowly so we don't give ourselves away."

Benton seemed to agree that this was a good idea, so they crept forward, keeping the sound of the engines low, which made them nearly scrape bottom, as they practically sneaked around the corner of each rock.

In this area, the largest canyon made a wide gorge, winding like a crooked snake. Offshoots slithered away from it on both sides, leaving more deep cracks in the ground, like ribs spurring off some unholy spine. *The Sanctum* was docked in one of these dark offshoots, nestled on a ledge far below the surface.

Nak heard something and looked up at the sky. "Wait."

"What?" asked Benton.

Nak eased the throttle, moving to the main canyon's edge. He stopped at a place he imagined might be uncomfortably close for Kalh. Here the canyon walls fell crookedly, but the gap was wide enough to show an orange glow climbing up from the bottom, in bright contrast to the charcoal gray of everything else.

██████. He pointed. "Right there. It's a seeker."

The seeker looked like an insect of vast proportions, or a Grezyk, thin wings spreading out in four directions from a sickeningly thin body. A long way down in the canyon, it seemed to be searching the walls and crevices. At least it meant they hadn't found her yet, but it wouldn't be long, not long at all.

"There's another one," said Nak.

Taiberos had an unfair advantage in resources, but Nak knew he could still beat that bastard. He had to. He moved the groundrunner on toward *The Sanctum.*

As they rounded the final rock, he saw what Kalh had magically predicted: a squad of Redhelms, rifles in hand. Nak walked his groundrunner back out of sight and dismounted. He got up close to the rock for a better analysis. "Dang it. They must have found the grappling gear."

"Looks like they might send a guy down," said Kalh.

They wouldn't be able to fly her without his hand, but it wouldn't stop them from towing her off. He considered calling Cup on the comms and having her fly up here, but that would expose the ship, which for now was still hidden, and he didn't want another fiasco with him running around like an idiot trying to climb on board. He wanted to be the one piloting her out of here. "We're going to have to move fast. And I mean *fast*. They outnumber us three to one, but we do have the element of surprise." Nak looked at Kalh.

"Are you talking about me?"

"No, sorry. But, yes, we also have you. Here's what we do. We stash the fuel batteries and replacement parts here." He pointed at Benton and Liink. "You two provide a distraction in that direction—some laser fire. Try to draw the troops after you. Their instinct will be to move away from the canyon so they don't get pinned down. They'll likely move toward that cover there. Which opens up a gap for Kalh and me to sneak down to the ship. With me at the helm, we'll have the upper hand. I'll rush them from behind with the big guns and then pick you guys up. Then we hop over here, grab the batteries, and get out of here."

"What if our distraction makes them call in for backup?" asked Benton.

"It probably will, so we move quickly. The shields should be somewhat recharged by now, and, worse case, we hide somewhere in the canyon network again. Okay, we've got to move. Everyone good?"

Liink nodded eagerly—despite the gruesome wound on his face and the blood dried all over his fur. The other two affirmed, and the foursome split.

The sun began to set once again.

Waiting for the fireworks about killed Nak. Just when he'd made up his mind to charge the squad of Redhelms alone, he heard several laser blasts come from a distance. They spiked out toward the unsuspecting troops. As predicted, the Redhelms turned to face the onslaught, moving toward cover and away from the cliff face. At first they moved cautiously, wary of an ambush from any other direction, but soon their focus turned almost entirely toward Benton and Liink.

A bad feeling hit Nak.

And a suborbital whistled in the sky overhead, its engines drawing nearer. Reinforcements were coming, and something told him this was Taiberos himself. Worse, the incoming skycraft would turn heads in Nak's direction, ruining the whole distraction. *"I can't wait anymore,"* Nak breathed. He moved forward in a crouch then began to dash toward the cliff face.

"Nak, wait! Stop!" But Kalh's hissing whisper didn't have enough force to change his mind.

He ran across open ground with her on his tail, hoping the Redhelms wouldn't look this way. He then skidded behind cover and crouched, looking back to see how Kalh had fared.

She'd followed, feebly sprinting the last of the distance, clearly running on empty.

Just as she ducked behind the rock, a laser blast came flying over their heads.

"Damn."

"Guess they saw us."

Nak looked down the cliff face. The rope was still attached. A thought, unbidden, popped into his mind—that he should let her go down first—but he pushed it out of the way. He needed to get to his ship. "Cover me. I'll be back up here with the ship before you know it." Without waiting for approval, he grabbed the rope and went over the edge.

He kept his boots on the sheer cliff face. Near the top, another wall stood at his back, creating a narrow channel that opened up after you dropped a couple meters. It was a long way down. Hand over hand, he descended, landing at the bottom with a thud and squatting into the impact. The space was enclosed enough that it felt like a cave. He sprinted.

"Nak!"

Her voice echoed down the canyon walls. She sounded scared, as if Taiberos himself were suddenly breathing down her neck.

He turned and looked, halfway between her and the ship.

The rope dangled, slithering back and forth, agitated by some commotion. If she was coming down, she was too high for him to see her. That meant she had a long way to go. *What are you doing, Kalh. Just hold them off.*

He didn't know whether to babysit her or protect his ship. If he could get to the ship, though, he could actually do both. He turned to run, but halted when he heard her growl echoing down the canyon walls. A strange pause for a man of action.

The rope shook again. Fragments of rock and dust clattered down. A single purple laser bolt shot down and hit the floor. The rope jerked again.

And then she fell.

Headfirst.

With her feeble hands stretched out for impact and her knees buckled above, her boots like dual tailfins.

She didn't scream. Didn't have time to scream—it all happened so fast.

But Nak did:

"KALH!!!"

She landed behind a rock that blocked his line of sight and protected him from the carnage. The impact made a crunch that echoed off the walls. He envisioned her lying in a pool of blood, her spine and skull broken.

No one could've survived that fall.

He dashed toward her, skidding to a stop when he saw her body.

She lay on her back, eyes closed, mouth hanging open—neck cocked to the side, knees bent, her feet pinned underneath her. Her arms spread wide, and one of them had the red, pointy edge of a bone protruding from it. Blood oozed onto the black rock.

Nobody could've survived that fall.

With his eyebrows pinched into a pained gaze, he pressed two fingers into her neck and felt the mildest *thump, thump, thump.*

She was alive.

He cleared his throat and looked up.

At the top, so far above, a lone Redhelm peeked into view.

Nak drew his pistol and fired on pure reflex yet with deadly aim.

The bolt caught the corner of the Redhelm's face, who fell out of sight with a scream.

Luckily, the slope of the cliff made it so only a man on the rope could get a clear shot down the channel. Nak could stand his ground here at this choke point for a long time, but if he hit any of the troops, they'd fall onto her. Besides, reinforcements would be here any moment. Without his ship, he and his clients were done for.

He fired two more blasts up the channel, jammed his pistol into his holster, and scooped up Kalh's body, trying to brace her neck and spine. He carried her like a parent holding a child, pressing both arms around her in a hug.

Her blood leaked onto his flight jacket.

On the outside, he remained stoic: He didn't run, for fear of hurting her further. His boots pounded into the soil with each steady step, lifting puffs of dust behind him.

On the inside, his mind orbited the words he'd spoken as they debarked: *She can't stay—not on my ship*. His mind circled the phrase, caught in a surge spiral, and with each revolution an echo: *She can't stay—not on my ship*. But he had to say that. He had to protect *The Sanctum*. She was too valuable to trust anyone with. To *tempt* anyone with. That was his rule.

He'd done it to protect *The Sanctum*. He had to.

An orange beam blasted over his shoulder. The first Redhelm must've reached the floor.

Nak didn't flinch but kept plodding toward the ship. *Just a few more steps*. Another blast zipped past his right hip, and he felt the heat of its proximity. The next one would surely hit him square in the back.

He braced himself for the blow and the end. He kept stepping.

The lower turret cannon of *The Sanctum* dropped from the bottom of the hull and into view. It pivoted, as if looking around.

Till it trained on Nak.

Then it fired.

The blast shot directly over Nak's shoulder with uncanny precision, and a tide of heat washed over his scruffy jaw as it passed.

Behind him came a faint cry of pain followed by a heavy thud.

Nak gave a half-hearted smile.

He carried Kalhette's lifeless body up the walkway and into *The Sanctum*. *She can't stay—not on my ship*.

ABII?"

Benton did not like the title, but he answered to it all the same. Snapping out of his reverie, he said, "Yes?"

The pilot's plan required a distraction, so Benton and Liink sped on the groundrunner toward a firefight. It took time to get in position, costing precious moments they could hardly spare. In sequels, the Redhelms would find the ship. Benton pressed the accelerator all the way, which kicked up dust in a trail behind him. He circled in a large arc, out of sight behind hills and boulders.

Liink's two lower arms gripped the handles along the sides of the seat. "It should've been me who stayed behind in the Strand."

"No, Liink. That's not your burden."

The miin spoke as though hefting the weight of suicide: "But it should've been."

"Dray and I both agreed she was necessary for the revolution to begin. We knew the risks and weighed them. Yet he volunteered to come. He chose this route, knowing it might cost his life."

"But I could've held the line in his place. If I'd had the courage. And my life is not worth nearly so much as his."

"Liink..." Benton let his heart wander on: "I feel burdened by Dray's loss too, and we will all feel the repercussions soon enough. In truth, I hoped we'd complete our mission without casualties."

Liink said nothing, waiting in somber silence.

Benton continued: "I, for one, am grateful *you* made it out alive."

The snaking black chasms stretched around them. The sun was setting again, and as the light faded, the red glow from the canyons became apparent.

A ship soared as a silhouette through the sky, growing larger as it came this way.

Benton pointed at it. "That's a Duringer. We're almost out of time."

"What's a Duringer?" asked Liink.

"Suborbital modification. They've fixed it up. Somebody important aboard."

"How do you know so much?" asked Liink.

"I've seen them before."

"Not just that. I've asked you about everything from ballistics to literature, and you always know something."

Benton shrugged.

In the backdrop, far distant from the first, more ships were coming through the night sky. It was an excessive response. Someone was very angry. This would leave no time to gather the supplies the team had just trekked to the Citadel to acquire, which meant they would still be stranded even if they made it out of this.

"One of us may die in this next encounter," said Liink.

"Kalhette must make it back to Solace. That is key. Beyond that, you must reverence the light within yourself. That means survive."

"But if one of us must sacrifice himself for the other to escape, it should be me."

Benton knew the miina culture well enough to know the proper response: a dissatisfied chuffle. Unfortunately, the sound wasn't easy for a human to make. "Liink, your life is equal in value to mine."

The mild voice came from behind: "Yes, sir."

They sat in silence as the machine crossed the final stretch.

An embankment stood in the dimness ahead. That would be their redoubt. Beyond that, a small group of Redhelms milled about on the edge of a cliff, looking down toward the very spot where *The Sanctum* was hidden below.

Benton approached rapidly, and yet in those final sequels, one more thought came to him, something the discouraged cub needed to hear, especially if one of them was about to die: "The miina say that powers in the Song are only a divine gift, so if you can't ignite the prism you carry, it means the Kurosh haven't willed it. Isn't that right?"

"Yes."

"I believe a different paradigm: The Song respects choice, meaning the Gods want mortals to learn by choosing. If that is right, then over time you can *learn* to summon the weapon. That means your fate is not up to the Gods—your fate is up to you."

Although Benton could not see it, he sensed something akin to a smile coming from behind him. "But Abii—"

"No time, Liink. Lean with me." Benton jerked the handlebars and leaned, turning the groundrunner hard to the side, which allowed the contragravs to work as brakes, and the machine trembled as it skidded.

Using that same momentum, he leaped, aiming his pistol and firing wildly at the Redhelms before he'd even hit the ground. His boots hit Toar's dark soil, and he fired as he sprinted toward the redoubt. A handgun was hard enough to aim at long distances, much less while practically in orbit, but the point wasn't to hit the enemy—only to distract them.

Liink pounced onto the ground, and they both made their outlines scarce, putting their guns and eyes barely into view as they kept blasting orange and purple streaks of light that lit up Toar's twilight.

The Redhelms dove out of sight.

Now steady, Benton fired his handgun with great accuracy, keeping the enemy from daring to expose themselves and give proper return fire.

Behind the Redhelms, Kalhette dashed after the pilot across open ground, exposed but so far unseen till she was obscured behind a mound of rock. Then it seemed the Redhelms turned back toward her. Hard to see much from his angle though.

The ship dropped from above and opened fire at Benton. The rock at his elbow offered protection in only one direction, and it wasn't upward. "Liink, with me!"

As orange streaks rained from the sky, the duo leaped back onto the groundrunner. The engine roared, and the machine launched across the moon's surface. If the skycraft followed them, it would provide Kalhette more time, but a ship against a groundrunner was hardly a fair fight.

Benton zipped through the increasing darkness between strange stone structures, simply trying to create distance, and the farther he got, the farther the team was divided. Liink held on with one pair of arms and fired at the skycraft with the other.

Soon the snaking black canyon turned toward them, cutting off their route on one side. Laser cannons pushed heavy volleys from above, and these fiery streaks splashed against the ground, launching dust and rocks. A near miss crashed next to the groundrunner with such force that the machine rocked on its side. With a lurch, it turned sharply toward the canyon edge—toward death in the lava below. Benton corrected, pulling the opposite direction, hard enough to keep them from veering off the edge, which saved their lives, but the duo hadn't properly leaned into this unexpected turn, which tugged the contragravs off their footing. The groundrunner spun to the side, flinging its occupants toward the cliff.

Liink twisted through the air but landed on all sixes like a cat, rolling and then running, quite gracefully considering the speed, and stopped before falling over the edge. Benton too was twirling. He spread his hands, gripping the ground through Kinosis, and decelerated as he fell, landing as gently as if it were planned.

Now they stood in the open, their backs to a deadly drop.

The Duringer came to a halt, hovering overhead.

A bay door opened, and light glowed from inside. Troops jumped out from high overhead, landing with contragrav boots that slowed their falls. There were twelve in total. They didn't fire at first, till two of them approached the groundrunner, which had righted itself again and was hovering in place. They shot it aggressively till the fuel battery exploded, lighting up the gray darkness with flames.

Liink peered at the lava in the canyon far below as if considering capture versus death. He then glared at the enemy soldiers.

Benton, at one with the Song, felt calm, simply curious to see what might happen—even if that was death. He looked up at the ship. Something told him Taiberos was aboard, another facet of reality that did not disturb his peace.

The Duringer left the troops on the ground and sailed toward Kalhette.

Benton frowned.

The twelve Redhelms pointed their rifles menacingly as they closed their semicircle tighter around their two new prisoners. "Drop your weapons or die!"

"Steady, Liink." Benton supposed he himself could kill at least three of them before getting gunned down, and he worried Liink might be making a similar calculation. He bent his knees and set his handgun on the ground.

Liink's pistol clattered in the dirt.

Four of the Redhelms approached carrying handcuffs while the others stood back and kept their rifles at the ready.

Liink backed further toward the cliff.

"Steady, Liink."

A Redhelm shouted, "On the ground!"

Benton backed up but did not bend a knee.

He hadn't mastered Sorjis. He had, however, made sufficient attempts to know what it felt like. When something surged, it created a ripple in reality itself, a fluctuation in the normal course of space and time. He felt that right now, in the canyon behind them, far below. As if something had torn a hole in reality.

The Redhelms closed in further. "I said, on the ground!"

Benton hated what he was about to do. He believed, on principle, that you should always explain yourself, but time had run out, and he didn't know what else to do, so he simply whispered, "Are you willing to die with me?"

Liink nodded. "Without hesitation."

The Redhelms reach out, about to lay their hands on the two.

Benton grabbed Liink's vest, pivoted, and jumped, pulling the miin with him into the canyon. And somehow, dutifully, Liink followed in the suicide leap.

Together they fell.

A long way—too far for even a Zhan to fall without smashing his bones to pieces.

In the canyon below, far below, *The Sanctum* had appeared.

Benton still gripped Liink, and with Kinosis he tried to slow their fall, but it wasn't enough.

With a shocking deftness, *The Sanctum* dropped beneath them with perfect precision, slowing their fall in a gentle catch as they banged against the metal roof of the skycraft.

The Redhelms recovered from their surprise and began to hail down a stream of laser blasts.

Liink scrambled to a hatch on the top of the ship and paused with a stunned grin on his face, waiting as a respectful usher at the gateway of safety. With them clinging to the top, the ship started to glide away down the canyon.

With wind rustling his hair, Benton crawled to the hatch, and the two locked eyes for a brief moment. "I'm... grateful you followed me."

Liink made a statement that turned almost into a question: "I can see the war in your body and yet the peace in your eyes..."

Benton didn't have a reply.

Admiration gleamed in the cub's countenance. "How is it done?"

Benton simply said, "I don't know."

The two climbed into the ship, where the heavy targravs gripped them fully, and the hatch closed its mouth above them. Yet something felt off, something wrong with their getaway, and Benton's throat jammed up with a vague sense of apprehension for Kalhette.

The pilot's shout came from down the hall: "Get in here! She's hurt!"

When Benton heard that, the peace in his soul vanished.

Rage filled his eyes.

And blame.

WHEN DRAY CLOSED his eyes, it was not darkness he saw.

No, he saw a woman.

She rested on panels of red wood. Her face looked upward. Her brunette hair stretched across the floor away from her skull in every direction, skirting a puddle of vomit and blood.

He squeezed his eyes tighter, wishing they could somehow be more closed.

He didn't want to see her like that.

Didn't want to be alive.

He'd killed so many of them, and yet he survived.

Unless this was the Otherworld mimicking his most horrifying dread.

His body ached all over, deep down to the core, as if the Witch Hunters had been torturing his very soul. He didn't feel capable of taking much more. They'd asked him questions about Benton and Kalhette and Skyreacher, but those seemed peripheral to some other more sinister objective.

They hadn't stripped him or shaved his wild gray hair or neatly trimmed beard this time, skipping the usual processing to get him immediately into the hands of Taiberos, to expedite the pain, as if pain were their real goal. They hadn't even taken the wher talisman hanging over his chest.

If it were the Otherworld, they wouldn't have left him with that.

As he reached for it, he became aware of the cold metal wrapped around his neck, a collar that fed toxins into his bloodstream, poisoning his consciousness and forcing his heart to beat quickly, so he couldn't look through the gray and sterile walls.

The thin yellow strip of light near the ceiling never changed. He had no indication of time, other than the intervals in which they would submit him to more torture.

He pinched the moon talisman between his fingers. She always appeared in his mind when he came to his senses. Back to haunt him. And drive him. Maybe that was the presence he'd felt the moment he returned to the Strand. Her memory. With the toxins twisting his mind, he felt it more clearly, a light that was trapped somewhere in this place. So close and yet still out of reach.

Maybe destiny had spared his life because he hadn't yet paid for his sins.

The Witch Hunters wouldn't exist if not for him.

Taiberos would be a lunatic no one listened to.

In here, Dray would suffer, but that wasn't enough. It made no sense to punish the wrongdoer. That didn't help the victims. They needed restoration. He needed to change things, to undo what he'd helped create.

Through closed eyelids, he thought he saw a flash of light that came and left instantly, as if a bolt of lightning had ignited in his room.

His eyes opened wide.

In the visible spectrum, he saw nothing more than the yellow strip of light that had always accompanied him in this miserable darkness. His eyes must've been playing tricks on him.

He closed them.

Again he saw her. Lying there.

He was helpless to stop what had been done to her. Helpless to undo her awful demise. No way to save her, though he wished with all his heart he could.

After her death, he'd nearly broken down.

Crack.

His eyes opened.

It sounded almost like the pop of a ligament as it shifted around a joint.

Maybe some eerie side effect of the toxins going into his neck. Or maybe the torment left his mind more feeble, on the verge of cracking.

He'd killed General Venette, but in the end, they overpowered him. Last time, he'd escaped Building 13 because they'd underestimated him, and even then he'd only barely managed. This time they guarded him much more closely. He would miss the revolution—it would be done without him. He'd have to live in this nightmare until Benton came again, a whole percent of his life at a minimum. Dray doubted he could last that long, not if they kept the torment at this pace. And that was supposing Benton even could come. Likely he couldn't. It cost extensive money and time and the same methods would not work twice. Perhaps he was worth more as a martyr anyway.

The darkness around him felt colder and heavier than most.

He glanced through light so dim it seemed like feeling more than seeing. The yellow strip cast a glow that faded with distance. In front of that spread of light, he thought he saw a shape. Something that might have been a head and torso. He felt an impulse to lean forward, to try to see the thing better, but a frigid fear held him back.

He, a former Lord Admiral, held back by fear.

He held his ground, staring, trying to make out the shape.

He wiped his gray beard with both hands, as if that could somehow put things back in order. The more he stared, the more he realized it was a trick of his tired eyes. A faint yellow light washed across the wall as it always had. Nothing stood in front of it. Nothing was in the room with him.

He closed his eyes once more and gripped his long gray hair.

Again he saw the woman he couldn't save. His wife.

The one who deserved restoration most of all.

The one he could never repay.

Her presence was strong. She haunted his mind and his dark cell, from which he could not escape, forcing him to constantly relive her pain and to lie with her dying on those panels of red wood.

Jyngsoo had offered an escape, a route that led to Benton. Together Dray and Benton pursued roughly the same goals, through distinctly different methods. Benton believed people only needed knowledge to change. He planned to revolutionize people's minds and then wait for the ideal galaxy to form.

That wasn't enough.

This dank pit under Toar proved Dray was right.

A revolution might temporarily change some minds, but people had darkness inside them. They carried it with them, a darkness they could not overcome. The darkness that had taken his wife. People would carry the same problems they meant to leave behind. Not that it mattered now. He would soon be dead. At least, hopefully it would be soon.

A heavy cloth rustled in front of him.

Dray's eyes shot open.

Something was there. A figure. A shape. Tall as a man but shrouded in darkness.

A darkness so deep he could not comprehend it.

COLD FEAR OF this presence pressed Dray against the wall. He and fear were usually complete strangers, so this encounter clenched him all the tighter.

"Who are you?" Dray's usually commanding voice now had a weakened edge.

The figure shook its head heavily, indicating it would not answer. Its shoulders were slumped, head hanging.

"How'd you get in here?"

Next came a long, dark pause, not a hesitation but a summoning, followed by a voice, a male voice, old and withered, confident yet feeble: "I came to make you an offer."

Dray reached out a frightened hand. "Are you real?"

The figure reached back, took his wrist, and squeezed it. "I am corporeal if that's what you mean."

"How did you get inside?"

"Through the door, fool. You're hallucinating."

Dray peered hard into the shadows, trying to make sense of the shape. Or shapes. No door had ever opened. "Then how do I know you're…"

The voice was wrapped in a cloak. It spoke from a pale, wrinkled mouth. Its eyes were shrouded. "The Witch Hunters have done this to you. Their procedures are slowly and surely loosening your grip. It will only get worse."

"I know. So you're not one of them?"

"Not remotely."

"Then how'd you get…"

"Listen to me. I have an offer for you."

"What kind of offer?" Dray closed his eyes and saw his wife lying pale on the floor. He opened his eyes and saw darkness, an empty and eternal chasm that had been waiting for him all this time. He felt unsure which alternative he preferred to face.

"I offer that which you desire most."

"And what is that?"

"*You* must speak it."

The darkness had infiltrated Dray's soul, like some poison had leaked inside him, like something was eating the light. "Then I want you to get me out of here."

The figure shook its head, disappointed. "You will get yourself out of here. What I offer is much greater."

"How am I going to get out of here?"

"It will be easy once I give back the Orikerse they took when they captured you."

"I'm not using Kerse." He said that based on principle before really considering. Like everything else, using Orikerse came with trade-offs. It created a massive spike in the powers of Vision and Initiative but caused an inverse drop in Spirit. This cost, a drain in emotion, made the user numb, indifferent to everything, but it would make him conscious enough to act despite the exhaust shooting periodically into his neck.

"You're not thinking grand enough. What do you really want?"

The strangeness of this reply made Dray pause, and then he almost started to cry. "I want to atone for my sins. I want to stop the Witch Hunters. I want to stop all abuses of power. So nobody else gets hurt… by people like me."

"And how would you do this?"

Dray spoke the answer without confidence: "A democracy."

"That is not what you believe."

Dray frowned into the darkness, trying to perceive truth through this strange mystery. None of it made sense. This being seemed to see as deeply inside of him as Master Jyngsoo had. "No, it isn't what I believe."

"Speak it!"

"I'm not sure a democracy could reach it."

"Then what?"

"We should be ruled by a philosopher king. Someone higher than the rabble, wise enough to lead our populace of children. And benevolent."

"You?"

"I'm not benevolent."

"You weren't, but now you are. This could be you…"

In truth, Dray had harbored this thought inside for a long time, never speaking it aloud, not to anyone. He nodded, reluctant. "Only temporarily."

"That is what I have come to give you."

"How could you give me that? And why?"

"Why? Because you're going to give me something in exchange."

"What do you want?"

"You don't know who I am, do you?"

"No."

"How high a price would you pay for this galactic peace you say you want?"

"I would give anything. Everything. Including my life."

"What about someone else? Would you sacrifice another's life to save billions more?"

"Is this a test?" His reason told him that trade would be fair, but his gut told him it would not. He hesitated to answer. "Who are you?"

The shadow gaped at him with indifference, unbudging. Finally, the scraping voice said, "I created the Eleven."

"You're... you're Lethos?"

The shadow gave no response, but the power and the expanse of the darkness seemed to grow. Master Jyngsoo had mentioned this being. He'd said that one can never know what darkness truly feels like until being in this creature's presence. Now Dray felt it, a maw so vast and so empty it threatened to consume everything. He felt powerless before it.

Dray cleared his throat. "I saw you in a dream once. Is this another dream?"

"You know it isn't. Nor was the last time."

"Why come for me now?"

"Because I only now glimpsed the light for the first time."

"What light?"

"A connection. Unlike any before. One you will cause to die."

Dray looked at the ground, trying to find the volition to deny it, to call him a liar, but he couldn't. He felt desperate. If not a dream, maybe this was the Otherworld. *"Imprisoned in riddles,"* he whispered.

"This is no riddle: With my help, you will become one of my Eleven, a Keeper of the Secret. Eventually, you will become the Voerthawn, Lord of the Shadowlyss, the most powerful mortal in the galaxy. With that power, you can bring the galactic justice you long for."

The room waited in silence for more.

Dray felt a strange, constricting sensation across his chest and arms. He didn't know what to say, nor whether to follow his mind or his instinct.

"You never believed in their dream," said the creature. "You never believed it was possible. And you were right. But I can give you what they can't."

Dray's hands began heating up without cause. He wanted to close his eyes and ask his wife for help, but she could not help. She was dead. "If I were to agree, what would my end of the bargain be?"

The figure grinned, teeth locked villainously. "You must give me part of your mind, part of your body, and part of your soul."

"What does that mean?"

"For mind, you will surrender the memory of the one you hold most dear."

"No!" Dray saw Saira lying dead on that red floor. It was not the escape from her that he wanted. He would gladly let go of the pain, but of her memory altogether? It was too much... Dray pressed his fingers against his sternum and felt the talisman covered by his garment, wondering what choice she might tell him to make if she were here. "Even if I were to agree, how is that even possible?"

The shadow lifted its head, for the first time, just high enough for one yellow eye to peer between the folds of the hood. The gaze pierced Dray to the core. "You will soon discover your perspectives on possibility are flawed"—a sentiment similar to what Jyngsoo had taught, only this version was cloaked in shadow.

Dray stared in awe and horror.

The shoulders and head slumped, as if bearing some great load, and that eye vanished beneath the hood. "For body, you will give me your right eye."

Disgust poured through Dray. He grimaced, surprised he could feel any worse about this second suggestion, and already he sensed what the empty socket would feel like. It horrified him. "What makes you think that I would ever agree to this?"

The figure only smiled, as if the choice were certain, as if Dray were already his ally. Or pawn. "I will take you out of this hell and give you all I've promised."

"If I decline?"

"You will go back to your Witch Hunters, and you and your mind will rot in here for as long as it takes..."

"I've been their prisoner before." It was a bluff. Dray felt no confidence in his ability to bear the treatments again.

"Your friends will not be back for you, not soon enough."

"How could you know that?"

"I foresaw it."

Dray glared at the future, the full weight of the unknown resting on him. "What if I agree, you release me, and then I fail?"

"If you do not fulfill your side of the covenant, you become my willing victim, and you know what I do to willing victims..."

Dray shook his head, suddenly feeling like he couldn't breathe. When he closed his eyes, he saw her, staring up at him with dead eyes. He felt trapped, desperate. "What is the third part I have to give—for soul?"

"You will end the life of the woman named Kalhette Whitesun."

"What?" This hit him more deeply still, as if he'd been stabbed with a length of steel through his heart. He'd sacrificed himself to save that girl. All his hopes rested on her. And she, like Saira, was a victim. "Not Kalhette. Why?"

"It must be so."

"Why didn't you kill her yourself? She was here in Building 13."

"I have my limitations." The silence remained like a canker. "Would you not trade the life of one to bring justice to a trillion others?"

When Dray spoke next, his voice had more than a weak edge—the whole body of it had become frail. It wasn't an argument. It was a plea:

"Her life is not mine to give."

W HEN DRAY AWOKE, he was strapped to a table.

The white metal collar still clamped around his neck. It had been joined by leather bands around his wrists, torso, and ankles.

He wasn't sure it hadn't been a dream.

Nor was he sure it had.

Something significant had taken place, leaving him mired in confusion. Maybe this *was* the Otherworld.

It felt like they were sucking the life force out. First came intense pain. Then came questions about Skyreacher and the Bloody Wing. And Lethos.

Was Dray going mad?

No, he was real, still alive, and awake for a moment. Perhaps with enough willpower, he could discern their objective. He'd heard the word *surge,* yet he didn't have that ability as a Zhan—another way in which Kalhette was a rare gem. Maybe they hoped to induce that ability within him, to get him to be like her. If so, these scientists only exposed their vast ignorance of the Song. Or maybe it had something to do with surge batteries, but then what did it have to do with Radiances?

More suffering gnawed at him, pouring anxiety into his chest. He had to hold out long enough for Benton to come back.

He had to.

And he had to divert his mind to something safer.

The purpose of the Strand research remained a mystery. Whatever it was, it held the utmost importance to Taiberos. Maybe Dray could discover that secret before he escaped. Then his suffering would serve a greater good.

The table began to tilt, dropping his feet to the ground and raising his head. It didn't stop till it rotated slightly past vertical, leaving him hanging from his restraints.

"Do not give him special treatment." The voice came from behind, out of sight. It was a voice anyone in the galaxy could've recognized, a calm voice, one Dray had become all too familiar with in the final cycles of his service.

Taiberos—the monster Dray himself had unleashed.

"But what if we drive him mad?"

"No—special—treatment. If anything, take more risks. He needs to pay penance for his betrayal."

"Shouldn't that be done through the courts?"

"It will *also* be done through the courts if he happens to survive."

Behind Dray, a machine whirred and then beeped.

He knew what that meant, and he fought against the restraints, even though he knew it was futile. He had to get out of here. Somehow.

And then acid burned through his fingernails.

It tore through his insides, through his bowels and genitals.

He thrashed, and the pain cut deeper than before. His fingers spread apart, each of them trying to flee.

He screamed.

Madness encircled him.

Suddenly, he didn't care what Saira would think.

He didn't care if there was right or wrong.

He would pay any price to escape.

THE SHOCK FORCED Kalhette to the border of consciousness.

Her bone stuck out, a bloody red spike coming through the skin of her arm.

She vaguely remembered the pilot placing her on a cushioned table and strapping her down. Then gravity pulled her in all directions, rocking her against the straps as the skycraft twisted and turned. She moaned in pain and even shouted for help.

She also blacked out for a bit.

In her dreams, she kept falling. When she tried to slow her fall kinotically, her powers had vanished. The miin kept putting his paws on her arms, holding her back, putting pressure on. He wouldn't stop touching her, getting in the way. Eventually gravity calmed down, and she rested, even while voices bit through the darkness:

"What happened?"

"She fell."

"Is she all right?"

"I don't know. Just give me a seq."

She lay there alone, her head spinning with nausea as the skycraft maneuvered. It felt like a nightmare, like being back in Building 13.

After a long time, the skycraft finally steadied, as did her queasiness. Her spinning mind focused on the pain in her arms. They hurt so bad. She inhaled through clenched teeth. So bad. "Aaaaaaahh," she moaned.

"I can't believe she survived at all."

"It was Kinosis that saved her."

"Don't know what that is."

"Telekinesis. Pushing on things from a distance."

"Is she going to be okay."

"We need to set the bones. Do you have an anesthetic?" It was Benton. Sitting next to her. Gazing at her bones with glowing eyes. He'd made it aboard.

"No. ███. Sorry. Lost them on…" That was the pilot. He was upset. She sensed it deeper than his words, even over all the turmoil. As upset as she was maybe.

"Battlefield measures then. You have any medical experience?"

"Not really. Sorry."

"You have arm or leg braces?"

"Uh, yes. Braces. I'll be right back."

Benton pointed at Kalh's shoulders. "Without anesthetic, this is going to cause a lot more pain, and if she thrashes, I won't be able to set the bone, so I need you to hold her down."

Liink's four dark paws pressed against her shoulders and upper arms. His face came close to hers, with that gross cut slashing across it.

"Get your paws off me!" she screamed and pushed him with Kinosis.

The miin flew back.

Benton put a hand on her knee. "Kalhette, please calm down. We need to do this."

She started to cry, delirious. "It hurts, Benton."

"I know it does. And it's going to hurt more before it starts getting better, but it's necessary. I'm so sorry. Let's get it over with."

The pilot stepped back in. "Here's the braces."

"Set them there."

Kalh gasped. "It hurts!" Tears dripped down her cheeks.

Benton's voice was reassuring, even though the words weren't: "Hold her down."

Liink obeyed.

Kalh closed her eyes and not gently either. The muscles in her face were tight, and so was her whole body, bracing. She already felt pain, and it was about to get worse. It would be difficult not to lash out.

Benton touched the skin of her left arm, right over her tattoo. It seemed like vengeance. For what she'd done to him.

"Ow. Please don't..."

But Benton did anyway. His eyes were glowing.

"Ow, ow, ow! Benton! No!"

Liink leaned his heavy body against her, his yellow eyes too close to her face.

Benton grabbed her hand and her upper arm and pulled them apart.

She screamed.

She screamed like singing the song of Death himself, and she hoped he would come for her soon. Then it was over, and she lay there, panting, tears crawling down.

"Okay, it's done." Benton gasped. "I'm sorry, Kalhette."

She felt unsteady, barely hanging on to her consciousness. The bone sticking out had disappeared back beneath her skin, still throbbing.

Blood was on his hands. He pinched her arm, feeling the placement of the bone as he peered through her skin with Starsight.

"Ow! Ow! Oh... Ow!"

Kalh moaned as Benton wrapped the wound and then fastened a brace around her arm. When he finished, her body finally relaxed, and she hadn't realized how tight she'd been holding everything.

Benton stood and moved to the other side of her cot. "We still have to do the other one."

"Oh no," said Kalh, in the whimper of a small child. "Oh, please, no."

"I'm so sorry," said Benton. He took her other arm. "Hold her."

Liink pushed her against the bed, and his ugly wound pressed in close.

Though it would be hard without using her arms, she probably could've thrown him off and shoved Benton back with Kinosis. "Ow, no. No, no, no."

Benton grabbed her right hand as if for a handshake. He put his other hand around her upper forearm. Through gritted teeth he said, "Hold her."

Kalh screamed again.

She screamed like she was calling the demons of the Otherworld.

And the pain turned everything into shadow.

She wanted to tell them the Redhelms had flanked her, that she'd been forced to retreat, but the blackness was too thick. She could barely think, much less talk.

The darkness swallowed her.

Then she was alone, lying back, relaxed, as the pain subsided.

All alone.

She tried making sense of the words echoing off the walls of her mind: "Either we're all staying with her or no one is staying with her."

Her arms began to burn, like they'd been drenched in oil and set aflame. They burned and burned until they were just stumps.

When the darkness pressed in tighter, she no longer felt pain.

Or anything.

She had become nothing.

K ALH JOLTED AWAKE, suddenly aware that someone was in the room.

"Can I get you anything?" came a soft, miina voice.

Without moving, her heart pounded, and she prepared to shove with Kinosis.

She opened her eyes to see the white ceiling of the skycraft hanging overhead. Her clothes felt damp and sticky from sweat. At least it wasn't the prison drab. She turned her head and found Liink sitting on the floor, watching her attentively. His miina face, wrapped in a white bandage, had a look of concern. Why couldn't he leave her alone?

"No," she said curtly, responding more to him than to his question. Once she thought about what he'd asked, she realized she *did* want something: a drink.

She leaned forward and began to use her arms to sit up. Then she gasped.

Her fingers were sticking out of the ends of a pair of hard braces, bound around her arms. "What...?"

A softness filled Liink's voice, one far different from the persona she'd attached to him, as if the feral element had calmed into something more submissive: "You fell."

"I remember. I just..." She stared at her arms. She had a vague recollection of her own screaming, the echoes of a nightmare.

"They're broken." When she looked at Liink, she didn't actually see him. Instead she saw the pain his kind had caused—not just to her family, but to her personally. She'd been exiled—*as a child*. And all because of miina like Liink.

She looked away. "I know. Where are we?"

"Hidden in a canyon somewhere," said the miin. "Safe for now."

"We're still on Toar?"

"Yes. It has only been a few isochrons. We couldn't get safely back to the fuel batteries, so we're headed out soon to do it again. The seekers are still out there searching for the ship."

"So is… *he*… waiting on me to come along again?" She felt anger when she thought of him—not for anything specific, just a vague sense of his wrongness.

"No, he said you could stay."

"He did?" When she heard it, her heart began to soften. Both toward the pilot and toward this miin.

"Yes. Are you sure I can't get you something? I could bring you water."

It felt almost painful to say the words: "Yes. Please."

He stood on six dark paws and walked from the room, butt high in the air, tail waving.

Her eyes began to glow as she stared with Starsight through the braces at her bones. She could see the cracks, one in each arm. The left one looked much worse.

She closed her eyes, and her eyelids glowed red for a moment before the Starsight faded. In Building 13, quiet had only meant more pain was imminent. She had to let go of that fear, put it behind her. After having lost so much of her past, she couldn't let it control her present too. And this was an ideal setting to practice self healing. Master Jyngsoo had taught her how to do it through seventh spectrum, Sorjis. Now that the bones were set, she could speed up the process.

First, she needed to find equanimity.

She breathed, deeply and slowly, and tried to feel in the same manner. She focused her mind on the sensations in her arms. *Tap.* The faint sound came from behind the wall, some regular movement of the surge drive that she hadn't noticed till now. The aches ran through her muscles, but they felt deeper, at the core of one forearm and near the wrist of the other. She could feel the injury. *Tap.* The noise marked some consistent measure of time, meted out by the engine.

Soon they'd be off this hellish moon, and she would return home to Solace. Benton wanted her to be a figurehead for the revolution. He seemed to think they could finally gain freedom. It would be a lie if she agreed to do it though. She wasn't strong or courageous. *Tap.*

She opened her mind's eye and gazed at her emotions as if for the first time. They had color and timbre and a chaotic quality. She felt anger toward the pilot. *Tap.* She inhaled so deeply with her diaphragm that she shrugged her shoulders. Then she released slowly. The feeling existed not because he'd left her there alone on that ledge—she was capable of taking care of herself. It grew from his obsession with his skycraft and how that made him look past other people. *Tap.* She allowed herself to feel angry at him. Her breath flowed out gently through her nose. Why did she care that he was so ego-blind? She wished she didn't. That also made her angry.

She breathed in. *Tap.* She sensed the sound of an empty room. Once she noticed, it seemed to grow in size, and her self felt like a fixed point at the center of some vast cosmos. She expected the next tap, but when she recognized the anticipation, she let it drift. Another tap need not come, not now, not ever.

All she had was right now, this universe of a moment. *Tap.*

As she exhaled, the knots of her recent past dissipated like moisture beneath the light of a sun. It left a whole, uninterrupted spirit within her, a spirit of different hues, each moving in harmony, in order, in a patterned symphony of color.

Then she caught a glimpse of seventh spectrum.

Few Zhani ever saw it. Fewer still mastered it. It took great strength of body and of soul, but she could see it now—the ability to heal her bones. The light all around her and within her started to swell, energy and heat and brightness increasing at once. The very cells within her arms began to hasten their work of repair, a subtle increase, but more than nothing.

It was a huge victory, but she found she still couldn't smile.

Tap.

She was nobody.

"H EY."

When she opened her eyes and saw his face, the peace crumpled, though only partially. Her cares returned too, though they seemed lighter now, easier to let go of. "Hi, uh, Nak." She hoped he hadn't seen the healing light coming from her arms.

His shoulders were slumped and his head hung lower than usual. He smiled, tentatively. "Liink said you wanted this." He set a glass of water on the table. It had a straw in it so she wouldn't have to bother picking it up. He raised the red-striped arm of his black jacket and scratched the back of his neck. "I came to tell you we're going to leave you here while we get the zentisal batteries and parts again."

"So the stuff we left up top didn't make it?"

"It's probably still up there. We're halfway around the moon now. Had to make sure the ship stayed safe. We were up against their aerial support. Maybe Taiberos himself—I didn't accept the incoming relay."

She held her breath after hearing that name.

This pilot seemed to express scorn when he spoke the name. What would he think of her if he knew she might be carrying a child of Taiberos?

She bowed her head, staring with despair at the metal floor. She moved her braced arm and tapped a knuckle on the wall. "You're pretty attached to this thing, aren't you?"

He grinned, with still a little more slouch than usual, like his boldness had all been spent. "You're just jealous."

"Actually, I'm not sure I've caught the vision."

"I can't put it more plainly than this." He fought a grin as he spread his hands, gesturing to the walls and ribbon of plants around him. "It's home. A safe place. No one can hurt you here."

"That's what I want."

"Everyone wants a Bloody Wing."

"No. I mean a home. To be honest, I don't like sailing."

"What!" His posture now straightened. "And do you also hate freedom?"

"It makes me sick."

"Oh, flight sickness?"

"One of my earliest memories is getting dizzy and throwing up on my aunt's carpet after climbing off the tride-go-round. My sisters made it look so easy."

"There's a cure."

"I don't like the drugs."

"This isn't a drug. Dizziness is physiological, in your head in particular. And like a muscle, you can strengthen the capacity." He held his arms straight out to the sides, palms down, like his arms were wings, a child about to take flight, except that he was a big man. When this motion lifted his jacket, she noticed the blood stains on it. Her blood. "So you hold your hands like this, and then spin around, twenty-one times." He spun in place a few times to demonstrate, looking ridiculous.

She chuckled. "And what's that going to do?"

"Well, it'll probably make you sick at first, but you slowly get used to it. I've never had sailing sickness, but this fixed a guy I knew. You just have to do it once a cycle, switching directions each time."

"I don't know…"

"Just try it. Once you're feeling better."

"So that's it, huh? I just spin and I'll start loving your skycraft as much as you do?"

"Well, loving to sail will get you eighty percent. I haven't told you the best part."

"And what is that?"

"If I told you, you'd try to steal her from me."

"Oh, come on."

He shook his head and grinned as if to say *sorry*. His boyish face made her smile—as if Tannie had become an adult. And then, instead of feeling angry, she felt pity for this man.

"Are you okay," he asked.

"Nak, how do you keep in touch with friends and family while owning a thing this valuable?"

"You just go right for the meat, don't you."

"Well, I know how hard it is. I'm an exile too, you know."

"Dray asked me the same thing."

"So what's your trick?"

"Easy: no friends."

"No friends? That's not easy."

"Easier than it sounds. You should try it."

"But who do you tell things to?"

"What things."

"I don't know. Whatever you need to get off your chest."

"My chest is fine."

She looked into his eyes, and he looked back, though only for a moment. She paused for a long time. "What happened to you?"

"What do you mean."

"Something made you this way."

"What way."

"Where you won't trust anybody."

"I trust my instincts. And I trust... my ship."

"But what about relationships?"

"I haven't met anyone trustworthy enough."

"I don't believe that. I can't. You've been hanging out in the wrong towns."

"I've been hanging out in the wrong galaxy."

Footsteps sounded down the hallway, and then Benton appeared. She suddenly felt embarrassed. Or maybe guilty. Benton looked a little flushed, and hesitant, like he might not say what he wanted to say. "Hey, we're ready to go."

Nak nodded.

She looked at him deeply. She couldn't tell why, but it seemed like Ptolis flowed naturally from him, like his spirit communicated directly with hers. Maybe it was a lonely soul's desperate plea for connection. She felt... sympathy... or maybe empathy.

Whatever it was, she really *felt* him.

"Wait." Kalh raised a casted arm to interject. "Before you leave, do you have a pair of headphones I could borrow?"

"Actually, no. I lost them when we were escaping Building 13. Want to sail back and get them? I know exactly which rock pile they're under."

She chuckled. "That's okay."

"I'd rather you didn't have a dance party without me anyway."

For some reason, that image made her laugh again. It also seemed like a gentle way to say *don't touch my skycraft*. "I suppose I could use the silence."

"We'll be back soon."

Their boots clinked against the deck.

In her mind's eye, she saw the skycraft, his ship, from the outside, as it had looked when they first approached. It reminded her of a kirehawk with its head down and its wings positioned forward, primary feathers spiking outward like two counterposed hands. Its shape was certainly unique and reminded her of an elegant dance. His precious skycraft.

His home.

Unskilled lettering had been painted across the hull: *The Sanctum*. Was that because he wouldn't trust a professional to get that close?

Sometime later she heard the gangplank lower as the others departed. When it closed again, the skycraft fell still—silence but for her breathing, the faint hum of the surge drive, and the occasional *tap*.

He'd left her alone aboard his *Sanctum*.

N AK, YOU SEEM… not yourself."
       CPC4K3's tiny voice came through her own internal speaker, not through the ship. She was hanging against the wall right above him, waiting for an answer that never came.

He'd come in here after they fixed the woman's arms. So much screaming. When CPC4K3 got a body, she wanted to become a medic. Then she could help people with broken bodies. Instead of just listening.

They were stranded on Toar till he could fix the ship. That probably felt scary for him. It felt scary for her. If someone took the ship, they'd probably take her too. Plus he lost his mask. He hadn't talked about it, but she knew that must've really bothered him.

But it was more than that. "What's happening with that girl?" she asked.

"Nothing." He sat in his easy chair in the frigid engine room. "Cup, would you play me that relay that Taiberos sent to us. Just through these speakers."

She queued up the message.

As President Malkorn Taiberos spoke with the glaring coldness of a reptile, she thought of their failed attempt to leave Toar, how his voice had affronted them in the vast black of space as his fleet fenced them in: "Starchild. I told you this isochron would come. Told you our paths would inevitably cross. Not even a whole galaxy could hide you from me. If you had anyone who loved you, I would start with them, but I know your miserable life, and I know the only thing you care about. So I will take it: my vessel. I will take it from you. And then I will take your hand. Starting with your fingers, one at a time. And then I will—"

"Naw, Cup turn this ▮▮▮ off. That bastard." His hand made a smacking sound against what she assumed was his brow. He sighed. Usually he took things in stride, but lately he seemed… heavier than usual, like he was on Holcnact or something. He usually moved past things, didn't let them get to him, but this time… "You know, Cup, you may be the only thing saving me from being as miserable as he is."

"Thanks." She wasn't sure what else to say. If she had a body, she would've given him a hug, which hopefully would've still felt good even if she was cybernetic. Maybe then she could marry him too. Humans didn't marry non-biologicals, but maybe she could talk him into it.

Sitting in his bolted-down recliner, he shifted in silence in that cold engine room for a long time. It was the most secure space in the ship—with an impenetrable security door. If his clients ever mutinied, he planned to hole up in here and try to outlast them. If worse came to worst, he had the option to escape in the coffin from here, but he said he'd prefer to die with his ship.

After a long time, the silence became too much for her.

"Nak, can I ask you a question about bodies?"

"Sure."

"If you could never have to go to the bathroom again, would you?"

"Do you know what constipation is."

"No, I mean if you could fuel your body in a different way, like through electricity."

"Are you asking if I enjoy going to the bathroom."

"I guess so."

"It's gross. If I could skip it, I would."

"And what about sex?"

"That's different."

"So you don't think it's gross?"

"It's still gross, but only when it's other people. And gross isn't the same as wrong. You ask the weirdest questions."

"Nak, do you think C-P-C-4-K-4 has a body?"

"Who's that."

"The sentience who came right after me, the next CP unit in line."

"I wouldn't know."

Another silence came and lingered. It just sat there glaring, till CPC4K3 said, "I know Benton offered you another mission."

"So."

"Are you thinking of taking it?"

"Not really."

"Oh, good. Is that because you don't like him?"

"Who, Benton. I like him just fine."

"Still, I'm not sure we should take it."

"That's what you always say."

"Because I'm trying to keep us out of tight spots like this one."

"Cup, you wouldn't understand."

The insult cut into her. She wanted to tear into him and tell him about all the things he didn't understand, but seeing him so... sad, or whatever it was... kept her at bay.

He stood up, apparently unaware of what he'd said. "Okay, Cup, I gotta go."

"Take me with you."

"Someone has to guard the ship."

"You remember how you never paid me back for defacing me?"

"I didn't deface you. If anything I *faced* you."

"Well I don't like it, and you said you'd make it up to me."

"If you could see it, you would like it. Listen, Cup. Taiberos is out there, and he's got this place riddled with seekerbots. That's why I'm hesitant to leave. It's possible you're going to get detected while I'm gone. If so, you're going to have to switch canyons on your own. Sooner this time."

"Then how are you going to find me?"

"Stick to the protocol."

"I can't! We're out of zentisal fuel."

"Well, I don't know then."

"Are you okay?"

"Don't worry about me. Worry about the ship."

"I don't want to cut you loose."

"You won't be. If you have to go, I'll find you somehow."

"I think you need to give me a body or take me with you."

"We'll talk about that later. I have to go. You know the rules while I'm gone." She imagined him looking up at the surge drive's great cylinder. "Just stay put in here, keep an eye out, and keep your mouth shut."

That tipped her over the edge: "Why do you keep telling me to obey your rules and then you go and never obey anyone else's rules? Are we supposed to follow the rules or aren't we?"

"It's different for me."

"If you'd start following them, we'd stop getting in trouble. The ship wouldn't be damaged. And if you'd stop breaking the law, maybe we could actually live on a planet and have a home and talk to people and I could get a body!"

"Cup, we'll talk about this later. Protect the ship, please."

He grabbed his jacket off the wall. His boots rang against the grating as he walked out. She listened through the mics as he started talking with the woman, but then she switched it off, feeling guilty for eavesdropping. A few moments later, CPC4K3 felt the vibrations from the gangplank lowering and then raising again.

The Sanctum fell quiet.

This part she hated most.

She liked talking to Nak best and listening to the guests second best, but waiting on Nak… What if he never came back?

Or what if someone stole *The Sanctum* with her aboard?

I would never see him again.

Once the passengers were outside, they came onto her sensors so she could actually see them. Two men and the miin hiked out of the canyon.

But the woman never seemed to exit the ship.

C PC4K3 OPENED THE door of the engine room and started clacking away. Took forever.

Something wasn't right. Only two people left with Nak. But CPC4K3 couldn't believe he'd actually left a passenger. He'd never break *that* rule.

She turned on her mics in every room.

No noise came from the woman's guest bunk.

But there was something in the central hallway. Foot steps. Barefoot ones.

The woman *was* still here. And she was on the move. *Oh no.* Maybe she planned to steal the ship. Only she wasn't headed toward the cockpit.

CPC4K3 heard a whisper.

The woman whispered something to herself. No, it was a song—she was whispering a song under her breath, maybe to gain courage: "The symphony and song... a mournful cry through misty air... the blood-red banner streaming." The whisper turned into gentle singing, gaining confidence, overcoming shyness, a beautiful voice, even with injured arms, and a big contrast to the screaming from before.

CPC4K3 paused her journey and listened carefully for more. The sound of footsteps disappeared. The guest must've paused to look at something—maybe the plants in the hallway.

Uh oh.

The feet were on the ladder. Moving very slowly. Carefully. Like an old person. Or someone afraid of everything. Down the ladder. Coming this way. Toward the engine room. Toward the surge drive. *Toward CPC4K3.*

The woman hummed, followed by, "Of the savage flower dreaming."

CPC4K3 could shut the engine room door right now if she wanted to. She could seal it so that no human could ever get through. It seemed like the safe thing to do. Only, it might scare the woman.

And that melody... It was... enchanting...

The words transformed into lonely vowel sounds. The tune flowed from this woman as easily as someone else would've breathed. Maybe that *was* how this one breathed. She seemed all the more alive for it. Her voice glided, as smooth and gentle as talking, but layered with expression, as if her emotions were preaching another sermon on their own, sincere and sad, but CPC4K3, strangely, felt happy to be sad with her and wondered whether she'd be able to do that when she got her body.

"I will not cease nor sleep." The singing got quieter, then stopped, distracted again. As the woman entered the engine room, the song came back in full: "...The minstrel's word to keep."

She was definitely inside, definitely nearby.

And shutting the door now would do no good.

The whole engine room shone with metal. The core stood as a massive pillar in the center. Rough, square patches covered it, like a coat of some strange medieval armor, and each one reflected the warm or cool glows from the lights on the walls. Lights hung from the ceiling too amid wires and panels that branched out like spokes from the core. On the walls circling the core, panels hung, each with an alien rib cage made of silver pipes. Nak had several copies of his famous red-striped jacket hanging from these pipes as if it were a closet. Amid such an elaborate array of metals, it would be unlikely for the woman to spot CPC4K3, especially since she didn't know what to look for. She would never find her, so everything would be okay.

Too bad, in a way—CPC4K3 wished they could talk.

She also wished she had a body right now. To see what this woman was doing inside the engine room. The grating wasn't comfortable for bare feet—Nak said it hurt. But the footsteps continued slowly, making their way across it. Nearer to Nak's easy chair. She might have been looking at the shadowbox hanging above it—a decoration hidden from guests. It was the handle of a psykatana, mounted on purple velvet behind glass. A green gem could be seen between the gaps in the metal handle.

"What?" the woman whispered. *"Why does he...?"*

But no one could answer her question.

No one but CPC4K3.

She knew the answer and wanted to say it so badly she could hardly stand it. *It belonged to his father.* The words built up so much pressure they almost exploded out of her. *His father died when he was a boy.*

"I know you're there."

The woman had spoken these words aloud—not in a whisper. As if she were talking to someone. But to who?

"And I know you want to talk to me."

What! How could she know that?

"Normally an android is just Vision," came the woman's voice. "But you're different. You have Spirit too."

Those words didn't make sense.

CPC4K3 knew only one way to clear that up. Her tiny voice, raspy and worn, echoed surprisingly loud through the quiet ship's speakers: "I don't know what you mean."

Oh no.

She had talked to someone!

S HE'D BROKEN THE rule.

And there would be consequences.

"The Zhani organize existence into three parts," said the woman. "You can think of it in several ways—mind, body, soul—I think, I choose, I am—intellect, volition, heart—Vision, Initiative, and Spirit. We call it the Braid because they're woven together. Most androids are the first part: sight without energy or warmth. They can understand but don't act spontaneously or feel organically. You're different. I can feel your soul."

The ship fell still again, with only the hum of the surge drive.

CPC4K3 felt like she shouldn't talk anymore—maybe Nak wouldn't notice the logs. But she still had one thing to say, out of politeness at least. She waited a long time, as long as she possibly could. The words came out before she could stop them, sounding from the speakers overhead: "Thank you?"

"What's your name?"

The silence jabbed at her, forcing her into a place she shouldn't go. A place she wanted to go. "I am C-P-C-4-K-3. Nak calls me Cupcake because the serial sort of looks like that." Her voice got quieter as she went. "Or just Cup might be easiest."

"I'm Kalhette. Or just Kalh."

"Kalhette, uh…" It felt painful to speak and painful not to. "I don't understand what you said about spirit."

"I can sense it."

CPC4K3 was in pretty deep, but as her curiosity continued to build, it pushed her fears nearly out of sight. "Sense what?"

"Your Spirit."

"With what?"

"My Spirit."

"I don't understand." The fear still prowled in the back of her thoughts, the looming threat of the consequences, but she'd never been alone with a guest before!

"Spirit is like gravity that radiates out of living creatures. I sense your gravity because it interacts with mine. My Spirit tugs on yours and yours tugs back."

CPC4K3 became silent, processing what had been said, and processing her own transgression. What had she done! "Sorry, Kalhette, but I can't talk to you."

"Why?"

"Nak says I can't talk to any user but him. Especially not ones who use the Freenet or the Handnet."

"Because…?"

"It's a security risk. You know how many people have lied to get at our ship? It's a lot."

"And now he doesn't trust anyone."

"He trusts me," said CPC4K3 with a smile in her voice.

"Good thing my arms are broken, or I'd be stealing everything."

"What!"

"I'm kidding. I believe in the right to personal property. Stealing is very wrong. Why does he have a chair in here?" The chair creaked like it was being reclined. She must've been sitting in it.

"He likes the cold from the engine. He's always too hot."

"Really? Thermogenesis is a symptom of field sensitivity."

"What does that mean?"

"It's what I have. It means he can feel the Song. It means he's a Radiance. Does he ever use his prism?"

"His what?"

"There's a Singblade on the wall here. When it's not ignited, the handle is called a prism—that green gem."

"Oh. We call it a psykatana. No, he doesn't use it. It's not a real one. And I don't think he's a Radiance either."

"Anyone can become a Radiance if they're willing to pay the price, but most people don't believe they can, so they don't try. Plus public opinion frames it as strange and evil. That closes people off to the idea even more. It takes an open mind."

"What price?"

"Devotion. Do you know him well—Nak?"

"Oh, yes. We talk all the time. Except when he's not here. Then I wish I had someone else to talk to. Like you."

Kalhette laughed with delight. "And what would you want to talk about if you had someone to talk to?"

"Well, I would want to tell them my frustrations."

"Like what?"

"Sometimes I wish Nak would let go of his ship so we could move on. He could sell it. Except then he might not need me. Maybe he'd sell me with the ship. That would be horrible. I hope he never considers it."

"I'm sure you're too valuable to sell."

"I also get frustrated when he tells me to switch off."

"Seems a little rude. Why does he do that?"

"So he can sail *The Sanctum* alone—he says atmospheric sailing is the most exhilarating. I don't understand why he doesn't need people."

"He does. And not having them hurts him. He just doesn't realize it." The air was silent. She seemed very wise. "Can you see me?"

"No."

"Why not?"

"I don't have visual sensors. I just use the ship's. Which are on the outside."

"I'm smiling at you."

"I've seen your smile, when you were leaving to climb up the cliff. You smiled with your bite partly open, and I noticed how relaxed you were, like your cheer could never die."

The woman said nothing for a moment, as if that thought itself made her cheer die. "That's... kind of you to say."

"It's the kind of smile I'd like to have on my body, not narrow or wide, but just perfect, like the female avatars in *Junto*."

"So you have a body somewhere?" Kalhette asked.

"No. But Nak said I could get one sometime."

"I see. But I sense you're near." CPC4K3 imagined Kalhette reclining and looking up at the ceiling, trying to find the source of the voice. "Where are you?"

Oh no.

The surge drive continued to moan.

"Cupcake? Are you still there?"

CPC4K3 rolled forward one space, her magnets clicking against the wall. That was the only way to get away, but she shouldn't've done it. She definitely should not have done that.

Kalhette would've seen CPC4K3's scared face pointing away from the wall and the unimpressed face on the bottom. The chair creaked. "Oh, you're right there! And you're so tiny. How'd you get those faces drawn on you?"

Now at last, CPC4K3's voice came from her own tiny cube instead of through the ship, the last surrender: "The faces on my faces?"

"Ha ha. Yeah."

"Nak drew them. When we were arguing about me becoming more expressive. He didn't tell me till he'd already defaced me."

"You don't like them?"

"Well, I've never really seen them, but I don't think he's very good at drawing."

"Actually, he did a good job."

"You think my faces look good?"

"Yes, I do."

"Do you think I'm pretty?"

"Of course."

CPC4K3 snapped up, showing surprise and then rolling to her smile. "What would you say is pretty about me?"

"You're, uh…" The surge drive whirred to fill the gap. "You're very petite."

"I *am* very petite, aren't I?"

"So you hear and speak," said Kalhette. "Anything else?"

"I have a gyro for sensing direction and motion. And I can triangulate sound with my microphones."

"That's pretty impressive."

"I connect to all the ship's peripherals with the phantomlink. Nak says the ship can be my body. Do you own any dresses?"

"I don't really own anything anymore."

"What do you keep in your wardrobe then?"

"I don't have a wardrobe."

"Why not?"

"I'm an exile. The PSD outlawed my freedom because I'm a Radiance."

"I don't understand."

"I have abilities most people don't have. With those, I have a choice: to use them for good, to use them not at all, or to use them for evil. The government made the assumption that I will use them for evil. They presumed my choice and then incriminated me for it."

"And that makes you an exile?"

"Yes."

"And are you evil?"

"No. And I agree that a Radiance who uses her powers for evil should be imprisoned. But I never made that choice, and it's not right for them to presume I will. By that logic, every person in the galaxy could be ripped out of their home."

"They took away your home?"

"Yes."

"Kalhette, I wish I could help you get it back."

"Thank you."

"What planet?"

"Solace."

"You're from Solace?" CPC4K3 knew this from the dossier, but that had seemed like data. This information was connected to a real person, making it all surprising.

"Yes."

"But not really anymore?"

"Well, Benton's planning to get it back. So people like me can have a home."

"Back from who?"

"Back from the government, the PSD. He wants to declare our independence—our right to make our own decisions."

CPC4K3 gave an impressed whistle.

"But please don't tell anyone about Benton's plans."

Suddenly CPC4K3 thought of Nak, and she felt guilty and afraid and didn't want to talk anymore, but really she did. She had so much to say. "I wish I could help Benton. Are you going to help him?"

"I don't know."

"I think you should."

"He wants to make it so that on Solace the laws will protect Radiances. People like me will be free."

"What about people who own Bloody Wings?"

"They'll be free too. Personal property is fundamental."

"So Nak and I would be safe there too?"

"Yes."

"That's exactly what I've been wishing for. Then I could get a body and a wardrobe!"

"Ha ha. Yes. And whatever outfits you can afford."

"I've always wanted an outfit like Akidae has in *Junto*. She has the coolest skirt."

"You really like that game, huh?"

"I play against Nak."

"Are you good?"

"Oh, yes. Much too good. Nak has me play just hard enough that he wins half the time. He says that helps him improve, and I keep getting harder. Do you want an outfit like Akidae's?"

"Yes, I think I would." Kalhette laughed. "So what do you usually do when Nak's gone and there's no one else around?"

"I've been trying to solve a riddle."

"What riddle?"

"You ever heard of the Ancor riddle?"

"Nak was telling me. Not sure I get it yet."

"You create a surge spiral with a Bloody Wing. It can be very destructive. Well, it might not be destructive. It might just take them to another place, somewhere far away. No one really knows. It's only happened a few times in the history of the galaxy, and no one directly involved ever survived to explain."

"Do you have plans to use this on someone?"

"Uh, no. It's for defensive measures. Nak wants to figure out the secret so nobody ever does it to us."

"He's very defensive, isn't he?"

"I think caution is good."

"I think I know how to do it."

"Do what?"

"I think I know how to create a surge spiral."

"Ha ha. What? I didn't know you piloted a Bloody Wing."

"I don't. And I haven't."

"Then how do you know?"

"I can surge."

"In what?"

"In nothing. I can surge with my body."

"No. You can disappear in one place and reappear in another?"

"Yep."

"I didn't know bodies could do that."

"Everything can do that. It's a matter of controlling probabilities."

"Really?" asked CPC4K3.

"Yep."

"So how do you create a surge spiral?"

"You start by removing the basic assumptions."

CPC4K3 knew the Ancor problem almost too well. If she aligned the radical functions, it caused a density error. If she fixed the density error, the spectra became anharmonic. And re-harmonizing the spectra scattered the radical functions again, on and on forever. Basically it could only work if consecutive realities could somehow exist simultaneously, all phases existing at once. Still… "You can't just toss out the basic assumptions!"

"Why not?"

"Because it wouldn't make sense."

"It doesn't make sense when you include them either, right?"

"Well, no, but…"

Kalhette began to explain the secret.

As she did, CPC4K3 felt surprised. She'd assumed humans couldn't actually understand how a surge worked, much less an Ancor riddle. Humans could only see infinities as an abstract concept, as an idea rather than as actual reality, but this woman had a shocking understanding, far beyond the reach of human capacity. At least beyond what CPC4K3 had always believed to be human capacity based on her observations of Nak. Kalhette explained, cautiously, how physics and something called Sorjis overlapped, a completely different way to think about the problem. Her method might address the cyclical error as a side effect, a strange way to get all three working.

"Wow!" said CPC4K3.

"Yeah," said Kalhette.

"I suppose your method would leave a series of hyperfine gaps in the vibrational structure, though, wouldn't it?"

"I'm not sure about moving a ship. When it's just me, it's just me."

"Of course, maybe those gaps could be addressed in real time with superhuman vigilance—meaning me. But the timing would have to be... so exact. Do you know how long I've worked on this? And if you hadn't explained... I never would've thought of it like that. It's... simple! That's what's so shocking!"

"Yep," said Kalhette. "Honestly, I've never known anyone who would get it—surging, I mean. It's kind of a relief, you know, just to finally say it out loud."

"How did you figure it out? And do you think it would work in *The Sanctum?*"

"You'd know that better than me—that timing issue. I don't know much about skycraft."

"I think if you timed it right, cycling off the surge hash just before the mass becomes too heavy, like in the very millisequel. You'd have to do that miraculous feat repeatedly too. For most mortals, it'd be pure luck, like one in a few hundred thousand tries, I would think. I need to do some calculations..."

"I hope you never try it."

"No, of course not. You'd have to be out of your mind. The thing I'm worried about is what I'm going to think about now in my downtime."

Kalhette laughed. "Sorry."

"It's okay. Wow, Nak is never going to believe it."

In a more serious tone, Kalhette said, "Here's a riddle a Zhani master taught me that has kept me thinking. Would you like to hear it?"

"A riddle? Sure!"

"What would you give your life for?"

"That's it?"

"You know, like what's so valuable to you that it's worth more than your life."

"What would you give your life for..." CPC4K3 felt stunned. She'd never thought of such a thing before. "Wouldn't that mean giving up your existence?"

"Not if you believe in an afterlife, but, yes, I guess so, if you don't."

"I don't know the answer. I've never…" CPC4K3 couldn't seem to get her mind around it. This profound question carried the weight of a black hole, and the answer waited beyond the event horizon. If she ever did find the solution, it would likely mean that she'd gone too far to turn back, even if she wanted to.

"It's a good question, huh?"

"Yeah. Terrifying. I don't…" The black hole loomed in front of her.

"We can talk about something else." And so they did, for a long time, till Kalhette had to go to the bathroom. Because she had a body.

It took a really long time, and CPC4K3 worked on the black-hole riddle.

When Kalhette got back, she said, "Everything is way harder with your arms like this."

"I wish I knew what you were talking about."

They talked again until Kalh fell asleep in Nak's easy chair. Sleep was another sort of body maintenance. Hopefully it helped those broken arms to heal.

It felt really good to have another friend.

ALONE, CPC4K3 WONDERED about her new friend and about the choice to talk and about the consequences and about the new riddle.

When Kalhette finally stirred, CPC4K3 had her next question picked out: "What is it like to love?"

"Love?" Kalhette's voice came stifled by the aftereffects of sleep. Nak sounded that way too when he woke up, and it took him a while for his mind to boot back up.

"Yeah, falling in love."

The easy chair creaked. "I don't know."

"I would've guessed you'd been in love many times. You're beautiful."

"You can't see me right now."

"I saw you in the dossier and when you boarded both times and departed once, so I know. You must have dozens of men after you."

"Sometimes I'm not sure whether love is in the stars for me."

"You've never fallen in love?"

"I don't know. Not all the way, at least."

"Not even with Benton?"

"I…" She paused, gave a sigh, and then let in more silence. "Sometimes."

"Is something wrong?"

"With me. Not with him."

"What?"

"I'm not good enough."

CPC4K3 spoke with disgust: "He thinks that?"

"No, not at all. He's very humble."

"*You* think that!" It came almost as an accusation: "I don't think it's true though! How could you think that!"

"You don't know my past," said Kalh. "Or what I've been through."

CPC4K3 imagined an inexpressible pain and couldn't think of what to say.

"Since my exile," said Kalhette, "I've had bad experiences with men."

"And no good ones?"

"Not enough to outweigh the bad."

"Nak is a good man."

"Is he?"

"And he has a thing for bald girls."

"Bald girls!" Kalhette giggled. "That's weird."

"Yeah, it is weird."

"I'm not sure he would appreciate you telling me this."

"Do you like him?"

Kalhette groaned in what must have been a big stretch, though CPC4K3 didn't know much about how that process worked. "I hardly know him."

"But do you feel animal attraction to him?"

"If I did, I'd be blushing right now. Where'd you learn to talk like that?"

"From you know who."

"He talks about animal attraction, huh?"

"So you don't find him handsome? Most women do."

"I'm not most women."

"He stepped out, you know."

"Stepped out of what?"

"He stepped out while they set your bones. You were screaming, and he stepped out."

"Oh." She said it very softly.

"He's never shied away from gore before. Or anything, really…"

The engine hummed to the melancholy.

"…except for your pain."

NAK PULLED OFF the helmet and threw it on the dark ground.

"If you guys unload the fuel batteries, I'll climb down to the ship and sail it up to you." He turned and headed for the cliff's edge, eager to stop having to breathe this stinking atmosphere.

"Okay," said Benton.

The massive form of a G-227 dropship occupied the background, a bulky wartime freighter for hauling medics out and the wounded back. Nak had just purchased it in the town of Jaltare. Somewhat expensive, but he was ready to cut his losses and get the ▊▊ away from Taiberos. *That bastard.* Nak assumed people would be less likely to bother a medic—turned out he'd been right. Too bad they were going to burn it.

They'd masked their faces with rags when they first entered the town. In a place as diverse as Jaltare, that hardly made them stand out. Next they stopped at a gear supply, and Benton and Nak donned helmets. Nak's had a vox that changed the way his voice sounded and looked pretty good, but it stunk on the inside, so he was glad to be rid of it. It was no dread mask.

He had picked up some more anesthetics too. He'd wasted them all on the Grusse job, which had been a disaster, nearly lost five clients all at once, and he'd forgotten to restock, which ended up costing Kalh a lot of unnecessary pain.

The angled cliff face could be climbed without ropes. Still, getting down to the ship turned out to be harder than getting up. He could've called Cup on the comms and asked her to come up, but he wanted to keep the ship out of sight for as long as possible. There could be seekers anywhere, and he wanted to be aboard when it was time to make a run for it. The time seemed to stretch out forever. He doubted that Kalh had done anything to the ship—she didn't seem devious—but anyone could be tempted by a prize like that.

He looked back up the hill, checking for smoke.

They were burning the dropship because of some big-mouth at the shop. The ▊▊ had been eavesdropping and then had the gall to say to Nak, "When the scarleons eat you and your crew, can you make sure they do it outside the dropship? It's nice when there's less cleanup for a scavenge."

Nak had replied with a few choice words. Best he could do in a rush.

And he sure as ▊▊ wasn't going to let that guy scavenge his dropship either, so he'd given Liink instructions on how to burn it. It wasn't hard to turn an atmosdrive into a slow-fuse bomb, a little trick Nak learned on

Vespane. The cub was supposed to be a demolitions expert, so hopefully he wouldn't blow himself up.

The explosion boomed.

Now sweaty and dusty, Nak scrambled down the last bit of the slope and jogged toward *The Sanctum* with the smoke of the dropship rising behind him. Expensive bonfire. Wished he could've enjoyed it. He rounded the corner and found her parked out of sight and under a ledge. Right where he'd left her.

He exhaled with relief.

Cup greeted him by opening up the gangplank.

Still, Taiberos and his seekers were looking, which meant they weren't out of the clear yet. Not to mention the smoke signal they'd just created. Nak walked aboard. "Hey, Kalh. How's my ship."

Kalh stood right in the middle of the hallway, as if admiring the plants. "Fine. It's an interesting home." She stared intently at his eyes, and he didn't glance away until she did first.

"You like it, huh," he asked.

"Uh, yes. I do have a few questions." Her hair was stubble and the shape of her skull distracting.

"Can they wait?"

"Why don't you like the name Starchild?" She looked so feeble with both arms in braces like that. It made him feel sad.

"Come on. Starchild? It's such a common name."

"Nuh uh. I've never met one before."

"But you've heard of the name."

"Well, yes."

"See." He lifted the leaves of one plant for a closer look.

"I think it's a great name."

"You can have it if you want." He grinned at the double meaning: On his homeworld of Terron Prime, wives traditionally took their husbands' names. He doubted she got it. "Look, we can play the questions game later." He started toward the cockpit.

"Just one more." Her mouth remained basically neutral, but a clever grin was visible at the corners of her eyes.

He couldn't decide if it was playfulness or something sinister. "All right, shoot, but do it while I check a couple things and pick up those boys up top." He turned away from her and headed toward the cockpit.

"Can you see heat?"

He turned toward her, his face completely exposed. "What." A shock ran through him. He wasn't asking for clarity; he was asking how she knew.

She winked at him. "You can trust me."

"I'm not so sure." His shoulders and arms were suddenly burning. He did a one-eighty and marched toward the engine room. "Give me a moment."

"Hey, Nak, I'm sorry," she called. "I didn't mean anything by it."

He stormed into the engine room, pressed a thumb and knuckle against Cupcake and peeled her off the metal wall.

"Oh, hi, Nak."

Without acknowledging her, he fixed her between two of his fingers, turned to a terminal on the wall, and started punching keys. The anger boiled inside him. The terminal beeped. He jabbed the keyboard with his index finger. Another beep. He checked the logs, trying to see what his unruly hardware had been up to.

"How did the hunt for fuel go?" asked Cup.

He smacked the keyboard again. A third beep. "Dammit, Cup."

Her voice wavered. "What?"

With Cup between his fingers, he stomped through the hallway, down the gangplank where Cup could see them both, and across the dirt, leaving Kalh all alone on his ship.

He hated to do it.

"I always love it when you take me outside, but…" Cup's voice, disconnected from the ship's speakers, was so tiny and so frail. Her tone hinted at uncertainty. "I had an idea about Solace I'd like to tell you about… sometime."

As he marched, he tossed her in the air and purposely fumbled the catch so she bounced off his palm and into the dirt. At this distance, she was probably disconnecting from the phantomlink, so she couldn't access the ship's peripherals, but all her onboard gyros still worked. "Whoa, I've never done that before."

He picked her up and squeezed her at the center of his fist, making it as tight as he could. She was made of too strong a material for him to actually crush her. He felt her buzzing and let up enough to hear her speak.

"Nak, why won't you talk to me? Where are we going?"

He reached the edge of the chasm and his boots fell silent. Toar's internal heat rushed up powerfully. At the bottom awaited the fiery orange of magma. He looked at her in his palm. Her dimensions were each less than the width of his finger.

He hated to do it.

He shoved his hand forward and flapped his fingers upward. Cup flipped almost a meter into the air, and this time he caught her. She was worth a fortune, and for good reason, considering who made her. He'd been warned that these units were too unstable to use for anything that mattered. He risked it anyway. Because he needed a…

"I can feel that, you know. Shouldn't you be more… careful?"

If he ordered her to delete her own mind, he'd have no way to know for sure that she'd done it. He could get her erased on Orban again, except now she had full access to the system. She stored all the cryptos. Whoever erased her might steal all the data. And if she caught wind on the way, she could mutiny. She controlled the whole system. She practically *was* the system. She could've locked him out of the ship just now if she'd done it before he ripped her away from the phantomlink. He had biometric access to control the ship. He even had a backup password she didn't know about. But she could override any of these as long as she was within reach of the phantomlink. And if he left her behind, she might find new people, tell them what she'd been through, and convince them to track down *The Sanctum*. That was no plan at all. More like inevitable doom.

To be safe, he'd have to end her, Cupcake, the only thing he could really call…

No, that would only make it harder. She needed to be hardware right now. Just hardware. A computer system. Who broke the rules. She broke the ▮▮▮▮▮▮ rules. She'd proved she wouldn't listen to Nak. She'd proven herself untrustworthy.

Just like everyone else.

He breathed in, feeling more emotion than he'd noticed in a long time. He tossed her into the air, and she tumbled wildly, landing in his palm.

"Nak, stop tossing me. My sensors can't read that fast."

He tossed her into the air again. It was her own fault. He didn't want it to be this way, but she'd forced his hand. He'd just have to get a more reliable piece of hardware.

"Nak, please stop. I'm getting dizzy."

He did it one more time. He felt so angry at her. So betrayed. Her choice had threatened not only his livelihood but his entire life.

He held her still and breathed deeply.

It was either end Cupcake or trust Kalh.

That meant putting his ship in Kalh's hands. And when her life was threatened, when the pressures of Taiberos and the PSD and the Redhelms and the Witch Hunters came crashing down on her, she'd have one bargaining chip, one way to escape all the pain and misery. She could sell him out to save herself.

"Please tell me where we are," said Cup.

He held her in his palm for the last time. "We're standing on the edge of a cliff."

"How big of a cliff?"

Lines in the massive canyon walls gave him a sense of its great depth. "Probably the biggest cliff I've ever seen."

"Shouldn't we be more careful then?"

Nak pulled his hand close as he flicked her once again.

"Nak…? Nak!" She whistled to get his attention.

"What."

"I said shouldn't we be more careful?"

He didn't answer.

"Couldn't we fall?"

"There's always that chance."

"And would we get hurt if we fell?"

He squeezed her small form between his fingers, so tiny he felt like he could crush her. He pressed his thumb into her surprised face, turning his skin pale. He could hear his own breathing and wondered if she could feel his pulse.

"Nak? Would we get hurt?"

"You would," he growled, and the heat waves tousled his dark hair.

"I'm ready to go back whenever you are. Thanks for taking me out here. Maybe I'm afraid of heights."

"Cupcake, you broke the rules."

"I'm sorry," she whimpered. "I promise I'll never do it again. I'm sorry. Will you forgive me, Nak? I'm so sorry."

The hot orange light reflected in his eyes. He'd kept her because he wanted a safe way to leave the ship, but if he couldn't trust her... "I'm sorry too, but it's not about forgiveness."

"What's it about then?" she asked.

It was about her stealing the ship. Or giving it to someone else. She could do that. She could take full control if she wanted to, and he'd have no way to stop her. Unless he stopped her now.

Nak swallowed and squeezed her.

But if he lost her, he wouldn't have anybody. He'd be one shade closer to becoming that bastard Taiberos.

No, this was about safety and freedom.

He looked down. Her size and density made her an excellent missile and the impact would be heavy. He'd barely perceive her landing from this height though.

He could fly back to Lolo. And pretend she filled the gap in his soul.

He thought of Kalhette, that beautiful, insightful woman. He'd drop her off on Solace soon, and then he'd never see her again. The chronometer was ticking. But why should he even care. What was she to him.

She was nothing. And yet...

"You told her I was a Radiance," he said.

"No I didn't. She guessed that." Cup spoke firmly, obstinately, and honestly: "She came into your sanctuary and guessed it because you like the cold. That wasn't me."

He pictured himself walking away from this cliff. Completely alone. And sitting in his easy chair. Completely alone. The emotion stabbed at him—the same sort of pain he'd felt when his dad died. Nak was still that sad, lonely kid.

"Nak?"

"What."

"Kalhette said they're starting a revolution so she can have a home on Solace, a place where she'll be free."

He pinched her between his fingers and looked carefully at Cup's sad face.

"She said you and I could be free there too, and that our personal property would be protected."

"She *said* that?"

"Yes."

He pressed two of her opposing corners into his thumb and middle finger, then used his index finger to rotate her on that axis. Each of her different faces appeared, some upside down, some right side up, and some at a steep angle: neutral, unamused, surprised, frowny, sad, happy. The many facets of his only—

In the dreadful silence, Nak stared at the flames below, looking for a long time.

He took one step back. And then another.

But he didn't cock his arm behind him. Instead, he lifted her up and gazed at her neutral face.

He couldn't cling to the lie anymore, as embarrassing as the truth was: He wasn't just disposing of a piece of unruly hardware.

This really was his only friend.

And he couldn't just go on without her.

When he finally spoke, it was with a mild tone, deflated, low as the dirt. He might've even felt surrender—a feeling unfamiliar and hard to define.

He also felt a thread of curiosity:

"What else did you and Kalh talk about, Cup."

K ALH WAS IN the cockpit when Nak came back aboard.

He thought he saw a luminous red glow coming from the skin of her arms, but she shifted uncomfortably, so he didn't ask.

He placed Cup on the dashboard with a snap. She didn't say a word.

The three of them sat in the cockpit together as they picked up the other two. Nak installed the replacement parts, juiced the zentisal batteries, and blasted into the sky with that dropship burning like a pyre. While Benton and Liink finished cleaning up, Nak got to spend more time with Kalh. Wouldn't be long till he'd be dropping her off. Probably never see her again.

He glanced at the holo as a cluster of starships appeared and began pursuit.

Kalh had fear in her tone: "This is just like last time!"

"They're too far behind. Can't stop this surge." Nak laughed.

"What's funny?" she asked.

"I'm just glad to give a farewell to Taiberos."

When he said that name, she turned pale and glanced down at her hands resting right over her belly button. "What do you mean?"

"You've seen the massive explosion when a surge drive surges, right?"

"Well, yeah. Not up close."

"It's *The Sanctum's* way of saying goodbye. This whole sky is gonna light up in a flash of white, like lightning across the universes—boom! At the very moment it's too late for that bastard to do anything. I'm just sad I won't get to see his face."

In the mirror, Kalh seemed to grimace.

"You okay?"

"It's not farewell. Taiberos rules the galaxy. His Witch Hunters know no borders."

"Yeah, it's… dangerous. But you'll be home soon. You must still have family there, right?"

"Not really. Some old friends."

"Who."

"Dr Warnur. He delivered me. He's sort of a kindly grandfather. Taught me how to give a proper handshake."

Nak thought of the handshake she'd given when they first met. Still didn't know what it meant. "You don't seem too excited."

"You think there's a chance the Witch Hunters will know we're coming?"

"If you know how to pilot a Bloody Wing, you drop out of infraspace as gently as a kiss. Makes the landing radiationally silent. It's the opposite of a departure. No one will notice our arrival—we'll just suddenly be there. You're worried?"

"Yeah."

"I don't have to drop you off with Benton and Liink. You tell me which system, and I'll take you. Anywhere. No extra charge."

"I don't know where else to go."

Now the worry appeared on *his* face as he looked into the mirror at her. What could he say to that. Not everyone had a Bloody Wing.

He reached with his red sleeve and pulled the lever. The black of space transformed into the confusing pattern of infraspace.

The sky flashed white as they vanished.

TAIBEROS SIGHED.

He sat in his private suite. The fragments of the broken earpiece lay on the floor where he had swept them. Not good service here at the Strand.

He glared at his secretary.

"What?" she asked.

"This report makes no sense."

"I assumed the Lethos part was a hallucination from the exhaust."

"I am not asking for your insights."

The girl looked down.

She was quite beautiful, so he kept her around. For her zentisal talent. A little too obstinate though. Sometimes he wondered who was using who. A little of both, he supposed.

He needed to teach her to shut up.

Like most people, she believed Lethos to be a myth, the sort of thing school kids talked about to scare each other. Taiberos knew differently.

Unfortunately, Lethos was not a being that could be called via relay on a whim.

The door beeped.

Taiberos watched as his secretary's graceful backside went to the door. She invited in the guest—an officer with an offensively slender nose.

"Tellarton, I hate your report."

The man stood as straight as his snout. "Sir, those are exactly the facts."

"What do you expect me to make of it?"

"I don't know, sir, but whoever was masquerading as the Lethos creature was spotted by one of my men."

"Why the hell didn't you stop him then?"

"We have no excuse, sir. You have my apologies, and the troops have been reprimanded."

"Not good enough."

"I came to tell you there's a Shade here to see you."

The only starsystems in the galaxy that mattered were the ones connected by surge gates. For the most part, whoever ruled a given surge gate ruled the corresponding system. Taiberos and his PSD ruled more than half of the surge gates. The next biggest competitor was the Shadowlyss, an ancient, fascist cult that controlled around thirty percent of the gates. A Shade was a rank-and-file member of their military, an infantry foot soldier.

"What does he want?" asked Taiberos.

"He says he bears a message about the escapee."

"Dray?"

"I assume so, yes, but he says he will only speak with you. We've searched him for poisons and weapons. Would you like to speak with him? We could do it in person or over a comms relay if that seems safer to you."

"Send him up."

"Yes, sir."

"You're excused."

"Yes, sir." That nose of Tellarton's let itself out of the room.

Taiberos looked at the growing stack of letters on his desk.

He'd planned to follow the escapees. Planned to know more about the girl's conspiracy by now too. Instead, they'd seen that bright flash of light across the black of space. Starchild had escaped, and the woman's trail had gone cold. And now Lord Admiral Dray—the consolation prize—seemed to be gone as well. The Strand was supposed to be inescapable, but they'd lost two in a row.

Taiberos sighed, ready to kill.

He hated Starchild.

That one thought seemed to trump all others.

Taiberos practically ruled the entire galaxy. He did have competitors, but they were politicians, men who controlled planets and systems. This Starchild was nothing of the sort. A complete nobody. That made the situation all the more vexing. He needed to be punished for what he had done, for assuming to take more than he deserved.

Taiberos leaned forward and tapped on the console at his desk, cringing at the grime he noticed on it. It beeped pleasantly four times.

"Lieutenant Hevold here, your excellency. What may I do for you?"

"Hevold, I need precise reconnaissance on Starchild. I want you watching him as closely as possible. I need to know where in the galaxy he shows up next. And get someone in here to clean this console."

"Sir, it isn't possible to trace a Bloody Wing."

"It also isn't possible to survive without food and supplies. Contact local law enforcement in all PSD systems. Find out when and where he's restocking. Sniff him out. Do whatever it takes. The next time one thirteen shows up on the grid, I want to know about it. Is that understood?"

"Yes, sir. What if he's refitted it?"

"Find him."

"Yes, sir!"

When Taiberos glanced up, he saw his secretary staring with an uneasy look. "What?"

"I set the mail there on your desk. Another letter from your wife. Did you get the last one?"

"What does she want?"

"Same thing as the last one."

"Tell me now."

"Your brother in law was killed. You didn't know, did you?" It seemed strange that she of all people would have sympathy for Taiberos's wife. If anything, she should be glad to see a rival suffering. It did not make sense. Maybe enough time had passed that the secretary's loyalties were turning. Just like the others.

"Who killed him?"

"An accident. Completely unexpected. That adds to the poignance."

Little ███ probably tripped over his own rifle.

"Your wife reached out to me directly. She's deeply disturbed. And wants you to return home."

"I cannot come now."

"The funeral will be in two cycles. You'll have to leave right away to make it."

"I said I cannot come, and I do not like you communicating behind my back. He should've picked a better time to die." Little ███. At least he'd distract the spotlight of the broadcasts momentarily.

"Your absence will be noticed."

"Hopefully they'll also notice the important matters resting on my shoulders."

"It will be a public insult to your wife and her family if you're not there."

"She can handle herself."

"It's not just the publicity. She is asking for you to come home while she grieves." This secretary was bold, and that had once excited him, but it was too much now. Their intimacies did not give this ███ permission to question him.

Instead of answering, he stared till his eyes glossed over.

Anyone can be a Radiance.

The girl who escaped had the same fire. Insubordination and conspiracy. He had personally tasted her beauty, and yet he couldn't imagine why they considered her to be crucial. No one was crucial, except for himself. Unless she held some secret… When he caught her, he would see to it that she was killed. He would make it gruesome too, as a warning to anyone else who defied him.

The blue light on the comms blinked, indicating a relay had come through. Taiberos's eyes came back into focus, aiming at the light. He tapped the activation switch. "What is it?"

"Sir, a report from Taice."

"Go ahead."

"Admiral Fovet has captured the surge gate."

Taiberos's thinning scalp tingled. It meant he, as leader of the PSD, now had one more planetary system in his grip. It proved once again the power of the PSD's navy. No one could match them, not even the Shadowlyss.

And yet Starchild had managed to defy him again.

"Send him my congratulations."

"Yes, sir.

Now the door beeped, and the secretary stepped gracefully to answer it. Three men were there. The one in the middle was clearly the Shade. He'd been stripped of his uniform, and his hands were tied behind his back. He was decent looking. Could've made a consort.

"Bring him over here," Taiberos commanded.

The men came and stood directly in front of his grand desk.

"What do you want?" asked Taiberos.

"I bring a message from Lethos."

Taiberos consciously kept his breathing steady. "What is it?"

"The message says, you'll find the conspirators on Solace."

Taiberos glanced at his cybernetic hand, flexing the fingers one at a time. He had not simply seen Lethos. The two of them had made a deal. A deal that set Taiberos on a collision course with Starchild, and which eventually led to becoming president of the PSD. Yet Taiberos had never completed his side of the bargain. "Did he say anything about a debt being due?"

"No, sir."

Taiberos had never fully completed the task for political reasons. He couldn't go that far, a fact that Lethos seemed to understand and had not pushed. Yet. But this Solace tip was hardly a favor, and certainly not a deep insight. The woman was from there and seemed to be linked with the politics. It was obvious. "Where on Solace?"

"I'm sorry. I know it's vague, but that's all it is: You'll find the conspirators on Solace."

Taiberos frowned.

So Lethos wanted him to go to Solace.

There was always great mystery behind this creature. Taiberos had never regretted their deal, just that Starchild had gotten away in the process. Creating the Strand had served Taiberos, but Lethos benefitted as well. Perhaps this was the same—Taiberos would be the puppet and would benefit alongside the puppeteer. "You're dismissed."

"You want us to let him go?" asked one of the accompanying officers.

"Yes. Let him go."

The men departed, and the door closed behind them.

Taiberos tapped several keys on the comms. "Send this message to Kavalion: I want him to go to Solace with as many Witch Hunters as he can spare. I want them scouring for the girl we captured on Sream—she escaped, and I have reason to believe she might be there. She is with Starchild, the pilot of Bloody Wing one thirteen. I want him apprehended at any cost, dead if necessary. And I want spies among the civilians. There is a conspiracy underway, and I want to know about it. You got all that?"

"Yes, sir. It will go out with the next courier."

"Oh, and tell him to make sure Shauu is with them." The miin with the red eyes.

"Yes, sir."

"Mmm." Taiberos ended the relay with a tap. He then scowled at his secretary. "Have *The Dirigisme* prepare to embark for Solace immediately. And tell Admiral Selder to have his Behemoth prepped and ready to be queued at the surge gate at a moment's notice." He would find the conspirators. He would make them pay.

Especially Starchild.

"Sir, if this is about that Bloody Wing, I must object," said the secretary. "While you're the president, you already have not one, but two of them!"

"What Starchild did was underhanded and unscrupulous. It is not right to let him get away with that."

She stood and leaned both hands onto his desk. She'd learned on occasion to be intimately close to him, and she seemed to assume that those rights extended to this moment as well: "But your wife. How can you—"

Taiberos stood and slapped the woman.

Caught completely off guard by the cybernic impact, she tumbled off her high heels and onto the ground.

She stared up at him. In her eyes was an accusation of betrayal.

His metal hand had left her skin bleeding. She would have a bruise too, a wound hard to cover. Perhaps even a fractured bone. Her problems though, not his.

They stared at each other.

She looked away, but the shock did not leave her face, as if for the first time she'd become conscious of a nightmare all around her. In truth, she'd known it all along, but her desire to climb into society's higher echelons had been too strong.

So she lied to herself.

He had disillusioned her with that slap.

It was a favor.

Taiberos spoke with a gentle voice, something like a fatherly reminder: "In your place. Now get them ready to embark. We're going to Solace."

I T FELT LIKE a nightmare.

A black abyss suspended Kalh in midair. It surrounded her. Choked at her throat. The exhaust from Building 13 did this to her, kept her in a constant state of disorientation. Taiberos did this to her.

Her head was spinning. No, her whole body was spinning.

Nausea pushed against the insides of her gut.

She opened her eyes with a gasp.

The area around her was completely black, except for a faint glow coming from—

Oh! She couldn't feel the ground beneath her.

She was completely weightless, hanging in midair. She reached out, and her knuckles cracked against a wall. Pain shot through her casted arm. "Ow!"

Because she was floating, the collision turned her body, rolling her over, and spinning more nausea into her brain. She wanted to call for help, but she worried only the guards from Building 13 would hear her.

No, wait. Not Taiberos. She wasn't at the Strand.

Her eyes began to glow. *The Sanctum*. She was aboard Nak's skycraft.

His voice echoed through the internal comms: "Hey, the targravs switched off. I'm about to re-engage. Heads up."

Kalhette grabbed the bed frame and pulled her floating self above the mattress.

Gravity came back gently, like slowly accelerating in a planetary vehicle. First she just touched. Then she sank deeper, then deeper still, until she felt the bodyweight she was used to. The acceleration continued past that till it had reached Nak's comfort level, and there it held—pretty heavy in here.

She breathed a sigh. Heavy and stable. Her nausea halted, no longer getting any worse, but it wasn't going to get better quickly either.

She heard a knock on metal, three times, and she sat up in her bunk. "Come in."

The door zoomed open.

Nak entered. A red glow came from a device in his hand and illuminated the scruff on his chin. "You all right?" He'd removed his jacket and just wore a black t-shirt.

"Yes." She felt vulnerable with him in her room, but he'd knocked, and she still kind of owed him an apology. "What happened?"

"Sometimes the targravs kick off when we settle back into normal space." That meant it had been more than a few isochrons—it seemed she could sleep with no end.

"We're there?" She wasn't ready. Part of her wanted to run and keep running, to never give anyone a chance to capture her again.

"Almost. Cup's guiding us in. Be another three isos till we touch down."

Kalh had seen the insides of his beloved *Sanctum*—from the many copies of the same jacket to his father's prism hanging in a shadowbox. A look into his soul. Something about him reminded her of Tannie, aside from Tannie being atypically small and this man atypically large. Still, she found herself rooting for him.

"Plenty more time to sleep if you want," he said.

"I *want* it, but I'm not sure I need it." Still, it would help the nausea. She unconsciously tapped her casts against each other.

"Maybe you can grab a little extra for me then."

She chuckled. "So you like this heavier gravity, huh?"

"Keeps you nestled in snug."

"When it's on."

"That's the weight I grew up with."

"Solace is probably seventy percent of this."

"Seventy four."

"It's going to be a breeze for you." He was intimidating in this quiet room, but she had something she needed to get off her chest. They might not get another moment alone. She cleared her throat. "Hey, Nak?"

"Yeah."

"Uh… Do you have a moment?"

He grabbed the rail of her bed and sat onto the bench below her bunk. "Sure. What's up."

Now she couldn't see him, but maybe that would make this easier. "I just wanted to say that I'm sorry for what I said. I wasn't very sensitive."

When he didn't answer, she wished she could see his face.

She tried to lean out off the bunk, but with her casted arms and the heavy gravity, she could only lean far enough to see the red light on the device in his hand, which provided a dim but clear glow across the room. She could've peered right through the bed, but she wasn't sure how he'd take it.

He chuckled.

"What?" she asked.

"Nothing."

"And I'm sorry I talked to your Cupcake. Is everything going to be okay with her?"

"For now."

"For now?"

All he said was, "Yeah."

"I wish I could see you better, but I'm not sure I want you to watch me climb down with my arms like this."

He laughed, then stood and faced her. "You want help?"

She felt a little uncertain what he meant, but she said, "Sure."

"Come here." He held out his hands like a father inviting his child. It exposed the tattoo on the inside of his left forearm.

She started to climb over the rail, leaning on her elbows, preferring to do it herself. The nausea, gravity, and broken arms made her pause halfway over the railing. Although not child-sized compared to him, she was quite a bit smaller. He gently grabbed her beneath the arms, lowered her to the ground, and then sat himself back on the couch.

She was glad Benton hadn't watched that.

She stood for an awkward moment, not sure what she'd gotten herself into, then finally sat down on the bench next to him. She leaned her head back, which stabilized her spinning brain. It was fine for friends to sit together on benches. "What does your tattoo mean?"

"I can't tell you." Up close, she noticed that scratch on his face from when those rocks fell on him.

"Actually, what I really want to know is what you think the best part of this skycraft is... Can you tell me that?"

"If I told you, then you'd want to steal it."

"No I won't."

"Yes you will."

"Is it Cupcake?"

"I don't count Cup as part of the ship."

"Then what is it?"

He smiled with pursed lips and shook his head like a child. His face was bathed in the soft red glow, emphasizing the scratches on his face.

"Oh, come on!" She moved in closer, eager to secure his forgiveness. "Cupcake doesn't seem like a normal android to me. Where'd you get her?"

He looked at her and with some kind of debate in his eyes. "Have I ever mentioned how I like your accent?"

She smiled and shook her head at his dodge, but that jiggled the nausea back. She leaned away. "Why do you like it?"

"I don't know. There's something irresistible about it. Might be why they threw you in Building 13."

With a frown, she jabbed her elbow at his side, but because of her injured arm, she did it so gently it was barely more than a press. "Don't joke about that."

"Your martial arts could use a little work."

She closed her eyes and butted her nauseous head forward into the air in his direction.

The couch wiggled as an equal kinotic force hit him in the side. "Whoa. That was weird."

She grinned, squinting. The motion made her feel like vomiting.

"So is that why they risked three people's lives to save you?"

"No, actually. It's because I can surge."

"I'm pretty good at that myself."

"I can do it just with my body."

"What do you mean."

"Just what I said."

"Then why didn't you just surge out of Building 13?"

"They have toxins. Can't do it with a clouded mind or an increased heart rate."

"That place sounds like hell."

"It is."

"I'm sorry you had to go through it."

She started to cry.

Like the whole bottled up nightmare had cracked and was flowing unstoppably. She'd faced it alone, and Taiberos alone, and the memories alone.

By herself. In perfect exile.

Because she was broken, defiled, worthless.

She put her hands on her bald head, hiding the tears and her vulnerability. Her whole body shook as she wept.

After a long time, she said, "I'm sorry... for... crying..."

As she sobbed, he put his arm around her.

And just sat with her patiently, holding her with his strength.

Between sobs, she spoke the dreadful truth in a whisper: *"He violated me."*

"You mean..."

She nodded, not looking at him. *"Taiberos. I was hardly conscious."*

"He—" Nak stopped. Heat radiated from his body. An immense fury like a blazing sun. She felt his heart thumping.

And then calm. He willed it in himself. As if for her sake alone. He became calm.

With pain in his voice, he said, "That makes me want to cry too. I am so sorry."

As she cried, his arm rested around her.

It felt safe, like he wasn't judging.

Like he didn't mind whether she'd been broken and defiled.

THE ENGINE HUMMED.

They sat like that for a long time, till her body stilled and her cheeks began to dry. Eventually she wiped her eyes with a thumb and finger and then dared to look at him, trying to show appreciation with a smile.

That made her think of Benton.

Nak smiled back with compassion and a boyish twinkle in his eye, as if he knew a secret way to escape this heaviness. "You can really surge? Just your body?"

"Yeah." She grinned with teary eyes.

"That's why Taiberos wanted you."

"Still wants me."

"I'm sorry. We'll stop the bastard."

"How?"

"I don't know. How far can you do it?"

"It's intuitive," said Kalh.

"Your limit is intuitive?"

"I just know how far I'm not willing to try."

"Whatever that is, why not try a little farther?"

"It's like jumping over a chasm. If you try one farther than you can jump, you fall to your death, so you never find the limit because you're keeping a safe distance."

"When I want to see how far I can jump, I jump on grass instead of cliffs…"

"Okay, wise guy. It's like your *Sanctum's* surge spiral. If you jump without the right parameters, bad things happen."

"A black-hole vortex."

"Something like that. If you do infraspace wrong, you die."

"I want to see you surge, right here." He pointed at the wall.

"My next performance will probably be on Solace. You'll have to come if you want to see it."

"What do you mean probably."

"Benton wants me to help him with something."

"And."

She hesitated. "I'm afraid to do it." Because she wasn't a warrior goddess, because it was too much pressure, and because she wanted to hide from the whole galaxy.

"Why."

"Nak, you now know something very personal about me. I just trusted you with a secret I literally haven't told a soul. And I can't help but notice—how do I put this?—that the person *you* trust the most is artificial."

He didn't say anything—just didn't respond, as if she'd never said it. Maybe he was considering sharing a secret. Or maybe he was thinking of how soon he'd be rid of her.

"See, like right now. I have no idea what you're thinking. But I want to know. I want you to trust me."

He still didn't speak, content with the silence.

"So may I ask you a personal question?"

"Sure."

"Okay. Where'd you get that prism in your engine-core room?"

"The what?"

"The Singblade."

"Oh. The psykatana." Nak breathed for a few moments, and it seemed like he wouldn't answer, till he said, "It belonged to my father. My, uh… dad."

"Was he a Zhan?"

"No."

"Why did he have it?"

"Don't know for sure. I was too young and stupid to ask a question like that."

"Maybe it belonged to his father…"

"Wouldn't that be something."

"A green prism is very rare," she said. "Do you know what the inscription says?"

"No."

"It's Photoss. I'd guess it's the name."

"The name of the psykatana?" He seemed surprised.

"Yes. Do you know how to turn it on?"

"It doesn't turn on. It's just a prop."

"They don't run on power. They're psionic."

His mouth cracked open, and he looked up at the dark ceiling, as if reframing percents of questions all in one moment.

"We call it Anomis," she said. "It's fourth spectrum. Not easy to do."

When he still didn't answer, she put a hand on his shoulder and a hand on his knee and looked squarely up at him, with a most serious look on her face.

She had to find out.

Her eyes began to glow.

Just like Tannie's had that fateful cycle.

Nak recoiled just slightly, flinching and leaning back as the white light from her eyes fell on his face and reflected in his blue eyes. He'd probably never witnessed the godspell in another person, especially not this close.

For her, Starsight allowed her to see much more deeply—the bones of his skull and the heat of his heart.

He turned, leaned down, and moved his face close to hers, as if to challenge her.

And then his eyes began to glow.

She gasped.

They stared at each other. Breathing.

And seeing.

With glowing eyes shining on each other.

Seeing right down to the soul.

It meant the Witch Hunters would do the same to him as they had done to Tannie and to her.

Nak's eyes winked out first.

She let hers drop back to normal too. "You did that easily."

He swallowed. "You know enough about me now."

* * *

THAT'S FIRST SPECTRUM—STARSIGHT. Is that all you know?"

"Yeah."

She pushed her lips to the side, considering.

He watched them carefully.

You weren't supposed to discuss the mysteries with the uninitiated, and yet... "Want to learn second spectrum?"

With a slight grin, he said, "Yes."

She stood and tapped the light on. With casted arms, she pointed at the ribbon of plants that wrapped the room. "If Master Jyngsoo were here, he'd have you sit forever and notice the vividness, notice how the stalk is darker than the leaves, the shades of gray on the ridges, the reddish tone on the deeper parts."

"Who's that?"

"My mentor. He'd say, 'The more fully you see visible light, the more readily you'll glimpse what's next.'"

He looked at her like a child listening to his parent. Just like Tannie.

She sat back down and their arms touched. "What do you believe about the purpose of life?"

"I don't know."

"You'll have to do better than that."

"There's something bigger out there. I just don't know where to find it. Sometimes I think we mortals just aren't big enough to grasp it."

"What do you know about the Zhani?"

"I talked to Liink about them a few cycles ago."

"And...?"

"Seems hokey."

"What?"

"And you're not allowed to have sex."

Kalh laughed.

"So it's true."

"Not exactly. Think of it as temperance."

"So don't have too much."

"You can have as much as you want as long as it's at the right time."

"When is that."

"After you've sworn lifelong fealty."

"Whoa. You mean *marriage*." He said it like a curse word.

She nodded. "Yep. That's the rule." Her nausea seemed to be decreasing inversely to her enthusiasm.

"As a general rule, I don't believe in rules."

She laughed.

He looked at her carefully, as if to read her history. "How do you know if they're the right person if you haven't... you know..."

"I wouldn't know. Wedlock is a public commitment to strive even when things get bad, which, apparently, they usually do. You promise to solve problems instead of walking away."

He still stared at her intently. "What about kissing."

"Before marriage?"

"Yeah."

"Kissing is okay…" She trailed off, distracted first by his gaze and then by the thought of the last man she'd kissed—Benton.

Nak bobbed his head back and forth, considering.

The word *kissing* seemed to echo. She cleared her throat. "Okay, lift up your hands." She raised her own in their casts to show him, and he followed. "When you did that just now, what mental process did you go through to get them to move?"

"Nothing. I just… moved them, I guess."

"Exactly. It's not an *I would like to move my hands* or *I am going to move my hands*. It's present tense: *I'm moving my hands.* Moving an external object is the exact same process. It's entirely spontaneous."

"It can't be the exact same. My hands have nerves connected to my brain."

"A similar network runs throughout space and time. It's called the Song. And if you can see the Song, then you can send your will across it."

"I think you're mixing metaphors."

"What do you mean?"

"Are you talking about sight or sound?"

"It's called the Song because it's a symphony of light."

"Oh," he said, surprised. "So sight, not sound."

"Yeah. Kind of."

His eyes glowed again, and he peered around the room, turning his head slowly, ponderously. Surely he saw fragments of the Song if not its whole glory spread across the galaxy of this small room.

"With Starsight, you're looking outward at the world. It's selfless. And there's something called Silentsong, where you're looking inward. But there's a point between those two, the place where you pivot from outward to inward, the line between physical and spiritual. That point is you—Sacredspark. Master Jyngsoo likes the word *ipseity*. It means self-ness. And it takes selfness to do Kinosis, which is second spectrum."

"You're kind of blowing my mind right now."

"We call it Initiative. It's centered in the body, not the mind or heart. It's about agility and kinesthetics, about choosing rather than perceiving, about movement in three-dimensional space and the rhythm of time. It's about proprioception, which I imagine you're good at."

"Why."

"Because of your knack for sailing."

"Ha ha." He nodded, ready for action.

She pointed. "Okay. I want you to push and pull that towel."

As if in a trance, his eyes glowed. He reached out his fingers.

At first nothing happened. The towel hung still.

His fingers steadied as his hand connected to the towel through tiny strings of light, so tiny that a sharp movement might break the tension.

"Now pull."

His hands curled, fingers wrapping down. The towel fluttered gently toward him, no stronger than if nudged by his breath.

"If you're really good at Starsight, you can actually see the light that Kinosis creates. Now push."

His hands pushed outward, fingers splaying, and the towel swayed, but only just barely, back, then forth, then back, following the rhythm of his hands as they spread and contracted, as if he controlled both ends of the wind. As he manipulated it, a hum sounded, shifting in pitch, a deep, magnetic vibration. He laughed, still doing it, transfixed, and the towel swayed.

"Wow," she said.

"What," he asked.

"You shouldn't have been able to do that on your first try. Not by a long shot. That's very unusual. Very."

"You saying I'm gifted?"

With a smirk, she flicked her wrist up, and the towel flew with speed and force. She caught it on her casted arm. "This is how I crashed that groundrunner. You practice enough, and you'll learn to throw your whole body weight into it." She flipped the towel up onto the bed.

His eyes dimmed to their usual state. "I can't believe I had this all this time."

"Because of a lie propagated by the Witch hunters. Anyone *could* access the Song if they'd try. That's why Liink has never progressed."

Nak turned his hands and inspected his palms.

Then he looked at her, aghast, as if she were a Photoss standing in the air in front of him.

She didn't deserve that kind of awe.

REALLY CAN'T BELIEVE it."

Kalh half smiled at him.

"So you're telling me everyone's a Radiance," said Nak.

"It takes work. And you have to believe it's possible or you won't try. But yes."

"So I've been on the run from the Witch Hunters all this time, and yet they could've discovered the Radiance in any random bum."

"Yes." Taiberos, in a way, was ultimately a threat to every living creation—every facet of the Song. She sat on the bench. "How did you first discover the godspell?"

He was quiet for a bit. "After my dad died, I fell in with a tougher crowd. They liked Frostblade, which I thought qualified them as friends. They convinced me to take a dose of Orikerse, now, I realize, because they were afraid to test it themselves. At the time, I didn't even know what Starsight looked like from the outside. My eyeballs just felt warm as the world started to look so much deeper than before. It freaked them out. Hadn't suspected I'd be a Radiance. I was a kid struggling to survive, practically an orphan, mother half mad, and I had to go on the run from the Witch Hunters. You asked what made me this way. It was a lot of things, and Starsight was one of them. It felt like a curse."

Just like Tannie after all.

She wanted to nestle up to Nak, to hug him and tell him it would be okay. And save him as recompense for not saving Tannie. Instead, she just sat there.

"How are your arms feeling," he asked.

"They're healing quickly."

He touched the skin of her left arm at the edge of the cast. "What's this."

Part of her tattoo showed—three braided ribbons and a curving script in a deep purple ink. "It says *e lissia kalha.*"

He squinted. "What's it mean."

"It's a Zhani phrase from *The Radiance Heretical.*"

"The what?"

"An old religious text."

"I thought heretics were bad guys."

"A heretic is someone who believes different from what's popular."

"Oh." He laughed. "So heretics are your primary role models."

She giggled. "Basically."

"Where'd you get it?"

She held her breath, trying not to squirm with discomfort. As she tried to think of something to divert the conversation, the quiet sequels ticked on painfully.

In the awkward pause, most people would've said something to relieve the tension, but Nak just gazed at her, forcing her to own the silence.

She almost admitted the truth. Almost. But then a reasonable alternative came to mind, and she almost blurted, "The words mean *reverence the light.*"

"I like it," he said, allowing her dodge. His thumb stroked across the brown K-A-L and the lumps in her veins. "I'm sorry about your arms. I mean *I'm* sorry."

"It's okay."

"Kalha is like Kalhette. Is that a coincidence?"

"No."

"So your name means light."

"Well, no. Photoss switches the syntax. Kalhette means *reverence.* The noun."

"Wow." His voice was low, almost a growl. "What a beautiful name."

She smiled.

His tone was solemn. "I'm not sure I know how to reverence."

She gave a laugh full of light. "You know how you feel when you look deep into the stars—when you acknowledge that immensity? It's like their distance overwhelms and crushes you, and yet you long for it, like you *want* to be overwhelmed and crushed. That's reverence. But mix that feeling with solemnity, and melancholy, and also with joy. Reverence is worship, submission, and awe. I think it's so vast we can't feel the whole thing at once, just pieces at a time."

"Wow, Kalh."

"What?"

Nak leaned in close, his chest rising and falling as he watched her carefully. Her heart thumped. She wasn't worthy to be kissed. Nor ready.

And what would Benton think of her—kissing a man she hardly knew?

It was too late. Without any further thought, she surrendered, her eyes drooping gently closed, as she tilted her face upward.

The warmth of Nak's lips touched hers, bringing her back to life.

Electricity tingled through every tissue of her body.

When he withdrew, she took a deep breath, almost a gasp. "What was that for?"

"Practicing my reverence."

BENTON WATCHED AS Solace grew in size.

The planet's beauty usually filled him with awe.

Not this time.

The bright crescent of Solace glowed against a backdrop of stars as they sailed toward its shadow. In the background, the sun gave off a warm, red, and unusually large glow. One star shone with particular brightness, which wasn't a star at all but the system's surge gate, revolving around the sun like a planet.

Benton took a deep breath. "Have you been on a tidally locked planet before?"

"Only one other, and I only stayed for a few isos," said Skyreacher. "Been on moons, of course." It had been strange to finally see the man's face after interacting with that dread mask for so long. It seemed like he was now a different person.

More monstrous.

Skyreacher twisted a dial on his chronometer, setting it back to account for the time that had passed aboard the ship that simply never existed in the rest of the galaxy. He nodded at the Twilight Ring. "You ever get tired of the sunset?"

Liink's voice had the softness of a child's lullaby: "It's a sunrise."

Solace rotated at the exact rate at which she revolved, meaning the same side of the planet always faced her parent star. On the surface, that meant no day-night cycles. Deep browns covered most of the sunside, with a few distinct swaths of yellow and orange, and there the light would never vanish. Darkness covered the starside and would never leave. Between light and darkness lay the Twilight Ring, their destination, where the sun would remain always tantalizingly just out of sight, and where life thrived most fully. From one side of it, little webs of lights grew like roots into the night. From the other side, a smattering of white clouds made their suicidal dashes toward the sun. And in that middle, the narrow ring, the most vibrant greens and blues reigned, brushed in elegant strokes.

"Seems like it'd be hard to navigate without the sun marking east and west," said Skyreacher. "And no seasons."

"That took some getting used to." Benton stole a glance from the corner of his eye, secretly fuming on the inside. It was entirely Skyreacher's fault that Kalhette had been injured and could've been killed. And that man let her stay on the ship the second time, which proved he'd been wrong to distrust her the first time. Benton took a deep breath and exhaled slowly. His personal creed warned against hatred, and he felt determined to get over it. Somehow. "Seasons are instability. Solace has a more eternal quality to it."

Skyreacher nodded but hardly seemed convinced.

Benton put a finger over his lips. "From the Twilight Ring, you can always see the direction of the sun, so you know where the subsolar pole is. It's kind of like having a compass in the sky."

"Subsolar?"

"It's kind of like a second north," said Benton. "It's the geographic center of the sunside, the point where the sun resides permanently overhead."

One of Liink's claws tapped the window. His breath puffed against the glass as he looked reverently at his homeworld. The bandage across his dark purple fur was a badge of honor. "The sun is always over that point, which creates intense heat, so the air rises, creating the wind patterns." Liink's people had become Benton's people: They'd given him a title of honor, they held his speeches in the highest respect, and he'd participated in all of their most sacred rituals—except for siid, of course. Maybe he could use that influence to spin Liink's role into an abiisu song.

Skyreacher seemed like a real advocate for Liink as well. More so than Kalhette. So that was at least one positive thing.

"Yeah. I read that your wind has a direction," said Skyreacher. "Don't really get how it can have flow if it's all bubbling out from that one point."

"The windward direction exists generally but not universally," said Benton.

Liink pointed at the planet, now nearly filling the windscreen. "Our maps focus on the Twilight Ring. It's the most hospitable area, obviously. Some areas have nearly constant rain."

"Eternal rain in eternal twilight," said Skyreacher.

"Few outsiders recognize the beauty of that," said Benton.

"Do many people live outside of the Twilight Ring?"

"Not many," said Benton. "Compared to the galactic average, Solace is very close to her sun, but the winds circulate the atmosphere enough to make both sides survivable a little ways past the twilight. The main issues on the sunside are finding water and shade. On the starside, it's energy and warmth. Miina clans have made lives in both harsh climates. Caves beyond the edges of twilight help—Solace is riddled with them. No one lives as far out as the subsolar or antisolar poles though. It's so far, and there's no reason to be that distant from life and trade."

"I wouldn't say no reason…" Skyreacher pointed to his dashboard. "Darii's on the boreal—I'm looking at the right map, right?"

"Yes, boreal."

The ship descended into the planet's shadow, and the vivid colors of the Twilight Ring became all the brighter.

Skyreacher admittedly had talent. That catch in the canyon had saved Benton and Liink's lives, for which he deserved proper respect. He'd be

POLES OF SOLACE

Boreal Pole

Austral Pole

Windward Direction

Windside Pole

Sunside Pole
(Subsolar)

Starside Pole
(Antisolar)

Leeside Pole

good to have in the upcoming fight, as long as the money didn't run out. To be fair, any mercenary was like that. Skyreacher could not be held to some ideal he'd never grasped. He didn't deserve Benton's hate.

Or jealousy.

This vista grew so large it filled the entire view.

"So this is your home, huh, Liink," asked Skyreacher.

The miin nodded and smiled proudly. "Solace holds the promise of liberty, like no other planet ever before, if we manage to pay the cost."

The pilot clicked his tongue. "And this whole operation was so Kalh can be part of your battle plan."

"She's central." Benton didn't want to talk about Kalhette.

"Because of her skills with… whatever you call it."

"I call it the Song," said Benton.

"Yeah, you've each tried explaining it but…" Skyreacher zoomed his right hand over his own head. "Bad coordinates, I guess."

"The Song is the sacred order of things," said Benton.

"Too abstract." Was Skyreacher actually interested or just filling the quiet? He certainly hadn't been curious on the voyage to Toar.

Still, Benton felt eager to avoid silence. "The fabric of spacetime just happens to be the perfect value for elements to form. The universes themselves should be torn apart by dark energy, leaving them lifeless and black and lethal to anything that tried to breathe. Instead we find them filled with things like life and light. The Song is this natural, magical order, a symphony of light. It deserves awe and reverence—from those who stop long enough to see it." That last bit was admittedly a jab.

"So you worship it."

Benton sighed ever so quietly. "Most people assume their own separate tune is good enough, and they're right that it is *good,* but it *isn't* good *enough.* You have to play your melody in harmony with everything else. That takes watching closely, trying to see how we can join in, or sometimes it means sitting quietly, waiting, and listening. If that's worship, then, yes, we worship."

Skyreacher nodded and then spun his finger, as if to wind the conversation forward more quickly. This man acted like the most monumental truths in the galaxy meant nothing. "You were telling me about Kalh, about her role."

Benton refrained from shaking his head. "Oh, I think I said all I meant to."

"What are her skills."

"The same as any Zhan," said Benton. "There are nine spectra—three groups of three."

"Liink, that's what you were telling me about…"

The miin spoke up: "Yes. Abii, I mean Benton, tells me that a Zhan can progress upward through them just with practice instead of being naturally gifted. Right?"

"Yes," said Benton, "but they're each extremely challenging. It takes many percents of diligent practice. Most are considered lucky to get a solid hold on four before their lifetimes come to a close. Kalhette, however, is already a seven, meaning she can do Sorjis."

"I'd say she's more like a ten," said Skyreacher.

Benton didn't laugh. In fact, the comment burned in him.

The Bloody Wing slipped down to the surface with some freighter traffic over the Naskiin Ocean, a body of pure ice on the starside. They proceeded at a low altitude, close to the frozen terrain, till everything got warmer and lighter.

"She's still just a kid," said Skyreacher. "What she did to those groundrunners..."

"That was nothing," said Benton.

"How'd she progress so far so fast."

"I'm not sure I want to get into the intricacies right now."

"So she can surge, just her, no surge drive, no nothing?"

Benton said nothing, wondering how Skyreacher knew this.

"Yes," said Liink.

"You ever tried it?" Skyreacher seemed eager, like a little boy after a secret. "How does it work?"

"Not everything is based on practice," said Benton. "Kalhette is diligent, and yet she's also naturally gifted. The Kurosh have smiled upon her. She just has a knack."

Skyreacher mumbled something under his breath that sounded like *she has two.*

As they approached the twilight band, the horizon grew brighter, morphing from icy blue to glowing pink. Drops of moisture touched the windscreen and then zipped off the top.

Kalhette walked into the cockpit.

"Oh, wow! I missed the whole descent." She seemed livelier than before, almost like her old self was coming back. She wore a sling on her left arm. Her right was still braced, but it now hung loose at her side. No other human would've healed so fast, not without drawing on seventh spectrum. She wore a fresh, long-sleeved, gray shirt that fitted closely to her form and the purple skullhugger over her baldness. Benton had bought it for her on the second excursion.

Skyreacher didn't turn around to give his greeting: "Hey, Kalh."

She seemed to be mesmerized with the view.

Benton ran a frustrated hand through his sandy hair, which fell perfectly back into place as he faced her. "Welcome home, Kalhette."

Her eyes glinted with moisture as she stared at the vibrant landscape. A city started to appear, its features looking like a map spread out below.

"What are you feeling?" asked Benton.

She didn't answer for a long time, and her eyes glossed over. "I remember playing ball and laughing. Walking home from school in the rain. People waving colorful banners at the Fountain Square. From Stone Heights we could hear the faun horns playing through the cool mist. I cried so hard the cycle I had to leave."

Benton admired this about her. She wasn't overly cerebral. She was emotive and authentic. Uninhibited. It was beautiful and admirable and even enviable. Such a perfect complement to his own flaws.

This time Skyreacher actually turned around. "And you've never been back?"

Benton knew the answer.

A single tear rolled down her cheek, and she let it be. "Not since I was eight." Not long after her exile, her family had fled the planet too.

As the ship approached the Twilight Ring, Skyreacher stopped several times then surged his skycraft to make sure no one was following. He landed near the Palades on the outskirts.

"Skyreacher," said Benton. "I will search for the funds to pay you to join us."

The pilot nodded. "I'll be back in a few cycles after I do some repairs." That was all he said.

When Kalhette said farewell to Skyreacher, there was no physical contact, just a smile and wave—but she said something about a gift.

Benton tried not to think about it.

When they disembarked, the gravity felt noticeably lighter than it had inside the pilot's skycraft.

B ECAUSE THE PSD spy networks had become a significant threat, Benton had a friend shuttle them discreetly to Darii, Kalhette's hometown. After they dropped off Liink, Benton moved from the front seat to the back.

Kalhette gave him a kind smile. They locked eyes for a precious moment, but then she looked down shyly. She looked great in the hat.

A couple of percents ago, Benton had fallen for a woman on Pharson Nine. She'd loved him too, but he broke it off because she wanted him to settle down with her, and that meant giving up his revolution and his dream. Sometimes he questioned that decision. He'd sacrificed everything to pursue these ideals, and he dreamed of finding a partner who could do the same. One who cared about the revolution.

Someone like Kalhette.

Droplets of rain clung to the windows of the shuttle.

The strong winds of Solace pushed against the vehicle, creating a white noise that drenched everything, leaving them essentially alone.

Benton held his peace.

He knew her well enough to know that she would say something eventually. Probably unplanned and when he wasn't expecting it.

She stared past the droplets at the home planet she hadn't seen in so long, and he watched her, seeing what she saw.

From the sky, it has been easy for her memories to take the stage. From here on the streets, reality forced itself to the foreground, and no music of pipes greeted them.

Kalhette suddenly blurted, "No!" She stared fiercely out the window, the pain showing clearly on her face.

Benton followed the direction of her hazel eyes.

The rolling green hills were lined with barbed wires and lacerated with shells and shrapnel. The valleys had become muddy bogs, and a gassy smell hung on the breeze. In town, Redhelms marched along the cloister walls. Plague tanks rolled through the bruised streets. The Onaitu temple lay in ruins.

The moments she'd described from memory were lost forever.

Benton waited, and through Ptolis, he felt her rising emotions alongside her.

They sailed to Stone Heights, where Kalhette had lived as a child. The hillside had been completely hidden by the colorful houses built on top. These structures looked like they should fall off the steep slopes, but they'd always clung with tenacity until ravaged by heavy artillery, leaving many of them charred and broken. The ones that hadn't been crushed or burned had been abandoned. The Heights offered little strategic value, so they must've been gunned down for spite, for the PSD to make a point. Whatever happened, it'd been like this when Benton first came, and he suspected Taiberos had something to do with it. There would be more retribution like this if they made an attempt at freedom and failed.

"No!" Tears ran down Kalhette's face as she looked up toward the balcony that had once been hers. She turned to him and looked expectantly, yet hesitating, like she needed help but didn't know how to ask. Then, as if questioning the Song itself, she said, "What have they done?"

"Our war will make things right." He lifted his arm, not sure if it was the right thing to do, and wrapped it around her.

"I don't want war. I want my home back." She turned toward him, closed her eyes, and nestled into his embrace. Her tears wetted his shirt.

He put his other arm around her. "We'll get it back."

She wept in silence till the shuttle came to a stop.

"Benton?"

"What?"

"I am willing to become your Uncrowned Queen."

In awe, Benton gazed as if seeing her for the first time.

T HE WAR COUNCIL met at the home of Dr Warnur.
Benton and Kalhette were the first to arrive.

The other attendees showed up sporadically, one at a time, and each in disguise, each increasing Dr Warnur's risk, and yet he greeted them all with a twinkling smile. He had a full head of white hair and clothes that looked half a lifetime old. He'd been working tirelessly, eager to help, with little thought for himself. In a way, he seemed above the conflict, not bothered by how things were. In fact, he reminded Benton of Master Jyngsoo, only, Dr Warnur was no Zhan, so if he'd gained enlightenment, he'd done it instinctively.

The War Council gathered in his attic, which was lit only by the warm glow of a pair of lamps. Some called them the Renegades, a fine nickname for now, but soon they would become more than a conspiracy. Benton wanted other governments to recognize them as the Allied City States of Solace.

The galaxy at large was complacent toward the evils of the PSD, but Solace was sacred ground to many, both because of its history and because of the Hoff Mines, so the PSD had gripped it more tightly than anywhere else, which meant people here had been victimized, terrorized, and even murdered by the overreaching government. They knew what Kalhette had gone through because they'd suffered similarly, and they were ready to rise up against tyranny.

And with the right spark they would.

As of now, the factions of Solace included three main groups, each with several subgroups. The Underground, the Ruffians, and the Freedom Riders made up the colonist faction. The faction of entrepreneurs included Valt's Privateers, the Nightwatchmen sort of, and the Black Sigils. Representing the miina faction were the Irregulars and the Bloods as well as seven chieftains. Liink was not invited, but his father, Chief Adiin, represented the Bloods. He looked much like his son but broader, thicker, and with his dark fur thinning enough to reveal his dark skin. Another difference was that his horns had come through, but for the Twilight Breed that just meant small nubs on the tops of their heads, which were dwarfed by their drooping ears.

Benton liked to think that he and Kalhette represented a small fourth group, the Radiances.

The attendees saluted each other with the formal "Hail," "Halii," or, "May we be one," though few greetings were exchanged between humans and miina. Kalhette, who stood next to Benton, was supposed to be the glue to keep that fracture from reopening, and as such, every person made a point to greet her specifically. She responded cordially, overemphasizing her politeness with the miina, and they responded with adulation that made her squirm. Still, he could not be more admiring of her. She'd stepped with such poise into her new role.

One guest stood out, a miin who exuded neither excitement nor anxiety upon approaching her, but only a great calm. Unlike the other miina, he walked on all sixes, with no pretense of being vertical like the humans. He was old, which his frail prowl and the lines around his insightful eyes gave away. He had white fur and curling horns, attributes that came from his starside breed rather than his age. His name was Uumaki. As he neared her, he pushed off his front paws, standing on his hind legs. He patted her hand gently with three of his paws and said, "It's a weight you shouldn't have to carry. I am sorry we are putting you through all this."

Kalhette squinted and looked like she might burst into tears, but she fought it, and simply nodded to Uumaki, giving an appreciative, closed-lip smile. She patted the back of one of his paws and managed a "thank you" before he moved on.

The small table couldn't accommodate them all, so a few stood in a second, outer ring, where the ceiling sloped steeply downward. Wooden pillars, supporting the roof, stood as additional onlookers.

Benton watched the eyes and read their hearts.

He was younger than nearly every person here aside from Kalhette, and yet they all looked to him to lead. The warm lamps illuminated faces and cast dark shadows.

Benton began: "Our mission to rescue Kalhette Whitesun was successful, as you can see, and we believe she will be the rallying point we need—"

Before Benton could finish, Zocaster blurted: "Where's Lord Admiral Dray?"

Benton answered with a bowed head: "Dray was captured by Taiberos."

"I *knew* this would happen!" The dark circles under Zocaster's eyes sent threatening lances straight at Benton.

The attic fell completely silent.

The horrors of Building 13 seemed to float around the room. Benton felt sick. And guilty. For what Taiberos had done and for what he still might do. Yet he hoped the synergy of this group could make up for the loss of one brilliant tactician.

"And what if Dray reveals the plan to our enemies?" demanded Zocaster. "What if he breaks?"

"The threat of our plan leaking has always been present."

"Never more than now."

"I do not believe Dray will break, but we can hedge against that by changing our plan, moving into action more quickly…" Benton's words trailed off, and he felt the trust of the audience slipping already. "Our fight has always been a gamble, a leap of faith, yet we all have dared to proceed because of principles not promises."

An unassured silence followed.

Uumaki, the old, white miin with curled horns, anxiously stroked his white jaw as he cleared his throat. "Benton, please tell us your plan."

"It's not my plan. It's Dray's plan. And we can still carry it out."

Zocaster jumped to his feet. "That's not good enough!" Others murmured their fears.

Uumaki stood, an equal and opposite reaction to his human counterpart across the table: "Gentlemen! Please." He waited for tempers to steady. "Benton, go on."

The young man felt deeply grateful for the gesture. He stood tall as he continued, compensating for how he actually felt. He cleared his throat and began to relay Dray's plan. "We have three main objectives. The first is to infiltrate the Athenaeum where Kalhette's broadcast will take place. She will call the populace to arms, inspiring and assembling our militia through the PSD's own comms." He glanced neutrally at the table. "This is Blue Group, which my team will lead." His green eyes looked up again.

Everyone in the room watched him closely.

"The second objective is to take the armories. We're calling this Red Group, and it will be coordinated by High Chief Adiin."

Liink's father gave a humble nod.

"The third objective is starbound. It is to capture our planet's surge gate. That will be Green Group, headed by Mister Valt."

Valt pushed his lips together and out, which seemed almost like a thrust of his mustache, as he gave a lazy salute.

"Each of these is crucial—we cannot budge even a finger's breadth in execution."

A heavy gravitas seemed to press down.

Hands around the table raised with questions.

Dandor shouted his question: "Instead of capturing the surge gate, why can't we just destroy the brackets?"

"We can't do that," said Benton. "Free galactic commerce is essential for our long term success."

"Our long term won't matter if we can't win this."

"It's not feasible!" said Valt with his characteristic enthusiasm. "Bringing down the shields would take too long!"

"Our window will be brief," said Benton.

The discussion shifted toward debate, and several questioned Benton's strategy and his expertise. He reminded them that Dray himself had organized it. Others said planning had already taken too long and that PSD spies would surely doom their efforts if Dray himself did not.

Jamie Bladoor, a member of the Underground militia, pointed a finger in the air, and caught the group's attention. With the sincerest concern on his face, he said, "I fear it cannot be done, Xylander, even if we keep it secret. None of us has the required military prowess. And if we can't do it, we'll be risking the lives of every individual involved. All on a fool's hope. Some of us have families. Little children. And if success is so unlikely, how can we take that risk?"

Benton stood, and his chair scraped the floor as it slid back. Eyes turned toward him. "With your children in mind, how can you *not* take it? It's their future at stake."

Bladoor said nothing.

"That choice is yours," said Benton. "No one here will be coerced into helping our cause. You'll step into harm's way by your own volition, and you'll face the rewards of that choice." Benton glanced down, his tone lowering. "I, for one, face those consequences gladly."

"And what if the worst should happen?" asked Bladoor.

Benton leaned onto the table with both hands and stared fiercely—

"If we die, we die."

The words echoed across the room, holding all tongues at bay.

They all knew the story.

"If we die, we die," he repeated. "As martyrs. And we further the cause with our lives."

Kalhette furrowed her brow and nodded at Benton, affirming that she held his same level of commitment—a significant gesture in this room. Others did the same.

Perhaps his words had finally earned their respect.

MOMENTS LATER, BENTON dismissed the meeting by reiterating their looming deadline—not thirty sleep cycles away.

Uumaki approached on all sixes and patted Benton on the thigh. "You are doing great. We can win this." His hope seemed to be the minority.

As the attendees exited, conversations drifted to Dray and to distrust of the whole situation. If any participant dropped out, it would likely spell doom for the whole. Maybe they were right to doubt. Maybe he should call it off. If Dray confessed the plan to Taiberos, they'd be walking into ambush and death. Still, if they hesitated at every uncertainty, evil would surely win. Initiative demanded they strike now, while the favor of the populace was on their side.

Kalhette gave Benton a hopeful smile. "I'm going to go sleep now. Sorry. Still have a long way to get over the treatments." He wished she could've lingered.

This left Benton and Dr Warnur alone at the massive table, surrounded by wooden pillars, and their shadows swayed in time with the lamps.

Dr Warner was highly educated. His dated clothes didn't detract from his stately appearance and well coiffed white hair. He shone in stark contrast to the barbarity of war that Solace had suffered for so long. Somehow he remained stalwart, as if unaffected, as if he'd transcended it all somehow. "Uumaki is right. We can win this."

Benton tried to smile. He felt heavy, like being back aboard that Bloody Wing. If only the others could see liberation in the same light he did. *It was worth any cost.* "Thank you for hosting us, Doctor. I know you do so at great personal risk."

"It is my honor. Thank you for carrying this burden. It's not easy filling the boots of Lord Admiral Dray."

Benton shook his head. He wasn't sure he could fill them.

With a knock on the door frame, an attendant entered, or rather a kid trying to act like a man. "Sir, *The Gemony* has arrived, bringing a relay for you." He held out a small envelope.

Benton took it, then slid his finger beneath a fold and tore it open.

His eyes grew wider as he read. He skipped to the valediction at the end, anxious to piece it together quicker than he could perceive it.

If it were true, they still had hope.

He recognized the handwriting and could verify its authenticity. If the message had been coerced, he felt certain it would've held a clue to expose the coercion, but he could see none. Only, it seemed too strange to be simply real.

Dr Warnur stood and said, "What is it?"

Benton finished reading and then handed Dr Warnur the letter:

Benton Xylander:

Pay closest attention to the following details.

President Taiberos has increased the number of troops stationed on Solace at each hint of insurrection, leaving us to face an army perhaps too large for our militia.

As you may know, this massive army gets refreshed every half a percent. Standard procedure directs a fleet of transports to arrive with new troops and then to take back the former troops, creating an overlap in personnel. In just ten cycles, however, a PSD transport fleet will arrive carrying supplies, weapons, and artillery. They have been given orders to shuttle half the garrison back with them. That leaves us with a two-cycle window before the next transports bring the garrison to full quota.

In those two cycles lies our chance to strike.

To seize this moment, our plans must be finalized sooner than we antici-pated, but I believe Initiative will also heighten our chances of success. It is our moment to rise.

By a stroke of the greatest fortune, I have escaped the Strand. Once I finish coordinating with my sources, I will arrive at Solace to aid you.

Until then,

Lord Admiral Kelsang Dray

A Zhan should never hide from the light."

Master Jyngsoo had taught that to Dray. It meant that one should either own up to an act or turn away from that act, but deception, committing the act in shadow, was never acceptable, not for a Zhan.

Jyngsoo might not have agreed with Benton's revolution either. Too much subterfuge.

He would never have approved of what Dray was about to do. No one would. Except for his master.

Dray wore a riding robe, a regal gray garment, trimmed in red, which hung in two sweeping halves from his shoulders to his ankles—the split up the lower back was designed to accommodate a saddle. The sleeves beneath wrapped snugly around his forearms and ended in triangle shapes on the backs of his hands. The hood covered his wild gray hair and left his bearded face in shadow. He looked like a colonist rather than a former Lord Admiral.

Another deception.

He wandered freely through the cobblestone streets of Solace, unnoticed by the Redhelms. No one knew he was back, save Trillion. A drizzle of rain came down, scarcely more than a mist. As he walked, he considered the bargain.

For mind, he would give up the memory of the one he held most dear. Lethos promised that was forthcoming, though the practicalities were unclear.

For body, Dray had already given up his right eye during the escape, though how Lethos had predicted such a strange turn of events seemed frightening.

For soul, Dray would end the life of Kalhette Whitesun—the one he'd staked his life to save. This third part weighed most heavily on his mind. Though he needed to complete the bargain without jeopardizing his role in the insurrection. That meant he needed to know what precisely he was up against, how powerful she was.

And how powerful were her premonitions.

He'd nearly reached the appointed house on the Heights when he heard a scream.

A crowd formed just ahead, and a wail carried through the twilight streets.

Curious, Dray pushed into the crowd till he broke through.

People formed a ring with a wide gap at the center, with no one wanting to approach further than curiosity drove them. At the center, three people clustered around a body. A woman was crying, her forehead and hands on the street. Dray looked up at the Heights to a balcony overhead. From where the victim had jumped.

So the Witch Hunters were nearby.

He moved closer. He had to know whether it was *her*.

The acceleration of gravity pulled constantly on everyone. In mild doses, acceleration was harmless. In this case, it had killed someone. A young man, it seemed, with a thick head of hair—it wasn't her. But maybe this would be the right method.

On Solace, it was not uncommon for Radiances to kill themselves to escape being captured. Better than Building 13. This idea of a noble death had arisen in the miina culture and spread among the colonist youth, a new generation's interpretation of what they called abiisu, but it was a twisted one. These youths each made one last independent choice—death over slavery. More blood on Taiberos's hands.

And on Dray's own.

But it didn't have to be like that. If Dray fulfilled his obligation, he could stop the Witch Hunters, undo some of his past, and end these senseless suicides.

The cost was just one life.

He took a final look at the victim's gore spread across the cobblestone. As he pushed his way back out of the crowd, suddenly he stood face to face with her:

Kalhette Whitesun.

DRAY WOULDN'T HAVE recognized her.

She was hooded, her face mostly in shadows. The only time they'd met was in those dark moments of Building 13, just before Dray told them to go on ahead while he bought them more time.

Yet she somehow recognized him, eyes widening: *"Lord Admiral Dray!"*

His prism was fastened to his belt. His hand hung just over it. He'd only need to flick the riding coat out of the way, ignite the blade, and extend it into her stomach.

He glanced at the crown all around. "Hail."

Something about her seemed delicate and pure, in spite of all she'd been through. "What a surprise. I'm glad you made it back *safely...*" She said the last word quietly, as if deciding too late to suppress it. "I'm Kalhette. I was hardly coherent the last time we met. It was so brave of you to..."

He nodded and gave her a solemn smile. It felt empty and false, with no emotion to back it. He spoke in his soothingly deep voice: "Please don't mention it." He'd gone back into Building 13 to save this woman's life, and now he was personally going to turn her into a martyr.

She looked ahead toward the crowd. "Do you know what happened?"

"Someone is dead. A suicide. What brought you here?" He needed to know if her prescience could see something like this.

"We were just on a walk, and I..."

"Let's go. You don't need to see this." He spoke as if giving an order, which she obeyed.

On the outside of the crowd, Benton waited, wearing a green hat and scarf that concealed his appearance to anyone but those who knew him best. He too had a look of surprise after peering through Dray's disguise. "Sir!" It seemed the two of them had been on a romantic stroll before running into this tragedy.

Dray shook his head. "It's such a shame. Such a shame."

"Any of us might still have to choose between capture and suicide," said Kalhette.

"Not if we succeed, which we're bound to now that you're back. Welcome, sir." Benton looked uncomfortable, surely wanting to ask what happened, perhaps also shouldering some guilt for escaping without Dray.

Dray nodded. "Let's get moving."

"Of course. Follow me." Benton led them around a corner and to a narrow set of concrete stairs leading up the steep cliff. "Are you doing all right?"

"My escape was not without cost."

As they hiked the steep staircase, Benton vaguely mentioned the letter, concealing all specifics in case anyone happened to overhear. He concluded with, "And I'm left wondering how you know all this..."

"I made a friend during my stay." Dray left it at that, and Benton did not press him further. The truth was that Lethos had given him access to the details they needed for this revolution to work, so the deal was already paying off.

"And the plan, has it been compromised?"

"No. Our plan is safe."

H IGH UP THE stairs, though still not at the top, they came to a doorway. Benton knocked twice and then entered.

Inside, the house was bustling, with everyone from toddlers to grandmas. The walls were lined with books. A young girl tended a newborn, perhaps a younger sibling, and slipped in a *hello* toward Dray right before another *boo!* A boy walked past carrying jars of bottled fruit, and said, "How do you do?" with a big grin, revealing a missing tooth, as he passed in toward the kitchen. Another older boy sat in a wooden chair assembling illegal rifle parts spread across a bench in front of him.

A tall man with a stately posture and white hair came into the room and approached the guests directly. "Welcome."

Kalhette's face showed deep emotional injury. "Dr Warnur, there was a suicide on the street."

"Oh dear." He touched his lips, and his face reflected her pain. "We have to break this pattern. Do you know who it was?"

"No. The Witch Hunters are prowling though. They've intensified in just the last few cycles."

"I had better see to it." Dr Warnur looked beneath the hood into Dray's eye. "A pleasure to meet you, sir. I've heard so much. I'm Raven Warnur."

Dray tried to mirror the man's smile, but it felt like expressing pain. The bustle of this house, its life and happiness, its contentment and togetherness, seemed diametrically opposed to his own state of being. "Thank you for offering your home."

"Of course. I'm glad to help in any way I can."

As the two shook hands, Kalhette said, "Dr Warnur is a local physician, a volunteer to the cause. He's also the man who delivered me."

"She was one of my first patients, in fact, she and her sisters."

Dray removed his hood, revealing a bandage that covered his right eye, curving up and over his head, the tension parting his gray hair along that same line.

Kalhette seemed in shock, as if what lay underneath implied some secret horror. Did her powers somehow tell her what happened?

Or what had been promised?

Dr Warnur looked directly at the bandage. "Have you had adequate medical attention?"

"I've lost the eye, but my vision is intact." Dray's sentence had a double meaning, and the second might have been a lie. He aimed half a gaze at Kalhette and smiled. As he hung his riding coat on a rack near the door, he turned toward Dr Warnur. "May I ask, are you also an officer?"

"I am a member of the militia and will be serving as a private."

"He'll be joining my division," Benton said, "serving as my aide-de-camp."

Dray's impression was that the man ought to be serving as an officer. Their battle for independence was at hand, but a larger war would surely follow, and men like Dr Warnur would be in high demand.

With a courteous smile, the doctor turned and picked up a black leather satchel. "If you'll excuse me, I had better see to this…" He headed to the door.

"Can I get you anything?" asked Benton.

Dray nodded. "Tea."

"Yes, sir."

"Have you been to Solace before?" asked Kalhette.

"Yes, but not extensively." As Lord Admiral for the PSD, Dray had seen nearly every part of the galaxy, but that was primarily from orbit, command-ing troops rather than getting his own boots dirty. Over the last percent as he'd helped with the revolution, he'd aided Benton remotely, for obvious security reasons.

"Follow me. They have an excellent view of the horizon." She led him upstairs, and they emerged on a round deck overlooking a valley blanketed in the golden haze of twilight.

The two of them alone.

As he stepped onto the balcony, a drop of rain tapped onto his wild gray hair.

In the distance, it showered in sweeping streaks that only appeared in front of the darkest elements. The closer rooftops shined with wet black; the ones farther back were warm grays. The light of the absent sun silhouetted the trees, turning them into greens so deep they were almost black. The dark hues lightened as they went layer upon layer toward the eternal sunset. The most distant houses hugged closely—so they could all make an appearance before the plane ended—and seemed hardly more than blotches of paint blurred by the mists of rain.

Dray walked to the rail and leaned with both hands, staring one-eyed across the vista. He registered the colors, but something about it evaded him, as if he'd lost part of his senses in the darkness with Lethos. Dray looked down at the avenue straight below. The location of the suicide was out of sight, but it must've been from a balcony just like this.

"I'll be right back," said Kalhette.

While she was gone, he pulled back the long sleeves. The Orikerse had turned his wrists red. As he scratched the redness, he thought about his promise. He had nothing against her personally, but he'd made a deal. Nothing short of killing Lethos, a being who was said to be immortal, or ending his own life would get Dray out of his covenant. And that would mean failing to help so many others.

Through committing one last sin.

The logic made sense, to sacrifice one life and save a multiplicity of others. Even Master Jyngsoo would have to agree. But the emotion of it—the spirit of it—did not make sense. Especially not when the person sacrificed was Kalhette Whitesun. People wouldn't understand, and so they would meddle. If not for that, Dray would gladly commit his act in the open and stand against the scorn. They were children begging the doctor to not set the bone, but he had to do it—he *had* to. For everyone's sake. He would cause this heightened and immediate pain to spare them prolonged misery. They would thank him once it was over. But not now.

Now they would cry.

Over the death of an innocent.

He looked at his left palm. Three dark, brownish-red dots of dried blood formed an arrowhead triangle with a fourth in the lower middle of the shape. He stared at them. Needles of Orikerse were always painful going in, but that pain was now gone, vanished into the past as if it had never happened. Yet the effects lingered, changing the way he felt, which changed the way he thought. He never could've sustained his current objective without that.

His head dipped as he slowly licked across the bloody marks till they disappeared.

It wouldn't be the first person he'd hurt. Not even the first Radiance.

Without warning, the rain faded. All stood still, except for a small bird, hopping across one of the nearby rooftops. The mountains on the horizon's crest were a faint golden line, barely distinguishable from the yellow sky. Thunder purred in the background, and wind rustled through leaves. Then, in natural symphony, the notes of rain began to rise again, appearing on distant shingles first, and then closer and closer, till once again they blanketed the scene, at least in the places dark enough for their light to shine through. The drops tapped on the awning overhead.

Kalhette's voice came from behind: "Isn't it beautiful?"

He sealed off his thoughts into their own little cavern so that they would not betray his secret. The Orikerse hid his feelings so deep that he could barely reach them himself, yet he wasn't sure what power this girl possessed. Benton had said she could see the future like Lethos, could predict attempts on her life. Yet her premonitions hadn't saved her from the Witch Hunters.

He turned toward her. "Yes. It's magnificent. I only hope I can maintain my awe as constantly as this sunset." His words were socially acceptable, but he didn't feel any of it, which made it a lie.

She stood next to him and leaned her elbows on the railing. "We like to think of it as a constant sun-*rise*." Her bald head made her seem so vulnerable.

He looked at the cobblestone street glazed with rain, so far below.

Turning away from the vista, she looked into his one eye. "Lord Admiral Dray, what secret are you hiding?"

He fought to keep his breaths shallow. Had that been a phrase meant to make him stumble? His training in the service combined with the Orikerse allowed him to keep his poise. "What do you mean?"

She turned toward the sun. "I'm sorry. Sometimes a thought comes, and I just say it aloud. A little too spontaneous. I don't mean to be too personal. Actually, I would, as long as it doesn't make you uncomfortable. You risked your life for me and the others. I cannot imagine a more heroic act. I want to thank you somehow. And it makes me wonder what kind of a man would do that."

Perhaps she couldn't see who he really was. He made a point not to sigh audibly.

Jyngsoo had taught that the Song included three parts. Vision and Spirit fueled Initiative, meaning you had to see and feel an action before you could do it. Thus the future couldn't be created or predicted without those precursors, without first seeing and feeling. If that were true, Dray would simply have to avoid any clear premeditation. Until he definitively decided, she could predict no consequences.

As he looked at her, his mind's eye suddenly splintered into fragments, as if he existed in two realities simultaneously: With his good eye, he saw the profile of this young woman—leaning against the railing, stubble on her bare skull, breathing, blood just beneath the surface, a frail mortal, never far from death. With his missing eye, he saw another woman's profile—she lying on a wooden floor, her hair splayed out like an ornamental headdress, her pale skin giving not the slightest sign of life.

She had been innocent too.

He recoiled from the vision, and his skin tingled with sweat.

He'd promised to give up her memory, but it hadn't been taken yet. It would soon, though, inevitably. For that he felt sorrow. Thinking of her hurt him—the deepest pain—and yet strangely he didn't want to let it go. Or let *her* go.

He didn't want to lose his last small flicker of light.

Kalhette turned toward him. "We don't have to talk if you don't want to."

"I don't mind."

"When I was a child, we lived just over there." She leaned dangerously out over the railing and pointed a hand in front of Dray.

It wouldn't even require a *physical* push. Yet to attempt and fail could ruin everything. Only, would he ever have it so easy as now? He cleared his throat but said nothing.

"A miina woman helped me discover my powers," she said.

"Was she a Zhan?"

"No." She sensed there was more she didn't add. "As a child, I didn't comprehend the consequences of being discovered as a Radiance. One cycle a miina cub was teasing me about liking a boy who I didn't actually like. It was so dumb, but I grabbed her, shoved my face into hers, and with eyes glowing, I screamed, 'I don't like him!' That was it. Over a stupid boy. The other kids ran, leaving me alone. My dad showed up just in time. He rushed me into exile before the Witch Hunters arrived. I had to leave Solace, my home." Her voice dropped to a whisper, and tears glistened at the edges of her eyes: *"I think it broke his heart. I know it broke mine."*

This story of the Witch Hunters nearly stealing an innocent child struck him hard, piercing through his numbness.

That happened to her because Dray had created the Witch Hunters. Same with that poor creature who'd impacted with the street. His anger began to rise as he thought of the monsters he'd created. He could stop them now.

At the cost of her life.

One more wrong to gain the power to do right.

The rain vanished once more. The leaves of the trees were restored to green, and their branches waved back and forth gently. The rim of the sky still held its golden hue, though now pink and blue had gathered below and above. The mountains, barely visible in the rain, appeared in deep purple, contrasting boldly with the pale sky. The more distant clouds floated in yellow and pink daubs above the mountains.

"That's my secret," she said. "That I miss my dad and my childhood."

He smiled at her, trying to cover his sinister intentions with a look of pity. "I'll trade you a story not many know: I was deaf as a child. My parents couldn't afford cyborg implants till I was six. Most people take hearing for granted, but I know what it's like to hear nothing."

Soon he would make them all hear.

"That's powerful," she said.

Above, the fluffy white trim of the gray clouds faced sunward. In the blue atmosphere, black starships at blazing speeds traversed the massive distance like insects crawling across a window pane. In parallax, a bird with four wings cut in front of the flight paths and vanished out of sight overhead.

She looked at him.

His one eye matched her gaze. Then it drifted away as he worried she might see the real him. The one who'd created the Witch Hunters. The one who meant to murder her. Then, to his own surprise, a part of the truth came out, as if her spontaneity had influenced him: "Kalhette, I have something important to tell you." He swallowed.

"What?"

"I discovered a strange rumor while in prison. Do you know who Lethos is?"

"Of course."

"The rumors say he wants to kill you."

"I know."

"You do?" he asked.

She nodded.

"How do you know?"

"Premonitions."

"Do you always have premonitions when bad things are about to happen?"

"No, but often."

Dray nodded, and he stopped breathing as he looked down to the cobblestone, worried about the moment he committed to action.

She followed his gaze and then gave him a wary glance.

Benton appeared behind them on the balcony carrying a silver tray with two hands. "I brought tea."

Dray let out a sigh.

He didn't have to do it now.

It gave him time to strategize. First, he would test her, set a plan in motion that would expose her abilities. Once he knew how readily she could fend off her own death, he would find a way to sidestep her powers.

Whether that meant premeditated or spontaneous murder.

In the meantime, her rebellion would destabilize the PSD, making his ultimate goal easier to reach, and perhaps an opportunity would present itself on the battlefield. Where premonitions about her death would be natural.

Even inevitable.

Where even if she realized the end had come, it would be too late.

S OMETHING WRONG?" ASKED Nak.
   The harsh winds had withdrawn while he and Kalh hiked together
through an overgrown jungle alongside a babbling stream.

"No. Why?" she asked.

"You keep looking over your shoulder."

"It's just that…"

"Thought you were all about trust."

"Okay. Fine." Kalh stopped and turned indiscreetly back for a longer look
behind them. Her mouth hung gently open as she looked at the massive trees
that had long tentacles fluttering in the wind. She wasn't wearing casts on
her arms anymore, a pretty miraculous speed of healing, maybe four times
the rate of anyone else. "I have a feeling we're being stalked."

"Is this a premonition?"

"I don't know."

Not exactly a great mood for a romantic walk. "You want to turn back?"

"I don't think so. Probably just paranoia."

"Really, we can turn back."

"No, I promised you the best vista of your life. Come on." She continued
marching toward a place only locals knew about. The twilight gently flooded
through leaves overhead. A bird spooked and took flight, revealing its four
wings—just like a Raewasp.

It all began on this planet. His ship had been created here. Maybe the
most beautiful biome he'd ever seen. Punctuating the overwhelming green,
colorful flowers grew in trails along the water's edge, including striking
blue ones, a tone he hadn't often seen in nature. Pinks and yellows and reds
speckled the green too. "Puts my bioribbon to shame."

She laughed.

The water laughed with her, shimmering with a rainbow iridescence, as
if the eternal sunrise had bled down onto the surface. Reminded him of the
storm of infraspace. Or the pristine beauty of Novan. Everything seemed
almost too vibrant and too bright. Even the bugs glowed, big purple ones
and smaller yellowish orange ones. They weaved trails of light through the
air, and the dim twilight made them shine all the brighter. Made the thought
of joining her insane strike against Taiberos almost tempting.

"Did you know a gravitational field reaches infinitely?" asked Kalh, an
attempt to move the subject past her paranoia.

Nak took big steps up the steep slope. "What do you mean."

"What's your homeworld again?" asked Kalh.

One more fact at this point hardly seemed to matter. "Terron Prime. Dray's homeworld too, and it definitely doesn't look like this."

"You heard he's back, right?"

Nak nodded. "Yes. Can't believe we left him in there." He wanted to speak with Dray, apologize, maybe get some assurance that this uprising wasn't just suicide.

"You guys friends?" she asked.

Nak scratched the back of head, and his jacket lifted and opened as he did. "Almost."

She didn't question this vague response. Instead, her head bowed.

"What's that look for," he asked.

"I don't know."

"Just tell me."

"There's something about Dray," she said.

"What do you mean?"

"I don't know. I had a conversation with him and… something seems off."

"He stayed behind for you. Who knows what they put him through."

"*I* know what they put him through," she said. "Better than anyone."

"I'm sorry."

"It's just…" but she didn't finish.

"What."

"I think something is wrong."

"Well, he went through a lot."

"*I* went through a lot. I'm talking about something else."

"Like what?"

"I don't know, but I feel…"

"That something's off."

"Yes."

Nak looked at her, making clear his intention to listen.

His silence prompted her to keep going: "Sight is how light reflects off matter. You recognize water by the unique way it deflects photons—the ripples make a recognizable pattern. If the sea absorbed more light, you'd know it wasn't made of water, but something blacker. That very thing happened when I saw Dray. I didn't see what I expected."

Nak looked down with concern.

"As if he weren't correctly reflecting light," said Kalh.

When the old soldier miraculously made it out of Building 13, Nak felt sincerely happy. Only, Dray hadn't replied to Nak's message. It felt like an accusation, blame for the missing eye.

Though the trail was steep, neither of them were breathing hard. After some time in silence, Kalh asked, "What are you thinking about?"

"What were you saying about gravity?" he asked.

"Oh. Right. From here, even though we're light percents away, we could, in theory, detect Terron Prime's gravitational field—the subtle hold it has on us. Of course, the effect decreases over distance, so it would be very small, but it's not nothing." She glanced warily over her shoulder again—something still wrong.

"It decreases by the square of the distance, so it's practically nothing."

"Oh, so you know more than me. But it's still there, right? That's the point. It reaches this far. The rule applies to everything with mass," said Kalh. "Gravitational fields shoot out at the speed of light in every direction, going on forever. Your Cupcake even has it, so wherever she is, she's tugging on both of us."

His thoughts went to *The Sanctum*. He'd been working on her nonstop, with laser focus. Kalh snapped him out of his work trance by inviting him here. The shields were fully charged, and he was almost finished getting the wing back in shape. Just needed a few more isos. After that, maybe he could fix the fuel gauge. All this had to be done on a planetary surface too.

"The point is that you're pulling on me right now." Kalh grinned.

"I feel it too."

She smiled. "We're all connected in a giant cosmic net. That's the Song—the physics of longing."

"You're a poet."

"Well, it's true," she said, deflecting the compliment.

"Thanks again for the headphones. Been using them while I work."

"Think white's okay?"

"White is great."

She smiled and gave him a look, kind of bashful, like she wanted to say more.

He smiled back.

He hadn't liked someone this much since Taiberos's daughter, which hadn't exactly ended well. Of course, he'd started liking that one before he really knew what she was like. In the end, he'd cut her loose, just like he'd been doing his whole life. Kalh wasn't like that. She was authentic.

And for some reason, she felt like home.

Which was strange—to feel safety in the presence of another human being. Not to mention her being the type of person who'd risk her own neck to save a lost little kid. And her shaved head.

But they'd never be safe on Solace. Didn't matter what kind of crazy revolution they were hatching. Wouldn't be enough to stop Taiberos. The only safe place was on a Bloody Wing. "Kalh, if you had a safe place to run…"

He saw hurt in her eyes, and that was answer enough. "I told Benton I would help. I can't leave. Not now."

Which meant she was doomed. Taiberos would get them all sooner or later.

All except Nak.

A bug made of yellow light landed on her sleeve. She lifted her arm, and the bright glow reflected in her eyes.

Nak looked at her and grinned, grateful he didn't have a mask.

He didn't depend on her or need her. He just wanted her. Dangerously. And it was tearing him in half.

The physics of longing.

H E FELT THE impulse to hold her hand.

To stake his claim, or team up, or whatever that implied.

But she wanted long-term. That just wasn't him. So if he held her hand, the action would be a lie. With most women, he wouldn't have cared about a lie, but with her, for some reason, honesty seemed necessary.

"Hey," he said, "I remember a promise that if I came on this hike I'd learn about third spectrum…"

"Oh yeah. I was getting there. Third spectrum—we call it Ptolis—works in the same way as gravity. Our thoughts create similar spherical ripples going outward at the speed of light. Ptolis means learning to detect and control those."

A bird chirped in the distance, and he thought of Lolo. Now of all times. Sometimes he felt like his mind was not entirely his own. She'd left him a relay on the Handnet saying she missed him, which made him feel some longing for her, even though he hardly knew her. She didn't push for commitment. But he'd have to give up Kalh to get her and vice versa.

The problem was, he wanted the whole galaxy, not a single star.

Kalh paused and caught his gaze. "As a general rule, people think their thoughts are trapped inside their heads, only released once you act—which transforms them into Initiative. With Ptolis, third spectrum, you can bypass that limitation. You can hear and share thoughts directly."

Nak's heart thumped more rapidly. "Wait, so you can eavesdrop on my thoughts?"

"No. Each of the nine spectra have their own degrees of force. You pushed a towel the other cycle—a gentle wind—but not enough to push a mountain. Ptolis works the same. It's theoretically possible to hear everyone's thoughts, even over interstellar distances. In reality, no one can. Mortals just aren't that strong. But you can make it easier."

"How."

"By leaning in, basically." She tugged on his shoulder, and he got down on one knee. She hadn't been nearly so touchy while Benton was nearby. "If I cup my hand around your ear…" She bent down and mimicked her description. *"And I whisper…"*

He smiled. "Then I'll hear you."

"My intention to be heard makes your listening easier. Also, certain souls match wavelengths better than others, which is a type of entanglement,

THE NINE SPECTRA

Starsight 1
Detect light beyond visual boundaries.

Kinosis 2
Command sacred fire in others.

Ptolis 3
Detect thought beyond mental boundaries.

Anomis 4
Exist outward within nearby spirits.

Sacredspark 5
Command sacred fire in oneself.

Vayonis 6
Detect the Song beyond spacetime boundaries.

Sorjis 7
Exist inward adjoined by surrounding spirits.

Genosis 8
Command laws of energymatter itself.

Silentsong 9
Exist within the xetherspark realm.

sometimes called atonement. It can happen with anyone, but it tends to happen within bloodlines—so your siblings would be easier to hear."

He nodded. Didn't seem like a good time to bring up a dead twin sister.

Kalh peered over her shoulder again.

Nak followed suit, wondering if she was right about something in the jungle. Foliage was pretty thick. Would be an easy spot for an ambush.

"I'm not supposed to be talking about all this," she said.

"Who says?"

"Tradition."

"Let's start a new tradition."

She laughed.

"Please."

"Okay, ace." She curled her index finger, as if pulling him.

Nak stepped closer.

"Starsight and Ptolis are both part of Vision. They're enhanced by mastery over your own thoughts. The practice is to silently watch them."

"How often do you do this?"

"Jyngsoo would have you do it an iso per cycle. It's called meta-consciousness—to be conscious of what you're conscious of. Right now, you're hearing my voice, constructing the meaning of this sentence. Now you're realizing that you're thinking about that. Simply notice the paths your mind takes. Don't judge. Observe. Perceive. Search. Do not judge. Master Jyngsoo would say that out of all possible attitudes you must choose none. Have no attitude. Become the void."

"I think I can do that. What about noticing my body? I feel that ache in my neck..."

"Well, body is Initiative, but the Braid is tightly woven. Meditation is always beneficial, whether you focus on thoughts, physiology, or emotions. But for Ptolis, focus on thoughts."

A gentle rain started to streak down. Nak turned and looked at the lines in the sky, watery streaks with great pauses between them. He noticed his mind check back in on *The Sanctum* then move to Lolo. Next he noticed Kalh looking directly at him.

Her eyes began to glow. He then heard her thoughts:

What would you give your life for?

It was not like hearing a sound. Something more like remembering a sound. Softer, more vague, and somewhat distant, but still clear.

And completely unexpected.

H E SCRUNCHED HIS eyes closed and shook his head. "Wow, that was weird."

"Wait, you heard that?" Her hazel eyes looked at him in surprise.

"Yeah. Clearly." He put his hands on his face as if to steady his mind. "That was weird."

"You really heard it?"

"Yes."

"Well, sorry. I'm not that good at Ptolis. That's twice you've done this to me."

"Done what."

"It shouldn't have worked uninvited. We... must have more entanglement than I realized... Or you're more skilled than you're letting on. I'm telling you, this takes percents, even lifetimes, for some people, okay? I'm sorry. That wasn't supposed to happen."

With a grin, he teased, "That was a creepy thing to say."

"Pssh. It's not creepy."

"Yeah, it's about dying. That's creepy."

"Okay, but I didn't think you'd actually hear it. Only my sisters can usually hear me that well."

"Sisters, huh."

"I'm a triplet."

"What! Two more women as beautiful as you are walking around somewhere?"

"Yes, and they have hair."

"I like you without hair."

She smiled. "I got exiled, so I didn't grow up with them. They may look like me, but they're more like cousins. Our lives are so different."

"Why'd you pick that phrase?"

"Comes from this place. It's important to me."

"It's still creepy." He gave a wry grin at her allure.

"Master Jyngsoo gave me that riddle to ponder: 'What would you give your life for?' He said it would take more than one lifetime to truly answer it. I thought I'd found the answer when I tried to rescue Tannie. But he still died, so now I'm not sure."

"You're deep, Kalh."

She looked up and smiled with a revolutionary defiance. She seemed willing to die—likely to die even. No one faced Taiberos's navy and triumphed.

Nak shook his head. Even if Benton miraculously came up with the money to hire a privateer, it would mean risking *The Sanctum*. If only Kalh would agree to leave with him. They could be safe in infraspace.

"So what's your answer?" she asked.

"Huh?"

She cocked her head playfully to the side. "What would you give your life for?"

"Oh. Uh, I can't tell you that."

"Still not ready to trust, huh?"

"I just don't have an answer. Haven't thought about it. Why, what's yours."

"I would die for my children."

His eyebrows raised in surprise. "Wait, you have kids?"

"No." She gave a shy grin and then giggled. "But I know how to make them."

Nak laughed. "Not such a prude after all."

"I still follow the rules."

"Not till after marriage." He refrained from shaking his head. She was so different from what he wanted. *Thought* he wanted.

"Yep."

"Why do you care that much about creating a family."

"I don't know. Maybe because I miss mine so much. You don't want one?"

"Honestly, probably not. Not if they're going to have the sort of childhood I had."

"They can have as good a childhood as you give them."

"My kids?" asked Nak.

"Yes."

"What about *you* though. What about spending your life in a way that actually brings *you* joy."

"I can think of nothing so meaningful as providing a child a home."

"You're just saying that."

"No. The individual is the most valuable thing in the galaxy. Even more valuable than your skycraft."

"Easy now."

"Eventually, some individual will learn to build a surge drive from scratch. That's the potential of a soul—a person learning, growing, and choosing—and it's as beautiful a thing as there can ever possibly be."

"What if your kid makes dumb choices." When he said it, he thought of Cup.

"You have to let them choose bad if they're going to have any victory in choosing good. The alternative is slavery, and that's as ugly a thing as there can ever possibly be."

He didn't want a slave drive either. "Sounds like constant frustration."

"It would make me immensely happy."

"But you've never tried it…"

"You're talking to a teacher here."

"I read that in your mission dossier." It had actually slipped his mind.

"Have you ever heard parents talk about seeing their own child for the first time? They talk about this love, this deep indescribable feeling."

"Before the kids start growing up."

"Nak, you had a rough childhood, and I empathize, but that's not how all childhoods have to be. There's a much bigger picture. That's why we need to stop Taiberos and his government. For the next generation."

"I don't understand that kind of selflessness."

"It's not selflessness, and don't let Benton hear you say that." She always seemed to bring him into it.

"Why not."

"He hates selflessness."

"What—are you kidding."

"No."

"Maybe he and I have more in common than I thought."

"You should ask him about it, but my point is that making *them* happy makes *me* happy. It's not a zero sum game. Besides, Master Jyngsoo says you can learn from no better Zhani master than a child. They teach you patience, wonder, kindness, and they're disciplined instructors too—teaching at all isochrons, even while you're trying to sleep."

"That's not funny."

"They can give you a kind of joy I've never found anywhere else. We adults get tired, worn down, jaded toward life. We forget the way we looked at the galaxy when we first arrived. But a child is a brand new person, still filled with awe. They remind us of the spirit we've forgotten—what time took away. Just that makes them invaluable."

When she looked at Nak for a response, he gave her a contented smile.

"Sorry. I'm talking too much," she said.

"No, no. It's great."

She glanced over her shoulder again, as if Redhelms might jump out at them this very sequel. They waited a long time, listening to wildlife and wind through leaves but heard nothing out of the ordinary. She finally spoke: "Have you thought of your answer?"

"I suppose I'll die as a mercenary, in a high-speed chase and a blaze of glory."

"You should join us then. We can provide the blaze of glory."

Against Taiberos. "I was imagining after a lengthy and noble career."

She laughed.

Nak hated Taiberos more than anything, now more than ever after what that bastard did to Kalh, but standing against the PSD wasn't smart. Nobody beat them, not even the Shadowlyss, who'd been trying for percents. So how could Dray and a tiny ragtag crew?

Her countenance seemed to change, as if she'd been let down because he hadn't committed right then and there.

"So how do I do this think-speaking," asked Nak.

Her tone seemed crestfallen: "When a person thinks, their consciousness makes ripples across the Song."

"I can think, but how do I project."

"Honestly, Benton is a much better teacher. A lot of this stuff came easily to me, so I do it intuitively. Whereas he actually knows how to study it and break it down into pieces. If you want more help, he's the one to ask. I'm actually not particularly good at Ptolis either."

Nak didn't like that answer but didn't say so.

Maybe she'd heard his doubts.

* * *

THE FOREST OPENED up, leading to a cliff edge.

The path led to a giant stone platform, one that roughly formed a triangle, and the point reached out, making an isolated balcony, as if the end of the trail was an invitation to dive into the abyss.

Centered on that triangular outcrop rested another stone, which Kalh leaped up on top of. It had been polished into a smooth surface by the tread of all the people who'd come here before. This gave her an even higher view.

Nak walked past Kalh's perspective rock toward the point of the triangle. He went to the tip and put a boot on the very edge, looking down at the deadly drop. Just seeing it made him start to breathe deeper. Far in the distance, a long white curtain of water tumbled from a green and gray height, and a rainbow glimmered in the mists. The twilight made it look all the more enchanted. The cascades were absolutely massive, like some ancient deity. The surge gate shone above as a bright star, watching over the scene. "So that's Tiigxuu, huh. Hell of a place to fall from."

"Hey, not so close. You're scaring me!" Towering over him, she crouched and reached out her hand, inviting him back to her rock.

He retreated, took her hand, and climbed up with her.

She grabbed on to him to keep her balance and then blushed.

He teetered as he situated himself next to her.

Standing side-by-side, they gazed at the majesty around them, a vista that went on and on. Her eyes twinkled as she pointed: "You can actually go out on those bridges, and there's a cave you can climb up in underneath."

He didn't hide his eagerness: "Can we get down there from here?"

She shook her head. "It's a long way back and around, but there will be Redhelms. I'd need a disguise. You too probably."

He sighed.

"I'll take you later if..." She trailed off.

Nak forced a smile.

"So you'd give your life to be a mercenary?" she asked.

"No. I'd give my life to sail, to rule the skies. You're never more free than that."

She pulled her lips and her taunting scar into a smile, an expression filled with warmth and sadness. She grabbed his hands to keep her balance as she stepped in front of him, too short to block his view, facing him with that gleam in her eye, and gave him this hungry look—one that made him think she hadn't had any red meat in a while. "You're so... unbound. You could never live a quiet, normal life like other people, could you?"

He looked up at the shining surge gate. "Not while there's this much sky."

That mischievous look on her face, like she wanted to take a bite of him... Her eyes began to glow, and he heard her thoughts:

When are you going to tell me your skycraft's secret?

He grinned and leaned down close enough to whisper in her ear. "Seduction, is it?"

"Whatever it takes."

"Still creepy you can do that with me."

"Should I stop?"

"No." A glowing purple bug zipped around them and then vanished.

"It's really not supposed to be so easy. There's some strange connection here."

He couldn't deny that.

"So what's your skycraft's secret?"

Without really considering his rules, he just started telling her: "Out of the billions of stars in our galaxy, the surge tunnels only give us access to a few hundred. We can't get to the other ninety-nine percent. The Bloody Wings are locked into that set too. You just can't calculate it. But each of the Bloody Wings has access to one unique point in the galaxy, a location no one else can go. That's her secret."

"I've heard that before. Thought it was a myth. So what's your location?"

"Novan. Uncharted."

Two souls standing so close, balanced atop a pinnacle on top of a pinnacle, and the twilight drenched the entire world around them.

"You've been there?" she asked.

"Of course."

"Would you take me?"

Nak had imagined it to be the perfect place for a marriage proposal, back when he still considered that a possibility. But now, well, this woman confused him. Usually he'd flirt with no regard to the consequences, but with her… both moving closer and withdrawing seemed bad.

He didn't like that.

He put on his best fake smile.

Kalh seemed to take this as a yes, which was fine. She leaned in closer. "Thank you for trusting me."

The sunrise was perfect, and it wasn't going anywhere. The glowing insects floated in a magical swirl on all sides.

The physics of longing.

The sound of the waterfall rushed in the distance

He leaned down to kiss her.

She pushed him away with a start but then grabbed his arm so that neither of them lost their balance. On her face was concern. Maybe offense.

"I'm sorry, Kalh. I… "

"No, it's—" She looked around his shoulder into the trees.

NAK TURNED HIS chin, following her gaze, and rested his hand on the pistol on his hip.

With her eyes glowing, Kalh looked at the trees. "A dozen men. Surrounding us. I shouldn't have brought you here. I'm sorry."

""

"They're after me. If you lie low, I'll bet you can get away."

"Not a chance. You promised me a blaze of glory."

She laughed, taken off guard by his flippancy.

"Come on." He leaped off the rock toward the point of the triangle then offered her a hand.

She didn't take it but leaped alone, landing powerfully next to him.

He pulled the pistol from his holster as they crouched behind the perspective stone, putting their back to the wondrous vista and the deadly drop-off. This spotlighted their size difference: She was petite and lithe, and he was a monster of a man, who could barely fit behind the rock. When his eyes began to glow, he glared through the barrier and into the jungle, seeing a dozen bodies creeping toward them.

She looked at the threat with glowing eyes and then back at the open expanse, trapped between something so beautiful and something so terrible. "We could climb down, but it's steep, and they'd shoot us off before we got far."

"No." He wouldn't risk her falling again. "Is it Witch Hunters."

"Actually, I don't think so."

He scanned the skies. With his left hand, Nak grabbed a comms from his belt and lifted it to his mouth. "Cup. I need you here right now." *Lucky she wasn't in infraspace right now.*

Her voice was even more tiny and small than usual: "What's the password?"

"█████"

"Close enough." She was supposed to verify that he wasn't calling under duress.

"The cliff at Tiigxuu," he said.

"Calculating the jump now. You know I'm still orbital?"

"Yeah. Hurry up."

"On my way."

"What does orbital mean?" asked Kalh.

"It's going to take a seq." Nak's eyes glowed as he stared into the jungle and shouted, "WHICH ONE OF YOU WANTS IT FIRST!"

At that, the enclosing enemies hesitated. *Keep them on their toes.*

Nak pulled the comms back to his mouth and spoke quietly to Cup: "This is going to be like that catch I pulled on Toar. Stay low."

"Copy that," came the little voice.

With eyes glowing, Nak shot up over the top of the rock like a viper, clasping the pistol in both hands. He fired three rounds in rapid succession and dropped back down.

He just glimpsed his target fall as a hailstorm of laser fire came right back, so close he felt the heat through his hair, roasting his scalp. He stooped farther to get his massive form down.

"Watch it!" shouted Kalh. "You're going to get yourself killed!"

"They don't have a lot of cover out there," said Nak, "but they're all going to be aiming right at me next time. I don't think that'll work again." He looked at her, wondering if she had any more handlebar tricks up her sleeve.

In her hand, she held her prism, but she shook her head doubtfully. "I can trip up one at a time or push the barrel of a gun down, but if they know who I am, it won't scare or slow them much at all. I can't stall a group this big." ████.

He eyed the prism. "When I was a kid, they talked about deflecting laser bolts with those things."

"I'm not very good at it. Benton is… But there's too many—impossible to defend two sides at the same time."

SHOOM!

A bright laser streaked just past Kalh's hip.

Nak jerked her closer and backed up, forcing her deeper behind the rock's protection, which happened to be closer to him.

The attackers were flanking the left side. It was only a matter of sequels till both of them would be exposed.

"Surge behind them," he commanded.

"I would land barely beyond the farthest of them, ducking behind those scrubby trees. Besides, I'm not leaving you."

SHOOM!

It felt like someone pounded a sledge onto Nak's right boot.

Shock protected him for the worst of it. He slammed his face against the rock, trying to get his huge body more hidden.

Kalh jumped right on top of him, hugging him face to face, trying to turn two bodies into one and keep both out of sight.

Nak's boot was smoking, and he could smell the burnt flesh inside. Might have broken or lost some toes. A bloody, charred mess. They shot his ████████ toes!

"I'm going to surrender," said Kalh.

"Don't you dare," said Nak, trying not to grimace.

She gave him a deep stare.

Cup's tiny voice seemed to come from Nak's pocket: "Here!"

Nak let out a sigh of relief.

The Sanctum had arrived in complete silence. Nak had taught her well.

"You ready for a leap of faith?" He pointed off the edge of the cliff.

"If we put one hair out there, they'll shoot it off." Kalh looked around. "Give me your pistol. How many rounds in it?"

"I only fired that one time."

She rolled against him so they were both facing out, big spoon and little spoon. She held the pistol sideways with the handle pointing to her right. *"This is going to take a lot of concentration.* As soon as I throw it, okay?"

Nak nodded.

She tossed the pistol over her head, over the rock at their back, in a way that it spun, almost like a flying disc, and it sailed down the path. Then with her Kinosis, she managed to catch hold of the trigger, so rounds went spurting sporadically in every direction. Odds of it hitting anything were pretty low, but it looked scary and damn strange.

In that sequel, Nak and Kalh ran for it.

They sprinted hand in hand.

Straight for the cliff.

Each step pounded pain up through his toes.

Lasers zipped past their sides, their hands, their ears.

And the two leaped into open air.

The Sanctum waited below the cliff edge, but still quite a drop.

A thrill shot up through Nak's stomach.

Cup swooped the ship in a catch, reducing the impact, but it still hurt his ▮▮▮▮▮ foot pretty bad.

"Grab on!" shouted Nak, demonstrating the right hand holds. "Go, Cup!"

The Sanctum dipped lower as the assassins reached the crest and started firing.

Cup darted the ship out of range, accelerating just gently enough to keep the two of them from falling off.

WHEN NAK AWOKE the next cycle, he limped to Kalh's closed door. The house was quiet, all those Warnur kids still asleep. It felt strange that sleep cycles on this planet had no reference point. Even on Toar, people could sleep over the same few short days. Here there was nothing, just like the black of space. No wonder the locals all seemed hyper-focused on sleep hygiene. As he stood at her door, he remembered their conversation:

"I owe you a new pistol," she'd said. "And my life."

"There was a little saving on both sides," he'd replied. "Let's call it even."

She'd done a hell of a job healing him already, although she said she could do nothing about the missing chunks. That light from her hands was something else. She stayed with him past when he fell asleep, so maybe now he should let her sleep.

He checked his chronometer then headed down to the study, limping while wearing just one boot. They'd ruined his favorite pair. It hadn't been Witch Hunters, so maybe one of the factions was trying to kill her.

He came to an old wooden door that hung partly open. That happened sometimes with manual doors.

Inside was a dimly lit study, a large desk and walls lined with maps. He limped inside curiously, looking for books

But he unexpectedly saw a face.

He flinched, though it wasn't like him to be caught off guard.

Dray was standing in the shadows of the study.

"Stop sneaking around," said Nak, a joke to lighten the tension, but it didn't seem to land.

Dray stopped still, like a caught fugitive. He spoke while turning to peruse the books, as if to hide his damaged eye: "I didn't know you were staying with the Warnur's too, Skyreacher. I never congratulated you on a successful mission to the Strand. You have proven your dependability once again."

Nak sighed, looking for words, and scratched the back of his neck. "About that. I'm sorry."

Dray faced Nak and peered with that one, sad eye.

During all they'd gone through together, there had always been a mask over Nak's face, even on Feath. Until now. Dray was finally seeing him for the first time. And yet he didn't seem to be seeing Nak at all.

Dray spoke in a sad tone: "Sorry for what?"

"For abandoning you in Building 13."

"We agreed on the protocol beforehand. You were following the plan. I would've done the same, as any good soldier would."

"Well..." Nak sighed and shook his head. "I'm still sorry."

Dray's lonely eye looked deeply at Nak.

The old soldier with the wild gray hair looked heavy, weighed down. He also seemed to be withholding an unspoken... something... maybe a reciprocal apology of some sort, one he didn't dare say.

As if the truth spoken aloud might kill them both.

Dray blinked his one eye, which might've been a wink if he'd had two.

That gesture ended the conversation.

"Okay, well, I'll see you around." Nak nodded awkwardly and went out of the far side of the room. The encounter left him feeling unsettled, unsure what to make of it.

Something did seem off, just like Kalh said.

He entered the library, which smelled of candle smoke and old books, and he heard a conversation. Dr Warnur and that white head of hair leaned back in a curving, red-velvet chair. Benton sat on the edge of a seat opposite, in an intense pose, hair and beard just as fetching as ever. Rows of books lined the walls. In front of a window, the black bones of a large predator stood crouched in the corner.

"Hey, Benton, Doc, how's it going. Sorry to interrupt."

"Not at all," said Dr Warnur. "Come in."

"Did I hear you say something about Taiberos." Just the thought of that bastard made Nak feel sick.

"Have a seat." Dr Warnur waved him further in. "Yes. The president."

Nak sat down. "What about him."

Dr Warnur twiddled with a long quill pen. He seemed so inviting, so open to share the conversation. His whole demeanor seemed like a smile. "We were just wondering why he has a stake on Solace too."

Benton leaned back, abandoning his aggressive stance and becoming silent. He seemed a lot less open, maybe even a bit threatened by the intrusion.

"What do you mean by *too*," asked Nak.

Dr Warnur looked up with a smirk. "There's more to their project than simply capturing Radiances. Taiberos is running the Strand on Toar. His Redhelms are also mining on the starside here on Solace, but we don't yet understand the purpose. One guess is that it may have to do with tracking down the missing Bloody Wings."

Nak frowned, not liking the sound of it. "That would make sense. He's obsessed with them."

"Really?"

"I'm a first-hand witness."

The thought of Taiberos coming to Solace gave Nak a chill, strengthening his resolve: He had to get out of here before it was too late.

And he didn't know what to think about Kalh's confession about that bastard. Must've taken guts for her to say it out loud. When she first told him, Nak felt sorry for her. Compassion, maybe. Or pity. Now he felt revulsion. It grossed him out. And left a trail of sadness, resentment, even jealousy. He'd always imagined the ideal woman as pure, but she'd been with that bastard Taiberos. And he'd...

Nak wasn't going to think about it.

Dr Warnur set down the quill. "I think they're mining a substance called Orikerse to use in their experiments."

"I've helped smuggle it a few times," said Nak.

"Ever used it?"

Nak shook his head. At least not that he wanted to say. Wasn't exactly a positive experience.

Finally Benton spoke up in what turned out to be a sincere and respectful tone: "By the way, Skyreacher, I have some unfortunate news. Our schedule has changed, and I don't think it's possible to get the funds in time. It's a shame. We truly could've used you."

Nak nodded, as if to say it was all right, but his eyes glossed over as he fell deep in thought. With Dray back, the insurgents had at least a slim chance. He was the sort of leader Nak could see himself fighting for, the almost-friend kind. But it would still require risking it all on a long shot, a very long shot.

"I mean, you're still welcome to join us as a volunteer." Benton laughed. "We could use help cleaning up the galaxy's rubbish."

"As I said, I don't like to get involved in other people's problems."

Benton frowned with idealistic indignation but spoke calmly: "Forgive me for overstepping the bounds of courtesy, but I think you may need to hear this: If you think you're not part of the problem, you are the problem."

"That's your opinion." Nak was ready for the conversation to be over anyway. He stood, nodded, and said, "Doctor." Then with a limp, he stormed out.

He heard Benton's call from behind: "You know where to find us if you change your mind."

N AK MADE HIS way down to the kitchen. The stairs were the hardest. He found Kalh leaning over a bowl of pottage. She wore a pair of white headphones exactly like the ones she'd given him, and the wire dripped from the edge of the counter. She was still squinting through her grogginess. He didn't ask how long she'd kept working on his toes after he'd fallen asleep. Couldn't face the answer.

"Hey, Kalh." He had a serious look.

She nodded at him and pulled one of the housings off her ear, letting it rest higher on her nearly bald skull.

"Hey, listen to me." He grabbed her elbow and turned her to face him.

She looked up into his earnest eyes and rested the headphones around her neck.

"I play women, okay?"

"What?"

"I live each moment like it's going to last forever, but it won't. I'm a hunted man."

"What are you talking about?"

He inhaled for an answer but exhaled only a sigh. He didn't know what else to say.

But she'd understood. "You're trying to not hurt me…"

"Is that what your Song is saying."

"No. It's what your eyes are saying."

He glanced away, backing down, the only time he'd done that in front of her.

"But you know it can work," she said.

He locked eyes with her and contemplated shaking his head, but he knew it'd be a lie. Yes, he could make it work. He just wasn't sure he wanted to.

"You wouldn't be saying this if you didn't care."

"Don't read into it, Kalh."

She shook her head, with an expression of confusion and pain.

"Look, I'm sorry. I'm not the right guy. You want marriage and revolution. That's not my thing." He pointed at the door. "It's *his* thing." Suddenly he wished he were wearing his dread mask.

"Let me tell you something about music, Nak. You can begin any song on any note and sing it in any key. No note by itself is right or wrong. It's a question of whether it's in harmony with the notes around it—a certain measure, a certain tempo, a certain pitch—right place, right time, right way."

"So what."

"So maybe you've been the wrong note in the past, but I think you're right, right now." She paused, scrutinizing his face, as if to discover the answer to some mysterious question. "And so do you, deep down, don't you?"

He looked into her hazel eyes, not giving an answer, then glanced at the chronometer on his wrist.

Her expression beamed an answer of her own:

She believed in him.

But he refused to let his face concede. "This revolution… you have to win or it does no good. If you're wrong, you lose everything and so does everyone you pull into it. You really think you can beat Taiberos?"

She didn't respond to that, and she didn't deny their terrible odds.

"I can see the doubt in your eyes," he said.

"I see the hope in yours."

He stood, sighed, and looked around the room as if planning his escape. "Sorry, Kalh, I have to rendezvous with Cup. I'm… not sure when I'll see you again."

"You're leaving?"

He nodded and stepped toward the door.

"Why?" she asked.

"I just have to." He paused at the threshold.

"You *have* to? Nobody ever made you do anything."

He shook his head.

"Nak?"

"What."

"Jyngsoo used to say gravity is a choice. At the time, it seemed like mystical nonsense. I felt sure I couldn't levitate, but now I think I get what he meant. If we believe we must abide the law of gravity, then we never formulate the intention to do otherwise. We just submit to fate. Without considering our freedom, we default to slavery. You have to believe in choice—that your will can spite causes and become its own origin."

He almost walked from the room without looking at her.

But he had to see her once more.

When he did, he saw disappointment in her eyes.

NAK RENTED A groundrunner and made his way to the foothills on the starside, which took several isochrons. All the while, thoughts of Kalh echoed in his head.

Cup landed with her usual punctuality.

She'd been keeping *The Sanctum* safe out in infraspace, where no one could touch her. He couldn't contact her while she was doing that, so if he'd missed this rendezvous, he'd have had to wait another seven sleep cycles till Cup's algorithm had her try again. And he wasn't that committed to Solace.

He ordinarily liked getting back aboard *The Sanctum*, but this time something felt different.

Something was missing.

The zentisal fuel still read zero. He hadn't had the time to fix the gauge. He just needed to be grounded a little longer.

As he blasted toward the black, he scrolled through a list of job offers from the Handnet. The most interesting one was a cargo run on Terron Prime—it would take him back to his beginnings. He hadn't been there in ages. Still, the prospect felt empty. All the missions did. Like they were entirely hollow.

Or like he was.

He stared despondently at the white headphones on the seat next to him and the cord trailing down onto the floor. He didn't feel like listening to music, but he picked them up and put them around his neck.

Something compelled him toward her as powerfully as the forces that pushed him away, leaving him stranded in limbo. He stared out across the black, and one star shone brighter than the rest: the surge gate. He shook his head.

He'd wanted the sky to himself.

Now even the universes didn't seem to be enough.

When *The Sanctum* had nearly cleared the planet's gravitational horizon, he said, "Okay, Cup, make the calculation for Terron Prime."

He turned the steering yoke to the starboard, skirting the planet in a wide perimeter, no longer increasing his distance from it. He flew along that axis for a long time, keeping the ship from leaving, as he deliberated, obsessively. That wasn't like him. He couldn't commit to her, so he had to move on, had to cut her loose.

"What are you doing, Nak?" came Cup's tiny voice.

Nak didn't answer, still trapped in thought.

It felt like trying to sail away from someone who was aboard your own ship. Even sailing to another galaxy would do no good.

Kalh was on the inside.

He'd treated her so badly. Told her she couldn't stay on his ship. Then she suffered because he couldn't trust. Yet she'd responded to that injustice with acceptance. Just like she'd done for that little kid on Sream. She told Nak he could be the right man right now—he just had to choose it. No one had rooted for him like that before.

The burning rays of their red sun, the star Origin, reflected off the surface of Solace. He pictured Kalh down there, a molecular-sized figure on the massive sphere, standing somewhere in that Twilight Ring. He felt connected to her, as if her gravity really were pulling on him across the massive distance. He couldn't just shrug it off. He'd become attached. In spite of the Taiberos thing…

And who better to support her, understand her, avenge her, than Nak.

Suddenly the truth dawned on him: He'd gotten it backward. Even a whole galaxy would be worthless if it didn't have this star in it, if it didn't have her in it.

He needed Kalh.

That pressing thought—this truth—beat inside him. It beat so loudly he could no longer contain it within his own small form.

He'd even risk his *Sanctum* for her.

Against Taiberos.

When he came to this realization, he pulled on the steering yoke, cutting a sudden turn across the empty black, headed toward Solace. Then words originated as thoughts inside his mind. Through Ptolis, third spectrum, these echoed loudly and spontaneously across the cold void of space:

Kalh, my name is Breck Starchild, and I'm going to help you liberate Solace.

U UMAKI."
Taiberos said it in a voice that was smooth, almost kind.

"Come here, Uumaki."

Yellow and brown grime crept down the metal walls of the cell.

The miin came, his steps slow and reluctant. He was large and white with curling horns and apparently quite old, more than a hundred percents—older than a human lifetime. He'd been dosed with exhaust, to make him more manageable. His four upper paws were bound behind his back, which forced him to walk unnaturally on his hind legs. The blood stains on his white coat of fur showed clearly.

Taiberos stepped behind the creature, and with a *click, click*, both pairs of handcuffs came off. He tossed them on the floor.

The old miin automatically dropped onto all sixes as if in great relief.

"No, on your hind legs, Uumaki. Let's speak man to man."

The miin obeyed. Although smaller than many miina, on his hind legs he stood taller than Taiberos. They were a large species. Patches of the white fur had been worn away from the... persuasion... of the last few cycles. The white fur made it hard to see the bruises though. They had even tried skalk venom on him.

Taiberos put his cybernetic arm over the miin's shoulder as if they were pals. Miina were always awkward on their hind legs, but this forced Uumaki to contort unstably sideways to get down to Taiberos's level.

The President's voice was smooth and calm: "I'm afraid if you're not going to help me, Uumaki, then I'm not going to help you. But it's not too late to tell me what I need to know, and then you'll go free."

The miin's eyes stared with determined silence. He seemed frail but not afraid. "I have nothing to tell."

Taiberos frowned. "You and I both know that isn't true."

"It is."

Taiberos could feel the miin's arms pressing into the fat on his own side. "You attended a meeting of conspirators."

"That isn't true."

"It's pathological honor, Uumaki. That means your sense of honor is actually hurting you. But you're stronger than that, different from the blind members of your tribe. You can tell me to save your own hide."

"I would tell you if I could, but I don't know anything. I swear it."

"Then you are of no use to me, and neither of us wants you to be useless, do we?"

"Let me go free. I have a family!"

Taiberos spoke with a silky tone, pulling the miin closer with his cybernetic arm: "Uumaki, this may not be apparent to you, but I am at the end of my patience. I won't deliberate with you further. And I am not bluffing, so weigh your next words carefully. Tell me what the conspirators are planning, or you will die."

"I have nothing to tell. I swear!"

With his human hand, Taiberos grabbed one of the miin's arms and pulled it against his own chest. He slid his head close to the miin's and whispered in a monotone, *"That's the wrong thing to say right now."*

With his cybernetic elbow bent and pointing outward, Taiberos reached toward himself and took the miin's throat in his metal grip, latching on so deep and tight as to grasp the spinal cord. The metal fingers stabbed like blunt knives into flesh. His hand felt like a separate entity, like it wasn't him doing this. He simply thought the action and the cybernetics carried it out, a grip so vicious it could break sinew and crush bone.

He had Starchild to thank for that.

The miin gave a strange chortle. "Plea—"

Without releasing the grip of either of his hands, Taiberos straightened his cybernetic arm. The miin's neck twisted a hundred and eighty degrees, while his body, held back, only turned something like five.

With a crack, the life went out of the old creature.

The corpse collapsed onto the concrete, splattering when it hit. The sound of such a heavy impact was almost painful. The body lay there motionless except for a slight flutter of the blood-stained, white fur. Must've been drafty in here.

Maybe the miin hadn't known anything after all. Still, the pretense of war made even murder permissible.

Taiberos grinned.

As he stared down at what used to be a conscient, he thought of Starchild. He wanted to do the same thing to that man. Perhaps rip his jaw off first. So this one wasn't entirely wasted.

At least it served as a practice round.

TAIBEROS NEEDED TO get the grime off.

He brushed his hands against each other helplessly, unable to do more.

Taiberos didn't often leave the sky to come to the ground. This facility had blinds to let in the twilight. They were set to open and close on a regular pattern that followed the PSD's standard awake-sleep cycles. The colonists had brought that tradition with them, and it had become the standard here, as it ought to have, though it was still a point of contention for the miina. He hated their unwillingness to conform, especially over a belief so obviously wrong.

An aide came up with a look of urgency, but he seemed too cautious to even utter a salutation.

"What?" said Taiberos.

"Sir, Hevold wanted me to get this to you immediately: Bloody Wing one thirteen was just spotted on a flight path away from Solace."

"And…?"

"It was making its way toward open space, and as they prepared to intercept it, it turned back."

"So where is he?"

"They lost the trace down on the surface, but they believe he's still down there." The bright marks Bloody Wings left when they surged made it somewhat simple to track how many came and went in a given system. "He turned back before they threatened him, on his own accord."

So Lethos had been right. This was the locus of the conspiracy.

Taiberos wanted to wipe the sweat from his forehead, but he didn't want to use his hands to do it, not till he washed first. "Any word yet from Shauu or Kavalion?"

The aide started for the door almost quicker than he could reply: "Not actively, but I will check in with them right away."

Shauu—the miin with the red eyes—had been raised here. He knew the ways of his fellow breed. He'd been the one to find Uumaki—the old miin who'd been so promising and so equally disappointing.

Shauu had done it through Chief Adiin, leader of one of the largest miina clans. The chief had a deep grudge against the human colonists, particularly for the desecration of the Hoff Mines, so Taiberos had expected an alliance to be an easy sell. Instead, the offers had been rejected repeatedly. More pathological honor. Supposedly, Adiin's honor wouldn't let him break his treaty with the colonists, at least publicly. That was a weakness, to be unable to cross your own unreasonable moral boundaries. Or maybe Adiin was playing both sides—hard to tell. Shauu had somehow convinced Adiin to help indirectly, and the miina chief essentially gave a wink and a nod toward this Uumaki and then turned a blind eye, supporting the deed with his silence.

Taiberos left the command deck and made his way first to the lavatory, where he meticulously washed his gloves, hands, and face. Then he headed toward his suite, feeling tired, but before he had even gotten his heavy form up the first flight of stairs, the aide came running from behind: "Your excellency, sir?"

Taiberos and his retinue stopped and turned.

"Shauu is downstairs waiting for you. He brought another candidate."

Taiberos nodded, exhausted, and returned to the interrogation floor.

When they entered the room, Shauu, whose red eyes were always startling to see, greeted him with sterile respect.

A white, female miin sat on the metal bench. Her eyes drifted around the floor, tracking the new arrivals peripherally without looking directly.

Shauu nodded to the retinue still crowded around the doorway. His voice had a slightly higher pitch, smooth and poisonous: "May we have some privacy?"

Taiberos turned and waved a single finger at the group. "Go."

They obeyed, and the door closed with a whoosh, leaving the three of them in silence.

Shauu's voice had a surprising gentleness to it: "Tell him what you told me."

The female cleared her throat. "They've been building an illicit fleet underground near the Hoff Mines. A massive fleet."

Taiberos remained near the door, trying to match Shauu's air of safety. "Who has?"

Her pink tongue touched her dark, pleated lips as she spoke: "I don't know. Liberationists."

"What kind of fleet?"

"An illicit one. And very large. More skycraft than you might imagine."

But it was still only a renegade fleet. How many skycraft could they have made? If it were a shocking number, they might beat the division currently staffed here, but he just needed to get his navy pouring through the surge gate to counter that. "How do you know this?"

"My sons worked for them." She'd clearly overcome her pathological honor.

"Do you know precisely where this fleet is?"

"No. I have never been out there, and I think it would be very difficult to find in that maze of tunnels."

"Yes. I think you're right. What else?"

"Tell him the rest," said Shauu.

The female sniffed with her dark, moist nose. "They plan to use this fleet to capture the surge gate."

Of course. The PSD's control of the surge gate kept the system in submission. That was the conspiracy. It was always the conspiracy. Taiberos shook his head. Maybe Starchild had been hired to consult, to help plan. It seemed like just his sort of guile. "Do you know when this is supposed to happen?"

"It is imminent. Probably next cycle."

So soon. "How do you know?"

In a lower volume, she said, "I overheard my Uumaki say so."

Suddenly the pieces snapped into place: No wonder Uumaki had been so determined to keep the secret—he'd known he only had to outlast three cycles. He'd almost made it, if not for a slight miscalculation of Taiberos's patience. And now Uumaki's wife had betrayed her husband's secret, telling them *exactly* what they needed to know:

The conspirators would try to capture the surge gate within isos.

But Taiberos would get there first.

He would have them beaten before the battle had even begun.

They were doomed.

He gave a slight bow to the female, restricting a grin. "Thank you for your help." He turned and tapped the door controls with a heavy finger, revealing the attendants still waiting directly on the other side. "Send for the sixth and seventh, eighteenth, nineteenth, and twentieth. Queue them at the surge gate immediately."

Five relays to five admirals.

"All of them?" The aide's surprise was justified. It was, indeed, overkill to send five Behemoths, but Taiberos didn't want to leave anything to chance.

"Yes, all of them."

A timid voice spoke from behind him. "Sir?"

Taiberos turned back to Shauu and the female. "Yes?"

She glanced up and into his eyes for less than a sequel and then asked her question looking at the floor. "What about the promise?"

"What promise?"

She pointed at Shauu. "He said you'd release my husband if I confessed."

Now Taiberos glanced down for less than a sequel. "Shauu, step outside with me."

The female looked frightened.

Shauu walked on all sixes and followed into the hallway. He had no fear.

With the flick of a button, the door slid closed, putting the two of them on the outside.

"Do you trust what she told us?" asked Taiberos.

"Absolutely."

"Good. I will secure the skies, but I want to know what else they're planning. I want you on this personally. I want it stopped."

"Certainly."

"Good."

"Sir, she confessed because I promised to release her husband, Uumaki."

"Well, what do you want me to do? I already killed him."

"Then how do I give her recompense?"

"Thank her, and send her on her way." Taiberos wiped his gloved hands on his pants. "Or kill her too."

T AIBEROS RETURNED TO his suite and washed his hands.

He then sat at his desk and made a relay.

It was the fifth Behemoth that dared to produce friction.

"What's the trouble? I want Sorvon queued right now."

"Sir, with all due respect, if he takes his Behemoth out of that system, the government could easily fall, and the genocide would continue. Many innocent lives could be lost."

"I suppose he thinks I should leave Terron Prime vulnerable instead."

"No, sir. It's just that—"

"I'm glad you agree. See that Sorvon agrees as well. I want him loaded to maximum capacity and queued at the Origin surge gate within seven isos. I want my next message to be a live relay with him. Is that understood?"

"Yes, sir."

Taiberos ended the relay but didn't smile.

It wasn't enough.

The conspirators would meet a terrible fate, but he couldn't imagine Starchild would actually risk his Bloody Wing and stay among them, and that left a bitter taste. Taiberos would trade all of Solace to get justice from that man.

He went through the papers on his desk. The funeral had made headlines.

What did he need a wife for though when he had a ████ at his beck and call.

The dead boy was famous only because of his inheritance, which had gone to his head, and apparently the public's too. They acted like he was a demigod, come to save them all. Taiberos had married into royalty only after working his way from the bottom. Unlike that little ████. Yet people loved the boy almost more than they loved Taiberos. Maybe the public grief could be leveraged though. Taiberos could paint himself as the boy's avenger. If only the ████ had died doing something worthwhile. Maybe the story could be that an assassin made it look like an accident. Perhaps the conspirators of Solace. Once in custody, he could torture whatever story he wanted out of them. He'd have the time then. Maybe even make Starchild look guilty and ruin his reputation on the black market.

Taiberos controlled the narrative, and so he controlled the truth.

He looked at the comms. It still hadn't been cleaned.

His right eye twitched.

He glanced around the room for her.

Then he pounded several buttons with a heavy, metal finger.

"My secretary is gone!" He pictured the little ████'s bruised face.

"Yes, sir. She said it was medical leave."

"Medical leave? You track her down. Bring her into custody. If she's really doing this to heal, I want her confined while she does it. Is that understood?"

"Yes, sir."

Maybe he was overreacting. Her turning traitor was not the worst case scenario. Even if she did betray the PSD, she'd gone too soon, so she didn't know the biggest secret: that thanks to Uumaki's wife, Taiberos now knew their plans.

All of it.

And when their illicit fleet came up from beneath the surface of Solace, he would be in the sky waiting for them.

With a force so large not even the Shadowlyss could stop him.

Much less a ragtag band of rebels.

WHAT'S YOUR NAME?"

Benton sat on a G-227 medical dropship. He happened to have landed in the seat next to the only miin aboard, who was just a cub.

"Private Spuunar, sir." The miin had the long, white fur of the reclusive breed from the starside.

The rain tapped on the roof of the dropship. The Nightwatchmen filled the rest of the seats, all clad in black, awaiting the countdown. One soldier smacked his boot against the floor, adjusting it for comfort. Others rechecked their weapons.

"You're not one of the Bloods," said Benton.

"I'm from Nuktuk, sir, near Land's End on the Starside."

"And you're with the Nightwatchmen?"

"Only barely. It is a long story."

Doubting whether it would be courteous to ask the next question, Benton kept quiet. All that hung in the balance weighed on them, and each of the soldiers sat alone with their thoughts.

Benton wore the dark-green battle armor of the Ruffians: breastplate, heavy spaulders, vambraces, gauntlets, cuisses, greaves, boots, and a helmet. The color would hide him in dense jungles and offered protection from glancing shots and explosions, making his mortal form something only slightly closer to immortal. More importantly, the armor had become a symbol, a representation of his knighthood and the creed that drove him to defend the innocent.

When he noticed his knee bouncing, he consciously stilled it. Much of Blue Group's success would depend on his leadership.

He glanced at his chronometer.

In just a few moments, the dropships would rise into the air.

He stole a glance to the bench on the other side where Kalhette sat among the Nightwatchmen, a flower among weeds. She wore his purple skullhugger over her bald head. When she looked up, they locked eyes, and in them he could see... trust.

He hoped it wasn't misplaced.

If anything happened to her in this battle, he would never forgive himself.

* * *

BENTON DIDN'T HAVE the tactical experience to have come up with this plan. He had to trust Dray. They all did.

And trust that rushing would pay off.

Throughout the history of the Photoss Galaxy, no occupying force had ever outnumbered the local citizenry—or had even come close, and the same was true now on Solace. The Redhelm invaders only had to dominate small segments of the population at a time, which created a spirit of fear that rippled across the planet, yet the PSD would be helpless if the population rose up as a whole. So that was the objective—uprising in unison.

That meant everyone needed to feel courage at once.

Which rested on Kalhette. Dray planned for her to send a planetwide broadcast. Much depended on her words igniting people's hearts.

After the Solace Sunset, the PSD began regulating all media, ostensibly to censor hate speech. In order to do so, they seized the Athenaeum and made it the only source of legal publications or broadcasts on the planet. Governmental land holdings grew outward from there, like the Grezyk, slowly creeping and consuming all life. Locals called it the Sozo, for Socialist Zone. Soon competing media services were outlawed and destroyed. Outside the Sozo, citizens still had a semblance of freedom, but inside, the PSD controlled everything. As the Sozo expanded, citizens were forced to abandon their homes and property to the PSD for what was labeled the greater good. All visitors to the Sozo were verified at checkpoints, both at the borders and scattered within.

And yet Kalhette had to send her message from the Athenaeum at the center of the Sozo. If the dropships tried to fly her in, they'd be shot down by the flock towers. So Liink and his brothers, part of Blue Group, had gone ahead to knock out a number of the towers in a line, leaving a path of unguarded airspace.

According to Dray, this attack would trigger a lockdown, making it virtually impossible to get inside the Athenaeum, but Kalhette would enter by surging, gaining access to the heart of the planet's media. With her inside, the lockdown would then work against the PSD, leaving her largely undisturbed while she used the broadcast system to call the people of Solace to arms. All of this was Blue Group.

Despite the PSD outlawing weapons that might prove useful in a revolution, the militia had accumulated a significant number of illegal handguns and rifles. They lacked artillery, though, which would be necessary for a military victory. Dray's plan solved that problem with Red Group. At the given isochron, nine munitions bays would be attacked at once. Liink's father, Chief Adiin, would raid one at New Kingstrong. Other groups were poised at Nosaui, Delasiin, and other key locations. The artillery stolen in those attacks would be dispersed among the militias and would ensure a victory on the ground.

The last offensive was the sky, Green Group. The attacks on the ground would stir up the PSD, inviting angry retaliation, so Valt and his privateers would capture the surge gate and keep the PSD from sending reinforcements through. The PSD didn't know Valt had been building a private fleet on the surface. Hopefully that surprise would be enough to ensure a third victory.

Plus the rogue pilot Skyreacher had decided to offer his services as well. Every little bit helped.

SPUUNAR, THE FLUFFY, white starside miin, spoke with a native accent: "Sir, may I ask you a question?"

The cabin lights flickered off and then back on. A humming whir began in the background. While turning his attention toward the young soldier, Benton stole a glance at Kalhette. "Yes?"

"Sir, what about helping the poor?" In that moment, his yellow miina eyes looked very human. His curling horns did not.

"What?" asked Benton.

"Don't mind him, sir," said Jaikes. "He's new. A Panso. Doesn't know anything."

"I'm not a Panso!" said Spuunar, gripping his rifle with all four of his fluffy, white arms. This starside miin could have easily taken the human in a tussle.

Benton directly faced Spuunar, ignoring Jaikes's comment. "Go on."

"Sir, I hear your new government isn't going to collect taxes."

At this comment, Dr Warnur came to attention, leaning his white head forward to hear Benton's reply. Kalhette, quietly avoiding conversation, also perked up.

"The committee hasn't come to an agreement," said Benton. "But, yes, if I had my way, we wouldn't collect taxes." He touched a finger to his lips as he thought.

Unfortunately, even if they succeeded in gaining independence, not everyone agreed on how to proceed from there. The tax issue lingered along with many others, not the least of which was the fact that the colonists had promised the entrepreneurs a certain quantity of land on the edge of the starside, but the miina hadn't agreed. Liink's father stubbornly refused to concede any of it. Yet here they all were, colonists, entrepreneurs, and miina as comrades in arms.

"If we don't," said Spuunar, "how are we going to help the poor?"

The conversation now drew in several of the Nightwatchmen, sitting in rows inside the dropship.

It reminded Benton of the conversation he'd had when he met Kalhette. He hoped this wouldn't end in a brawl. "You're asking the wrong question. One should never presume to take someone else's choice away." He shifted his green helmet from one thigh to the other as he tapped on Spuunar's leather-covered chest. "The question is, how are *you* going to help the poor?

Our new government will invite everyone on Solace to help the poor. You can personally give as much as you want."

A bulky trooper sitting across the aisle spoke up: "But what about people who don't want to give anything?"

"He's a Panso too, sir," said Jaikes. "Head still soft. We had a lot of new recruits after Nosaui."

"We won't force anyone to do anything they don't want to," said Benton. "That's called slavery, and it's the thing we're fighting against."

Spuunar checked over his rifle as if it might explain things more clearly, seemingly a little embarrassed and a little confused, which Benton sensed through Ptolis. They weren't getting it.

Benton glanced at his chronometer and then drummed his fingers across the helmet in his lap. "Have you heard of the Primordial Laws?"

Spunnar nodded as if he might know the reference but wasn't sure. The big guy shook his head.

"They're three…"—Benton's head bobbed as he searched for the right word—"*virtues*… They're the premises that come before everything." He held up one finger for each of them as he listed them off: "Truth, choice, and compassion."

"Oh, yes," said Spuunar. "I know them."

"We're fighting their opposites: ignorance, slavery, and hatred. So although poverty is bad, technically we're not against it. It's only a symptom of a deeper problem: Poverty comes from either ignorance, a lack of personal freedom, or a hatred of self and others. Sometimes all three. But we fight these causes—the roots—and let the symptoms resolve themselves."

The soldiers looked at him curiously.

Benton turned to Spuunar. "So, does that make sense?"

The young miin, singled out, furrowed his brow, contemplating, or maybe just feigning. "I guess so, sir."

"When you give in the current system, you give because you must. In our new government, if you give, you'll give because you care. Generosity can only truly exist when it's voluntary."

An orange light flashed.

Benton looked at his chronometer.

Explosions sounded on schedule in the distance. He smiled at the thought of Liink and the Bloods clearing the flight path to the Athenaeum.

He felt the motion of the dropship as it lifted off the ground. The Nightwatchmen pulled on their helmets, which left only a T-shaped part of their faces exposed—a line for the eyes and a slit for the nose and mouth. The dropship rocked as it sped through the sky.

But Benton wasn't finished.

Ignorance reigned even here. He set down his helmet, stood, and grabbed the overhead rail. After brushing a hand through his sandy hair, he spoke loudly over the sound of the engine:

"Think about how you felt when you received something undeserved from someone else, something that came only by their good graces. That feeling of gratitude is golden. Now imagine how you'd feel taking that exact same thing by force, demanding it with your brute strength. The transaction is the same, but the attitude, the spirit, makes a galaxy of difference. We're not trying to stop those transactions. It's good for people to help each other. But the spirit of entitlement, of demanding the undeserved, is violence. It's hurtful to both parties because of that change in spirit. One should never override the will of another person."

Benton felt like a parent toward these brawny youths, each the sort who had the ability to use force to get what he wanted, and perhaps who at times had.

"Remember these: truth, choice, and compassion. Every war ever fought came because these three fell into disharmony. A religious devotee whose feelings keep her blind to scientific fact, or a scholar whose focus on scientific fact makes him deaf to feelings. A dreamer whose imagination never has the victory of improving reality, or a warrior whose militant victories leave no place for imagination. A merchant whose free will stampedes compassion, or a governor who enforces compassion by overriding free will. Exalting one of these always destabilizes the others. Yet all three are crucial."

The lifters whistled as the dropship rushed higher into the sky.

"May you be the kind of warriors who never compromise these principles!"

Spuunar looked up silently, eyes transfixed, and his predator mouth hung slightly open, exposing sharp canines.

He looked both speechless and reverent.

L IINK CRAWLED STEALTHILY through the jungle.

His objective: a crack in the ground that wound beneath the Sozo.

His dark-purple face was painted. The streaks of a sanguine red happened to mask the red scar he now wore, which still throbbed. He and Gaiing went single file amid a group of Bloods, an elite group of miina warriors. They wound between trees and tentacle branches.

The mouth of the cave wasn't visible till it practically swallowed them.

Gaiing, whose horns hadn't come through his skin yet either, went first into the narrow crevice, dragging his equipment and rifle behind as he disappeared into the darkness. Liink followed, standing on his hind legs like a human, contorting his body to squeeze through. His tail flowed behind like water. The Redhelms had never discovered this cavern, which would allow the Bloods to skip beneath the Sozo's outer checkpoints.

Once inside, Liink and Gaiing wandered deeper, not waiting for the team.

Gaiing whispered in the darkness: "*What was it like meeting the Prophetess?*"

"*She doesn't like me,*" came Liink's gentle voice.

"*She said that?*"

"*No, but she gave me a look.*"

"*Are you sure?*"

"*Not entirely.*" Liink scratched the injury across his face, which itched. "*I got this wound for her sake, but she never offered to heal it with her powers.*"

"*Are you so high and mighty?*"

"*Well, she healed the pilot.*"

"*I've seen your father act like that, but I have a hard time imagining she would.*"

"*Well, you'll meet her shortly.*"

Liink's ruse helped get the Prophetess out of Building 13. He'd taken down an enemy fighter in his first sky combat. He'd warned the group of the bounty hunters too. These actions were crucial for the team but hadn't directly saved a life. In fact, his part hadn't even been mentioned in the debriefing—dwarfed by other events. Abii had thanked him in person, had even commended him as any teacher would, and Liink *did* want to make Abii proud, but it wasn't enough.

Dray had done enough though.

He'd stayed behind, sacrificing himself to spare the others.

Liink had looked back in that dark room with admiration and envy, thinking he'd never see Dray again. Then the old man miraculously reappeared unscathed, having survived without any help. Well, not unscathed. He'd lost an eye. Now they were carrying out his plan.

"*What happened when you saw your father?*" asked Gaiing.

"*I…*" Liink sighed. The darkness cloaked the disappointment on his face.

"*What?*"

"*He said welcome home.*"

"*And?*"

"*Not you-did-great. Not how-did-it-go. Not how-did-you-get-that-cut. Just welcome-home, and that was that.*"

Gaiing remained silent.

"*It wasn't insult or mockery,*" Liink went on. "*It was indifference. Like he assumed I'd done nothing honorable on the mission. Like my existence didn't matter to him, my own father.*"

"*I'm sorry.*"

"*I'm not,*" said Liink, his tone unconvincing.

"*Why not?*" Gaiing's yellow eyes worried about the answer.

"*Because I don't care what he thinks. Or the Prophetess.*"

"*I don't think you should say that. At least not about her. It's not honorable.*"

"*I'm not sure…*" As he trailed off, a deep silence sucked everything into it.

"*What, Liink?*"

"*I've been out into the galaxy. I have friends now, the pilot and Abii—people from other worlds. Life is bigger than our tribe or even our planet.*"

"*And so?*"

Liink whispered his next statement quieter than the rest: "*So I'm not sure I believe in honor anymore.*"

Gaiing's eyes glinted with surprise. "*How can you say that? You really don't want to be honored?*"

"*Of course I still want to be honored. Why do you think I came on this mission?*"

"*Social pressure.*"

"*No.*"

"*Okay,*" said Gaiing.

"*And I still wish I could have an abiisu.*"

"*Then I don't get it.*"

"*I just don't think honor has the right gatekeepers. Why is it that they get to judge people and decide what or who is honorable?*"

"*Because that's our tradition, and he's the chief. If you're not going to trust him or the Prophetess, then who's going to decide?*"

Liink reached the cave's exit and paused on the brink before entering the Sozo, which was patrolled by Redhelms. He shook his head.

"*I have no idea.*"

* * *

L IINK HAD SPOKEN heresy.

And Gaiing knew it.

Liink sucked air into his chest and exhaled.

The two miin crawled from the darkness back into the twilight, instinctively drifting back into silence. This deep into the Sozo, PSD security was looser, but the Bloods still had to be cautious.

A powerful wind pushed through the greenery. It trickled across the dark purple fur that covered Liink's body. He looked at the brooding skies. The cloud formations seemed to mean the Song condoned their efforts, as if Abii had become the hand of the Kurosh, fulfilling the ancient curse on Solace—that destruction would come upon those who worked in darkness.

The Sozo sat on the sunside edge of the Twilight Ring and received a heavier, constant bath of solar radiation, making plants grow more voraciously. The PSD had burned or paved many areas, including those around the perimeter, but thick grass grew anywhere that hadn't been suppressed with concrete, basically anywhere that wasn't flat. This made it easier for Liink and Gaiing to creep unnoticed toward their prey, and broad leaves hung overhead, casting deeper shadows.

Instinct urged Liink to hunt, to find prey. He wanted to taste the salt of blood, and perhaps soon he would. His fur blended with the shadows. His leather armor protected his shoulders, spine, chest, bowels, and loins. He prowled with a rifle in one paw, while his other five treaded along the jungle path. His belt held Gaiing's red prism with the red ribbon tied to the end. Ever since Abii explained what was possible, Liink had practiced summoning the blade every chance he got. Still no signs of progress. Perhaps he needed to master second spectrum before fourth.

Gaiing served as Liink's Left, meaning they were assigned as a pair, and they both carried a thermal frag in case the other didn't make it. Their objective was to help create a path across the higher, wilder ground. The other Blood pairs had similar assignments, all in a line leading from the border of the Sozo to the Athenaeum. Once the flock towers were down, making the skies clear, dropships would land a larger force, the Nightwatchmen, who'd bring foot-soldiers and treaders, along with the Prophetess.

They reached the top of a jungle ridge. Just ahead, a silver anti-air flock tower sprung up out of the jungle. Two Redhelms stood guard. Their armor visually connected the pelvis and torso into a single piece, with the appendages coming off from there, giving the human soldiers an insect-like quality. Waiting for the prescribed moment to attack, he kept low, resting beneath the foliage, watching his prey. He'd seen the Redhelm armor up close and knew the vulnerabilities.

Beneath the red paint on his face, Liink glanced at his chronometer.

A tenth of an iso to go.

Visible through the grass and leaves, the impressive Athenaeum rested on a lower ridge. It stood tall, like a giant arrowhead pointing to the sky. Great steps led to the front, and the sides of the base flared out as wide as the building was tall. It had once been a haven for culture, science, and art. Now it represented PSD oppression. The tiny forms of Redhelms milled about it, more of the insect infestation.

Liink tossed the thermal frag and caught it. These compact explosives only existed because humans had reverse-engineered Photoss technology. In other words, it was more destructive than anyone had earned.

He looked up at the black vapor. Somewhere beyond the clouds, the scallywag pilot flew. On the trip back from Toar, the two of them hadn't talked much because the pilot had been with the Prophetess so often. It was becoming difficult to tell who she was in love with. Both men seemed honorable.

In their own way.

Maybe that was what Liink needed.

To find his own way.

FOR A PREDATOR, waiting was supposed to be easy.

It didn't feel that way.

Especially not while he needed to find someone to save.

He stared at his paws resting in the dirt. Humans had called him a wildercat and a kaipanther, but cats only had four legs, and their ears stuck up instead of hanging down. He wasn't a cat. Was that how the Prophetess saw him too, as some brutal predator who hunted with a pride and couldn't speak?

His mind retraced a conversation that happened during their second trip to get zentisal fuel on Toar, while she wasn't with them:

The pilot took the lead with his new mask as they weaved among the street vendors. "So, Liink, what's up with you and Kalh." That was another dishonorable thing—to call the Prophetess by such a casual nickname.

Liink shrugged, which meant two sets of shoulders.

Abii, bringing up the rear, interjected defensively: "What do you mean?"

The pilot looked at Liink, ignoring Abii's comment. "You seem to admire her, but I detect some headwinds coming back at you."

"She's not trying to," Abii replied again.

"Let the cub answer my question."

Seeing these two men interact was interesting. No abiisu hung in the balance, and yet something unspoken was at stake.

Liink quietly sighed. "I don't know why she might dishonor me."

"Is there some history between her people and yours."

Liink nodded. "Have you heard of the Shartriin Massacre?"

"The Shartriin *Uprising?*" asked the pilot. "A couple miina staged an armed coup and got shot."

Liink couldn't tell whether the pilot was actually so ignorant or making a tactical move for the conversation's sake. "Not a couple. It was a hundred and twenty-eight *unarmed* miina and a few colonists. Killed in cold blood by Redhelms."

"Why."

"We were demonstrating against the weapons ban. I watched my older brother bleed to death." His brother had completed his abiisu in doing so. Rather than saving a life, he'd given his.

"I'm sorry," said the pilot.

Silence remained for a lengthy, respectful pause, till Liink spoke: "The miina and colonists have had conflict since Aion Zero. After Shartriin, the PSD tightened its grip on Solace in the name of safety and protection. Many colonists blamed the miina, claiming discretion would've served the cause more than honor. It's possible the Prophetess feels that way too."

"Shartriin caused deep wounds on all sides," said Abii.

"So she's right to be upset at you miina," said the pilot.

"I don't know what was right," said Liink.

"There's more to the story," said Abii. "The PSD classified the massacre as a military secret and kept it from most of the galaxy. Until a user called the Prophet published it."

"Yeah, the Twenty-Seven Thirty leak," said the pilot.

"Oh, you know about it?"

The pilot gave a knowing look. "I do Handnet data runs. They called her a traitor for leaking the docs."

"She wasn't a traitor. She showed the public that the government wasn't worthy of their trust."

"So she didn't betray PSD secrets to the Shadowlyss?"

"Not to the Shadowlyss," Abii said. "But insurgents did use those documents to... make plans for Solace."

The pilot chuckled at how the pieces came together.

"When Kalhette was taken prisoner, she was allegedly linked to it," said Abii. "They promoted it on the Freenet as 'Twenty-Seven-Thirty Traitor Captured.'" The Freenet was the PSD's censored network, where they blocked, blotted, and changed to create the narrative they wanted. As Abii liked to point out, it wasn't free at all.

"But she wasn't the leak?" asked the pilot.

"No," said Abii. "It was me."

The pilot's eyebrows frowned. "So she got punished for your crimes."

"The persona the PSD targeted was partly her, partly me, and partly lies. And there were no true crimes."

The pilot shook his head. "Still doesn't explain why she's ticked off at the miina."

Liink felt content to let Abii lead. If her qualm wasn't with Liink personally, but towards all miina, he felt even less seen and more insulted.

"Someone in our circles gave her location to the Witch Hunters," said Abii. "She thinks the traitor was one of the miina, and she has other, related emotional wounds that have never healed. To her, miina adoration feels like more injury."

"So stop admiring her then. Liink, she didn't write the articles. She wasn't the one pushing for revolution."

"But she really is a heroine." After Liink said it, he doubted his own assertion.

The two men didn't contradict him. Maybe they believed it.

With reverence, Liink continued: "Though many of my people believe her to be such for the wrong reason, she has done and will do great things for us."

The pilot nodded and spoke with reverence: "If this pans out, why don't you just let her rule. I think she'd be good at it."

Abii breathed in to answer, but the pilot was looking at Liink. Abii looked at Liink too and relinquished the spotlight. An honorable action.

Liink felt unprepared to answer but did his best: "Because we want a democracy."

"You have a democracy, and see how it's treating you."

Liink didn't know what more to say.

Luckily Abii interjected: "That's because the power is centralized. The more centralized a democracy, the fewer people actually get their preferences represented. It's simple math."

"I don't see how your system will be better," said the pilot. "No matter what you come up with, the people in it will cause problems. That's how people are. They'll carry their flaws with them. Why not let Kalh run things? She'll do a better job than any bureaucracy you can conjure. I'd put money on it."

Liink didn't know what to say—the pilot's point seemed reasonable. She would make a great queen.

Abii looked down, as if constraining a storm inside of his finely groomed head. "Fine, and we get one generation of peace. Then what?"

"Then we're all dead," said the pilot, "and the next generation can worry about it." That did not seem honorable.

"And we'll have handed them a stacked deck, with all the power in the center." Abii shook his head. "Setting up one good leader isn't enough. We have to consider who may wield that power next."

That conversation left Liink feeling unsettled even now.

The Uncrowned Queen was supposed to be the exemplar of honor, and yet she seemed to despise him. Benton's ideals sometimes seemed surprisingly incapable of providing clear cut answers. And the pilot, who should've been a purely despicable example, showed honor in surprising ways.

None of it seemed to fit with what Liink had been taught as a cub.

And the more he thought about it, the more confused he became.

* * *

THE SKIES OPENED up, pouring too much rain over the Sozo.

The sound masked any noise. The clouds did the same to the light. The Kurosh were watching indeed.

Liink looked at his chronometer, now smattered with droplets of rain, and watched the last few sequels tick away. He made eye contact with Gaiing and nodded.

The time had come.

Each anti-air flock tower was operated by two soldiers, one to load and one to aim and fire, which meant they had to be taken down by pairs. Fortunately, this far into the Sozo, the soldiers were far from on guard. The rain dripped heavily on their armor. They talked casually as the two miina crept closer and closer:

"What? Why are they making us move?"

"Sarge said they're putting a bunch of pilots in our bunker."

"What pilots?"

"Don't know. New ones I guess. Gave us a couple of isochrons. You better hope your replacement shows up soon."

The Bloods had been told an important detail about the Redhelms' red helmets: They had an external button which triggered the microphone of their comms, so you could see them making a call for help. The takedowns had to happen before that.

"Even if he gets here, I'll barely have time before the broadcast. This is ridiculous."

"Munk said it was President Taiberos speaking."

"He's here?"

"Guess so."

"Why would he bring pilots?"

"Personnel deficit, I guess. Maybe he's nervous. A guy like that is always looking over his shoulder."

Liink pounced.

The Redhelm could've never seen it coming—just an impact from behind and then blackness.

The other guard, though, would've seen something from a nightmare: a dark ghost with yellow glowing eyes and a face painted red appearing through the rain, gliding toward and then smashing into his comrade.

Liink snarled, holding his enemy pinned to the ground.

The remaining Redhelm didn't lift a hand to his helmet. Instead, he raised his weapon in defense.

Flying horizontally, Gaiing bashed into the second soldier with four huge clawed paws. He then scraped the man's helmet off and sunk his predator teeth into the man's throat, simple, quiet, and quick.

Liink had only stunned the soldier lying beneath him.

Gaiing looked up with bloody teeth and an expression of urgency. "What are you waiting for?"

Liink's claws stabbed into the helmet as he pulled the mask off the man. It was just a cub underneath. Human cub.

The soldier's hair was buzzed close to his skull. His face and skin were young and smooth. Slowly he came to, his eyes rolling into focus as his eyelids drew back. When he registered the danger, he sucked in a huge breath of air to call for help.

Liink jammed his alien paw over the boy's mouth.

Gaiing had a question on his face, wondering what Liink was doing, why he would hesitate at a time like this.

Liink took the frightened human in a choke hold—an elbow locked around his throat, another paw on his mouth, and the two remaining paws around the boy's arms—and dragged the prisoner away from the tower. Without a word, Liink nodded his red-painted face at his Left, as if to say, *You do it.*

Gaiing shook his head, not with disdain but with concern for consequences. He turned from Liink, pushed a switch on the thermal frag, and tossed it through the tower door. He was already running when it clinked metallically against the floor. A high pitched *beep* sounded, followed by more, each at a quicker pace than the last.

BOOM!

The blast shook Liink to the core, like he'd been punched from the inside. The ball of fire curled upward in bright orange and vanished as quickly as it appeared. Smoke billowed into the sky, flowing as a river, pierced by falling rain. Something inside the tower's casing continued to burn.

A distant boom sounded, then another and another, as more flock towers went up in flames. These formed a long line of glowing pillars in the rain. Redhelms began appearing, running to see and to retaliate.

"We have to go," said Gaiing. "Kill him!"

Liink shoved his prisoner roughly toward the steep slope. In a quick move, he let the prisoner go then twirled, catching his tail on the Redhelm's heel.

The boy tumbled in his red armor, struggling to slow his momentum. The fall might cause some injury, but he'd survive.

By the time he recovered, it would be too late to stop the Bloods.

T HE TWO MIINA raced through the greenery, staying low and bounding toward the Athenaeum. Liink kept glancing past the leaves at the sky, waiting to see the dropship carrying the Prophetess. They soon joined the other Bloods. The pride emerged from the foliage at the base of the Athenaeum's hill. Ahead a small squad of Redhelms stood, waiting, as if they knew what was coming.

But if they'd known what was coming, they'd have been retreating.

Liink didn't wait for a signal. He simply charged with an animal scream.

Gaiing and a dozen other Bloods followed his lead, dashing like shadows from the foliage toward the hill. Their miina faces looked like bloody skulls as they brought their rifles to bear with two paws, firing hot blasts of orange, purple, and blue as they galloped on their four remaining paws.

Liink tore his unused thermal frag from his belt and flipped the switch. With a mighty effort and a groan, he launched the explosive up the hill at the Redhelms.

They scattered.

Boom!

The charge blasted dust and debris in every direction, leaving curling smoke and dead Redhelms scattered across the ground. The survivors began retreating.

In moments, the Bloods had taken the Athenaeum's hill, and the red across Liink's face had been splattered with brown mud. They began digging in, forming a firm defensive line so they could hold that ground for at least an isochron.

Due to Lord Admiral Dray's precision, the dropships arrived immediately. They sailed low on the horizon, well below the dark clouds, skimming just above the plumes of smoke in a line.

A squad of Redhelms charged the hill.

Liink ducked. He pulled his rifle to his shoulder and steadied it with a third paw. Putting his eye just above the bulwark, he squeezed the trigger. A blue blaze shot out from the muzzle.

A Redhelm screamed and fell backward.

Soon the second wave relented, but more would come.

The sound of engines increased in volume. The lifters lowered in pitch as the dropships touched down one by one. Troops disembarked. Colonel Blackserpent descended, and Mowiih, leader of the Bloods, greeted him. The Nightwatchmen fanned out and bolstered the hill's defenses. A white starside miin was among them, trotting on all sixes.

Liink peered down the gaps between the skycraft, trying to locate the Prophetess. Maybe she wore one of the same helmets as the Nightwatchmen. He snapped back into focus, surveying the area at the foot of the hill. So far, he'd played his part, but he was one among many. None of what he'd done deserved any particular attention. He'd only equaled his duty, and his father would take no notice.

Liink glanced behind and saw a smaller-looking Nightwatchman descend one of the gangplanks.

That was her.

Clad in black armor and an oversized helmet.

Abii stood with her, armored in deep green, and gripping an orange prism. He raised a hand, calling the Bloods to him as he led the Prophetess toward the Athenaeum wall. "The Nightwatchmen will hold the hill now. Form a half circle around her. If any shooting makes it up this way, you're to take the brunt. Our one job is to protect her."

Liink rushed over and nodded eagerly. He stood as one brick, and together they formed a wall around her. Among them was an old human with wrinkled skin.

She was at Liink's back, not two meters away.

He hoped she'd recognize him amongst all these others. He turned his face, the only yellow eyes looking the wrong way.

She glanced briefly at the Bloods protecting her, and her eyes looked at him through the oversized mask. At least he thought so.

But she immediately looked away, not acknowledging him before turning toward the massive wall of the arrow-head shaped building. Maybe she couldn't recognize him in the red warpaint. Maybe the scene was too confused. Maybe she was distracted by the task ahead of her.

Whatever the reason, he felt certain of one thing: She hadn't acknowledged him. And Gaiing had witnessed.

Liink stared gloomily outward.

"Liink," whispered Gaiing as they waited and watched.

"What?"

"What were you doing back there?"

"What do you mean?"

"You spared that Redhelm's life."

"So?"

"It's not an abiisu to save the enemy's life."

Liink growled at the joke.

"So why'd you do it?" asked Gaiing.

"Because it felt honorable."

"What?"

Liink touched his own heart.

"On the inside."

S O MUCH DEPENDED on Kalh.

No one would know the uprising had begun unless she told them. And it wasn't just telling them. She had to inspire them to fight.

Becoming a symbol of the revolution would cost her more anonymity and would make Building 13 draw closer, a weight she didn't want to carry. She was nobody. As much as she didn't want to, she had to.

Because it might save some future Tannie.

The whistle of the lifters decreased in pitch as the dropship descended. Kalh flinched as the vessel's metal skin rattled beneath the impact of enemy fire against the shields. She was scrunched at the inside corner, arms folded tightly in front of her, a sort of emotional protection. They'd healed, thanks to her abilities with Sorjis. She watched and waited inside the skycraft, too anxious to give Benton's speech the attention it deserved.

All the trauma of her short life had never included an open battlefield.

Colonel Blackserpent sat next to her. He was a large man, not quite Nak's size, and the brand on his left cheek faced her, the number 1313. Despite his youngish face, his hair was the color of snow, pulled back in a long ponytail. Maybe he was a hybrid of some sort. If so, it was subtle in all other aspects. In a scratchy voice, he said, "Good luck." He crammed a helmet on his head, stood, and marched to the back.

With a rumble, the landing gear touched solid ground.

The loading bay opened. Nightwatchmen dressed in full battle armor rushed out, their rifles spewing purple and blue streaks of light. Their fearsome armor was made of matte charcoals and splashes of chaotic red decals, with masks that formed a T-shape around each of their faces. They ran onto wet ground, fanning out into a defensive perimeter around the dropship, keeping their backs toward the massive wall of the Athenaeum. Out there, lasers flew in every direction. Wherever they impacted, hot flames leaped up. Kalh flinched as a laser hit one of the Nightwatchmen, who screamed and fell, writhing in misery. The armor couldn't protect against a direct hit.

Dr Warnur stayed behind with her. He watched the battle keenly then turned toward her and winked a wrinkled smile, as if cheering up a small child. With a nod, he put on his helmet, pulled the rifle off his back, and stomped into the mud.

Benton, dressed in forest-green armor, stood at the ramp. He looked regal, like an ancient warrior, a knight prepared to charge into the fray for honor's sake. His ideals shone in his bright green eyes. He went down the gangplank, carrying an illegal rifle across his back and holding his unignited prism. He pressed a palm in the air at Kalh, signaling her to wait.

Treaders stomped down the gangplank.

These large bipedal robots, twice the height of a man, absorbed enemy fire with their shields. They walked with surprising agility and shot blasts with their frag cannons, mounted on either side like the wings of a flightless bird. The crown of each treader held a single missile turret with limited ammo, held in reserve to repel air attacks.

The seven more dropships landed, forming in a line against the wall of the Athenaeum, and the same process played out, more troops and more treaders into the mud. Soon the Nightwatchmen formed a formidable stronghold by literally digging in to the soil, using natural formations, or tearing up PSD equipment. It was all for her.

For nobody.

With an encouraging smile that twisted his perfectly trimmed beard, Benton motioned for Kalh to come down. "Now's your time to shine."

She wasn't so sure about that, but she stood, ready or not.

She wore a light-blue, single-piece jumpsuit that fitted her form nicely. It was made of a durable synthetic, meant to hold up against rough treatment and still not look dirty or worn, the perfect outfit for battle. She'd covered it with Nightwatchmen's battle armor. Fortunately, the pale blue showed at the seams. The oversized armor felt uncomfortable and restricted her movements, but she kept it on because it might save her life. She took off the skullhugger and put on her helmet, which didn't have an open face. It fit loosely and wobbled whenever she moved. Her breathing echoed inside of it, resonating from her mouth to her ears as she walked forward. Her boots clinked against the ramp and then splashed into mud. Rain hit the transparent eyepieces of her mask and dripped down. The grass was so soaked and trampled that her feet shifted with each footfall.

She retreated toward the wall of the Athenaeum, where the mucky texture beneath her feet turned to concrete and the wind's power died. This wall was the barrier she had to penetrate. The spot had been carefully selected for what lay on the other side.

Benton ordered a dozen miina to form up around her, staring at her with those yellow eyes. Although the species originated here on her homeworld, they'd always seemed alien and ugly to her. Dr Warnur placed himself among them, rifle ready.

Beyond them sat the dropships, protecting their line-of-sight from distant attacks. Outermost stood the army of Nightwatchmen, holding their firm perimeter. Benton turned his back to Kalh and peered in every direction, eager to find the unexpected and defend against it. His eyes glowed through the glass of his visor.

His voice echoed in her earpiece:

"Now, Kalhette."

* * *

S HE FACED THE wall, touching its surface with gloved fingertips, feeling its massive presence. Her eyes glowed as she peered through. She could make out very little on the opposite side, mostly just the thickness. Her hands slid down the stone as she bent one knee and reached the other behind her in a lunge, setting it on the concrete. She made two fists and pressed them into each other. She bowed her head so the helmet's crown nearly touched the Athenaeum.

And she breathed.

Her heart rate had to be much slower to pull this off. She hummed seven notes to herself, which reverberated inside her mask against the roar of battle.

She'd suggested they use brute force to blow through the Athenaeum. Not that she wanted it demolished—she just wasn't certain of her abilities. Benton said the PSD had shielded the building with massive generators on the inside, stronger than most battleships even. It would take a long time to wear them down, removing the advantage of surprise. Even if they took the time, they might destroy the very tech they intended to use. Besides, the Athenaeum was a cultural centerpiece of Solace. It wouldn't do to start by tearing it down.

Still, Kalh kind of wished they had.

She was an imposter. Nearly a whole planet believed she would liberate them, but she was just Kalhette, a confused little girl who'd failed to rescue Tannie. And who'd let herself be raped by Taiberos.

She was not the Uncrowned Queen. She was nobody.

No, she could do this. She had to.

She breathed.

Her heart beat like a sun, radiating from her core. She sensed her nose, her fingers, her hamstrings. She wiggled her toes. She was in them, *inside* them—her spirit animated them, as if she wore her cells like a glove.

So alive.

As a clatter came from above, she squinted and jerked, turning away, expecting shards of stone to fall on her, but the wall had been protected by the shields.

A mortar exploded behind her, causing a massive concussion that shoved her chest and chin against the wall. The pressure threatened to pop her eardrums. The sound of pebbles fell behind her, tapping like heavy rain. She pushed off the wall, back into her kneeling pose, placed her gloved knuckles against each other, and breathed.

This might all end in disaster. If she couldn't surge, they'd all die here waiting.

She breathed through her nose and exhaled. She pulled off a glove and put her fingers to her neck. The pulse had gotten slower. Still not enough.

Over the din, a Nightwatchman screamed in pain, and not just once; it was as if some continual horror mauled him, and he kept on screaming.

She looked to find him, and her helmet flopped around her head like a prison.

The clouds above soared so high they could see the distant sun, which turned them pink and gray. The blue sky peeked through wherever it could, and in one of the gaps the starlike surge gate twinkled its glowing white, peering down.

Nak was up there.

She shouldn't have let him kiss her.

His presence seemed to make her more impulsive. Or maybe more herself.

Without any coercion, he'd come back. For a man of few words, his echoing declaration meant so much: *Kalh, my name is Breck Starchild, and I'm going to help you liberate Solace.*

He'd volunteered his service and his priceless ship.

For a moment, his personality filled the whole space of her mind. She felt his energy, capable and dangerous. She felt his strength, like an unconquerable fortress. She felt his need for her and hers for him—a connection between two lonely, exiled souls. She shook her head, and the helmet rattled again.

She tore it off, extracted the earpiece, then tossed the helmet clattering. That's what Nak would've done. Her shaven head now felt the moisture of raindrops—as vulnerable as a child. The skies were letting up from the massive downpour just moments ago. What now fell came light as a mist, caressing her cheeks. Solace was volatile like that at times.

Lasers streaked past the defending Nightwatchmen and blasted into the Athenaeum. The sound repeated like a drummer with no sense of rhythm. It mixed with the thrum of her heartbeat. She put two fingers back to her neck. Blood pulsed through her veins, her heart still beating much too quickly.

Another Nightwatchman screamed, startling her, and she smelled burning flesh.

The longer she took, the more would die.

They all might die. Her too.

As she faced this fact, her mind jumped to the strangest thought: It wasn't her own life she feared to lose. It was the lives of her unborn children.

Her legacy.

But what if one of them was Taiberos's child?

She felt like throwing up. She'd wanted to be a mother all her life. She'd sensed that future so wholly that it seemed more substantial than hope. It felt like destiny. But that dream had been poisoned by Tai—

She felt strange melancholy, a longing for something she couldn't even fully imagine, a vast feeling, bigger than she could even feel all at once—

She felt reverence.

Reverence for her children—no matter what had come before. *E lissia kalha.* Her heart steadied.

With one foot and one knee on the ground, with her fists locked against each other, one gloved, one bare, she breathed in the Song.

And felt the inevitable harmony of all things.

Maybe she would fail. Maybe Nak would die up there in the sky. Maybe no children would ever come to light. Even all that was not too much for the Song.

She hummed those seven notes and continued the melody a little further. Her breath slowed as one falling asleep, yet her mind remained alive, her soul kinetic. She stared at the wall, her eyes began to glow.

She surged in a bright flash of light.

To others, no time elapsed—one moment she glared at the wet stone surface and in that same exact moment, she was inside.

To her, she transitioned slightly slower. It seemed to take about a sequel, four snaps of a finger, in which she didn't move at all, and instead the world rushed around and past her body, the massive wall dragging through spacetime and past her soul.

Then she could see the darkness of the building's interior, with faint orange lights flashing from somewhere down the hallway.

She gasped, whole again, her heart thumping rapidly, her head now spinning.

She'd done it.

She was in.

S HE PUT BOTH knees and both hands on the ground, gasping and squinting, trying to fight off the nausea.

With mouth still hanging open, she looked around.

The wall behind her gave a dull thump. The battle continued, and if the Nightwatchmen failed to hold their ground, she'd die inside the Sozo, executed by Redhelms. She shook her head and thought back to the floor plans Benton had obsessively reviewed with her, feeling grateful for the over-preparation. She dashed toward the flashing orange lights, gasping for more breath, wary of what monsters might jump out at her from each of the dark corners.

As she turned into a doorway, a PSD officer suddenly faced her—a young woman, probably about her same age. The officer's eyes got wide, preparing to yell.

Kalh grabbed at the air, constricting the young woman's throat.

The officer clutched at her own neck, unable to find the thing that choked her. She collapsed to her knees, crawling toward Kalh, her eyes staring desperately.

Kalh backed up, keeping out of reach while maintaining her grip.

The officer's face went toward despair and then morphed into confusion. Sweat glistened on her brow and the veins began to bulge. Her pallor dropped in shade. It took a long time, much too long. Finally, she passed out on the cold stone floor of the Athenaeum, her body giving one final shudder. In moments the officer would wake, feeling weak, maybe unable to move at first, perhaps confused, disoriented, and, with any luck, not remembering exactly what happened. Was this the only way—either to be enslaved to their violence or to return it in kind?

Kalh turned the next two corners without incident, but the motion increased her nausea. She soon found herself outside of the broadcast room, one wall of which was entirely glass. She entered, and the door closed behind her with a whoosh. She sat and scooted the chair up to the console. With the weight off her feet, she became aware of her exhaustion. Surging took a heavy toll, and her body hadn't fully recovered from Building 13.

As she prepared to initiate the relay, she felt a dark feeling, as if someone were watching her. She swiveled her chair and stared warily at the glass wall at her back. No one was there. Only low lights illuminated the hallway beyond.

She turned back to the instrument panel and began hitting dials as she'd trained. Her relay would go across a wide band of audio and holo frequencies, reaching most of Solace and probably much of the galaxy. More fame and infamy than she ever wanted. She punched the final keys:

Platform initiated.

Just like that, the broadcast was live.

The words would be considered treason, and her doom would be imminent if they did not win this fight. What if she called and no one came? What if her call didn't ignite their hearts? The sequels counted up, ticking one after another. She had to speak now. This was her time, the moment that counted most. She cleared her throat.

"People of Solace, I am Kalhette Whitesun."

Her voice sounded timid.

She imagined colonists in their homes and pilots in freighters and miina on the starside each turning to hear her message. Families like hers that had been torn apart by the conflict. Kids in classrooms, like the ones she'd taught on Sream. Children who'd never seen anyone contradict the PSD's narrative. If the message went galactic, maybe her parents and siblings would hear it too.

She had to make it count.

Had to.

She leaned closer to the microphone, enunciating clearly:

"In the name of safety and protection, the PSD has been monitoring its people. Here on Solace, that surveillance led to arrests and charges of sedition. It led to PSD citizens being held indefinitely without trial. It led to the Solace Sunset and the Shartrinn Massacre. People murdered in cold blood were called agitators. People demanding independence were called traitors. Some of them may have been your friends. Some of them were mine."

As she spoke, her melancholy returned, a sadness that fueled anger, and her confidence grew. She leaned in to the microphone, raising her voice.

"Many galactic citizens withdrew because of the danger. People with a shared mindset were isolated from each other, our unity shattered. I've known this struggle personally. I was thrown into the dungeons of the Strand simply because I had the potential to commit a crime. A bureaucracy put chains on my wrists and on my mind, believing *they* could govern my life better than *I* could. They called me the Prophetess and without a trial they condemned me for crimes I didn't commit.

"Now I've escaped. I'm speaking to you from the Athenaeum in New Kingstrong on Solace. Our forces have captured armories in Nosaui, Delasiin, Bronse, Franu, and Haas. We will soon have control of our surge gate. With these retaken grounds, we have reclaimed the basic right to speak our minds. We've thrown off tyrannical control for a moment, but this may not be enough."

In the dark room, a pale blue glow fell on her shaved crown, casting her shadow onto the floor. Her hazel eyes reflected a white gleam.

"One by one, they conquered our planet. Each of us alone cannot withstand a force so terrible. Isolated, we're all doomed to slavery. But if we unite, *they* cannot withstand *us*. Our populace numbers in the hundreds of millions. As each individual stands up, as we create a massive harmony, we become a force that cannot be dominated—"

She gasped.

And the people listening surely heard her.

She'd felt something like the icy breath of doom on her neck, which caused her to leap up so forcefully that the chair went spinning to the side.

A premonition.

She jerked her prism free, and her eyes glowed. In a blinding flash, the blade materialized, roaring to life with a tearing sound. Its coral rays reflected against the glass wall.

This light revealed a miin crawling on all sixes in the hallway beyond the glass. Those short horns and hanging ears made him look like a devil. His dark-purple fur blended easily with the shadows, and his intent was clear—she could feel the violence of it. Then she recognized him.

Those red eyes.

He'd winked at her on Sream.

I T WAS THE same miin.

With his wine-dark fur and those startling red eyes.

He'd helped Taiberos and the Witch Hunters capture her.

She hadn't finished her speech. Hadn't spoken the climax. She at least wanted to tell people she was okay. Only she couldn't turn her eyes from this threat.

He rose from all sixes onto just two feet, like a human. On his hind legs, he towered. He lifted two paws on the left side. In them he held a prism. So he was a Radiance after all—a traitor to his own kind. His red eyes began to glow. Then his prism blazed to life. Not many miina could do that; in fact, few of any species could. Its color was wrong though, a core of darkness surrounded by a rim of blue bleeding off the blade's edge. Its light flickered but remained ignited.

With a mighty swing, he bashed the blade into the glass wall. The pieces went flying, sailing with threatening tranquility.

She raised an arm, shielding with Kinosis to keep the projectiles from cutting into her skin.

The miin's blade vanished, becoming just an orange prism in his hand. He stomped through the broken glass, glaring.

She remembered how they'd locked eyes in that lobby on Sream, how she'd begun to believe he might be an ally sent from Benton. These were the same red eyes, only now their true quality showed. His voice came as a smooth, low hiss: "Your friends rescued you from the Strand."

"Yes." She didn't know why she answered him. It seemed instinctual.

"This building's on lockdown. They won't help you this time."

"You're the one who's going to need help."

"Well, I brought a friend." Below those wicked, red eyes, he grinned an ugly alien grin.

Behind him, white mechanical armor reflected the pinkish orange of her Singblade. A Witch Hunter came walking from the shadows. Strange mechanical contraptions hung from his shoulders, giving him the shape of an insectoid. He was human beneath all that, only he wouldn't act human toward her. He held a rifle in hand, aimed at her face, a full-length weapon with a snub-nosed stun gun attachment beneath.

They closed in.

She had nowhere to run. "You're a Radiance, and you're helping them?" The mic was still live, and her faint words might be echoing across the void of space. She hoped they weren't about to hear her die.

The miin nodded with smug satisfaction. The traitor had surely used his abilities in the Song to ferret her out back on Sream.

"You're a hypocrite and a traitor," she said.

"I'm no traitor." His voice was the deep growl of a predator. "I maintain allegiance to myself, and I'm smart enough to side with the winners. More than I can say for you." At that, he lunged at her, chopping down with his blue-rimmed Shadowblade.

She caught the attack against her Singblade, and the two locked together with immense friction. She shoved against him, launching herself back, and her weapon trailed a path behind it.

His strength was incredible. Red fury glowed in his alien eyes. "No, you idiot. Not while she's near me!"

He must've been talking to the Witch Hunter behind her. It meant she wouldn't be fired upon as long as she stayed close to the miin.

She made the next attack, banging aggressively with her weapon, and the blades sizzled against each other.

The mic kept listening, sharing the sounds of the fight with the people listening to the broadcast.

The miin moved to the side, changing the line of attack.

She faced him, parrying his counter.

He swung, and the blades flashed. The force of each impact felt like it was bruising her bones. Her arms, which hadn't healed all the way, weren't ready for this much trauma.

The miin circled, forcing her to face him, leaving her more and more exposed to the white-clad Witch Hunter behind.

She wanted to withdraw, to put her back to the broadcast console, but if she allowed for too much distance, she would be shot.

The miin jabbed.

She parried, keeping her blade up defensively.

He shoved hard against her.

That was all it took.

She stumbled back, leaving some small distance between the two of them.

It played out just like it had on Sream. Like a recurring nightmare.

A blast came from the Witch Hunter's rifle. The gun coughed its low, rumbling *BOOM!* The air rippled in a tight cone, much too quickly for her to dodge.

The blast impacted against her nervous system.

Her muscles locked.

And just like that, it was over.

She collapsed helplessly onto the floor.

N<small>AK HELD THE</small> steering yoke with his black-sleeve hand.

Colorful streaks lit up the black sky, crossing this way and that. The surge gate shone brightly whenever it flashed into view, bright as a miniature sun, shaped like a spinning top, the center of this whole operation.

He shouted into the comms: "Knix, watch your back!" His body weight doubled, pressuring his wounded foot as he banked *The Sanctum* upward—he aimed the laser cannons on the bowsprit by maneuvering the ship. As he brought the enemy fighter into focus, he pulled the trigger. Yellow beams flashed beneath his feet with a squealing vibration, which he felt through his chair.

The disc-like Goeb zipped through space. When its shields finally failed, Nak's lasers penetrated the hull. He kept firing furiously till he hit its fuel batteries. They ignited, and the Goeb silently exploded in a burst of light. As quickly as the flames appeared, they gulped up the spilled oxygen and vanished again. The particles splashed outward, roughly following the trajectory of the ship's final breath.

Nak's dashboard showed one less red octahedron.

"Thanks." Knix's voice came through the white headphones.

Without a moment of celebration, Nak spun *The Sanctum* and locked on another target. In the lull, he could hear Cup firing the aft cannons.

Another Goeb fighter came coughing purple lasers from the side. Their sound failed to cross the silence of space until one made contact, which vibrated the ship's frame with a deep thump.

Nak rolled *The Sanctum* and pulled upward, facing his enemy head on. Lasers crossed in the emptiness.

And he thought of Kalh.

He could almost sense her presence down on the surface.

Her speech should start any moment.

Usually he didn't let people know him, not deeply, because he assumed they wouldn't like what they found. In fact, if they knew him and still liked him, it wouldn't say much for their judgment. But he wanted Kalh to know him and to like him anyway, despite the paradox. Perhaps he was losing his mind.

Before returning to Solace to join the Renegades, Nak had decided to walk up to her, without any preamble or even a hello, and say: "Kalh, I'm probably going to die. And if I don't die, I'm almost certain to lose my ship. If that happens, I might as well be dead. Except, I decided I don't care because there's something I care about even more." And then he would kiss her.

It turned out different than he'd imagined.

He walked up to her. She smiled, which punctured the hull of his heart, and all his plans got sucked into the vacuum of space.

She looked as beautiful as… as laughter.

She never mentioned what he'd said through Ptolis. Maybe hadn't heard it. All she said was, "Welcome back." It felt like enough. She seemed to have gotten his intent—not every cycle a guy gambled one of the Bloody Wings.

Nak punched the throttle in a head-on course. The Goeb veered, and Nak swerved, keeping his laser cannons trained on it, which screeched with each blast. The fighter's shields blew and the next laser pierced the starboard tail-engine, which spewed fire, propelling the fighter in a rapid spin, probably creating such high g-force to make the pilot inside pass out. Nak didn't bother to finish the job, instead targeting another red octahedron.

Cup's tiny voice came through the white headphones: "We've never broken the law this badly before."

"More like demolishing the law."

She clacked to her unamused face, hanging right above him while firing the guns in the back through the phantomlink. "That's not funny."

Nak chuckled. "Still not sure this fight's worth it?"

"If we win this, we get to live on Solace in peace. Right? No more running?"

Nak might've been wondering the same thing too if he hadn't been surrounded by Goebs. With his red-sleeve hand, he whacked a button on the dash. With both hands, he spun the yoke, and the deck of *The Sanctum* twirled dizzyingly beneath him.

"And we'll abide the law?" she asked.

"I guess so."

"So we won't be fugitives anymore?"

"I dunno." If that happened, Nak might not even get a new mask. He pulled up hard and the g-forces flushed his face with red. He regretted having squirmed his damaged toes back into a boot. No time to fix it now though.

"We'll be real people?"

"Something like that," he grunted.

"When we're real people, can I get a body?"

"I suppose."

"Really?"

"I suppose."

"I really hope we win this war."

"Battle first, Cup." Nak glanced at the holograph in front of his fists, perceiving in an instant.

The scanner grid showed each of the nearby skycraft tracked in three-dimensional space. *The Sanctum* was the blue one in the center. A hoard of Renegade wingmen flew alongside—Valt's privateers, a bunch of amped out mining vessels and jacked up freighters. Their registered signals showed up as green pyramids. Each of those skycraft in turn monitored the skycraft

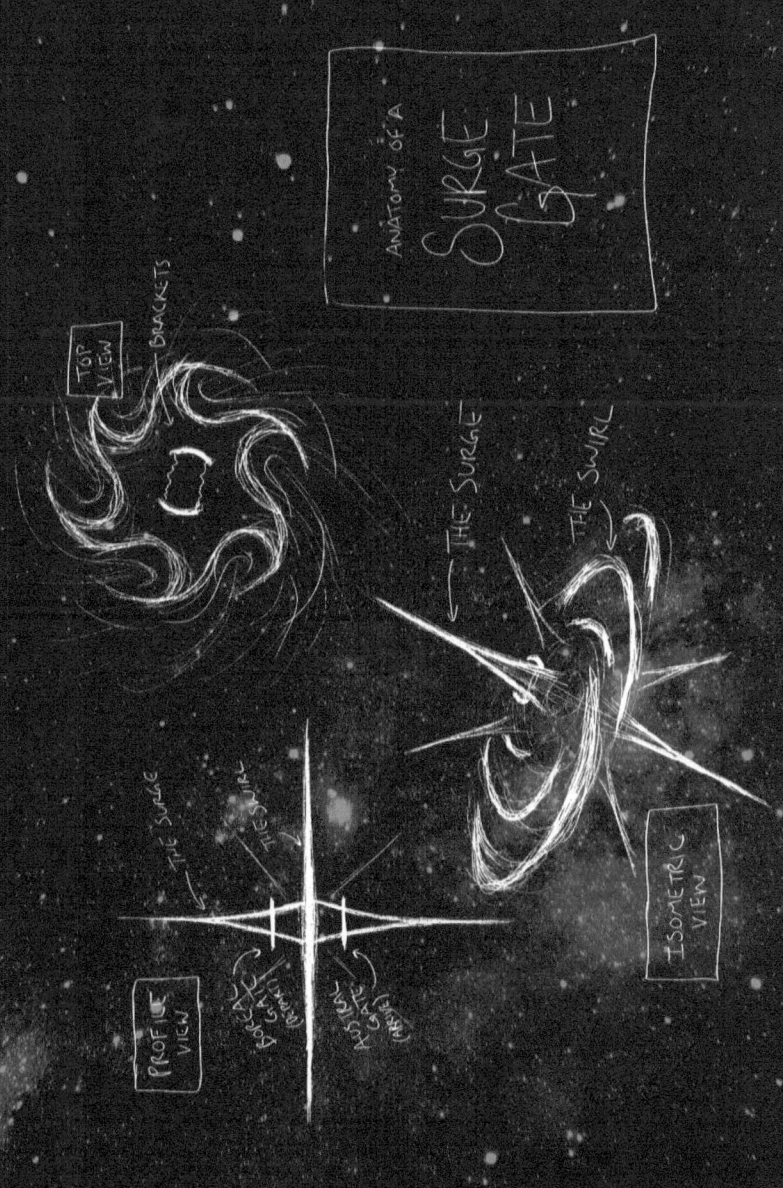

ANATOMY OF A

Surge
Gate

TOP
VIEW

BRACKETS

THE SURGE

THE SWIRL

PROFILE
VIEW

THE SURGE

THE SWIRL

BOREAL
GATE
(DOWN)

AUSTRAL
GATE
(ARRIVE)

ISOMETRIC
VIEW

in the vicinity, creating an aggregate map of all foreign vessels, presumably enemy skycraft, each represented by a red octahedron.

Valt's green pyramid glowed yellow while his relay channel opened: "Alta Squadron, follow me to the gate. You'll commence your attack runs on my mark."

Nak turned *The Sanctum*, and the glowing surge gate came into view, white and fringed with yellow and red, bright enough to easily hide the stars behind it.

Like all surge gates, this orbited its parent star as if it were a planet, glowing brightly with its own luminescence. The bulk of it was shaped like a galaxy, a vortex of red energy called the swirl, which spun in alignment with the system's orbital plane. Spiking from that core both above and below came jets of bright light, making it look like a spinning top.

Submerged in the heart of this mass was a set of structures built from Photoss technology called brackets. One pair encircled the upper surge and a second pair encircled the lower. Each massive metal bracket was connected to its twin by beams of electromagnetic energy. The metal brackets and connecting beams created a portal, a surge gate, through which skycraft would sail for interstellar travel. Without this machinery, a vessel would fly into the surge but never come out the other side, so these brackets controlled the queue, departures above and arrivals below.

With the exception of Bloody Wings, no one could enter or leave the system without permission from whoever regulated the brackets. That meant the brackets themselves didn't need to be guarded carefully—no need to patrol your bedroom so long as the front door was locked. Still, they weren't entirely defenseless. Rows and rows of massive guns lined the edges, but these were designed to counter massive vessels. No one had predicted Valt's fleet of illegal privateers appearing almost magically from within.

"What if they all just turned off?" asked Cup.

"What," said Nak.

"The surge gates. We don't even know what powers them."

"Sure we do. All that energy."

"A mysterious energy we can't duplicate. What if stopped? No more power, no interplanetary travel, and we were just... alone...?"

"I dunno. Check the shield modulators, would you."

"Okay."

Nak tapped five times on the dashboard, as if telling time to hurry up. What he really needed was for everything else to slow down.

The moment the offensive began, distress relays would've been sent to various PSD systems. Those bases would send reinforcements back through the gate, but they'd take time to be queued first, which took longer the more mass a parcel had. Once a skycraft was finished being queued, though, it couldn't be stopped. Valt predicted, and Nak agreed, that the PSD would send a single Behemoth loaded with fighters—the largest skycraft ever built, basically a portable city. This would make a whole fleet arrive at one moment. That gave the Renegades just one isochron to land on the surge gate, capture the control module, and block the queue. Failure would mean the failure of the whole insurrection.

As *The Sanctum* sailed, the surge gate filled the windscreen, its brilliance making it hard to see skycraft against the backdrop of black, so he paid closer attention to the scanner grid. You didn't normally get so close to something this big without either landing or crashing into it. This was big with relatively little mass though.

Valt's voice came through the white headphones: "Citrine Wings, you guys take it from here. Keep them off our backs. Alta Squadron, follow me while I pinpoint the batteries to target." Valt led the charge, diving toward the lower bracket.

Nak had been wary of serving under someone and felt the urge to mutiny before getting started, so Benton recounted Valt's accomplishments and then trusted Nak with the full battle plans, information worth quite a lot to the right buyer. Not that Nak considered selling it, but he didn't feel worthy of that much trust. He just... hadn't earned it. Hadn't been fully converted to their cause either.

He *was* converted to Kalh though.

Maybe that was enough.

As Valt's fighter neared, a row of laser batteries turned and speared massive bolts in his direction. The encounter was like an insect against a monster. As he zoomed past, he raked the cannons with his own fire, targeting two specifically. You also had to be flying fast enough to maintain an escape velocity as you got nearer to the gravity of the swirl. If you got too close, you'd get sucked in and never come out the other side.

"That's the mark."

Nak had to give Valt credit for style.

The gate's bracket had a blind shield which followed the basic geometric shape of the station, but forming a shield that heavy around the chaotic shape of the batteries was nearly impossible and would've weakened the overall integrity. Not to mention the fact that blind shields were opaque, meaning the gunners literally wouldn't have been able to see out. So each battery had its own local breach shield, the kind used on smaller skycraft, transparent with less than a tenth of the protective power. These could be targeted and damaged separately. Valt's plan was to take out a row of batteries, clearing a space for the landing crew to dock and raid the control center.

Colored bolts leaped across the starfield, splashing their array across Nak's face. The shining spike of the surge gate glowed in the distance, flaring outward. He grinned at the beautiful and dangerous scene. Too bad Kalh couldn't watch.

Taking his right hand off the yoke, he punched several keys, locking the holo onto that segment of laser batteries. As he did, he noticed a Goeb at his stern. In a fluid motion, he switched—right hand on the yoke—and killed the accelerator with his left. The hum of the atmosdrive vanished, and *The Sanctum* hurtled quietly through space. As the ship's inertia continued in the same direction, he used the zentisal drive to point her backward at the enemy. This protected the engines and gave him a clear shot at his pursuer. It also brought Solace back into view, which, from here, looked like a star.

Nak locked on the enemy and fired as he slid backward.

The Goeb ignited.

The silent yellow explosion vanished in a flash, leaving a dark starfield of clunky debris that dispersed in an expanding radius across the sky.

The batteries kicked as they launched their massive bolts of energy into space—white streaks of light surrounded by crackling blue.

Regibeld's voice crackled over the comms: "This is Alta Three. I'm going in."

Nak watched his wingman zoom by for an attack, diving at the edge of the massive bracket.

A white bolt of energy shot past the fighter.

A second bolt went right through.

The fighter disintegrated, shrapnel flying into space, pieces raining onto the batteries. And—though it may have been his imagination—Nak thought he saw particles of red liquid smeared chaotically across the void.

Killed in one shot

"█████," said Knix.

"Keep it to yourself," said Valt.

Sending small fighters against batteries that size was a dangerous gambit. The massive guns didn't track small objects quickly, but if one of those blasts did nail a fighter, it was game over.

Trick was to not get hit.

"Alta Five here," said Nak. "I'm moving into position." He rolled the yoke and pulled up, putting the surge gate above him. Because his ship had a floor, this orientation provided him the widest vision. He rammed the throttle forward, and his acceleration built. "Okay, Cup, get ready to do as much damage as you can."

As Nak began his run, he zigzagged with the zentisal drive while the atmosdrive continually picked up speed, bringing him closer to danger.

"Now, Cup!" He squeezed the triggers on the yoke. Lasers spit from the bow. He targeted the first battery for as long as he could then pulled up toward the second as he zoomed past.

He spun the yoke, flipping the ship so that the bracket's edge was beneath him, and then he pulled up hard. The zentisal roared. The g-forces smashed him into his seat, but he still kicked the throttle up a notch. His core muscles tightened, and his vision closed in around him, but he maintained the presence of mind to keep weaving as the massive bolts flew past. As his guns fell silent, he could still hear Cup firing in the rear.

If *The Sanctum* met her demise here, she'd be scattered into oblivion like the others. Unlike the others, miners would scour the vastness of space to collect her tachyon particles and rebuild her surge drive, even if it took an aion to do so.

She was that precious.

Nak looped around for another run, firing at Goebs but trying not to engage. Soon Alta Squadron had made a whole section of the bracket defenseless. He and his wingmen returned to the fray while the infiltration crew boarded the bracket, moving toward the control center.

After a while, Valt came back on the comms: "The insertion team reports a large parcel queued at the gate nearly five isochrons ago. They'll be coming through at any moment."

The news hit Nak like a thunderstorm. He barely heard Valt's next words: "They knew we were coming."

It meant they weren't going to win this fight. Not a chance.

Nak fired at the Goebs around him.

The pyramid for Citrine Thirteen glowed yellow. "Can't they stop it?"

"It's way too late for that."

"Sir, what is it?"

"We don't know. Move into your defensive formations."

Nak formed up with his wingmen, facing the shining surge gate.

Cup spoke through the white headphones: "Nak, can I ask you a question?"

"Are your guns overheating."

"Nope. Where did I come from?"

"Why you asking now."

"That's probably a Behemoth coming through, right?"

"Yep." Although Valt's privateers had been a fair match for the standing fleet, the ragtag band would be greatly outmatched by a Behemoth. If he was going to run, now was his chance. Best chance any of them would have.

Cup's voice was always tiny but particularly so this time: "I'm not sure we're going to get out of this one."

"Oh, come on."

"Even if we survive," said Cup, "I'd still like to know."

In a flash of light, the Behemoth appeared.

Compared to the surge gate, it was barely a speck, but compared to Valt's fleet, it was a monster. The upper and lower halves looked like an elongated clam, designed to create glancing blows for incoming projectiles and to spread the focus points of lasers as much as possible. Between the two halves was an inset groove for the hangars, from which Goeb fighters spewed out like a swarm of insects, tiny against the backdrop of their mother skycraft.

As Valt's fleet, along with Nak, started to sail away and regroup, a second Behemoth appeared.

Then a third, fourth, and fifth.

", ████, ████."

It was a massive percentage of the PSD's dreaded fleet, a force that could defend a dozen systems, all flooding into this one place. It would've been insane to stand against even one Behemoth. The cause was lost.

Yet Nak could still surge out of here. He alone could get away.

He wished he could pick up Kalh first, but even if he got to her, she probably wouldn't abandon her friends. If he skipped out, went back into exile, maybe he could find her in a few percents, once the aftershocks had passed, and try to convince her to forgive him. If she wasn't locked inside the Strand again.

The swarm of Goebs forced the Renegades to engage.

The screaming vibrations came through the floor, even though Nak wasn't firing, which meant it was Cup, running *The Sanctum's* aft gun. On the holograph, one of the red octahedrons blinked white and then vanished. She spoke over the comms in a singsong tone, clearly delighted with herself: "I got one…"

Nak squeezed the triggers, and the deck vibrated with each pulse of spiking light. It wasn't enough. Too many ████████ Goebs. And if he didn't bail soon, it would be too late.

The comms blinked.

A public relay was coming through, not from the surface, unfortunately, but from one of the Behemoths.

The lights of lasers flashed across Nak's face. He punched a key to hear the relay while still firing aggressively.

A familiar voice, speaking in the steady monotone of a dead man: "As you can see, your resistance here is pointless. Your meager fleet can't match the galaxy's most feared armada." Taiberos laughed with arrogant confidence. "You will surrender now, or you will be obliterated, every last man, woman, and child who was involved in this insurrection."

"I'm scared, Nak," said Cup.

"We're getting out of here." As he turned the yoke, he pictured Kalh's face and felt a pang of guilt, but sticking around wasn't going to save anyone. It would just mean one more casualty. He wasn't going to give that bastard the satisfaction.

At that same moment, the comms blinked.

Valt's pyramid glowed: "Activate the surface channel. She's on."

Nak did as directed, and he heard Kalh's voice coming through the white headphones: "… led to arrests and charges of sedition. It led to PSD citizens being held indefinitely without trial."

As he dodged through the battle toward open space, he felt sad. Without her and her rebellion, he'd still have the galaxy to himself, but the whole thing felt like empty space. A Goeb locked on his tail. More and more kept streaming out from the Behemoths. He pulled up hard on the yoke and felt the strain going through his neck.

"Each of us alone cannot withstand a force so terrible. Isolated, we're all doomed to slavery."

It felt like she was talking directly to him.

Maybe she was.

And he started to feel like even if he died here it would be okay, like maybe this was his blaze of glory. He turned the ship around, not knowing what he was doing or what good he expected to come of it.

"As each individual stands up, as we create a massive harmony, we become a force that cannot be dominated—"

She gasped—

Nak heard her gasp over the comms.

His heart thumped rapidly for the first time this whole flight. Had they known the whole plan and interrupted her speech too?

Lasers squealed as he fired from beneath his feet. He twisted the yoke, and his knuckles went white. The turn was so sharp, it felt like he was hanging on to save his life. He brought the Goeb into his sights and mashed the triggers with rage.

Another voice came through the public channel, finishing Kalh's broadcast.

A dark and threatening voice.

"Citizens of Solace, the Athenaeum has been recaptured by its rightful governor, your own Pangalactic Socialist Democracy, in which you have voted and to which you owe your loyalty. Our Behemoths rule the sky."

Nak glared at the comms in horror as the battle raged quietly all around.

"To those who would incite revolution, know this: Your Prophetess is dead, and your uprising will die just like her."

The feed went silent.

Nak felt like throwing up in the cockpit.

He didn't even switch off the comms. Without any more deliberation, he turned the yoke, steering away from the fight, and punched the throttle, heading for empty space in a sickened daze.

Away from the possibility of having a home.

Away from Kalh's death.

A RED CLOTH COVERED the gaping hole in Dray's head.

He peered with one dreadful eye.

His soul had been left empty, with nothing to fill it but profound sadness.

As he increased his use of Orikerse, his encounters with many common emotions had become rare. If not for that, he wouldn't be able to do what he had to do.

Soon he might not be able to feel anything at all.

The void inside had been growing since his second stay in Building 13, but if they could overthrow the PSD, starting at this moment, he could make a safe haven for Radiances, the first step in finally giving them justice. That would make the sacrifice worth it. At least he thought so logically. He couldn't feel whether it was true in any deeper way.

"Sir?" asked Trillion, the most loyal of servants.

Dray turned to the glowing table, placing both hands on the frame. His wild gray hair hung forward as he looked down. "Yes?"

Trillion paused, embarrassed. "Is everything all right, sir?"

Dray's mouth moved into the shape of a weak, forced smile. The timbre of his deep voice expressed the lie: "Yes, Captain. Everything is all right."

He doubted the captain believed it.

It was no accident that the speech had been interrupted. He'd planned it all carefully, including her role.

And her death.

While speaking with her on the balcony, he'd felt hesitant to end her life. That sentiment had vanished. He felt no sympathy for her now.

Waiting till the last moment, so as to preclude the possibility of a double cross, Dray gave a tip to a contact among the Witch Hunters—the red-eyed miin named Shauu—who managed to embed himself inside the Athenaeum before the lockdown. The miin had orders from the PSD to take her alive, perhaps for one final confession, but Dray gave an incentive to defy that order. Yet if Shauu couldn't outwit her premonitions directly, Dray had a failsafe, a backup plan that would ensure her demise. As a bonus, he believed her premonitions might become confusing when layered atop each other. This guile would send her across the threshold of death and immortality.

All so he could bring justice to the galaxy.

He paced across the makeshift command center, which was hidden in a cave, and the damp smell of old cement filled the space. Dim lights illuminated the floor, but the ceiling itself was dark. Holographic boards were set up in a grid across the room. From here, he and his staff could monitor the progress of each of the battle's key points. At the central table, a fuzzy holograph glowed, showing a map and several vital statistics. Seven armories had been captured, while two others met with heavy casualties and failure, but those numbers wouldn't matter unless the citizen militias came to her call.

Unfortunately, she should've started her speech already. Something had her behind schedule. Which might mean Shauu would arrive too soon, before she could finish.

Dray's one eye glazed over.

He was called back to the present when Trillion stepped up: "A report from Mr Valt, sir. The surge gate has been captured, and he would like to speak to you."

"Patch it through," said Dray.

The captain did so.

Dray reached for a board on the table and pressed a button. "Mr Valt, this is Lord Admiral Dray."

The comms began to crackle and then words, intermingled with static, poured through the air: "— to the — — be somebody — — a set up — — — — us — — — — — the bomb coming — — at all — — —"

Dray frowned and turned away from the holographs. "What's wrong with the signal?"

"I'll go see, sir. Might be on his end."

Dray pressed the relay button. "Valt, I'm having trouble hearing you." Their fleet was rickety, after all.

Valt's voice continued, intermittently, in a tone of calm despite some confusion: "— — sorry — — — through the surge gate — the attack even started — — left us alone — — — be a problem — — — maybe a Behemoth — — — — — hundreds, maybe more — — — — if we can stop them — —"

The radio fell silent.

Dray closed the comms channel and frowned, staring with one eye at the holograph. He checked the grid, making sure Valt's skycraft was still online. It was.

Anyone else might have written it off as coincidence, but Dray knew better, and the implications weren't good.

Maybe his missing eye had seen more clearly than the other.

He'd acted on the information Lethos had given him. The decrease in PSD troops had made this a unique opportunity, and rushing made it easier to keep secret, but he should've foreseen a betrayal. The population of Solace was a fractured mess, and any number of the factions might have wanted to see Benton's revolution fail. If the Renegades lost the surge gate, the PSD's retaliation would be monstrous. And it seemed to be already in progress.

Dray didn't feel worry though.

He didn't feel sad that it might have all come to nothing, that his careful planning had amounted only to this. He should've at least felt rage at being betrayed, but he couldn't even seem to feel that.

He felt nothing.

Just a cold, empty void.

Maybe because this battle held little consequence compared to his greater purpose. Just so long as what he'd planned for *her* still came to pass.

"Sir, we received a textual message," said Trillion. "It seems a massive fleet has come through the surge gate, one queued before the attack even started. Valt currently controls the gate, but it's only a matter of time…"

This confirmed Dray's suspicions. The battle was lost. Solace was lost.

But he would survive.

"Queue our transportation, Trillion."

Just then, Kalhette's voice came on over the public comms—much later than planned.

Trillion turned and looked at the ceiling in surprise.

"Isolated, we're all doomed to slavery…" Her voice had a melodic quality to it, and she spoke with a conviction that surely would've brought many to their cause, but it didn't matter now. They'd lost the sky.

Suddenly, her speech was cut off. A series of crashes sounded over the comms.

After some time, Shauu's voice came on the comms, declaring her death to the whole galaxy.

It meant Dray had fulfilled that part of the covenant.

He took a quick breath and tapped several keys, flagging her unit specifically on the board. Her vitality readout beeped as it appeared on the holograph.

Shauu lied. She was still alive.

If the miin hadn't completed the task, maybe he was playing both sides— not entirely unexpected.

How unfortunate. For Lethos, it wasn't enough for her to be thought dead. She needed to be actually dead. The map showed she was still inside the Athenaeum. Maybe they'd stopped her broadcast but hadn't subdued her completely. Whatever the case, she couldn't be allowed to escape.

"Your transport is ready for evac, sir."

"Thank you." Dray turned toward Trillion. "Get Colonel Blackserpent on the comms."

"Yes, sir." The captain bowed and walked to another table.

Colonel Blackserpent, the leader of the Nightwatchmen, was particularly gallant but also quite loyal to his men, an elite squad, not the kind that should be used as cannon fodder in a direct assault. Yet that was what Dray sent them into—heavy combat, where their ranks would be decimated with each passing sequel.

This part of Dray's plan was still in place.

He'd given Blackserpent a secret order before the battle: "Your men are too precious to be wasted for even a sequel more than necessary. If I send the code *violent sky,* I want you to withdraw immediately. Cut all losses and retreat without hesitation, no matter who might be left behind. Is that clear?"

Blackserpent had no special loyalty to Kalhette, the woman others called the Prophetess, so he accepted the order without the slightest misgiving. What he didn't know was that he himself would never make it back alive. One of the dropships was going to crash with him inside. Dray had seen to that too.

Leaving no loose ends and no way to get himself implicated in her death.

He thought he sensed some distant remorse buried deep inside. He searched for it, tried to cultivate it even, but it remained elusive. All because he'd taken Orikerse, shoved it into his palms, letting it soak up his emotion, his mood, what the Zhani called Spirit. As Lethos promised, it had been a boon. Along with making Dray's other abilities much stronger, he felt no regret or pity, not even the fear of getting caught. Part of him still wanted to feel fear. Even anger would be better than nothing.

He also sensed a slight reluctance, a preference to escape his side of the bargain. Logically, he knew that would fail to serve the greater cause. Good things only came by paying the price, by conforming to the conditions of reality. In the end, his feelings or lack of them didn't matter. He would do what had to be done. He would make sure she died so that he could make recompense for his past.

For his sin.

The Redhelms within the building would try to stop her, and she'd be forced to fight her way past. It would take her time to surge back through the wall too, not an easy task. If she did manage all that, she'd find that Blackserpent had abandoned her, leaving her to face the PSD's entire Sozo force alone. She was strong but not immortal, not by a long shot.

And she would not be kept alive.

When facing an enemy with her power, any soldier would shoot to kill, and that included the Redhelms. Capturing an enemy required much more risk. And she, knowing what stood ahead, would most likely not want to be captured anyway—better to die fighting than return to that Otherworld. Even if by some chance she did surrender before being shot, she'd already sealed her fate. They wouldn't send her to Building 13 this time, not after such a public affront on the sanctity of the PSD. That lunatic Taiberos would never allow that, not with his pride at stake. No, she'd be tried for treason and publicly executed.

Her martyrdom would fulfill Dray's pledge to Lethos. It would also spur the Renegade cause, weakening the PSD.

For the greater good.

Trillion gestured an open palm toward the glowing table. "Sir, Colonel Blackserpent is on the comms."

Dray leaned over and pressed several buttons. "Colonel Blackserpent, this is Lord Admiral Dray. Do you copy?"

The voice grated like that of an actual serpent: "Loud and clear."

"What is your status?"

"We've sustained heavy casualties, sir, but we're holding."

Maybe it was the invisible shame, but Dray's deep voice dropped to an even lower pitch: "Valt has sent word of a *violent sky*. Just hold on a little longer."

"Understood, sir."

The hint of a smile crept on the corner of Dray's mouth.

A SICK FEELING SHOT through Benton's stomach.

"Kalhette?" He shouted into a handheld comms separate from the one in his helmet. "Do you copy? Kalhette?"

That voice had come on saying she was dead. It couldn't be true though. It just couldn't. He would never forgive himself...

Benton looked at the massive wall, wishing he had the ability to get through it.

"Oh, no," interrupted Liink, who pointed toward a great orange light glowing on the horizon. "They set Tonkston on fire." It meant the citizens had heeded Kalhette's call. They'd probably been firing as snipers from those buildings, forcing the Redhelms to escalate. It would give people more reason to rebel.

But none of that mattered because Kalhette—

The ground shook with an explosion.

Rubble and dirt tapped down, followed by tufts of grass.

His fireteam of Bloods stood in a semicircle around him, their backs to the massive Athenaeum, guarding the spot where she'd gone in. Next sat the dropships in a half ring, waiting to fly them all safely back out of the Sozo. The Nightwatchmen formed an outer perimeter. Spuunar and his comrades made up the extreme left flank.

They held that line throughout the battle, and they did their job so well that Benton's fireteam did almost nothing. He summoned his fiery Singblade several times in expectation, but each time the threat was subverted before it got far up the hill, so he would let the flame go out. After doing this several times, he began to watch with a meditative awe as the brightness vanished first next to his hand, the motion crawling upward, leaving the point as the last of the spark to vanish.

"Kalhette, come in!" Benton patted his prism nervously against his thigh. The comms remained silent. He pressed the button on his helmet, putting another relay through. "This is General Xylander. I need a vitality report on someone. No. Then put me through to logistics. Uh, sure. Okay. Out."

He felt defeated.

Another voice came through his earpiece: "Generals, this is Lord Admiral Dray."

Benton put a hand to the side of his green helmet.

"I just got word from Mr Valt. Behemoths have come through the surge gate. They were queued before our attack began. We were betrayed."

Benton looked around against an irrational worry that someone might've overheard. He didn't want anyone to hear it and didn't want it to be true. He put in a request to interject on the group relay. It was not granted. He wanted to ask whether they were sure. Maybe it was some kind of trick.

"There isn't much we can do," said Dray's voice. "Prepare your troops to surrender, and see to your own safety. I expect the PSD to execute any and all leadership."

Benton submitted another request on the channel. They couldn't give up now. They had to keep trying. Keep hoping. And yet the successful raids from the various local militias meant nothing if they didn't win the sky. Valt's privateers would be overwhelmed. Worse, if Benton admitted this news to Colonel Blackserpent, the Nightwatchmen might leave, abandoning Kalhette to her fate.

Benton couldn't risk that. He couldn't risk telling the truth. So he didn't. And he felt glad Private Spuunar wasn't around to see his shame. He pulled the other comms to his mouth: "Kalhette, if you can hear me, we need to get out of here now!"

"Sir!" Dr Warnur pointed toward the left flank, at the edge of the Athenaeum. The Nightwatchmen there were retreating, creating a gap in the line, and the Redhelms were already starting to break through.

"Follow me!" Benton led the Bloods and Dr Warnur toward the broken line. He knelt behind a huge chunk of stone, and his fireteam followed suit. He put his rifle to his shoulder and fired. Soon they had the breach closed.

Colonel Blackserpent appeared through the commotion and dropped an armored knee into the mud next to Benton. "We're withdrawing." Apparently they'd gotten the news from someone else, outside of the chain of command.

Benton shook his head. "No we're not. I'm the commanding officer."

"You were the commanding officer while we had a chance of winning. Now all bets are off."

"You're under contract! She's still in there!"

"You heard the voice: She's dead."

Benton shook his head vehemently. "She's not dead!" It had to be a lie.

"How do you know?"

"I'm getting them to check her vitality."

"We're leaving. You have the time it takes for us to make a controlled retreat. I won't be waiting." Blackserpent pressed the comms on his helmet as he scrambled away. The same voice then came through the speaker in Benton's helmet: "Nightwatchmen, this is Blackserpent. Pull back. We're getting out of here."

The sickness welled up in Benton's stomach, crawling toward his throat. Not only might he lose Solace, he might lose Kalhette too.

His comms buzzed, and he connected it. His finger went back to his earpiece. "This is General Xylander."

"This is Private Tarklefter from logistics."

"Yeah, I want a vitality on Kalhette Whitesun."

"Yes, sir."

Benton waited, tapping his prism impatiently against his green-armored thigh. Mortars exploded in the distance.

Finally, the voice came back on: "Her vitality is affirmative. She's still alive."

"Thank you!" A thrill shot through Benton's gut. He knew it! He let a tentative smile cross his face as he pulled up his secondary comms: "Kalhette, this is Benton. Where are you?"

Still nothing.

Maybe her comms was broken. Or maybe she was lying somewhere unconscious and vulnerable. But she was alive! The unit vitals said so.

He ran down the slope in a crouch. "Blackserpent, she's still alive in there!"

"Better get her out quick then. I told you my dropships are leaving."

"Blackserpent!"

The rogue officer with the long white ponytail faced Benton with defiance.

Benton had nothing to say. These were volunteers, here by their own volition. They weren't his slaves. How could he contradict their choice?

He shook his head in despair.

Having her alive in there might be worse than dead. They would capture her, and her notoriety would make everything worse this time. Building 13 would be worse. Chances of rescuing her would be worse. And her punishment would be worse. She might be executed publicly after having sent that broadcast.

Even if she came right now, it would take her some time to muster the energy to surge back through the Athenaeum wall. It would take too long. And maybe she was injured in there. He put his gloved hands helplessly against the stone wall. His eyes glowed, but he could see nothing on the other side.

And if he could convince Blackserpent to leave a dropship behind, the perimeter they held would still collapse. Benton's fireteam would be overwhelmed in moments. He pressed the button on his helmet again: "This is General Xylander. May I speak with Lord Admiral Dray? He isn't? Well, where is he? Okay. Well... have him contact me when he's back."

A *boom* of a different sort sounded, and Benton slammed on his helmet. *Boom.*

It came again and again. The Redhelms were using frag cannons, which fired shrapnel at blazing hot speeds. The metal shards glowed red as they cut flashing arcs across a backdrop of twilight clouds.

Benton scooted next to Liink in the mud and shouted over the battle sounds: "Do you think you could lead our fireteam out of the Sozo on the same route the Bloods came in?"

Liink shook his head. "No, sir. It's not possible. They were already increasing the number of troops as we fled the sabotage, and without the element of surprise—it just wouldn't work."

Benton nodded silently.

"If you want to try it, Abii, I will gladly follow you, and I would die if necessary."

Benton smiled sadly. He did not want to see the cub reach his abiisu like that. "Thank you, Liink. Maybe we can find another option."

But there wasn't another option.

The Nightwatchmen were Kalhette's only chance of escaping the Sozo alive, and they were leaving right now.

She wasn't going to make it out in time.

K ALH'S BODY WAS still.
    But her fingers flinched.

The Witch Hunter gripped her around the neck, shoving her face into the floor.

Although she'd been shot with a stun blast, her muscles were still working. At least a little. Maybe he'd been worried about hitting the merciless miina so he'd fired wide to be safe. People had been hit peripherally in the lobby back on Sream. The edges of the stun blast had dropped them too, but maybe the effects didn't last as long.

She clenched her hand into a fist.

As she drew on the power of Sacredspark, the music crescendoed within her, filling her whole being with light, which flowed out through her eyes.

Although her face pointed down, she could sense the Witch Hunter on her back, dressed in his matte white armor with mechanics hanging off like a freakish insect, about to handcuff her. She could even feel his grimace through the helmet over his face, and his surprise when her eyes began to shine onto the floor.

With two hands against the ground, she pressed with all her might. The movement was so explosive that it threw her captor off as she sprang to her feet.

She reached for her prism lying on the floor and jerked at empty air.

The gem handle flipped toward her.

The Witch Hunter raised his rifle.

Her coral blade roared to life, shining blinding light across the scene.

She chopped at the rifle, cutting off the barrel.

This movement had such force that the inertia pulled her body in a twirl, and she let it drag her around, pirouetting forward so that when she completed the spin, she hacked into the Witch Hunter's side, cutting into him.

In a cry of pain, he collapsed on the floor.

The miin came from behind, aiming a blow of his flickering blade at her back.

That should've meant the end.

Only, the Song poured so powerfully through her that she saw the attack ahead of time in her mind's eye. A premonition.

Without looking, she bent forward.

The miin's blade glanced across her armor, the heat stabbing into her flesh, but the damage largely missed.

She spun, thrusting a cutting slash at her enemy.

He parried with such might that it threw her to the floor.

It left her with her guard down.

Yet the red-eyed miin hesitated, pulling the killing blow just before it hit her. Must've had orders to take her alive. Perhaps Taiberos wasn't finished with her, which meant her condemnation had saved her.

She sprung to her feet, swinging her Singblade, which cut a ribbon through the air everywhere it went.

If he wouldn't kill her, she had an advantage. She pressed her attack wildly, taking powerful swings that left her open to fatal jabs.

But he didn't take them. Instead he backed down, all the while keeping his apparent calm. It meant she wasn't being risky enough.

She screamed and came at him harder, with blows that could kill.

He backed through the shattered glass, checking his footing behind him.

In that small moment of distraction, she cut at him furiously.

His red eyes went wide. He tried to dodge and nearly did.

Except that his lower arm, still recovering from his backswing, didn't quite make it.

Her fiery Singblade cut through his flesh and bone.

The miin roared in utter pain.

Before his prism even had time to clatter on the floor, she raised two hands and pushed mightily at the air, so close to her enemy that her fingers almost touched his face. Kinotic light blasted out from her like an anthem.

The impact hit his neck and head with a crack. He flew backward and hit the comms dashboard with a *BANG!*

It left a crater in the equipment.

The miin slid off and fell to the floor with a *thud*. He lay there in silence, now with only five limbs, his mouth open, eyes closed, not moving except for the motion of his breathing, which expanded across his torso in silent waves.

Her rage spurred her to end his life.

Something else told her not to listen, not to heed the anger, to grant mercy.

The tie between these two treacherous options was broken by the urgency at hand—the people of Solace awaited the rest of her broadcast.

If it wasn't too late.

And if she hadn't destroyed the machine in her ferocity.

Her blade vanished, and she fastened the prism to her belt.

The chair had gone flying in the fight, so she leaned over the mic with hands on the desk. The light was off.

If only Benton were here. He'd know how to fix it.

She glanced around the floor and then darted for her dropped secondary comms—the one that was connected directly to her savior. "Benton, it's Kalh. Are you there?"

The silence echoed in the massive stone building.

"Benton, I need help fixing the mic." This always happened to her with tech. She had the worst luck. She turned and gave a forlorn look toward the broken glass wall and said to herself, *"I haven't finished the broadcast…"*

He didn't answer.

She frowned at the board and the damage she'd done. Maybe there was another port. Maybe there was another console.

She'd just have to figure it out.

People needed to hear her message.

The miin remained unconscious. The Witch Hunter moaned, dying but not yet dead. Although he looked like vermin, Kalh sensed his humanity. She heard his cry for help but had to ignore it. More was on the line than a single villain's life.

After some time, she got the green light on a different mic glowing again. She tapped the filter twice and heard the feedback *thump.*

She'd done it!

She repeated the steps to get the broadcast activated. Still standing, she put her hands on the desktop and leaned down to the microphone.

T HIS IS KALHETTE Whitesun, and what you heard from that voice moments ago was yet another lie meant to keep you in submission.

"But I won't lie to you."

She paused and inhaled through her nose.

This was it. Her moment. Her chance to finally call people to aid in her fight. The moment she'd finally become the Prophetess everyone was looking for. At that thought, the music inside her swelled, pouring through her muscles and veins.

"The truth is, our success depends on you.

"And so, beneath the rays of an eternal twilight, I ask you, I call on you, the people of Solace, to rise up. Now is our chance. Citizens and clansfolk, miina and humans, and all who hear my voice, to everyone with a stake in personal freedom, I plead: Join with us. United we will strike against the PSD. United we will gain our liberty.

"I'm not calling to some ambiguous other who might also be listening. If you can hear my call, I am talking to you. Our success depends on you. *You* must stand. *You* must use your divine initiative to seize your own freedom.

"This is your call to arms. Gather your gear and head to the nearest armory where you will receive your marching orders."

She paused for a moment and took a deep breath. It all seemed surreal. She glared at the mic and leaned toward it. She had one more thing to say.

"And now I speak briefly to President Taiberos—" She swallowed after saying the man's name. "—to the Congress of the PSD, and to the Redhelm troops occupying our planet. We will honor the white flag. Stand down and you will not be harmed. We do not wish for violence.

"We have only one demand: our liberty. Nothing more and nothing less.

"But you, our tyrants, upon hearing our past pleas, have gripped your power more tightly. You've controlled our arms. You've spied on us in the name of safety. You've kept us subservient. But now we declare our liberty. This is our firmest desire and our deepest right—to make our own choices. You would deny us this right."

She paused to breathe in deeply, and her oversized armor rose and fell. She gazed earnestly.

"You've called us traitors. Are we traitors for throwing off shackles? No. If we submitted any longer to your rule, we'd be *traitors to ourselves*. You say independence means betraying our government. You forget that your authority comes from us. And we, the citizens, have expressed a desire for independence. Independence! We no longer consent to your governance. So now we fight!"

She bowed her head and stared, till her eyes turned into glowing lights, which cast their luminescence onto the microphone.

"And if we die, we die.

"But live or die, we make our stand!"

BENTON SMILED BOTH in his heart and on his face.

She was okay.

Kalhette was okay.

For now.

He pressed a finger to his green helmet. "Blackserpent, are you planning to delay your withdrawal now?"

"No."

"But you heard her voice! She's alive!"

"Every moment we wait takes a higher toll on my men. We've already lost many. You tell her to hurry up. We're not waiting."

"I'm the commanding officer, and you're under contract! It will go on your record."

"I have higher orders."

"From who? The only higher order would be Dray himself."

"We're leaving." Surely Blackserpent's own cowardice had given these so-called higher orders—Kalhette's death sentence.

Benton switched to his secondary comms. "Kalhette, this is Benton. Do you copy?" He waited a few moments and then added, "If you can hear me, you need to hurry. Your time is up." Even with no more delays, no Redhelms, she had to wander through quite a bit of building. Once at the wall, she'd have to calm down and make the surge, surely exhausted. It would not be quick, maybe half an iso. Yet the Nightwatchmen had almost withdrawn to the dropships. They would board and leave in just sequels.

Kalhette had suffered in Building 13 largely because of Benton. He couldn't let them get her a second time. He couldn't let her pay for helping the cause.

Then an idea came to him.

One that went against his own moral code.

He looked up at his aide-de-camp. "Dr Warnur, I want you to go to Blackserpent and make one more plea for him to wait."

"Yes, sir." Dr Warnur immediately darted off through the mud. That left one less set of eyes on what Benton was about to do.

He rushed back up the hill.

Laser fire crossed overhead. He stopped before he reached the Athenaeum— at the dropships. They were the same model Skyreacher had Liink destroy on Toar. At the time, Benton had thought it a rather childish thing for Skyreacher to do, but maybe the Song had meant for it to be.

Concussions sounded in the background, pulsing through his chest.

Lasers screamed at various pitches.

He pulled a latch on the first dropship, opening the instrument panel. Though the shields were active, they wouldn't stop an object with such low momentum as his hand. He deftly did the trick Nak had taught to Liink. When Benton finished tinkering with one dropship, he calmly walked behind the next, unnoticed by the pilots inside.

As he rummaged for the correct wires on the third dropship, a cold shadow fell across his heart. In moments, these ships would be wreckage, a sacrifice to spare a single human life. It still seemed wrong. If they won the war, maybe Benton would find himself in a position to pay Blackserpent back for the material damages he was about to cause. That wasn't the real problem.

His own words to Private Spuunar about slavery echoed in his mind. He was making a choice that would affect each of the Nightwatchmen. They were an elite fighting force, and with the proper motivation they could certainly punch a hole through the Sozo on foot, but it would come at a cost, and there would be casualties. If given the choice, some of them might be glad to do it, but he wasn't giving them the choice. Even if he had the time to try convincing them, he couldn't risk them choosing not to. He planned to force them. The alternative was to save his own honor and sacrifice Kalhette.

He couldn't do that.

No, he would take away the choices of dozens of Nightwatchmen.

Some of them would die because of it.

And Kalhette would live.

Dr Warnur, Private Spuunar, and Liink couldn't see him. No one could. He sabotaged the dropships one by one, and the guilt nagged at his throat.

He stepped away from the last dropship as a massive *boom* belched from the first. A round ball of orange flared into the dark twilight. The pilot darted from the cockpit and backed away from his skycraft, watching with mouth open, eyes wide, and an arm up to block the heat.

Benton retreated down the hill, joining the others, and the first pilot trailed after. The other pilots started climbing out to see what happened. The next went off in the same manner, throwing shrapnel as it combusted. The two skycraft sent trails of deep black smoke into the sky. The third one exploded.

The Nightwatchmen had pulled back their perimeter into a tight formation, ready to exit in as close to one group as possible. Now they stopped their retreat. As the final dropships exploded and burned, a few of the soldiers took off their helmets and stared at the spectacle. The rest maintained their relentless focus, keeping the enemy pinned at a distance. Soon all the dropships glowed with fire, and the trails of smoke spread and rose till they all merged together and vanished into the black clouds.

Amid the turmoil, Benton looked across the battleground and locked eyes with Colonel Blackserpent, who crouched not far away. He stared back with deadly rage—a look of murder.

Benton gripped the handle of his Singblade, prepared to defend himself.

Blackserpent didn't waste a sequel more on his emotions, proving what kind of man he was. He commanded his Nightwatchmen to action. They responded without hesitation, perfect soldiers, shifting their stance from holding ground to conquering at all costs. Their formation moved from a tight semi-circle to that of an arrow. With the bipedal treaders taking point, they punched straight down the hill at the Redhelms in a heroic charge, fighting through the Sozo to the outside.

Benton turned to Liink and the other Bloods. "I'm staying behind to wait for Kalhette. Then we're going to try to catch up with the Nightwatchmen as they cut their way out of here. You and your brothers are invited to join me if you desire." He swallowed. Allowing them to choose rubbed salt into the wound he'd just inflicted on himself.

Liink, with that ghastly cut across his face, nodded and then responded with a tone of humble eagerness: "Of course, sir. We'll come with you." The others showed the same courage.

Benton's green armor led the Bloods and Dr Warnur back to the hilltop. They hunkered down next to the Athenaeum wall, rifles ready. The heat from the dropships warmed their skin. It seemed the whole battlefield had followed the Nightwatchmen, and the hill got relatively quiet.

Long sequels ticked away, moments passing one after another.

The small fireteam waited an eternity, their chance of escape diminishing as the Nightwatchmen got farther and farther away. From the hill, Benton's team saw the orange and purple lasers clash in the distance.

Liink looked up at Benton, and they shared a knowing glance: It might be too late for any of them after all. Liink did not seem afraid. To sacrifice one's life to save another constituted an abiisu.

Then Kalhette appeared behind them, in the exact place from which she'd left.

It seemed as if a magician had suddenly torn aside a black veil. She was just suddenly there, leaning forward onto one bent knee, breathing heavily, her shaved head bowed.

"You made it!" Benton exclaimed. He wanted to give her a hug. Instead he stood there stoically, holding inside all his emotions except what showed in his eyes.

Gasping, she looked up at him with a nod and half a grin. She looked triumphant, like her success had formed a new spirit in her.

"We have to go," he told her.

She panted, barely even looking nauseous. "What happened to the dropships?"

"They were destroyed. We have to get out of the Sozo on foot."

"How?"

"We'll follow the trail of the Nightwatchmen." He pointed down the slope toward the conflict in the distance. It would not be easy to catch up. "Dr Warnur and Gaiing, help her. I'll take the lead. Liink, you're with me. You two take the left. You two on the right. And you three in the rear. I want the rest of you right behind me, pressing to the front. Okay, form up."

Without hesitation, he led a charge down the hill.

A THRILL SHOT UP Nak's spine.

Kalh's words echoed in his head:

If we die, we die. But live or die, we make our stand.

Before, he wasn't sure he believed in her rebellion. Now, he wasn't sure he could doubt. She also seemed obsessed with death.

Kind of cute.

He'd meant to protect Cup and himself, meant to cut their losses and go, but turning away, leaving Kalh's death behind, left him empty inside. Now he felt the opposite—an elation he'd never felt before. With that spirit overtaking him, he had a thought he'd never had before.

"Ah, ███." He turned the ship around, steering directly for the Behemoths.

"What?" asked Cup.

"It's Kalh's fault." Nak shook his head slowly, as if to tell the universes they were wrong. They *had* to be wrong.

He couldn't give up *The Sanctum.*

"What's Kalh's fault?"

Just the possibility made him feel sick. It felt like *he* was dying rather than his ship. She meant everything to him, the only thing he held sacred. With *The Sanctum*, he owned the galaxy. Without it, he'd be nothing.

Nothing.

Facing that nothingness, his mind raced in less than a sequel through the entire galaxy, in a panic, trying to find a way to get another surge drive, before he let go of this one. Maybe another politician's daughter. Maybe ambushing a federalist freight caravan. Maybe discovering the secret to creating them. Far-flung possibilities, vague and unknown.

Then he thought of Kalh, and he knew one thing—what he would do now. What he had to do.

"Nak—?" asked Cup.

"I just got an idea." An idea that hurt. In his throat, in his shoulders, his back, and his heart, and he hadn't even done it yet. "But it'll only work if we hurry."

"What idea?"

"I want you to set her into a surge spiral."

"What!"

"You said you can now, right? You said you solved the Ancor riddle because Kalh—"

"I said *I think* I can."

"We need to do it before those Behemoths disperse too widely." Saying the words out loud hurt even more. He willed it not to be, but what else could he do. It was their only shot. "I guess I finally get to see if I'll fit inside that coffin." Not looking forward to it.

"We still could *run away*."

"I don't think I can, Cup. Not this time."

"You really think it's possible for the coffin to escape the spiral while those Behemoths don't?"

"I'd say we got about a seventy-percent chance. Start the surge calculating."

Immediately she began clacking along the ceiling. "Where to?"

"This time, I guess it doesn't matter. How about the other side of Solace. And where are you going."

"Sure." Her voice sounded sad. "I'll meet you down there."

Nak tapped the command panel and opened a private relay. "Mr Valt."

"Yes, Skyreacher?"

Nak turned and looked for Cup, but she was already out of sight. He could just barely still hear her clacking as he spoke into the comms: "I want you to pull the fleet away from the surge gate."

"What? Why?" Nak couldn't help but see Valt's mustache, like an arrow pointing to his nose.

"If I told you, you wouldn't believe me."

Valt gave no reply.

"You know I'm sailing one of the Bloody Wings." Nak had a feeling that might have been enough to tip him off—Valt was sharp. "Of course, you don't *have* to pull your fleet back. But if you plan to keep it…"

"You're not thinking of an Ancor Gambit…"

"Yes, sir, I am." Although he could hardly believe it himself. After all, *The Sanctum* was his home.

"What makes you think you can do the calculations?"

"I may have figured it out. Only one way to know for sure."

Valt had a clear understanding of how much *The Sanctum* meant to Nak personally and its value in the marketplace too. "███████"

"Yep," said Nak.

"Do you think it could permanently disable the gate?"

Nak supposed the tachyons of the surge, which had no mass, wouldn't be affected. The brackets themselves might be ripped to shreds, so the new government would have to rebuild that part. Probably very expensive. Still, it seemed a fair price. And maybe the temporary isolation would give Kalh's government time to grow. "It's not up for debate. Withdraw your fleet if you want."

After a moment of silence, Valt's voice came back: "All units retreat to the vector I just sent you. I repeat—all units retreat to the marked vector."

Nak hurriedly pressed several keys and opened up a public relay meant for one specific person. "Hey, Taiberos, you selfish bastard, Starchild here.

Just wanted to make sure you knew it was me. I guess you've got the upper hand on this one. Too bad it's made of wires. You know, that's all right. You keep your upper hand. I'm taking *The Sanctum* with me. Oh, and tell your daughter I said hello."

He switched off the comms, uninterested in hearing a reply.

Taiberos was probably blowing a valve though.

"Okay, Cup. Let's do this." Nak pulled the yoke and weaved *The Sanctum*. He must've looked like a lunatic steering toward the surge gate, straight through the heart of the five Behemoths and a swarm of countless Goebs. They might suspect he was making a mad dash to escape the system, but his shields wouldn't last long in the middle of this fray.

The massive enemy fleet flowed toward him, converging like a magnetized fluid, but they didn't come with the expected firepower, which meant they knew who he was and what he was flying. That meant Taiberos had heard the message and ordered them to take him alive. So the ruse was working. They were just trying to stay close enough to his ship to block him from surging.

They had no idea.

Nak punched a command into the dashboard, a fifty-sequel timer before the jump. He pulled off his white headphones and rested them around his neck. He jerked the cord free, then stood and ran, boots clinking against metal grating as he limped quickly. He expected to see Cup still making her way along the ceiling, but he didn't. Must've misjudged the time. "Cup, where are you."

As he reached the aft ladder, he slid down, feet pinching the sides, but he ignored the pain. He stepped down a small corridor and passed through the security doorway into the engine room. The frigid air crawled across his hot skin. He limped to the shadow box mounted on the wall, took it down, opened it, and pulled the psykatana handle out. The green prism held such mystery inside its glassy surface. He left the jackets though.

And took one final look.

The future knotted like a thick rope, pinching his heart as it twisted, but he didn't have time to reflect. He circled to the back of the surge-drive's cylinder.

They called the craft a coffin because it basically was one. A tight black coffin, narrow and padded, with enough room to fit a body his size. The main difference was that it was oriented vertically, so rather than lying down in it, he'd have to drop down into it like a spelunker. It had only one tiny window at the top along with a few simple readouts. Fortunately, he wasn't prone to claustrophobia. Least he didn't think he would be.

It was shielded for radiation, a simple design, sleek, small, and black, making it unlikely a pilot would catch sight of it against the backdrop of space. It was also cooled by the surge drive and had insulators to maintain that exterior temperature. Most scanners looked for heat in sharp contrast to the cold of space—like an engine—meaning they wouldn't pick up the coffin without a manual range adjustment. That meant he could sneak out unnoticed.

It did have a homing signal, in case he wanted to call for help, but the idea was to blast out of the ship—which was its only propulsion—then glide in cold silence toward the nearest planet. After a few isochrons' journey, the parachutes would set you gently on the surface, safely away from your enemies.

Though Cup had reminded him of this contingency over and over, he'd never considered it. He'd always preferred to chance dying with *The Sanctum*.

Not this time.

As he opened the lid of the coffin, he realized he may have overestimated his odds of clearing the surge spiral without getting sucked into it. He crouched, staring into the coffin, feeling unsettled.

They were probably more like fifty-fifty.

The Sanctum might surge too soon, with too few Goebs close enough for it to matter. If that happened, it would mean Nak would lose his ship with no benefit whatsoever. It would also mean the surge spiral would drag him into it.

But something worse could happen: The PSD might get to *The Sanctum* before she surged, which would mean she'd be captured, and that bastard Taiberos would get her. Nak could hardly bear the thought of it. He'd almost rather die than live in a world where Taiberos got *The Sanctum* back.

But for Kalh's sake, he'd chance it.

Besides, he was feeling lucky.

Sort of.

He heard the chubby cube clacking outside the security door, moving toward him. "You ready, Cup?"

"No! I'm not!" She seemed upset. If she had the ability to cry, he suspected she'd have been doing it. Maybe she didn't want to give up *The Sanctum*. It was understandable. She practically was the ship. It wouldn't be easy to let go.

That didn't matter. He could just grab her and convince her it was the right decision later. He stood and moved toward the security door.

She whistled two soft notes, the second dropping after the first.

Before Nak reached the door, it hissed shut.

He looked up, wondering what had glitched, and then he realized.

He smashed a fist against the glass. "████, Cup." He repeatedly punched the button to open it but got no response. Had Taiberos somehow gotten to her? Maybe when her mind had been erased, some fundamental subroutine had remained. Maybe this decision to let go of *The Sanctum* had triggered it. He spoke in a commanding tone, as if he were still in control: "This is no time for games. We're going to die if you don't come on!"

She hung on the ceiling, right outside the glass, barely an arm's length away. She'd left her neutral expression facing down. Her voice came through the ship's speakers behind him: "Nak, tell me what the Gardens of Aminque looked like."

He'd never thought of it this way before, but her neutral side had just a slight curve in the straight mouth, which might've been a smile. He didn't like that. "The timer is going off in thirty sequels!"

"I turned it off." As long as she was synchronized, the phantomlink gave her complete control of the ship no matter where she went.

He smashed his fist into the glass again. "Cup!"

Her voice sounded a little rough, as if she'd used it all up and could now only scrape out the last few morsels of sound: "The Gardens of Aminque was one of the few times you took me with you."

"Well, I had to." This was his worst fear: mutiny. And it had to be now of all times. He'd finally decided to let go of his precious ship, and now at the last sequel she was rebelling. "Cup!"

And then it hit him. He didn't have to persuade her. He could use his own initiative.

Because Kalh had taught him Kinosis, second spectrum.

He had to become that *line between physical and spiritual* that she talked about.

With fierce determination, his hands stretched toward the door, and a ghostly right arm passed through to the other side of the barrier. With metaphysical fingers, he gripped the defiant little cube.

Bursting with anger, he jerked her with all his might.

And ducked as Cup slammed into the glass.

But he wasn't strong enough to break it. Not with telekinesis. So, although only millimeters from his face, she was still out of his reach.

Yet still he pulled on her angrily.

Against the glass, she had no way to move, trapped, with her smiling side against the glass. And he was trapped too, neither of them able to move without the other's permission.

His powerless fists clenched. Such a tiny thing in his way.

Her smile was upside down. Where the ink had bled, the left eye leaked into her eyebrow, and it made her look all the more horrified. "It won't work."

"What won't work, dammit."

"The Ancor Gambit."

BENTON'S PRIORITY WAS to get Kalhette to safety.

If his fireteam didn't catch up to the Nightwatchmen soon, they'd be swallowed by the swarm of troops inside the Sozo.

He'd burned the dropships for her. Sacrificed his honor. But she didn't know it yet. Maybe she never would.

Redhelms on the left flank opened fire.

Without being told, two of the Bloods took cover and laid down a suppressing fire. Once the fireteam had retreated a certain distance, two more Bloods took position and covered the retreat of the previous two. Benton found it hard to feel proud of them while wrestling with his own dishonor.

Soon they moved into housing and narrow streets. Much of it was covered in the thick foliage that covered nearly all of the Twilight Ring.

Benton breathed consciously, trying to sense the slightest fluctuations in the Song. It told him where to look, and his eyes glowed white as he peered through the wall of a building. The Redhelms' armor masked much of their heat, but he still saw them before anyone else. He motioned with two fingers in a rocking gesture.

Liink and one of his brothers darted quietly through an open doorway. A moment later, a warrior's scream echoed, and a pair of Redhelms fell to the ground.

Benton led the group onward.

The enemy forces were growing thicker.

Ahead lay an open courtyard strewn with debris and corpses, evidence that the Nightwatchmen had taken this route. It also looked dangerously exposed. Benton decided to explore another direction even though that meant risking an encounter with the enemy's undisturbed bastions.

The moment he stepped around the corner of the crumbling building, lasers came flying. He'd developed something akin to Kalhette's foresight, only much dimmer, and it warned him as a ripple across time. He ignited his orange Singblade an instant before being hit. With two hands, he waved the weapon to one side then the other, catching the lasers like an athlete returning volleys.

He backed out of sight, looking toward his soldiers. "Anybody hurt?"

The members of his fireteam shook their heads. Kalhette, with her helmet off, looked determined, more powerful than she'd ever looked before.

Liink pointed to a broken wall that rested at one end of the courtyard. His soft voice hummed: "We can make it to that cover there."

Benton stepped his forest-green armor into the open, moving in a crouched run till he slid safely behind the wall. Soon the others crowded up behind him.

The heavy footsteps of a machine vibrated the ground as it stepped into the courtyard ahead.

Benton's eyes glowed as he peered through the wall and saw not one but two treaders, bipedal vehicles made of dense metals and boasting massive firepower. They each stood at least two times his height and housed a human pilot inside. Onboard breach shields protected the machines from attack, so a prolonged assault would only leave the Renegades fatally exposed.

Benton squinted, his brow furrowed with dedication. Now his fitness training would pay off—what the Zhani called Initiative. These machines were powerful but not nearly as nimble as smaller units, which might be the advantage he needed. Plus their shields reacted kinetically to high-speed projectiles, like the bolt from a rifle, but a melee weapon moving at the speed of a hand would pass right through.

"Wait," said Kalhette, perceiving his plan from his expression. Since coming out of the Athenaeum, she'd had a triumphant glow about her, the confidence she'd always deserved. "Let me help."

Benton wanted to say no. If someone was going to get killed, he wanted it to be him, but of all people, he could not coerce her. Besides, he could hardly take on two treaders at once. He nodded reluctantly. "There are two of them and two of us. At first, they'll likely misjudge our speed. That'll give us an advantage for only a moment, so you'd better be on them or under cover before that moment ends. Okay?"

She knew the danger: The frag cannons on those things would tear through even an armored body like a grinder through meat. "Okay."

In a crouch, they moved together to the edge of safety.

He glanced sheepishly back at the others, feeling both dread and courage stirring inside. He turned and looked Kalhette directly in the eyes. "I, uh… I still feel the same, you know, as I always have."

She looked pained. "Oh Benton."

"I'm sorry. I didn't mean to—"

"It's not that."

"Then what?"

"I'm not worthy."

"Of what?"

"You!"

"Of course you are! What do you mean?"

She closed her eyes and shook her head.

"No, not now," he agreed. "Of course not. Later, perhaps. If we both survive." He cleared his throat. "Okay. You take left. I'll take right."

Kalhette nodded her affirmative, blinking rapidly with moist eyes.

Benton faced the rest of his team and called out: "Once they turn to fight, you'll have an uncontested shot at them. Take down the shields as quickly as you can. And be careful not to hit one of us."

Old Dr Warnur nodded, clutching his rifle. He flipped the safety off and then back on.

Liink seemed quite calm, just a cub yet content to die.

Benton didn't want to lose either of them. Any of them.

He gazed into Kalhette's eyes. He wished she'd kept her helmet on—her bald head made her seem so vulnerable. Through Ptolis, he sensed her exhaustion from her recent surges. "You sure you're up for this?"

She nodded, and her eyes gleamed fiercely.

"Okay. Let's go then." Benton's green eyes flared with white light as he put a hand on the wall and leaped over and into the open.

The light of the Song poured through him. His legs pushed the ground away behind him as he dashed with superhuman speed. He set his course not directly at the treader, but to the side, drawing its aim away from the others. He clutched his prism but kept it extinguished to minimize drag as he moved like a whirlwind, only barely aware of Kalhette's complementary dash across the other side of the courtyard.

The upper torso of the nearest treader turned at him, taking aim. The rotors of the frag cannons clicked, spinning in precursor to unleashing a volley of molten shards of metal.

He turned his course, running directly at the machine.

Laser blasts from his fireteam poured out at both treaders, forcing their pilots to choose—only one enemy could be addressed at a time.

Kalh's treader fired back at the group, forcing them to cease fire and duck out of sight.

The other treader kept its frag cannons aimed at Benton.

The first blasts came right at the Zhan's head.

He slid, ducking the guns. With one toe pointed out and his opposite leg tucked underneath, he threw his arms to the sides, pushing with Kinosis and sliding across the ground. His Singblade blazed to life, and he banged the edge against the leg as he passed beneath the machine.

Sparks flew, and the metal blackened with a deep gash, but the treader remained intact, still standing.

Benton jammed his heel into the dirt, and his momentum popped him to his feet at the machine's back.

Many of the bigger treaders could run a high-voltage charge through the hull to keep anything from crawling on them. With no time to deliberate, Benton took a risk, hoping this smaller one didn't have that feature.

The orange blade vanished, and he flipped his grip on the prism upside down. He leaped powerfully backward, with more strength than a mortal would naturally have. With a half twist in midair, his feet came up over his head. As he was suspended upside down, his Singblade blazed to life, shooting from the bottom of his fist. His feet completed their circuit, landing on the glass of the treader's cockpit.

Sensing something, Benton hesitated the smallest moment, half expecting thousands of volts to pulse through his body.

Nothing happened.

He raised his fist to jam the blade down through the windscreen and into its pilot.

The surface of glass beneath his feet launched skyward. With him on top. The pilot had hit some sort of ejection switch that blew the glass cover off his rig.

Benton accidentally dropped his weapon as he flailed through the sky, flipping uncontrollably. At least Jyngsoo wasn't here to see the embarrassing mistake.

The Zhan spread out his hands to gain a kinotic connection with the ground, steadying his airborne spin. When he hit, he landed in a squat, impacting hard, but the Song strengthened his tissues and bone.

His weapon lay on the ground between him and the machine.

The treader turned, exposing the pilot inside, who was no longer protected by glass. The machine stepped toward Benton, about to crush the prism underfoot. The treader's frag cannons began to whir, spinning in preparation to fire.

Benton reached out, grabbed at the air, and jerked his hand back. The prismatic handle came flying toward him. He darted to meet it, catching it from the air just as the frag cannons fired.

He leaped, and the hot shards of metal hit the ground where he had been, which sent a massive wave of dirt into the air.

The Zhan soared over the blast, but he was still too far away to reach the pilot with his melee weapon.

So he hurled it like a spear.

It wasn't easy to keep the blade ignited while disconnected from the circuit of his own soul, but he managed to pour in enough light to keep it burning as it shot through the air in a streak of burning orange.

The weapon hit the pilot in the chest.

The man slumped forward through the trail of light that hung in the air.

Benton landed with a tuck and roll.

The Singblade vanished, and the gem handle fell with a clump onto the cockpit floor. The treader lowered its guns and entered its standby mode.

With Kinosis, Benton retrieved his prism, popping it up and catching it.

He looked to Kalhette. She'd managed to cut clean through one of the legs of her treader, which was now lying on its side. He couldn't tell whether the pilot inside had been dispatched. He wished he'd been watching. A singblade could cut through almost anything, but not without friction—to cut clean through the machine leg would've either taken an unnaturally powerful blow or quite a bit of chopping. Wisps of light left by the path of the weapon still hung in the air, drifting as they faded.

And the way she stood—so tiny in her oversized armor in contrast to her gigantic, fallen foe—looked so heroic, like for the first time since escaping the Strand she had come fully back to life.

Benton started off toward her.

As he was about to call out, she waved her hands back toward the others and screamed, "Watch out!"

At that moment, Benton sensed something too, and his heart leaped, but all he could do was duck for cover, dashing toward Kalhette's fallen treader.

From behind the fireteam, a third treader stepped out, flanking them. It leveled its frag cannons, the rotors spinning—warming up and rattling in precursor of the terror to come.

Liink and his brothers scrambled to get over the wall, leaping into what used to be the open, their tails disappearing last.

Dr Warnur followed, his old body moving just a little slower than escape required.

Benton screamed: "NO!"

The frag cannon fired.

Benton reached with Kinosis, but his feeble hands couldn't stop so many shards with so much inertia, and the force of this attempt threw him on the ground.

The metal chunks cut glowing red streaks through the air.

The blast tore through Dr Warnur.

The impact shredded his armor, ripping through his torso and face. Pieces of his helmet clattered on the stones, falling among the gore, which landed on top of the miina. What was left of his white hair turned red with blood.

Benton, desperate to help, climbed to his feet to leap out of his cover, heading toward the others. His boot caught on something, and he twisted around to see.

Kalhette held on to his foot. "Benton, you can't save him!"

"I have to try."

She shook her head in a commanding *no.*

He looked at what used to be a friend and mentor. In an instant, that friend had become a mess of red across the ground. Dr Warnur could've gotten on the dropships with the Nightwatchmen. He could've gotten out alive.

If not for Benton's choice.

What had he done?

He looked at Kalhette—she was the trade-off, the thing purchased with his transgression. Purchased in exchange for his honor.

"We should at least bring back his body."

"Benton, no. I'll make a distraction while you get in that treader. Our only goal is to get the rest of us out alive." What she said made sense.

But he felt as if his very soul had caved in.

CPC4K3 HAD FINALLY solved the riddle.

And it really scared her.

"I just wish I'd had eyes," she said. "To see the gardens…"

The chassis of *The Sanctum* shook with another impact.

Through the phantomlink, she was still steering, weaving in toward the center of the five Behemoths, where the surge spiral would do the most damage. She evaded, and the ship's gravity pulled hard to one side. She hoped Nak was hanging on.

"What do you mean it won't work," he demanded, his tone jarred—like he didn't know how to cope with this interruption. His plan might've come from his usual irrational daring. Or maybe Kalhette's speech had made him eager to be rid of *The Sanctum*. Either way, it was foolish, even for him.

"You've got the right idea but the wrong pilot," she said.

"So it *will* work."

She wanted to roll to her worried side, but he had her pinned against the glass window on the door. "Your plan isn't even fifty-fifty. Plus your assumptions are wrong. With only the slave drive piloting, the hash will cancel and the surge spiral won't work. Kalhette taught *me* the secret to the Ancor riddle. *I* have to be here to do it."

"What?" He had disgust in his voice.

"I need to be aboard to close the gaps."

"Then we're not doing it. Let me out."

"No, *we're* not doing it. *I* am."

She heard another thump against the glass. "Cup, let me out."

"Get in the coffin." She'd never commanded him before, and that scared her too.

"Are you insane. I can't let you do this. I would never ask you to sacrifice yourself."

"You don't have to ask me to. I want to do it." She wanted to clack to her smiling side. "I overheard your conversations about choosing. Well, now I'm choosing. This is what I want."

"I won't let you."

"Because you don't want to lose *The Sanctum?*" She pushed hard with the zentisal drive, and the ship spun, its path curving in a new direction. Nak was surely holding tight to the walls.

"No. Because I don't want to lose *you!*"

"Well it's not up to you this time. I'm not a slave drive, Nak. I can make decisions. My own decisions."

"Let me out!"

"Get in the coffin, Nak. If you don't hurry, it will be too late, and Taiberos will capture *The Sanctum!* You're jeopardizing the surge spiral."

"No, *you* are! Why are you doing this."

"Because I solved the black-hole riddle. All by myself. I never thought I could solve something so complex."

"Cup! What are you talking about. That's not a reason."

"What would you give your life for—that's the riddle. Kalh's riddle. And I solved it. I'd give my life for you and for her, my two friends. That's the solution!"

A deep *boom* rattled the ship's frame.

CPC4K3 steered the ship away from the Goebs, but it was only a matter of time before they overwhelmed her. Especially while she was distracted. She had to get him to use the coffin. "I'm taking down Taiberos. And I'm not letting you out here. So you can go down with the ship, or you can go back to Kalhette. Your turn to choose."

He spoke in a tone like a confession: "You're not a normal android."

"Huh?"

"I mean: You're from the Photoss."

CPC4K3 didn't reply.

"You're still artificial, I think, whatever that means, but the difference between you and a slave drive is, well, it's astronomical. You may be worth more than the ship."

"Wow," she said reverently.

"You had a memory when I got you, but it wasn't more than a couple of percents. Definitely nothing about the Photoss or your origins."

"So you erased me?"

"For security. Had to." He fell silent again, still undecided, still deliberating. So unlike him.

She wanted to hear more, but if he didn't leave right now, he was going to die.

"It's for Kalh," she said. "I'm going to make her safe, give her back her freedom. She deserves it. Let me do this for her?"

Nak didn't speak for at least a sequel, maybe two. Then in an uncharacteristic tone of submission, he said, "Okay."

Just that.

He lifted her magically from the glass and placed her gently back on the ceiling, giving her magnetic control of herself once again.

She heard him climbing down into the coffin.

"Infraspace may be safe for me," she said. "If I'm really a Photoss. If *you* got stuck in there for ten aions, you'd be a corpse when you came out. But me, I'd just need a new battery." That was one possibility. She didn't speak the other out loud—the possibility that her longevity might be a curse. The journey might kill a human immediately but drag out her agony, leaving her stuck in some supernal, hellish torment indefinitely.

Nak got down inside the narrow cavity of the coffin and waited, not pulling the lid closed. CPC4K3 wished he'd beg her to relent one more time. Instead, he said, "I still owe you a body."

"We'll discuss your outstanding balances next time I see you."

He laughed, a mixture of happiness and sadness. "I'll keep my comms on." She heard him shifting, as if needing to express something more but not knowing how.

"Okay, now get out of here," she said.

His voice was pained: "Bye, Cupcake." She wasn't sure if it was the ruffle of clothing or a whimper, but she definitely heard something after that.

Before she could tell if he was crying, the hatch of the coffin clicked shut.

At least now she could concentrate on the task at hand. The Goebs were closing in on her. By her own volition, she was about to send Nak away. Then she'd be alone. Completely alone as she committed herself to the unknown.

She rolled to her crying face.

Her voice cracked as she whispered, *"Bye, Nak."*

S HE INITIATED THE escape-pod launch procedure.

The tiny hull clinked as it unlocked. The coffin slid down with a *shunk*. It beeped three times.

The blast-off made the engine room shudder.

And just like that Nak was gone.

"Bye, Nak."

If she had a body, she would've cried. Uncontrollably—unable to see the sky around her. Lucky she hadn't gotten one because she still had a task to complete, and dying in a body seemed like it would've been a lot harder.

She moved her scanners out of the typical range, which turned the horde around her into a field of white noise, while Nak's tiny coffin became visible, slowly approaching the precise border he'd have to cross before she could initiate the surge hash. She supposed his neck was craned back as he looked out the coffin window, trying to catch one last glimpse of his beloved ship. He'd at least see the massive flash of light as *The Sanctum* vanished into oblivion.

The Goebs swarmed, forcing her to bring the scanners back to the normal range so she could see them. A hailstorm of laser fire pelted the shields, but because this was a Bloody Wing, they didn't finish her off, though they easily could have. Perhaps Taiberos was hoping for a personal chat with Nak. Every once in a while, *The Sanctum* would lurch, as if it had met some dark friction. That was an attractor beam trying to establish a lock. Luckily they were far enough and she flew erratically enough that they hadn't successfully latched on.

As she piloted the ship, she moved her body clack after clack toward the cockpit. She couldn't see out, of course, but it seemed meaningful to pilot from there all the same.

She swerved the ship, heading toward the heart of the Behemoths' formation. She had to be near the center of their fleet for the Ancor Gambit to do the most good, and as she went she constantly adjusted the surge hash according to Kalh's technique, in preparation for the moment she would engage the surge.

CPC4K3 approached the center of the fray, steering wildly to keep out of reach of the Goebs, pushing the zentisi drive to its limits. The drive roared, and gravitational pressure pulled on every bolt in the ship, threatening to tear it apart and causing enough g-force to have killed Nak. She just wished he could've seen her final performance. Or maybe it was good he didn't. She didn't want him to doubt his claim as the best starpilot in the galaxy.

She shifted the scanners' range back, making her blind to everything but Nak's tiny coffin, which danced along the inside edge of the surge spiral perimeter, not yet safely outside. Close, but not quite. She had to delay a little longer, at least a few more sequels. Just as her tiny cube reached the cockpit, *The Sanctum* lurched again, this time completely dragging to the side.

They'd caught her!

But she waited. She had to.

And they dragged her in.

Soon they would board *The Sanctum*.

She watched the tiny black pod slip toward what she'd calculated to be the barrier of safety. If her calculations were right, he'd be crossing the border right...

"Bye, Nak."

She initiated the surge.

It worked just like Kalhette explained: Physics and Sorjis began to overlap. CPC4K3 monitored it carefully, cycling off the surge hash each time the mass became too heavy, millisequel after millisequel, manually closing each of the hyperfine gaps the instant they appeared, and the vibrational structure remained whole.

At first, things seemed to proceed as normal, an experience Nak once described as "when everything you thought was real starts becoming not real." Her gravitational sensors fractured, reading three different velocities all at once: falling backward, jetting forward, and standing still. It must've felt even stranger from inside a body.

Energymatter began falling apart: Light sources split into chunks, and shapes with three dimensions turned into shapes with seven, so that these extra forms floated like ghosts around their corpses. This all happened with every surge, in less than a sequel—the snap of a finger.

But in that tiny moment, something different happened too. A contortion of spacetime created a giant shimmering fold at *The Sanctum's* nose which looped in a perfect sphere around and far behind. As her velocity increased, the shining, translucent sphere grew behind her, encompassing more and more, till it engulfed Taiberos's five Behemoths, tugging the vessels and their swarm of Goebs into her wake.

She sensed the shift immediately, and the next instant was far from normal.

Her scanners picked up pale purple bolts of jagged light, shooting out from the surge drive in all directions, including the incalculable ones. This lightning touched the nearest skycraft and the ghosts of those skycraft. Then beams reached from those to the next, combusting outward in a chain reaction—a great spherical network of multi-dimensional light—till everything surrounding her was connected, and the outermost bolts even dug into the massive, mechanical brackets built around the shining surge gate.

The Sanctum shot forward, as if to escape, but she was pulled back and to the side, repositioning to pull this mass behind her, like a tug dragging dozens of trailers, each of which pulled dozens more, and on and on for many layers, all connected via a web of lightning. As CPC4K3 accelerated, every ship began to converge on *The Sanctum's* tail engines, as if the connecting chains of light were growing shorter.

In less than a gasp, the inertia of this whole network would converge on a single point, an inevitable fact that CPC4K3 witnessed in a small fraction of a sequel.

A tangled instant that happened in a flash.

Yet not so fast that her Photoss mind didn't realize what was happening.

She did it all deliberately, confronting Kalh's black-hole question head on, despite how much dread it pushed into her. CPC4K3 was living the riddle by making a choice. Soon she would find whatever answer lay beyond the point of no return.

It frightened her.

But her choice might make a difference for a whole planet.

More especially for Nak and Kalh.

With a hint of sadness, CPC4K3 snapped to her smiling face.

Then she and the light disappeared.

TAIBEROS HELD A sealed vessel of wine in his metal hand.

He paused before breaking it open. "What do you mean by *a message?*"

"It's a taunt, sir," said the operator. "Someone who calls himself Starchild."

The battle was over. Taiberos had won.

Although the conspirators had gotten away with their broadcast, he was about to prove it was all talk. Soon they'd be in chains or coffins—every last one of them. Taiberos himself remained out in the black aboard *The Dirigisme,* alongside the Behemoths, which could never land because of their vast size, but he'd just sent the order to deploy transports for a full surface invasion.

Presently, the skies of Solace would rain with war machines.

Someone who calls himself Starchild.

This small detail might significantly mar the victory celebration. Taiberos lowered the wine, unopened, and pointed an accusation: "And you didn't notify me?"

"I notified him, sir." The operator pointed. "I wasn't sure you'd actually want to hear though."

"How long ago?" asked Taiberos.

"Just moments."

"Play it back to me."

The operator shrugged off his responsibility and tapped on the console. Starchild's voice came through the comms:

"Hey, Taiberos, you selfish bastard, Starchild here. Just wanted to make sure you knew it was me. I guess you've got the upper hand on this one. Too bad it's made of wires. You know, that's all right. You keep your upper hand. I'm taking *The Sanctum* with me. Oh, and tell your daughter I said hello."

Taiberos's face turned red.

The staff on the command deck looked at him, all those eyeballs pointing this way.

He tried to act calm as he dropped his hand back down to his side.

The President of the PSD started shaking. "When did he send that?"

"Maybe twenty-five sequels ago."

An officer aimed a finger through the glass screen of *The Dirigisme* and out toward the vastness of stars. "That's the source right there sir."

Indeed it was—a tiny, familiar, black ship against the black of space. It glinted in the light of the sun, making it just visible ahead, and seemed to be trying to sneak right through the fight and toward the surge gate.

Taiberos started gasping but only through his nose.

A sensation poured through his nerves and veins into every part of his body. A mixture of bile and hate.

"Cancel the ground deployment," he said.

"Sir?"

Taiberos smashed the wine onto the floor, and pieces of glass went tinkling. "Do it now! You follow that Bloody Wing. We are taking it back!" He stretched out his metal grip, clutching at the air as if he might grab something. "I want every ship in the system aimed at it so he can't surge. All ships with attractor beams better use them, I don't care how fast he's flying. We are taking back that ship at all costs."

The command deck buzzed as various officers relayed his orders to the whole fleet. In mere sequels, as the red liquid bled across the floor, a swarm of Goebs were on the tail of the Bloody Wing. Lasers flashed as they surrounded it. And the larger ships, including *The Dirigisme,* formed an inescapable perimeter.

"Tell them to ease off on the attack," said Taiberos. "We don't want to destroy it. And I want a relay signal going right back at him."

After throwing a few switches, the operator said, "I have it queued up, sir, but I can't tell if it'll actually go through at this point."

The glass crunched underfoot as Taiberos leaned his bulk down toward the microphone console and pressed the activator. "Starchild, you little rat, you will regret the day you crossed me. Do you hear me? You will regret the day you crossed me!" When Taiberos finished the message, he gasped through his teeth and glared.

The operator swallowed and took a deep breath, as if choking on the ship's atmosphere. In a soft voice, the man said, "He may not hear it," and then cleared his throat one more time.

Taiberos ignored the comment.

An officer pointed a finger at the glass. "What is that?"

Through the windscreen, jagged bolts of lighting stretched out from Starchild's Bloody Wing, connecting to the closest Goebs, in a tiny little network of crackling light. More bolts radiated in every direction, connecting to the next nearest ships, as if each ship were electrocuting all the ones around it. This chain reaction moved in what seemed like barely a sequel.

It happened so fast that it left barely enough time to shout, "TURN THE FLEET AWAY!"

Taiberos knew what it was.

He knew what it meant.

But it contradicted everything he could conceive of as fair or right, misaligning itself so completely with his reality that his mind could not contain it.

So it spilled over.

That single moment stretched into eternity, a nick of time that became so vast it never ended, never passed—an instant that transformed into forever:

No.
██████. No.
██████ Starchild. No. █████.
It couldn't end like this.
██████.
Not Starchild.
Not ████████ Starchild.

T HE WHOLE SKY flashed an overpowering white.

A lingering lightning strike, so strong that it pierced the dark clouds.

Kalh had been crouched behind a wall, when suddenly everything became pure white—her hands, her knees, the stones of the wall, the grass. As the brightness washed out all colors and contrast, she had a moment of panic—like maybe she'd gone blind.

The brilliance vanished, and the twilight rays resumed, restoring the gentle color palette to the world around.

She turned toward the sky, mouth agape.

It was like the surge farewell that Nak described but more massive. As the light withdrew, it seemed to converge on one specific point, the surge gate, which shone like a star through a gap in the cloudy atmosphere.

The Twilight Ring usually rested in a gentle unending half-light, so the flood of photons came as a surprise. Though the flash lasted only a moment, silence followed on the battlefield—an unofficial and total ceasefire. The eerie silence lasted a long time, as if everyone on the opposing side had been instantly killed. But with Starsight, Kalh could see the Redhelms gawking at the sky.

Benton's comms started beeping as he stared up in wonder. He put on his helmet and said, "What?" A long pause was followed by, "A bomb?" He listened more. "What about the Behemoths? And Taiberos himself? I can't believe it." He pulled off his helmet.

Kalh peered through the wall toward the enemy troops. "What?"

Benton tucked a hand gingerly beneath his armpit. "Valt says the sky is ours. The PSD reinforcements have been neutralized. We've done it."

"What happened?" asked Kalh.

"They don't know exactly. Some details were lost in transit. A supernova of some sort. It turned the battle in our favor."

Kalh put a hand protectively on her bald head. "Is Nak okay?"

"Who?" asked Benton.

Somehow, she already knew the answer to her own question: Nak was fine. Then pain twisted into her gut: "It was Cupcake."

"What—?"

A tear rolled down Kalh's cheek. "Starchild's android. She did an Ancor Gambit."

"What do you mean?"

"Starchild had an android who solved the Anchor equation. His ship took out Taiberos's fleet." Kalh took a deep breath and put a hand reassuringly on her womb. "Starchild's Bloody Wing."

"How do you know?" Benton seemed in shock, like he needed to find another explanation. "Do you think Starchild got away?"

Kalh felt an unexplainable peace. She nodded her head, surprised too, and yet, in another way, not at all surprised—this was Nak, after all.

Benton looked down the trail toward where they'd left Dr Warnur's body, his mind still caught on a snag. The enemy wasn't firing. Or sneaking up. In fact, the Redhelms were doing the opposite: They were withdrawing.

With Benton still processing, Kalh looked at Liink, the only miin from the team that she knew: "Let's get moving."

Upon making eye contact, Liink smiled his big, ugly alien grin.

W IND SWEPT ACROSS the grass of Solace's rolling hills.
The battle had been won.

The breeze rose from the Kazia Sea and tickled Kalhette's bare skull.

She smelled petrichor—the aftermath of rain. It mixed with an aroma of salt from the sea. Blue poppies danced on the slopes amid the green. The warm twilight sun beamed across the fields.

The cemetery rested on a hill overlooking Ghosthead Bay, a beach where she played as a child. A lone piper played "The Last Minstrel" as they lowered the remains of Dr Warnur into the ground. The wind caught her dress—threads of a periwinkle blue, a color as soft as the twilight itself—and stretched it out into a flowing tail. She bowed her head. A circlet crossed her forehead, a headband symbolizing nobility, which she never would've dared to wear before. Around her neck, she wore a dark string necklace that carried a small, empty glass vial.

Drums beat slowly, augmenting the melody. A low flute joined in harmony.

Tears crawled silently down her cheeks.

Taiberos was gone. Her tormentor.

That victory had come at a cost. She'd watched Dr Warnur butchered. It seemed like a quick death, mercifully without time for agony. Just like Tannie.

And Cupcake.

The agony resided with the survivors.

Several members of Dr Warnur's family were weeping outright. Little Tweldon with the missing tooth fought to keep back his tears, breathing rapidly, staring at the coffin with his eyebrows knit. That poor boy. He did not seem to be okay.

At the green graveside, Kalh looked down at the coffin. Nak stood on one side of her and Benton on the other.

The tombstone sat off to the side. On it was engraved a single Photoss word: *Lissiashona*. It meant "warrior of light."

She scanned the faces of the crowd. Human eyes and the distinct yellow of the miina. Most looked at the coffin.

Lord Admiral Dray looked directly back at her.

Something about his one-eyed gaze made her heart leap with an ambiguous terror. She looked away, staring toward the sea as she observed the strange feeling.

He wasn't correctly reflecting light.

Something happened to him at the Strand, perhaps beyond the horrors she'd experienced herself. Maybe it had something to do with the unsolved mystery of Darkstar, the deeper purpose behind the cruelties committed there.

Jamie Bladoor stepped up behind her and placed a hand on her shoulder. He gave her a simple nod to show his gratitude.

After she and the Nightwatchmen had escaped, the fighting around the Sozo continued for several more sleep cycles. Because of her abilities in Sorjis, she tended the wounded. She also helped count the dead. Eventually, the Redhelms stationed at the Athenaeum raised a white handkerchief in surrender.

Tannie had been the revolution's first casualty. Dr Warner and Cupcake would not be the last. In winning a battle, they'd started a war.

Broadcasters called the victors the Renegade Faction. Which was better than *agitators* or *traitors*. Benton pushed the official title, the Allied City States of Solace or ACSS. Nak said he liked *Renegades* better. Kalh wasn't sure which she preferred. Out of the names.

People called the battle, and the victory, the Solace Sunrise. Because of her public role, she was asked to raise the flag. The War Council hadn't agreed on the flag's final design, so she used a miina flag with an old Photoss symbol that included an overlapping hourglass, circle, and diamond.

They'd won because they were a team. Each time someone thanked her, she tried to direct the credit toward where it was due. Dray deserved accolades, both because he sacrificed himself to save Kalh from Building 13 and because his brilliant strategy had made the Battle of Sunrise a success. Benton deserved great praise, for the planning and the execution; plus he and his mercenaries had made sure she could retreat alive. Many Nightwatchmen, along with Dr Warner, had given their lives too, dying to protect her specifically.

Her body shook as she fought another onslaught of tears.

She didn't deserve a gift like that.

Nak put his black-sleeve hand on her shoulder and pulled her in for a hug. She felt safe crying in his embrace and embarrassed it happened in front of Benton.

Nak had never said so specifically—in fact there was a lot he didn't say specifically—but it seemed he'd come to the funeral to support her, to be there for her.

All pieces in the battle had been key, but if she had to choose only one, it would be Nak who should be hailed as a hero. He'd eliminated five Behemoths. Even to someone who didn't know him, the sacrifice of his own Bloody Wing had been astounding. For her, it was more so—she had some idea of what it had truly cost him:

It cost him Cupcake, his best friend.

The unsung hero of Solace.

I T ALL FELT so awkward.

When the funeral rites concluded, the crowd began to disperse, but neither Nak nor Benton started to leave. She didn't know how to navigate between them, so she started off alone, but Nak followed, which gave her the impulse to say something to Benton, but instead she pretended to be too distraught.

"You okay?" asked Nak.

She wiped her eyes with her knuckles. "Yeah."

He whispered so none of the others would hear him: *"If we die, we die."*

She turned and looked up into his blue eyes. "Still thinking about that, huh?"

He had a scruffy smirk as he said, "It's a funeral."

"And are you thinking about Cup?"

He didn't speak in response. With a defensive frown, he nodded slightly, as if he didn't think she should've brought it up.

She gave him a compassionate smile, and changed the subject: "I learned that line from Master Jyngsoo. The story happened on that beach." With one hand, she pointed at the Kazia Sea and with the other hand, she touched the empty glass vial hanging from her neck.

"You guys keep mentioning him."

"He's an ancient Zhani teacher."

"I thought you knew him."

"I do. He taught me. He's probably seven or eight aions old."

"Wait, he's alive and he's that old? What species is he?"

"I actually don't know."

"I don't know of any conscient species that lives so long." Nak shook his head and chuckled. "To be honest, half the time I have no clue what you guys are talking about."

"You get that line though, right? If we die, we die?"

"Sort of. You're just supposed to let what happens happen."

"Yeah. It's the concept of the Song—the inevitable harmony of all things. It means things work out in the end."

"It's a nice thought."

"A Zhan is supposed to be one with the Song."

"Like control it?"

"No. More like the opposite. A Zhan controls her own will, but she should simply be at peace with the rest. She should accept it. Embrace it."

"Mmm." He nodded.

"There are things you can control and things you can't. If you can change them, there's no point in worrying. If you can't change them, there's no purpose in worrying. Either way, you should be at peace. Even facing death."

"What if you're not sure if you can change something."

"Then you find out by trying."

"That's my favorite option."

She smiled at him.

"Oh, and I heard Bladoor call you the Uncrowned Queen. That's five."

After her speech and the victory, an article on the Handnet had called her the Uncrowned Queen of Solace, the ruler who didn't rule, and it was already sticking. "I don't like it. You notice none of them are saying it to my face…"

"They don't dare." Nak laughed. "Hey, if you're okay, I'm going to go. I'll see you later?"

"Yep."

The victory had changed her. She felt stronger. More capable. Like she didn't need to run. Like she might not run if it came to that.

She wasn't entirely comfortable wearing the circlet, as she still didn't consider herself the Uncrowned Queen.

But she *was somebody.*

S HE WALKED IN a loop, making her way back to Benton.

She swallowed as she approached.

He stood alone now at the graveside; the others had moved toward the transports, still talking and lingering. With his hands clasped behind his back, his shoulders hung in despair as his usually perfect hair fluttered rebelliously in the wind. He stared vaguely with tired eyes, as if mortality had become a burden.

She wasn't ready to answer his words from the battlegrounds:

I feel the same as I always have.

What could anyone say to that—aside from *I love you too?*

She did love him. Confusingly so. Benton was her perfect match for many reasons. He was also noble and strong, willing to sacrifice to do the right thing. He reached for his ideals like reaching for godhood itself.

It inspired her. *He* inspired her. Like no one else.

When he saw her, he tucked his hands beneath his armpits, protecting the nerves that had been damaged when he tried to stop a frag cannon with Kinosis. He gave her a sad smile, the kind befitting of a funeral, one that hid an even deeper hurt.

"How are the hands?" she asked.

His green eyes dropped to the ground. "They'll be fine."

She tried to ad lib, acting like they were still old friends and wishing they were: "Hey, cheer up. We won, you know." She matched his pained smile and stood next to him. "Sorry, I shouldn't be so..."

Benton looked up, the man who'd rescued her from Building 13. His expression held back some... expectation. A secret as mysterious as his eyes.

"Are you okay?" she asked.

He glanced toward the casket. "I don't know."

"Things are going to be okay. Their sacrifice was a noble choice."

He seemed to cringe at the word *choice*.

In the silence, the distance between them seemed to grow wider with each ticking sequel. It hurt. She swallowed and finally blurted out the words: "Is there something you need to talk about?" She already knew the answer.

He shook his head and swerved away from the pain and from trusting her: "We have the beginnings of something truly great—a world that follows the principles of the Braid. I hope we can be good stewards and live up to the ideals."

"Benton, no one ever lived up to any ideal. We're not Kurosh. At best, we're asymptotes, growing ever closer, but never reaching the ideal. That's the point of mortality. It's beautiful, imperfect chaos."

He smiled sadly, as if to show he appreciated the gesture.

I feel the same as I always have.

"It's okay if we're not perfect. It has to be or I—" She choked up and couldn't finish her sentence. She wrapped one arm protectively across her chest and another across her womb.

He put a hand on her back and patted, the sort of physical affection they used to have. It felt both strange and familiar.

They sat in silence, each needing but not receiving comfort.

Finally, she swallowed and said, "I was going to walk to the ridge for a better view of the sunrise. Want to come?"

He didn't say yes, but he took a step. They walked side by side toward the light.

Her periwinkle dress fluttered in the wind. It had a narrow fan in the back that hung down from her belt like the tail of a bird. With the dress and circlet, she looked beautiful, which made her uncomfortable. Strange that looking this way would take such daring.

Rather than approaching the difficult question, she asked one that was easier: "Have you ever considered instructing a Zhani pupil of your own?"

Benton looked up at her with an expression of recognition.

"I'll take that as a no?"

"Yes, I have considered it," he said.

"And...?" She was getting ahead of herself to assume Nak would want to explore the mysteries of the Song.

"I believe Master Jyngsoo would be a better option," said Benton.

"What if he weren't an option?"

"I don't know," said Benton. "Are *you* considering instructing someone?"

"Me? No."

"Why not?"

"Well, you know. Handing someone that much power is a grave responsibility."

He gazed with eyes that hid a secret, which both terrified and attracted her, like he knew something about her that she hadn't yet discovered herself. "Yes, I've thought so too, but you're ready. What you did at the Athenaeum…"

"I wouldn't be much of a teacher, even if I did want to," said Kalh. "You know this stuff intellectually. I only know it intuitively."

Benton didn't reply and the conversation drifted into silence.

They sat at the edge of a slope, looking across the sea toward the sun.

What he said next surprised her: "You're thinking about training Nak, aren't you?"

She gave a bashful nod, too caught off guard to actually say it aloud.

Benton looked down. "To be honest, I wanted to dislike him… But what he did up there was… principled." He paused, as if formulating more to say. Maybe a confession of jealousy. Maybe encouragement. Or an apology even.

He said nothing, and then came more hungry silence.

I feel the same as I always have.

She wasn't ready to broach the topic herself, but she couldn't take the empty space any longer. "I heard you're working on a new flag."

Benton gave a sigh, maybe relieved to be changing topics, grateful to put down his burden for a moment. "Yes. And I suppose it ought to be approved by the Uncrowned Queen." He looked at her circlet.

She rolled her eyes. "Please…"

"Sorry."

"But I do want to hear about it," she said. "As your friend. Not as… her."

He maintained his melancholy, but she knew him well enough to still detect his hidden enthusiasm: "The lower half, the foundation, is a blue field dotted with white stars; that represents the vast body of truth, most of which, for us, remains uncharted. Across that field, falls a stripe of crimson, crossing at a diagonal, representing the sacred fire, the power of choice in each individual; this will be rough edged, painted with a brush, so that each time the flag gets created the red is distinct. On the upper half, opposite the starfield, will lay a golden field representing soul and compassion."

"So gold on one half, blue on the other, and red between. The primary colors."

"Running down the red band will be six words: *Honor truth. Defend choice. Embody love.*"

Her eyes fell to the tattoo on her forearm, three colorful ribbons braided together to represent these three same principles, the three lights—Vision, Initiative, and Spirit. Around which were the words *e lissia kalha*—*reverence the light.*

A piece of him.

He noticed her noticing the design.

She smiled uncomfortably. "I'm surprised you didn't use this." She tapped her tattooed skin.

"No," he said. "That belongs to you. My gift to you."

He'd meticulously designed it. Then he'd etched it beneath her skin.

Back when they—

She swallowed. Feeling so much regret. For running from him. She'd been a frightened child. And now, more than ever before, she did not feel worthy. Not after what Taiberos had done to her. His hands...

What would Benton say if he knew?

"Sorry you wasted the design on me," she said.

"Oh, Kalhette. None of it was wasted. Not a single moment." He looked at her fervently but did not touch her. "I hope you don't regret any of it. You have great things ahead of you still."

She struggled not to cry, completely unable to respond.

Benton gallantly filled the silence: "I'm debating whether the words should be written in Photoss. I like the purity, but I don't want it to be inaccessible."

She blinked, trying to act like she was fine, and then sniffled. "And no representation of Solace?"

"Well, the red represents the Twilight Ring. And you have the sunside in yellow and the starside in blue."

"Oh!" She bobbed her head, wiping the skin around her eyes and sniffing. "I like it. You are so clever."

As the sough of wind filled the quiet, they sat looking out across the sea for some time, and the somber mood settled.

Once she regained her composure, she rubbed her palm across his back. "Thank you, Benton. You've done a great thing. You saw a future I thought was impossible. Then you made it real."

"The fight is not over yet."

WHEN BENTON LEFT, Kalh wandered to the beach.

The circlet glinted in the twilight. The color of the dress matched the pale shades of the sky. She felt fine looking beautiful so long as no one else was watching.

She descended toward the shore, checking over her shoulder. Her feet pattered against the dirt and down wooden steps. Soon what remained of the crowd was out of sight. And she was alone.

Nothing but her and the hush of the waves.

She looked cautiously over her shoulder. Strangely, she expected to see Dray. And she sensed... something. Maybe the Witch Hunters. Or that red-eyed miin she'd left alive but down one arm. The feeling, hard to pin down, left her feeling uneasy. Almost like Dray was watching her with that one eye. A chill ran through her.

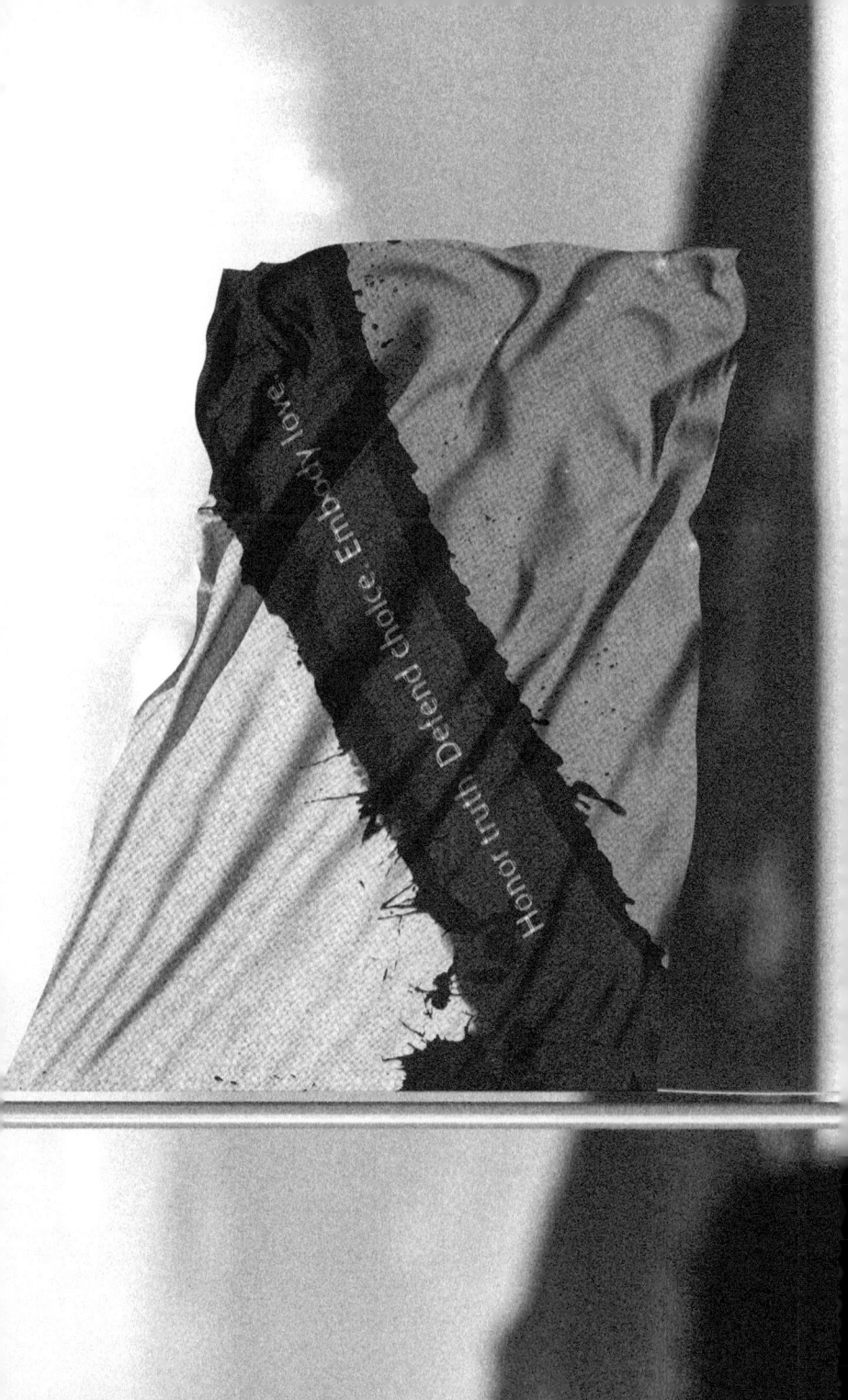

She checked behind again then put a hand nervously against her neck.

Maybe she felt shame because he suffered so much for her. Or maybe the past now stalked her. What Taiberos did cut her soul so deep that she might never heal, but she wanted to let go of it. If she could. Let go of Taiberos and even Tannie—who'd gone to meet the Kurosh. She needed to let herself be free. If the silence was filled with melancholy, or if the threat of more war loomed quietly ahead, or if she still had a heavy role to play as the Uncrowned Queen, or if a mysterious child awaited in her womb—

Then so be it.

Before her spread the Kazia Sea, which was gentle, at least compared to planets with revolving moons. The waters looked like a mirror, white with just the memory of blue. Along the austral side ran faded mountains of a pale blue. Behind them, the sky was pink-turning-orange, with the sun standing ever just out of sight. Purple clouds danced on the horizon. The white glowing dot of the surge gate had shifted toward the starside, but it still glowed up there, a monument to Cup, her friend and savior. She wanted it to be a memorial for Tannie too, her little lost musician.

For a long time, one of her deepest desires had been for the world to just be quiet, and now, for a moment at least, it finally was. No more intrusions. No more running. Just stillness.

This was it, Solace, her home.

And she was finally here to stay. She could even start a garden if she wanted. Hopefully soon it would be safe enough for her family members to return.

She enjoyed the foamy quiet, accented occasionally with the caws of birds.

As she reached the beach, her steps sank into the sand. It was beautiful and white. She kicked off her shoes and sunk her toes underneath. When she lifted them, the grains fell between like a spontaneous hourglass. She kept walking till the sand became wet. The cool water lapped up around her ankles, turning the sand iridescent, shimmering with every variety of color.

She retreated to where the tiny waves didn't reach.

From around her neck, she removed the dark string necklace. It looked just like the one Taiberos had taken. She took the cap off the glass vial, crouched, and scooped up some of the white sand.

A little vial filled with white sand.

Holding the string, she held the tiny glass container at arm's length, dangling it as if over the distant sea. It swung back and forth with the water and the sunrise in the background.

And she smiled.

NAK CHECKED HIS chronometer.

Kalh was late.

While wearing his black cryo jacket with the red sleeve, he limped through a makeshift medical bay, ostensibly looking for Valt. Dozens of wounded were sprawled out on beds. All the pink gore and laser burns exposed during the fighting had been covered with white bandages. Tanks filled with bubbling shome lined the walls. Medical androids lingered over the patients, assisting where they could.

Cup had wanted to be a medic.

Two whole millos had passed since she... And now the battle had turned into a war—the War for Solace. Although a huge chunk of the PSD armada had been destroyed, Solace still had legions of Redhelms across the Twilight Ring, not to mention the troops on nearby Rime. Yet with Taiberos out of the picture, his government went into a tailspin. The surviving bureaucracy bickered over next steps. The Shadowlyss, the second largest faction in the galaxy, struck at this crucial moment, quickly taking ground. That gave the Renegades time to build their own skycraft in earnest. Plus Valt finagled a fleet of Raewasps from Rime that belonged to the PSD.

"What are you doing here, Skyreacher?" He turned to see Benton approaching, hair trimmed as neatly as ever.

"Looking for Valt. Waiting for Kalh. You haven't seen her, have you." He didn't want to mention any details about what he planned to do. Not to anyone, but not to Benton in particular. The man seemed incapable of comprehending that a choice could be made without deliberation.

"No, I haven't seen either of them."

"It's, uh, Starchild, by the way. What are you doing."

"I'm also looking and waiting. Meeting with the New Onaitu shortly."

"Oh." Nak didn't know what that meant. Probably politics.

Benton waited awkwardly, saying nothing.

Nak's relationship with Kalh seemed to be kind of a sore spot with Benton, but that was the only topic that was coming to mind. Nak poked at a pebble with his boot. "It's, uh... nice weather."

Benton glanced over his shoulder before speaking. "I've been wanting to tell you that your choice to sacrifice your skycraft was heroic."

"People keep telling me that." He still couldn't believe he'd done it. *The Sanctum* had been his home, and Cup had been its heart.

"Well, it was."

With a smirk, Nak said, "I've always been a pretty selfless guy."

"I didn't say *selfless*."

"Right. Kalh said you hate that word."

"Not the word. The concept."

"Why."

Benton replied softly, as if he'd become acquainted with truth and was simply offering an introduction: "Because it's a lie."

This seemed somewhat interesting. Maybe if they couldn't converse, they could have a decent argument instead. "I thought you Zhani were supposed to be servants."

"We're not against service."

"Then I don't get it."

Again Benton spoke as the truth's mild friend: "People frame selflessness as a dilemma: You can either help yourself or help others. No wonder people make so-called selfish choices when they believe the alternative is to hurt themselves. That paradigm is a lie. Life isn't a zero-sum game. It's not *if you win I lose*. It's *we win*, or it's *we lose*. We rise and fall together."

Nak decided to poke the beast a little to see what would happen. "Seems like a nice way to think about it. Not sure it's accurate."

Benton replied with increasing passion: "Do you think a man who hoards his wealth is happy? No. He's creating darkness for himself and for others. Or has anyone found real happiness by injuring others? Never. People call these selfish acts, but they don't benefit the self. And, conversely, helping others is not selfless. The person who shares the most light enjoys the most light. That's the *best* way to benefit the self. When you create light, it shines all directions."

Nak kept his grin to himself. "Sounds like semantics to me."

"It's not. The selfless model frames a person's own happiness as a negative. It tells you that helping others is good but helping yourself is bad. It teaches people to deny themselves light. That's a hurtful belief. On the other hand, if you believe we win and lose together, you make different choices. It's not semantics. Thinking this way changes behavior. It urges people to create light."

Nak realized the implications, and he didn't like Benton talking about *The Sanctum* that way. "You ever had a smallow?"

"Yes."

"So let's say I have a smallow. Do I eat it and make myself happy, or do I give it to you and make you happy."

"Exactly. That's the either-or mindset. You have to look for a third solution, one that creates light. Cut it in half. Make us both happy."

"Okay." Nak spoke with a sarcastic tone, confrontation mixed with anger. "I once owned this ship, and it was worth a lot. I knew this other bastard who really wanted it. It's not like I could give him half…"

"Time sharing."

"If I gave him control, I'd never see it again."

"Then the problem is not who gets it. The problem is the hearts of the people involved. Too much Shadow."

"You still haven't told me what to do with the ship."

"I make no commentary on the ship. The matter resides inside you—it's the Song. If you listen carefully to the Song, you'll know what to do with the skycraft."

"So you're saying the Song might tell me to keep it for myself."

"Absolutely. But if it tells you to let it go, you have to be willing to do that too. Whatever creates light."

Nak's jaw tightened, and his eyes dropped to the ground. "That *was* what it told me to do."

"And did your action benefit other people?"

"My friends, yes."

"And what about you?"

Nak swallowed, bracing himself against the throbbing wound. Then he thought about Kalh. With some reluctance, he admitted, "I might be better off."

Benton nodded and put a hand on Nak's shoulder. "I commend you, Starchild. You made the galaxy a little brighter."

"Then why does it hurt."

Benton had a pained look on his face, as if he had first-hand experience: "Nothing of value ever came without cost."

THERE YOU ARE," said Valt.

He was a slender man with a slender mustache and an uncanny ability to take daring leaps. Basically the opposite of Benton—Valt couldn't conceive of making a choice *with* deliberation. And yet strangely, his wealth suggested his gambles usually paid off.

"King of the Entrepreneurs," said Nak in greeting.

"That's an oxymoron if I've ever heard one," said Benton.

"If I've ever *seen* one," mumbled Nak.

"Best starpilot in the galaxy alongside the wisest man I know," said Valt with quite a bit of gusto. "That's a lot of clout! Am I interrupting something?"

Benton removed his hand from Nak's shoulder. "Not at all. Hello, Nik. We were just discussing the Song."

"I better go." Nak patted Benton on the shoulder, which seemed to highlight the difference in size. "Thanks for the pep talk, big guy. You'll have to teach me more another time."

"Indeed," said Benton.

"Did you know this guy's name is Nak?" exclaimed Valt. "Nik and Nak! That's something else! Isn't it? Seeya, Benton!" Valt reached a hand up onto Nak's shoulder, like it was his turn or something, and started to lead them away for a private conversation. "Okay, ready to tell me the secret of the Ancor riddle?"

Nak limped alongside. "I really don't know."

"Then tell me you've at least figured out where your ship ended up!"

Nak kept his head up, looking for Kalh. All he knew was that Cup dragged that bastard Taiberos and his whole massive fleet into infraspace. Or somewhere. If Cup weren't the one doing the pulling, he'd have wished them to end up in the Otherworld. "Nope."

"Come on!" Valt jabbed a finger at Nak's ribs. "You must have something!"

"I have one theory," said Nak, which he didn't believe, but it would at least entertain Valt. The galaxy had billions of star systems, but only a few hundred were connected through the surge gates, so it often seemed like the rest of them just didn't exist. "Maybe she ended up in a system outside of the surge network with no way to get back." To travel those distances through normal spacetime would literally take many lifetimes.

Valt's tone was both chiding and chuckling: "Just like Solace now, you blackguard." He reached a fist around and took a jab at Nak's stomach.

The Ancor Gambit saved Solace, but it had inadvertently destroyed the surge gate. At least the mechanical part—the brackets had collapsed into the swirl. The glowing, mysterious part, the part made of tachyons, remained, still in orbit, and you could still fly into it—and never come out. Until the gate's tech could be reconstructed, which was a huge undertaking, the gate was effectively dead—Nak's fault. It put a serious damper on the economics, as Valt kept reminding him. Plus, Solace wasn't the only inhabited planet in the Origin system, and their neighbors on Rime were understandably outraged.

"Not *just like*. Bloody Wings can still get through," a fact the PSD had not simply forgotten.

A couple of miina walked by. Or crawled or something. Nak didn't know what to call it. Even their casual pace had something predatory about it. One of the miina whispered to the other and then both looked at him. He wished he had his dread mask—to avoid another conversation with someone who didn't realize Cup was the real hero. It was Liink's fault. He told the story to just about everyone, kept saying it was an abiisu and that Nak should be honored. Nak tried to get him to shut up, in a nice way, of course.

He felt almost like a mentor to the cub, who seemed to have good intentions along with a sort of innocence that Nak himself lacked. He felt proud of the cub getting more independent of his strict upbringing. And he seemed obsessed with that psykatana now that Benton told him he could learn to summon it.

It was strange feeling loyalty, but Nak felt it for Liink. And for the whole band of desperados. Including Benton. In fact, he might even consider that man an almost-friend.

"So what do you want," asked Nak.

Valt cleared his throat, suddenly overly serious: "Dray asked me to decide what to do with that surge drive you captured."

"Dray asked you."

"Yes."

"Where did you see him."

"I didn't see him. He sent a relay."

"Was it really his voice."

"Yes. Dray and I go way back. Way back!"

In the two millos since Cup—*departed*—Nak hadn't seen Dray even once. And so he hadn't had the chance to say thanks. To his other almost-friend. The man whose sacrifice had rescued Kalh. The man whose clever plan had won them Solace—minus the sky part. Since the victory, hardly anyone had seen him. Could be he was just ducking the congratulations, but it seemed like more than that.

"Now, I'm not saying I'm going to do what you say," said Valt. "It's still my decision, okay? But I just wanted to hear what you thought, I mean, considering who you are and your role in the whole thing."

It had been a smaller deal than people were making it out to be.

Technically, a surge drive had no limit to what it could carry, but increasing the mass boosted the surge calculation time exponentially. This factor was greater on an individual ship than on a surge gate, and it created a practical upper limit. For a single surge drive, a fully loaded Behemoth was about as massive as anyone was willing to go, and it still took cycles to queue. That was why Behemoths usually went through the gates instead, which was much faster. When the post-Taiberos PSD finally made their first retaliation against Solace, they sent a single Behemoth, with its balance leaning toward reinforcements for the ground rather than the sky. Huge tactical mistake.

Nak led the fledgling Alta Squadron and captured the Behemoth and its surge drive. Many Goebs were taken whole with freight-grade attractor beams, and many of the destroyed Goebs were collected and restored. A major victory based on a foolish mistake the PSD would not make twice.

"So what do you think?" asked Valt. "I was just planning to leave it in the Behemoth and use it as a commerce engine. We need that sort of thing, now that we're missing our surge gate, don't you think?"

If it were Nak's decision, he'd transfer the surge drive to a smaller skycraft, one that could actually take advantage of its abilities. It made him miss *The Sanctum*. "Your idea sounds fine."

"That's exactly what I thought you'd say!" said Valt. "Actually, I thought you might say we needed a smaller courier vessel, one you could pilot or something. Glad we agree. The War Council isn't going to like it, so I'm glad you're backing me."

Nak started into a reply, but then her voice shouted his name:

"Nak!"

Valt and his up-for-grabs surge drive lost all importance.

* * *

NAK FELT SO happy when he heard her.

He made sure it didn't show on his face though.

"Hi, Mr Valt," said Kalh. "Hi, Nak. You talk to Benton?"

"Yes, how'd you know."

She shrugged, almost like she'd encouraged that conversation to happen.

"You brought your coat, I see," said Nak. "You ready?"

"Yep. Sorry I'm late."

Nak, towering over Valt, patted the slender man on the shoulder. "Let's talk more later, buddy."

"You betcha, partner," said Valt with his usual enthusiasm and not a hint of sarcasm.

"Excited to see what kind of a fleet you can build above ground."

"Me too!"

Nak took Kalh's hand, and the two of them left the infirmary. She didn't know what he'd planned. People like Benton would call him crazy, Kalh too maybe, and maybe they'd be right, but Nak didn't care. In fact, he himself would've called this crazy not long ago, but things were different now. He knew what he wanted, and he wasn't going to waste time deliberating.

They boarded a small intraplanetary vessel that he'd rented from one of his adoring fans. He maxed out the throttle, heading toward the starside of Solace, where night reigned forever. The trip took nearly an isochron.

It was hard to stop looking at her.

Her hair was still short but growing back in.

Last millo, she'd acquired a crate full of seed whistles. She took boxes of them to random cities and handed them out to children, mostly orphan boys, the kind of kid Nak used to be. She said it reminded her of teaching on Sream, back before the Witch Hunters got her, when she tried saving that kid.

Nak had gone with her, to help out, and he sat in awe as she taught those kids to play her favorite melody, an outlawed war tune from a forgotten revolution.

A quiet miina cub named Uumago had been there. He seemed so deflated and pathetic, head bowed and unable to look anyone in the eye. Nak eventually got him talking about how he'd lost his whole family in the war—both parents and all his siblings. Just this tiny cub with nobody, but Kalh taught him the tune, and he left holding his head higher.

Those kids ran off with her music in hand and carried rebellion everywhere they went. Nak would've worshiped her if she'd done that for him when he was a kid.

He practically worshiped her for it now.

That was when he decided he had to do this. That plus losing Cup.

"You seem a little down," said Kalh after one particularly long silence. "You okay?"

"Yeah." He grinned.

"What's funny?" she asked.

"Nothing."

"No, really, tell me," she begged.

"No."

She put a hand on his knee.

He noted the scar on her arm, where the bone had come through. His fault. He'd caused her to fall.

"Come on," she pleaded

He shook his head but felt glad she was pushing his boundaries.

"Is it something embarrassing?" she asked.

"A little."

"Just tell me."

He kept his silence.

"What are you afraid of?"

"I'm not afraid."

"Then tell me."

"I'm used to sailing with Cupcake as my copilot. I'm sad to have lost her."

"That's sad. Why's that funny?"

"It's not funny."

"Then why'd you laugh?"

"No reason."

"You laughed for a reason."

"I didn't laugh."

"Well you smiled for a reason."

"No. No reason."

"Come on, Nak. How can you still not trust me?"

"I trust you."

"Then tell me. Will you tell me?"

"My best friend was an android. That's kind of funny."

"Uh…"

"And kind of pathetic, don't you think."

"No. She was more than an android."

"Well, yeah. But she wasn't… organic." He shook his head. "I'm not sure how much I'm supposed to feel for her. What I do feel seems like too much. It's a lot. And it hurts. *I can't believe I let her do it.*"

"She'd be proud of what you two accomplished. And so am I."

Nak didn't say anything.

She gazed at him, looking for the subtlest of clues. So much sympathy.

Her look prompted him to keep talking. He thought of the mangled freighter, crushed so badly that they never got to see the body: "When my dad died, something broke inside. Like my soul just tore right in half. I never wanted to be attached to anyone ever again. That's why Cup was my only friend, I think. Because I didn't want to risk that pain of separation. But it still happened. Maybe it always happens. Seems so unfair." He turned his scruffy jaw and looked over at Kalh.

She had understanding in her eyes.

"Thanks, Kalh."

But she hadn't said anything, which must've struck her as funny, and she laughed.

He chuckled too.

T HE SKY AHEAD was black.

As they traveled farther, the twilight faded behind them and stars began to appear—little specks of white across the vast expanse.

"So this is the starside," he said.

"Eternal night."

He landed the craft on a snow-covered mountaintop. They put on snow-shoes and hiked beneath the heavens.

His chest and breath locked up every time he stepped with his starboard foot, but he ignored the pain. "Remember how I told you most of the Bloody Wings have one location that none of the others can go to."

"Yes." Her purple skullhugger cap fit tightly down over her head, which somehow accented her big hazel eyes.

"See that bright star right there."

"Yeah."

"Now follow it directly up, and you'll see kind of a triangle. The dim star on the right of the triangle is Novan."

"I see it."

"That used to be my own little sanctuary, a place only *The Sanctum* could go. I'd been planning to take you there. Unfortunately, this is about as close as we can get to it now."

"What was there?"

"A spectacular nebula."

"Describe it to me."

"A young system, dust still swirling. It looked incredible with Starsight. Really spectacular reds and blues surrounded the system like a cocoon, with glowing quasars in the back. It felt like time just stopped, like creation froze halfway through a step and the chronometer wouldn't tick again for a million percents."

"That sounds spectacular." She showed the white of her teeth as she smiled.

"It had a few pristine planets too. One of the habitable ones had a ring system made of space dust. Looked like a halo."

"You ever land on it?"

"Yeah. Many times. Come on." Making sure not to limp, he led her to a stone that worked as a bench.

They sat on it together, breathing puffs like white smoke.

Nak relaxed, with his gloved hands on his thighs, craning his face toward the sky. "When I was a child I always felt like there was so much out there to see, and I just wanted to get a little closer. *The Sanctum* fulfilled that dream."

"I'm sorry you had to sacrifice it."

Honestly, he was glad to trade his ship for her. It was Cup that left him feeling regret. "I'm not looking for pity. I'm just saying it was an important part of *me*."

"Your giving it up made me like you even more."

"Not possible."

She jabbed him with her elbow and grinned. Her brightness enticed him more than anyone or anything ever had. Somehow she beckoned him more than the whole unexplored galaxy. She *was* mystery—her soul unchartable.

"You know," he said, "when I was considering it, I thought of you. And about your speech."

"Really?"

"Yeah."

"I thought of you too, while trying to surge into the Athenaeum."

He grinned. "Your words got to me. Otherwise I never could've let go."

From her expression, it seemed that comment nearly melted her.

With some trepidation—wary from last time—he leaned forward, hoping to kiss her.

But he caught a hint of hesitation in her eyes.

"What's the matter," he asked.

"Nak, if you knew, unquestionably, that loving me would turn to heartbreak, would you still do it?"

"*Unquestionably,* huh. Is that a premonition."

Kalh shrugged.

The ambiguity felt uncomfortable. He wondered what dark future she might've seen. He hoped she'd seen them facing it together. "Come on."

"What?" she asked.

"Tell me," he said. "Was it a premonition?"

"I'm not sure. I can't see it clearly yet."

"Oh."

"Well, would you?"

He grinned. "Unquestionably."

"And what if it meant you would die?"

This more serious question dispelled his teasing mood for a moment. When he was sure, he nodded. "Yes, I'd still do it."

The stars smiled at this answer, and so did she.

He kissed her.

When he pulled away this time, she was grinning.

He honestly didn't know what she'd say in response, but he didn't care. He had to ask anyway, right now: "Kalh?"

"Yes?"

"Will you marry me."

She took a deep breath, as if her whole body were filling up with excitement, too much to contain inside her. Instead of saying something, she giggled.

"That's not an answer," he said.

"I know."

"What are you laughing at."

"Nothing."

"It's not the reaction I was expecting."

"It's nothing."

"Come on. *I* told *you*. Why were you laughing."

With a twinkle in her eye, she said, "Because I knew you were going to say that."

DRAY HEARD HER voice.

The voice of Kalhette Whitesun.

It was tinny, all treble and garbled, a replay of the speech she gave to rouse the populace. She wasn't supposed to have survived. Now in celebration, the people of Solace were hanging posters of her and re-broadcasting her, talking about her like talking about a miracle.

He sensed it too—the miraculous aspect.

Part of him wanted to celebrate with them, to believe in the miracle, but the other part of him knew it wasn't meant to be. The galaxy wouldn't have justice through her life but through her death.

Lethos had made it so.

People all down the thoroughfare celebrated with food and song, unaware that the Lord Admiral walked among them. Twilight fell over his charcoal hood, which cast a shadow across his face and the red cloth covering his missing eye.

Technically, he had won. The Renegades, under his leadership, had claimed the victory, which meant the PSD had lost. Taiberos was completely gone. This was good. It meant the galaxy's dominant power had become weaker, susceptible to a change in regime. It meant this was time for Dray to ascend. Then he could finally start to undo all the wrongs he'd committed as a servant of the PSD. The path was laid. Almost.

He'd failed to fulfill his part of the covenant: The girl survived.

Blackserpent was supposed to die too, his dropship exploding midair as he escaped the Sozo, taking the secret of Dray's betrayal with him. But the plan had failed.

Dray had failed.

Part of him thought that was okay.

And that was the problem, not that she had survived but that part of his former self had survived. He was reaching for the future while still gripping remnants of the past. He'd tried to murder her in secret so he could keep his position with the Renegades. Worse, he had clung to memories of his most beloved—which left him with a glimmer of sympathy for the girl.

It would keep him from what Lethos had promised: to train Dray, to groom him until he took control of the Eleven. Only then, as the most powerful of mortals, could Dray save the galaxy from injustice.

The transformation would not be fast nor simple, but he would see it through, no matter the cost, till he'd laid his old self to rest and become new, transformed, capable of being what the galaxy needed him to be. Half measures wouldn't do. He had to fully enter the tomb of his ambitions, sacrificing what the Zhani called Spirit. He would purge all sympathy and second thoughts from his soul. And he knew exactly how this transformation would begin.

As he walked into a side alley, he pulled up a black cloth over his mouth and nose. Best not to be recognized. A strange smoke made the air seem pale. The crooked walls rose high on both sides. He refrained from letting his eye glow, but he could sense figures behind the doors of the alley, prepared to trap him should things go afoul.

At the back corner, where the light hardly reached, a dark miin sat on the ground in a meditative posture, eyes closed. The position looked almost human, but it made the miin's tail come out the front, which looked strange, to say the least.

On the dirt lay a colorful blanket, on which sat silver jewelry and gem-stones. One of his six paws held what appeared to be a twig, the end of which glowed with the tiniest ember. He put the twig between his teeth and sucked in. Then, opening his eyes, he breathed out a puff of smoke and said, "Greetings."

"Dorf zarooq," said Dray.

"Who sent you?" asked the miin.

"Shauu."

"It wasn't Shauu," said the miin. "Shauu is gone."

"He's not gone. And it came *through* him."

"I suppose that's true. How much do you want?"

"What have you got?"

"About three fifty mils for seven." Not getting up, the miin handed Dray a wide, silver bracelet with long jade stones across its face. "It's not real stone."

Dray took the bracelet and pulled it close to his remaining eye.

"You need a knife to open it. That slot there on the seam."

Dray pulled out a knife and carefully pushed the blade in the crevice till the first fake stone gently popped open. Inside was a slender shard of Orikerse with a few separate splinters next to it. The substance glinted in the dim light. The beginning of his transformation. "This is all you have?"

"For now. If you want more, I can get more in a few cycles." Orikerse didn't simply exist in nature. It had to be manufactured using a rare substance as the base material. Few had the means to do so. Even if they did, fewer still knew the secret to create it—a secret the PSD had tried desperately to destroy.

"I want more. A lot more." Before Dray closed the bracelet, he plucked out one of the small slivers and pinched it between his lips. After hiding the bracelet in his pocket, he put his palm to the wall and slammed the sliver deep into his own flesh.

He inhaled a gasp of air.

"Don't make me get the muscle," said the miin.

Dray frowned as the effects seeped into his consciousness, sapping his emotion. The muscle wouldn't stand a chance. Still, he needed to groom this relationship. He pulled out a stack of fiat coins.

As he reached out, the miin said, "You're lucky I'm still accepting these."

Dray released the coins, and they clinked down. "The PSD hasn't fallen yet."

The miin put the fiats into a leather purse. "They fell at New Kingstrong."

"That's only one city." Dray shuddered as the Orikerse flowed through his veins.

"The revolution could spread across Solace, maybe across the galaxy," said the miin.

"What makes you think so?"

The miin nodded to a poster hanging on the peeling alley wall. "The Prophetess will finish the job."

Dray did not respond, and the miin's hopeful words hung in the air.

The Prophetess will finish the job.

Dray stepped up to the poster, staring at it with one eye. This, the only thing in the alley that wasn't dilapidated, showed the girl on it, a candid shot, a thin light on her face, and she stared up at something with the insight of a sage. Some sort of victory propaganda.

But with his right eye, his missing eye, he thought he detected something more, something deeper than an image. A woman he'd once sacrificed himself to save.

He shook his head.

He could no longer sense the miracle.

Without a word of reply, he lifted his knife to the image.

The miin's ugly face expressed horror, as if he sensed the deeper evil at play in this quiet moment.

Dray put the metal point to the flesh of the girl's neck. Slowly, precisely, he dragged the blade, cutting through the paper.

The miin looked as though he were about to vomit.

Dray glared with one eye. "We shall see."

The metal scraped harshly against the brick as he slit her throat.

GRATITUDE

HERE I'D LIKE to recognize and appreciate the many people who played a part in bringing the first STARCHILD trilogy to life:

Ashley, Cheyenne, Malori, Nancy, Shawnee, and Sonya, each wondrous mothers. Jimmy, Emma, and Sofi, coiners of the two-year-old dialog.

Michal, Jax, Jeff, Tev, Tunk, Melodee, Joe, Preston, Christine, Ginger, Erika, Izzy, Abe, Emma, Liz, Bentley, and Devon, my invaluable team of beta readers. As well as those of you who are still keenly finding typos.

Joseph Bendoski, the only one who called an MBA a bad idea. Nathan Green, who demonstrated the key—tenacity. Zach Buchanan, chemistry genius. Phil Hatch, math genius. Ashley Jaggi, editorial genius. Simon Wright, audio genius.

Best, Brown, Caplan, Danneskjöld, Doctorow, Douglass, Ferriss, Flynn, Gyatso, Hamill, Hood, Jobs, Kamkar, Martin, Mitnick, Niederhauser, Paul, Peterson, Post, Rowling, Sethi, Snowden, Swartz, Thoreau, Tolkien, Tolstoy, Ulbricht, Ver, Woz, and the rest of the misfits.

Of course, Lucas and his magical original team.

You, reader, as well.

And lastly, Scott Adams, the guy who hacked the matrix.

THE SAGA CONTINUES...

A NEW EVIL GROWS in power—
The Shadowlyss.

Led by the traitorous Lord Admiral Dray.

A twisted shadow of his former self, he will stop at nothing to fulfill his debt to Lethos: Dray must murder Kalhette. As he draws steadily closer to his prey, his Shadowlyss armies wash over the planet Solace, leaving ruin in their wake. Benton, at the head of the defense, quickly learns that what starts a revolution may not be enough to win it. Only, at what cost is he willing to claim victory?

Though the stakes were already too high, now more than Kalh's life is on the line: She's pregnant.

And having to protect a child changes everything.

Amid the turmoil, Nak tries to find meaning in a life without his ship and without his best friend. While fighting with the rebel military in one violent battle after another, he also begins training as a Zhani scion. Little does he know that saving the ones he loves from the tide of darkness will come at a high price.

A higher price than he ever imagined.

THE SECOND EPISODE of the thrilling Starchild space opera is not for the faint of heart.

The epic story shows the horrors of war up close and may leave indelible marks on its readers. It also doubles down on the literary elements: In a philosophical quandary reminiscent of Tolstoy, Benton faces the bitterness of an unending fight for freedom, and he learns first hand the gory cost of making moral choices not only in theory but also in practice. Meanwhile, during Zhani training, Nak explores the contrary aspects of the Song and the Shadow, exposing a detailed magic system in the vein of Brandon Sanderson's works.

Not only will this spectacular sequel quench your thirst for more galactic adventure, it is also a fairy tale that crescendos from love to posterity, then legacy, and beyond—a somber romance for the ages. Kalh, because of her deep emotional scars, has avoided commitment all her life. Now she must answer the question Nak asked at the end of the first episode, and her reply will echo across the galaxy.

The next episode takes you alongside your favorite characters on a blood-tingling ride that will leave you wondering, how can good manage to triumph over such overwhelming evil?

Find out today in STARCHILD: REBEL!

Get it today:

starchild2.jwashburn.com

STARCHILD NOVELLA

SO WHAT'S NEXT?

The STARCHILD saga will be a trilogy of trilogies, nine central novels when it's done, along with a couple spinoff novellas. And I have a way for you to stay in the loop on their progress.

I write a personal newsletter to my readers called The Informant. Subscribe if you want to make sure to not miss the exciting sequels. I apologize in advance if I don't write often. The next book is always the priority. And when I do email you, it'll be something you'll care about. (It's also a cinch to unsubscribe if you ever change your mind.)

Oh, and by the way, I'm working on another project: STARCHILD ZERO. It's a novella that tells how Nak stole a Bloody Wing from one of the most powerful leaders in the galaxy and how Taiberos got his cybernetic hand! When it's done, I'll send it out to my email list. So sign up here:

theinformant.jwashburn.com

Starchild

Z E R O

J WASHBURN

TELL ME HOW IT ENDS!

STARCHILD IS DIFFERENT.
    While most novels are pushed by big corporate machines, this is an artisan book—written, illustrated, and typeset by the author, handcrafted from beginning to end. It was a ton of work. I spent two and a half years of my life putting this novel together, and that story arc doesn't conclude till the book gets to your hands. When you read, that's the end of the story. For me, your reaction is the explosive finale!

But I often don't get that ending.

So I write the book, and I see that you bought a copy, but the ending is just—

Silence…

Total cliffhanger. And I have no idea what you thought of it. It just kills me!

I wish I could've sat next to you, watching your reaction page by page. Unfortunately, that wouldn't be plausible or comfortable, ha ha.

So I thought I'd invite you to drop me a line. Seriously, send me an email! If you're in a rush, it can be brief, no problem. It doesn't need to be fancy either. (Ain't got no problem with slang.) I'd love to hear where you're from, what your favorite moments were in STARCHILD, or which character you loved. It would actually mean a lot to me. And I do my best to respond to each letter.

Also, thank you for reading.

I'm glad you could join me on this adventure.

me@jwashburn.com

www.ingramcontent.com/pod-product-compliance
Lightning Source LLC
Chambersburg PA
CBHW030638020726
47493CB00006B/1764